Deadly War of Words

A Mystery/Thriller

Jed O'Dea

Jed O'Dea

Published by PELL Resources Publications

ISBN 978-0-9974555-4-0

DISCLAIMER

Novels by Jed O'Dea:

Tucker's Discovery

Deadly Cold

Unsustainable

WHA-CKED

Jed O'Dea

This book is dedicated to the life of John Powers Mason, Knoxville, Tennessee

CHAPTER 1

"Attack him where he is unprepared, appear where you are not expected."—Sun Tzu, 554 BC–496 BC, Chinese general, author of *"The Art of War"*

Wood Buffalo National Park, Alberta, Canada – June 19th

Gabriel Lakatos focused his Canon 18x50 binoculars on a lone bull bison grazing on the prairie's northern wheatgrass. He leaned on the warm hood of his rented Toyota Land Cruiser to steady himself as he zoomed in on the old bull's severely scarred head. As Gabriel lifted the brim of his outback hat which was pulled down low to shade the lens of the field glasses from the glare of the ever-present sun, he said, "Chief, this guy is scarred and too ugly to mount on the wall behind my desk in my Manhattan office." Lakatos took a deep breath in the cool, still air and was about to say something else to his chief of security when, without warning, his chest exploded.

The old bison, frightened by the incredibly loud sound made by a Barrett M82 sniper rifle, hustled away from where the .50 caliber round sprayed dark heart and lung matter broadly across the hood of the silver SUV.

Gabriel never got a chance to have a dying thought. There was no final opportunity for the billionaire to ask for forgiveness for his sins or share final words with loved ones. The time between existing and not existing was measured in microseconds.

Although Lakatos met his destiny before he knew that there was an immediate threat to him, his security team instantly recognized after their boss's internals splattered onto their Ray-Ban Aviator sunglasses that they, too, might have only seconds left to live.

Lakatos had felt safe from his adversaries in this remote location in the northeast corner of the Alberta Province. He had a .405 Winchester rifle by his side, loaded with 300-grain big bore buffalo cartridges to take down a 2,500-pound bison. To add to his sense of security, two former Delta Force unit soldiers who doubled as hunting guides provided around-the-clock personal security for Gabriel. At the very moment of his death, it never occurred to him that he might not be safe from his numerous enemies. In his home in New York City, yes. But here, in northern Alberta, nah. Privately, he worried more about being trampled by moose, bison, or caribou and continuously stepping in bison piles than any human treachery.

And only those with a need to know were supposed to be aware of his itinerary. Virtually no one should have known where he was.

The sixty-nine-year-old financial genius decided to check off a bucket list item. He was in Alberta to investigate the status of one of his oil sands investments near Fort Chipewyan. The short, overweight, and physically out of shape Lakatos had a bulbous nose from indulging in too much Scotch over decades, a full head of gray hair, bags under his eyes large enough to hide the lost continent of Atlantis, and visible blood vessels in his left cheek. Gabriel was a teenager the last time he did a pushup. His physical appearance was quite a contrast to the two security guards who protected him and who had taught Gabriel how to handle the Winchester. They were thirty years younger than their boss, rugged, tall, muscular, and athletic.

Lakatos's chief of security—a big target at 235 pounds—hesitated an instant too long. The delay allowed the sniper to complete the rifle bolt action and peer into the high-powered scope. The six-foot, four-inch bodyguard swan-dived into the mud behind a fallen tree for cover and hoped that the sniper didn't see him.

The rotted log the chief hid behind provided no resistance—his left arm was blown off at the shoulder.

The other security guard had just enough time to jump behind the Land Cruiser before he heard his chief's scream. The guard nervously used his left hand to mat his Saddam Hussein-like mustache against his face when a single bullet tore through both the driver's-side and the passenger's-side doors of the SUV. The shot missed him by only inches.

In torturous pain, the chief screamed pitifully for help—his arm lay next to him on the ground. Mustache hesitated, hid behind the hood where the engine block protected him, and asked loudly, "How bad?"

Only ten yards away, the chief answered, "My arm is gone. I'm bleeding out."

Mustache responded, "If I try to run to your side to help, I probably won't make it. Can you take your belt off and use it as a tourniquet?"

Before the chief could answer, Mustache heard the next shot.

"Chief?"

No answer.

"Chief, damn it, answer me."

Still, no answer.

Mustache considered his options. He was pinned down, lying in the mud, and using the engine block as his shield. No one was likely to come to his rescue here in the middle of fucking nowhere. Although it was still morning and daylight lasted 18 hours this time of year, he concluded that he had to stay put and wait until dark to move—if he could survive that long.

Few people ventured into the Canadian far north to explore Wood Buffalo National Park in the Alberta Province and Northwest Territories in Canada. The population density of the Northern Alberta Region averaged less than one person per square mile. So, Mustache suspected that no one had heard the sniper fire.

"Does a rifle make a sound if no one is there to hear it?"

Mustache thought, "If people did hear the rifle fire, they would assume that the rifle sounds were from hunters."

The sniper had positioned himself comfortably on a rock formation roughly 500 yards from Mustache's vehicle. He surveyed the area around the target through the powerful scope a full 360-degrees and determined that there was still no one in the area in a radius of at least three miles. The marksman pulled out his satellite phone and made radio contact with his team.

The sniper said, "Main target down. Mission complete. Request extraction."

The moose ignored the sounds of the incoming helicopter. Mustache prayed that it belonged to law enforcement. But the chopper landed close to a rock outcrop hundreds of yards away from him.

After only a few minutes on the ground, the Bell 407GXP lifted and flew a circle around the Toyota. It came no closer than 200 yards from Lakatos's remaining security agent. Mustache considered dashing for his chief's Remington rifle, which laid on the ground only twelve yards away but decided to wait for a more opportune moment. He crawled further under the engine of the SUV to hide and to avoid being in the direct line of sight of the sniper. Mustache pulled out his 9mm Beretta, looked skyward, stuck his gun hand out from under the Toyota, and fired wildly in the direction of the helicopter knowing full well that it would be a miracle if he hit anything.

The sniper had no experience shooting from a moving platform like a helicopter. He had never trained for it, but even from 200 yards, the shooter had no problem hitting the large gas tank in the Toyota.

The sound of the explosion startled the caribou, causing a herd to flee and the whooping cranes to take flight. Black smoke rose into the empty sky, flames licked the top of scrub pines, and Mustache's DNA was spread over an acre of wheatgrass.

The shooter in the Bell helicopter faded into oblivion—unnoticed by any humans.

Wood Buffalo National Park

A rugged twenty-four-year-old outdoorsman thought he had the most fabulous job in the universe as a ranger for Parks Canada. His job, along with two other rangers in his unit, was to monitor the 17,300-square-mile park for any unusual or environmentally problematic activities and to report back to the park warden with his observations.

Most of the time, the independent survivalist observed the park in one of the Park Canada Bombardiers, but today he was driving a bright red three-year-old Jeep Wrangler randomly around Ruis Lake. It was slow and hard going. There were no roads, paths, or well-worn trails to navigate—only mud, grass, and stumps to overcome. Two hours into the survey he felt like he'd already fought twelve rounds with Mike Tyson. His was definitely a young person's job.

But he loved it. He loved being outside in God's country, breathing in clear air, and smelling the pine sap. He enjoyed the aloneness, the privacy, and the lack of human contact. The ranger, a wiry sportsman, contemplated why he was such a loner. He sadly concluded that he just didn't really like people. Most every person he met was self-absorbed, selfish, and boring. Except for maybe his sexy female coworker. His mind wandered to thoughts and fantasies about her.

He pulled out a protein bar, sipped on bottled water, and continued to survey the park until he noticed black smoke rise into the blue sky maybe ten or twelve miles away. He immediately concluded that something was on fire that contained man-made plastics or oil-based products; a natural forest fire would produce gray or white smoke. He called the park warden on a government issued satellite phone. The warden instructed the ranger to check it out, confirm or deny his suspicions, take digital photos of the scene, and advise him of what course of action Parks Canada should consider.

The ranger's teeth jarred as he crossed a ravine created from storm water earlier in the spring and wondered why Jeep didn't design the Wrangler with better shock absorbers. Ninety minutes later, he had managed to fight his way to within a mile or so of the source of the smoke. The ranger noticed that whatever was on fire generated less black smoke now and must be burning itself out.

The ranger looked up at a collection of eight black vultures circling at maybe 600 feet overhead east of his current position. He regarded vultures and other scavengers as part of the natural order of things. But this time, he was overcome with apprehension about what he might find at the burn site. For another thirty minutes, he struggled to get the Jeep across the treacherous landscape until he interrupted the meal of more black vultures scavenging two carcasses that were much too small to be bison or moose. As he got closer, the indigenous smells of wildflowers and honeysuckle were overpowered by the rancid odor of burning plastic and rubber.

His first clue that the dead were human was the burned-out empty Toyota Land Cruiser. Otherwise, it would have been hard to determine what the vultures were devouring.

The ranger pulled out his handgun and shot into the air to scatter the large birds before he approached the remains of the dead.

Usually, he was unaffected at the sight of partially eaten dead animals. This was different. He couldn't hold back nausea creeping into his throat.

CHAPTER 2

"There is nothing more deceptive than an obvious fact." — Arthur Conan Doyle, 1839-1930, author of *"The Boscombe Valley Mystery"*

Fort Chipewyan, Alberta – June 20th

At the Fort Chipewyan Detachment, Royal Canadian Mounted Police officer Douglas Butterfield was forced to wait eighteen hours for the forensic specialist to arrive from the Calgary Detachment's Science and Identification Services. He predicted that the longer it took for the medical examiner to reach the crime scene, the fewer remains they'd have to sample and bag. Based on the digital photos taken by the park ranger and forwarded from the park warden, there wasn't too much left of the victims' carcasses to inspect as it was. He dreaded going to the murder site with the investigative team—Butterfield knew it was going to be ugly.

The six-foot, two-inch twenty-two-year-old blond police officer had never investigated a murder. He felt a little insecure and wasn't sure he was up to solving a multiple-homicide case. He'd graduated from the academy only eighteen months ago, and since there were very few murders in his territory, he feared his rookie status would be on display. Although his hardworking parents had instilled in him a sense of self-worth, self-confidence, and purpose, his ex-girlfriend had obliterated his self-esteem. He was reliving their last argument when his depressing thoughts were interrupted.

"Officer Butterfield, please come in," his P25 Motorola radio announced.

"Go."

"This is Royal Canadian Mounted Police Detective Rod Nelson incoming from Calgary with our forensic identification officer. We'll be landing a 350 at your doorstep. Make sure all is clear. We're ten minutes out. Over."

"Copy. Over"

"Holy shit," thought Butterfield. His heart started to race at the excitement of meeting the RCMP Major Crimes Unit's renowned homicide detective. Rod Nelson was famous for solving the most difficult and high-profile crimes in the country. Doug had watched interviews with the detective on national television many times. Butterfield felt light-headed, unburdened, and relieved because the lead for solving the homicides was obviously transferred by higher ups to Nelson.

"But why?" Butterfield wondered. "Do others lack confidence in me to close the case? Or is it because this crime includes the murder of a well-known, high-profile person?"

He listened to the unmistakable sound of approaching rotor blades. The Eurocopter AS-350 piloted by the homicide detective landed gently in the parking lot of the Fort Chipewyan Detachment.

Rod Nelson waited for Officer Butterfield to emerge from the detachment building, but no one came out. The rookie heard on the two-way radio, "Butterfield, are you coming or not? We picked up some grub and refueled at the Fort Chipewyan Airport. Time's a' wastin.' Grab your gear and get in."

Officer Butterfield clumsily ran double-time from the front door of the detachment to the helicopter carrying a computer bag and an unharnessed backpack.

After the young officer climbed in, Nelson asked, "Who did you piss off to win the assignment here in Fort Chipewyan?"

Butterfield said, "I asked for this assignment. I grew up here."

"Oh." Although Nelson already knew where Butterfield was raised.

The forensic examiner looked at Nelson disapprovingly for his comment and wondered what the purpose of his question was. The detective had a reason for everything he did.

On the way to the murder scene, Nelson and the forensic examiner briefed Butterfield about the importance of the case. The more Butterfield heard, the more grateful he felt that the case lead was transferred from him to Nelson.

Young Butterfield knew that Gabriel Lakatos was famous but didn't know much more than that. He learned from the seasoned investigator that Lakatos was one of the most polarizing figures in the world.

Nelson said, "Victim number one, Lakatos, was a radical left activist who proselytized his Far-Left ideology and was worshipped by those who shared his one-world-government philosophy. He was a philanthropist for liberal causes, a visionary for advancing socialism, and creative in motivating chess-like pawns to sacrifice their time and effort for his beliefs.

"Lakatos was a financial junkyard dog and had many enemies with a motive to have him executed. He made fools of and ruined the careers of financial advisors on Wall Street."

Butterfield said, "That narrows the field down to a few hundred."

Nelson continued, "The billionaire artfully destroyed the reputation of a few politicians who had opposing views to his. High-priced lobbyists on Washington's K Street failed their customers because victim number one implemented financial moves that reversed the value of their client's product or service."

Butterfield added, "A few hundred more people with motives."

Nelson barked, "No shit, Sherlock! Will you let me finish? Even whole nations suffered after the genius manipulated the value of their currency. Angry citizens disliked him for his refusal to pay his own taxes while expecting middle-income taxpayers to fund his socialist values. Members of the radical right hated him because they were convinced that he funded a deep state shadow government. Capitalists of all makes and models reviled him for his apparent hypocrisy—he sponsored socialism, but he made his wealth as a capitalist.

"His 'Free Society' activist philosophy reinforced a belief that everyone was equal in health, skill, knowledge, energy, drive, intelligence, and upbringing. Yet, he believed in a world where superior thinkers—like himself—would make decisions for the 'lesser-intelligent' masses. He supported open borders, late-term abortion, the anti-Israel movement, the LGBT agenda, and opposed voter ID laws. In short, he was committed to degrading America into a socialist state."

Butterfield concluded, "He sounds like a real sweetheart. Too many people with a motive and means to kill him. Too few with opportunity. What's the story on the other two victims?"

Nelson answered, "Their sin was to fail at their job as his bodyguards. The unsub probably killed them just to eliminate witnesses. We're definitely dealing with professionals."

CHAPTER 3

"There are risks and costs to a program of action—but they are far less than the long-range cost of comfortable inaction."—John F. Kennedy, 1917-1963, 35th President of the United States

Wiscasset, Maine – June 21st

The breeze off the river was warm and soft. It smelled of life's wonder and stimulated Tucker Cherokee's philosophical juices. Enjoying the moment, he took the rare opportunity to meditate, contemplate about his coordinates in the universe, do a little self-reflection, and ask the enigmatic and unanswerable questions:

Why am I here?

What's the purpose of my life?

Do I have a destiny?

He pondered these questions because he didn't know exactly why he had started down his current path. It was fraught with potential treachery, and he'd already experienced enough of that in his life. He wondered whether he had a character flaw and why he chose to expose himself to danger.

Yet, here he was pushing the envelope, coloring outside the lines, and trying to accomplish "mission impossible." When he came to a life-changing crossroad, he invariably chose the most challenging pathway.

Tucker, CEO of the defense contractor Entropy, LLC, thought about casting a line out into Sheepscot River as he watched a family of geese land without grace on the slowly moving water.

He was startled out of his deep thought when his encrypted satellite phone rang. He recognized the number.

"Hi, Tank, what's up?"

Jorge (Tank) Alvarez was Tucker's best friend since childhood and always had his back.

Tank asked, "Did you hear about the murder of Gabriel Lakatos?"

"Tank, you're the fourth person to call me about it. I told the others that we had nothing to do with it."

Tank said, "I know because you would have tried to involve me. I called to see if you want to engage me in damage control. A couple of the foundation members are likely to bail on us if they even suspect that murder is a tactic we intend to employ to achieve the mission."

Tucker said, "No, but thanks. That burden is mine. However, Maya and I will leverage Lakatos's death to the foundation's advantage. Have you caught wind of who or what organization may have ordered the murder?"

Tank said, "No, not yet, but I'll keep my ear to the ground. Call me if I can help calm anyone down. I suspect you're going to get a few more inquiries today from foundation members."

Tucker disconnected the call with Tank, looked out across the river, took in a deep breath, and waited with dread for the next call. He'd rather have a root canal than talk to more anxious members.

Maya Cherokee entered the back deck, placed her hand on Tucker's shoulder and said, "It's done."

He asked his lovely bride, "Did Lawrence Slaughter acknowledge his text? He was the last one on the list who hadn't, right?

"Yes, all fifty-two people on our list, including Slaughter, have read their messages. Our crack cyber team sent each of them emails, texts, messages on social media, or blog posts from sources whose footprint was falsely linked to a North Korean IP address. As we agreed, the message was simple and was the same for all of them:

"You could be next. It's time to repent."

Maya was always composed, but today her beautiful and exotic facial features—her almond-shaped eyes inherited from her second-generation Chinese father, her royal blue irises from her Norwegian mother—showed stress and uncertainty.

"You know, Tucker," she said, "we may have just taken the first step toward some serious trouble. Like Gabriel Lakatos, the people on the list who we just threatened are powerful. Some, I suspect, are vicious if not downright evil. Sweetheart, I hope we know what we're doing. I'm having second thoughts, and I'm a little frightened. I hope we're not past the point of no return."

Tucker smiled and joked, "As Baghdad Bob used to say, 'We're absolutely in control.'"

Mountain View, California

"How the hell did they get this phone number?" Lawrence Slaughter, CEO of California Media Group, admonished his chief information officer, Pratap Desai.

Desai answered, "There is no way anyone could have gotten your secret phone number by hacking into our system. I stand by my position that we have the world's best anti-cyberattack program, the best possible firewall, and the best possible anti-virus, anti-malware blocker."

"Well," Slaughter continued, "then how the hell did I receive this threat as a text message?"

Desai controlled the anger metastasizing in his mind and asked, "With whom do you text on that phone?"

Lawrence removed his Gucci sunglasses and exposed his mud-brown eyes to Desai's insubordinate stare. "You for one."

"And?"

Slaughter's serious expression revealed the deep lines on his face as he combed his thinning chestnut hair with his fingers and imperceptibly shook his head.

"Get me a new phone and number. Encrypted this time." Pratap Desai was dismissed.

Slaughter silently reviewed the potential people who knew his phone number and who might even remotely think of betraying him. It was a short list.

Lawrence Slaughter groaned as he lifted his bones out of his study chair and wandered with a stooped-over posture to his office bar to pour himself a glass of brandy. It was only the second time in his seventy-five-year life that he tipped a sniffer before 10:00 a.m. The news about the demise of his old friend, Gabriel Lakatos, depressed him. He also knew in his gut that the text he received on his phone was directly linked to Gabriel's murder.

It was not well-known that he and Gabriel had built an international cabal over four decades to include wealthy, elite, and powerful members with the goal of achieving a one-world governing body. He drank his brandy, contemplated his situation, and concluded that whoever or whatever organization could pull off the assassination of Lakatos could also get to him.

He poured himself another drink, lifted the glass, and said, "To you, Gabriel."

Fort Chipewyan

The homicide investigative team completed their round-trip by helicopter to the murder scene in Wood Buffalo National Park and back to the thriving metropolis of Fort Chipewyan with its 1,260 residents. The park ranger who discovered the murder victims was coerced into joining the team on their return flight. They washed up, dragged their tired butts back to the detachment, had food delivered, and settled in on building the murder books.

"Doug," asked homicide detective Rod Nelson, "do you have a whiteboard or flip chart around here? I want you to write down in big bold letters what we know as fact, what we suspect, and what are our action items. Get a Magic Marker or Sharpie."

"We don't have either, but we do have a projector. I'll plug in my laptop, and we can view everything on the wall in PowerPoint."

Nelson said, "Whatever. I miss being able to walk the wall, but we'll make do with what we've got." To the others in the room, Rod said, "So, while Doug here is setting up, what facts, Doctor, do you think are relevant to the case after you examined the scant remains of the three bodies?"

The medical examiner answered, "The number one, most important fact is that they were murdered. This was not a hunting accident."

Nelson quipped, "How many years of medical school did you have to endure to come to that conclusion?"

She ignored him and continued, "As you know, by the time we got to the crime scene, there wasn't much left of the victims after the vultures and other scavengers feasted on them. But based on the presence of larva and pupae, the time of death was around thirty-six hours before I started my examination or about four hours before the park ranger discovered the bodies."

"That's not a fact, Doctor, that's an assumption," said Rod Nelson.

The thirty-two-year-old medical examiner got her back up and tersely responded, "I said the murder was 'around' thirty-six hours before we arrived at the scene and that's a fact, Detective Nelson. Unless you are a medical examiner, you have no right to question my findings."

Detective Nelson was a graying, grisly, fifty-two-year-old no-nonsense kind of a guy with haunting eyes, thin lips, and a cleft chin. He put his calloused palms out revealing the hands of a man not afraid of hard physical work and said, "I solve crimes by questioning everything. Get used to it."

Doug Butterfield cleared his throat to break the tension and said, "OK, the projector is working, and we can begin documenting the case. So far we have two facts listed." Doug looked over at Nelson to see whether he objected.

The young park ranger added, "It's a fact that the victims arrived at the crime scene in a Toyota Land Cruiser. Gabriel Lakatos of New York City, New York, rented the vehicle in Fort Smith and two other drivers were listed on the contract. Identification found on the bodies and in the vehicle match the signatures on the rental contract. But I understand, Doctor, that final confirmation will occur when we get the DNA results back from the samples you sent off to the Calgary lab."

She took her designer prescription glasses off, massaged where they pinched her nose, and added, "We should have lab results back within two or three days. Until then we should consider the victims' identities as 'what we suspect' and not a fact."

Nelson said, "Correct. Lakatos could want everyone to think he is dead and send a look-alike out hunting. Although, admittedly, that's unlikely."

Butterfield contributed, "It's also a fact that all three were killed by a large-caliber projectile from a high-powered, long-range rifle. The slugs that passed through the two security guards were recovered, and forensics determined the bullets to be .50 BMG. It's also a fact that we found evidence—only 550 meters away—of a helicopter rail impression on the high grass."

Detective Nelson said, "So far, the evidence points us in the direction that a sniper assassinated a well-known person who has many enemies. The killer was extracted by a team with the financial and personnel resources to have access to a helicopter. So, it's a group or organization that planned Lakatos's murder and who were also ruthless enough to kill the two security agents to eliminate witnesses. This narrows the field down considerably."

The park ranger added, "Or an enemy wealthy enough to pull it off."

Nelson asked, "How did the killer know to be within 500 meters of Lakatos in a park bigger than some countries? Ranger, did we check for transmitters on the Land Cruiser? And Doug, were you able to determine where the helicopter took on fuel?"

Both answered, "No, sir."

"Well, let's get on it, eh?"

CHAPTER 4

"A person often meets his destiny on the road he took to avoid it."—Jean de La Fontaine, 1621-1695, poet.

Wiscasset, Maine – June 22nd

Tucker and Maya Cherokee walked along the bike path in the wooded section of their guarded estate. Maya said, "I know I supported the creation of the foundation up until now and as you say, 'someone's got to do something about it.' I think it had a good chance of doing something meaningful."

Tucker interrupted, "Had? Past tense?"

Maya held up her right hand, palm out, and continued, "I know it was our plan for the foundation to evolve into a secret organization, much like the Freemasons, Skull and Bones Society, or Illuminati. But the murder of our nemesis, Gabriel Lakatos, by who knows who made me realize just how treacherous our plans were. We don't need to do this, Tucker. Our scientific discoveries made us a fortune. Let's take advantage of it and buy a damn football team with it or something.

"And just as a reminder, Love, we were once targeted for assassination by heads of nations who felt threatened by our discovery. Hired mercenaries poisoned you with a radioisotope and attacked your hideout with Stinger missiles. And don't forget this." Maya pointed to a scar on her neck. "I was shot by that Chinese assassin bitch. Do you want to be exposed to that kind of danger again?"

Tucker said, "You mean that assassin you killed."

"That's the point, Tucker. I was lucky then. Others like her could come after us again. Except for this time, they'll be domestic killers."

Maya stepped over a tree root and picked up the pace as her comments got more passionate. "I know you remember the fear we experienced. Hell, even the president of the United States once said he wished you were dead. We had so many enemies that we were placed in witness protection on the other side of the world for six years."

He added, "We spent those six years wisely, getting trained in self-defense."

"Tucker, damn it, we're lucky to be alive. Admittedly, we had a lot of help from Tank. You could say we have it all and won life's lottery. Why blow it? We should count our lucky stars, sit back on a beach somewhere, stay in a protective cocoon, and smell the roses. Most people in our life situation and good health would be content to live their lives enjoying all the benefits that accompany wealth. There is no reason for us to change orbits. But no, instead, we're embarking on what, potentially, could be our most dangerous journey yet."

Tucker listened to the logic of the physicist, Dr. Maya Li Cherokee, as she presented her compelling one-sided argument against pursing the mission of the foundation they worked so hard to create. He listened and tried not to interrupt as she made her closing arguments.

As they continued their walk, he couldn't help but observe that she was not only brilliant and a wonderful person, but she was also drop-dead gorgeous.

Maya added, "And don't forget, we have a fourteen-year-old daughter to protect. Star provides more love and inspiration than we could expect in two lifetimes. God outdid Himself when he made Star."

Although cute as a button with her curly auburn hair, aqua-blue eyes, and cheerful disposition, Star exercised parts of her brain that the rest of humanity had not yet discovered. Maya and Tucker tried to keep the knowledge of her special "perceptive" skills—for which they had deep respect—hidden from the public.

Tucker tried to keep up stride for stride with his more athletic wife. Maya looked over at the man she loved and saw a fit, above-average in height man, still in his early forties, confident, and well trained in the art of self-defense. She saw a man with an unusual heritage of Cherokee Indian and Irish bloodline. He had a unique facial appearance that she found handsome and intriguing.

Maya said, "OK, it's your turn."

Tucker said, "You have skills at filibustering."

Maya punched Tucker's shoulder.

He said, "Last year when I shared the idea of my new project with you and Star, you didn't tell me I was crazy. You didn't tell me it was impossible or that it was too dangerous. Instead, you said that TV pundits, talk radio hosts, and conservative newsletters all whine and complain about the biased and sometimes dishonest media reporting, but that no one has ever offered a solution. When the German magazine, Der Spiegel, announced that their star reporter made up facts and the main stream news media sort of shrugged it off, you said 'it's about damn time someone does something about it.'"

She said, "Don't beat me over the head with my own words. That was then; things have changed."

Tucker reached out and touched Maya's left hand with his right and said, "You went on to say that the media abuses the First Amendment in the Bill of Rights. I remember you telling me that although the media is constitutionally granted the right by our forefathers to lie or be intentionally misleading that you believe the writers of the amendment forgot to mention anything about honesty, integrity, or transparency.

"As we often discussed, the profession of journalism allowed itself to become a tactical tool of the ideological left in their war against limited government, personal responsibility, and capitalism. The high standards they hold for themselves turned out to be mediocracy to us. Since the media abandoned the Canons of Journalism and failed to self-regulate or adopt a method of professional quality control, we decided to tackle the mission to effect a change in the inherent culture of the media and fight back."

Maya said, "None of that has changed, but we didn't know the risks back then."

Tucker added, "We formed The Media Transformation Foundation and attracted others who were willing and able to support the mission, but who wanted to do so from the shadows. We planned and strategized for months. We developed a framework for a solution to encourage journalists to report the news according to a code of ethics without screaming their ideological predisposition."

Maya said, "That was before I understood it to be life-threatening."

"Maya, we're action oriented—doers. I wonder if it is our destiny?

Why are we here?

What's the purpose of our lives?

Do we have a destiny?

"We were ready to launch our first mission or war front against the liberal media when we learned about the death of Gabriel Lakatos. I hated the bastard, but our newly formed foundation had nothing to do with his demise. I do wonder, however, who was responsible—I think I'll buy them a drink if I ever learn the truth.

"Lakatos funded groups to influence the mainstream media with distorted information. He's partly responsible for the current state of dishonesty reported by news organizations. Lakatos led a group of hateful, like-minded people who promoted the concept of a one-world government, socialism, communism, and totalitarianism. His death should help our cause, not hurt it."

Tucker took both of Maya's hands in his and said, "Will you come with me to the foundation's first meeting in Carlsbad? I can't do this without you."

CHAPTER 5

"The world will not be destroyed by those that do evil, but by those who watch them without doing anything."—Albert Einstein, 1879-1955, theoretical physicist

Carlsbad Caverns National Park, New Mexico – June 24th

Under a clear cloudless baby-blue sky, Tucker watched magpies float effortlessly against an easterly wind, which carried just a touch of the pungent smell of drifting sage. He turned 360 degrees to take in the mosaics of scrubs and grasses, yucca, flowering cactus, and tarbrush that sparsely touched the desert landscape.

It was not always a desert. Two hundred and fifty million years ago, an inland sea once covered the land where Tucker stood. Under what is now the Chihuahuan Desert, high ancient sea ledges and deep rocky canyons persisted. Over time, sulfuric acid dissolved the limestone from fossil reefs, leaving behind 199 caverns in what is today Carlsbad Caverns National Park.

This was the location selected for the inaugural meeting of The Media Transformation Foundation.

Tucker "persuaded" park management to grant him use of one of the caves, known as the Mescalero Cave, housed in the caverns. The specific cave's existence was virtually unknown even to some of the park rangers, but Tucker's sizable contribution to the Carlsbad Caverns National Park for maintenance and research provided Tucker some latitude to outfit the cave and close the park to the public.

Tank had performed advanced security surveillance at the site before the decision was made to buy access to the caverns. Tank ultimately secured the national park on Tucker's behalf for a series of meetings.

Tank Alvarez was the operational leader of the newly formed and nonexistent-to-the-outside-world secret organization. Tank was critical to its success and directed the foundation-approved and maybe a few unapproved operations. Tank formed White Knight Personal Security, LLC, a decade ago; added his mentor, Powers, as a partner; and grew the business to be one of the premier security firms in the country. Tank carried an intimidating six-foot, seven-inch, 310-pound muscular frame, which when matched with his close-combat fighting skills made him a one-man fighting machine.

Tank's partner, Powers, was a former Green Beret officer, a former Special Forces trainer, and a former one-term senator from the State of Maine. He would gladly lay down his life for anyone in the Cherokee immediate family. Tank and Powers both loved Star like she was their own daughter.

Tucker selected Carlsbad Caverns for the meeting because it allowed the foundation to conduct business without fear of eavesdropping. No satellite or drone surveillance was possible in the cave, and GPS couldn't track members inside. There was no cell service, no Wi-Fi access, and no other means of overhearing the members' discussion or learning about foundation tactics.

To maintain secrecy, it was decided that discussions would be conducted only in person. There would be no emails, use of social media, use of private servers, texting, or phone calls between members of the group on its business.

Over the last several months, Maya and Tucker had established the requirements for entrance into the foundation, recruited members, and raised funds.

Members included industry giants, social media entrepreneurs, a congressman, an evangelical leader, a talk radio host, military leaders, successful business executives, a retired judge, a cybersecurity contractor, a Hollywood producer, and a former attorney general and mayor. For their own protection, members did not know each other.

Leadership of the foundation could be the most important and most challenging task of Tucker and Maya's life. The foundation's mission was just, honorable, unselfish, and necessary. Collectively, the members of the foundation could change the course of humankind, just as America's founding fathers had done hundreds of years ago.

Maya and Tucker argued passionately about tactics. It was Tucker's opinion that the foundation couldn't win a war against the liberal press if they limited activities using strictly legal tactics. It was a risk, but he believed that they'd be wasting the funds donated by the foundation members if the money was only spent on lawyers who filed suits.

As they sat in the underground meeting room, Tucker asked Maya to critique what Tucker intended to say to each foundation member when they arrived: "We missed the starting gun. The dark side declared war against us decades ago, but we never understood it to be true or treated it like war. We are at war with an enemy that uses Saul Alinsky tactics. To catch up, we must plan our attacks as we would conduct a war against a foreign aggressor. We must drive a stake through the hearts of those that participate in false news reporting.

"Our foundation has ultimately adopted two documents to represent the basis of our strategy: Saul Alinsky's *Rules for Radicals* and Sun Tzu's *Art of War*. One of the reasons we've decided to operate under such extraordinary secrecy is that the foundation may need to use traditional Alinsky tactics—the same tactics adopted by the enemy."

Tucker added, "As it is said, 'What's good for the goose is good for the gander.' We're not going to win this war with love. We must fight fire with fire."

Maya stood up and walked around the cave, gestured with her hands, and said, "The foundation members may appreciate all your metaphors, but I think you might want to add that we spent many months researching the fundamental root cause of the wrongheaded thought process that has afflicted mainstream journalists. The reason that we might be successful and the difference between our approach and the approach that others before us have tried may be Tank's unorthodox and untraditional methods of encouragement."

CHAPTER 6

"Give me the power of the money and it will not matter anymore who is commanding." – Mayer Ansel Rothchild, 1744-1812, Illuminati

New York City, New York - June 24th

The Owl—as her friends called her—wore oversized, round black-framed glasses with thick lenses. Even without the magnification her glasses offered, her round brown eyes were abnormally large on her slender face and four-foot, eleven-inch frame.

She was retained because she suffered from a body-clock disorder that was always ten to twelve time zones off. She couldn't sleep at night and couldn't stay awake during the day.

Her target was Margaret Mellon, the famous and reclusive trustee of the Mellon Bank family fortune. After many dull evenings waiting just to get a glimpse of the rich bitch in the lobby or outside the building entrance, the Owl finally caught the woman in her crosshairs as she clandestinely left her New York City penthouse in the dead of night. The Owl zoomed in on Ms. Mellon and took a couple of digital photos. The paparazzi wannabe photographer was surprised to see the middle-aged fashion-conscious socialite unescorted and wearing jeans, a cheap sweatshirt, and a Yankees ball cap. The Owl, a nocturnal nineteen-year-old runaway from Dayton, was excited about maybe getting a never-before-seen image of the fastidious clothes-horse in such a common-looking outfit, alone, without her chauffeur or security guard, and getting into a taxi.

A *National Enquirer* reporter paid the Owl to be a paparazzi snitch. The spotter's job was to notify the columnist if she saw the lady leave her Park Avenue penthouse and to take photos, if possible, with the Sony digital camera he had provided her.

When the *Enquirer* reporter received the 3:30 a.m. electrifying text from his spotter with photos attached, he instructed her to grab a taxi and have the driver follow the diva to wherever she was going and to call him back when they arrived at the woman's destination.

The girl's cabbie followed Ms. Mellon's Yellow Cab across the George Washington Bridge, onto Route 46 in the direction of Hackensack. She watched as the woman's taxi turned off at the exit to Teterboro Airport in New Jersey. As instructed, the nineteen-year-old called the reporter to inform him of the development. He, in turn, raced to the airport to execute the time-honored process of bribery.

The secretive Ms. Mellon was greeted at the airport by her bodyguard and was escorted to the Atlantic Aviation terminal where the pilot, copilot, and personal flight attendant had prepared the family-owned Learjet 70 for departure. Mellon's four employees surrounded her as they walked on the tarmac, up the jetway stairs, and into the aircraft cabin.

The Learjet had already departed from Teterboro by the time the gossip column reporter got to the airport to meet with his source. The reporter bribed the air traffic controller for the flight plan and learned that the famous woman was headed to Lubbock Executive Airpark, Texas.

The *Enquirer* journalist contemplated his next move and elected to call a paparazzi photographer friend of his in Dallas to see whether it was possible for the photographer to reach Lubbock before the world-famous heiress arrived and whether he would follow her to her ultimate destination.

The photojournalist said, "Do you have any idea where Lubbock is? It's a fucking five-hour drive at best. Can't get there in time, unless, of course," he said with a wry smile, "you pay for a chartered flight."

The reporter, sensing a big story, agreed to reimburse the photographer. "You better make it worth it."

The photographer's roommate was a pilot for a regional airline. The pilot chartered a Cessna and arrived at the Lubbock airport twenty minutes before the Learjet 70 was scheduled to arrive from Teterboro. The camera monkey's longtime friend and pilot went to the Avis rental car counter to ready a four-wheel drive SUV while the paparazzi photographer found a strategic location to set up his tripod, his Nikon Digital SLR, and his long-range zoom lens. He was pumped; it would be a prize-winning shot of the diva in her commoner's attire when she deplaned.

A sudden, sharp pain pinched the photographer's right shoulder. He blacked out.

Forty minutes later, the pilot, who had rented an SUV from Avis, found the photographer lying on his back on a concrete walkway. "Wake up! Are you alright? Geez!" By the time the paparazzi photojournalist came around, the Learjet had landed, and its reclusive passenger was nowhere to be seen.

So was whoever had caused the photographer to pass out.

Lubbock, Texas

Margaret Mellon, the heiress to the Mellon Bank family fortune, looked over at a man who called himself Powers—no first name—in the back seat of the Range Rover Velar and said, "Thank you for taking care of that bottom-feeding gossip shutterbug for me. Those leeches are on my back constantly. I was hoping I could lose them on this trip."

Powers tried to display a rare smile, but the muscles in his face forgot the right positions long ago. He said, "You did."

Ms. Mellon asked, "What do you know about the meeting I'm about to attend, and what is your role in the, uh, foundation?"

"My job will be to make things happen." Powers stared through the tint of the blonde woman's sunglasses and directly into her aqua eyes. He said, "You and others in the foundation will decide 'what' things have to happen."

Margaret said, "If we can do a tenth of what we need to do, you'll be a very busy man."

Carlsbad Caverns National Park

The Range Rover pulled off the main road after a long drive from Laredo until it reached a barrier that blocked the entrance to the park's nearly empty parking lot. Tank stood intimidatingly by the barrier chain and motioned the driver to roll down the window.

Tank, expressionless, said to the driver, "You'll have to surrender your piece before we allow you to pass through the entrance, and you won't be able to enter the meeting. You'll have to stay in your car, unarmed. I'll return your weapon when you leave. You OK with that?"

Margaret Mellon's driver said, "First of all, how do you know I'm carrying? Secondly, I provide security for my employer. I have a concealed carry permit. It's my job."

Tank responded, "The passenger in the back seat with your employer is my partner. Powers sent a text to inform me that you are armed. No matter how tough you think you are, there is no way you will get past me and my partner, who is at your back with a weapon. Further, we'll not allow your employer's cell phone, iPad, tablet, iWatch, or any electronics of any kind past the entrance to the cavern. Understood?"

Ms. Mellon said, "Malcolm, it's OK. Please comply. It's the rules of the game."

"Powers," asked Tank, "did you pat down Malcolm's boss while in the car, or do I have to do everything?"

"Now just a minute," responded Margaret.

Powers said, "Don't worry, we're not the TSA. What we call a 'pat down' is just running a wand around you to make sure you don't have any electronic devices on you. It's not invasive. And, yes, Tank, Ms. Mellon has electronics on her person."

Tank waited.

"OK, OK, here." The Mellon Bank family heiress turned over her cell phone and mini-iPad.

Tank said, "Thank you, ma'am. Sorry for the inconvenience." He removed the barrier and allowed the Velar to pass.

Powers escorted the secret foundation member into the Carlsbad Caverns entrance where the sweet and overpowering smells of yucca flowers gave way to the damp, musty odors of algae, mold, fungi, and guano by the time they reached the Mescalero Cave. The national park is home to hundreds of thousands of Brazilian Free-tailed bats, which exit the caves at dusk on their nightly forage for food.

Margaret entered the cave and was immediately greeted by world famous hosts.

Tucker said, "Thank you for coming, Maggie. It's good to see you again. The lovely and brilliant lady by my side here is my partner in life, Maya."

Margaret extended her hand to Maya and said, "You are more breathtakingly beautiful in person than you are on television. I understand that you are also a brilliant particle physicist."

Maya said, "Thank you." She turned and beamed, "The young lady here with us is our daughter, Star. We are the only people you will ever meet that are associated with our organization outside of our security and operational staff."

Margaret said with melody in her voice, "Do you mean people like Powers and Tank? How do you intend to maintain a low-profile, secretive foundation with such high-profile people like you, Maya, and Powers? I think when you were the science advisor to the president and a vice presidential candidate, you were on more magazine covers than most Hollywood actresses, Maya. And wasn't Powers a former senator?"

Tucker answered, "Fame has a short half-life. It's been years since either Maya or Powers were in the spotlight. We'll be careful not to tie them to the underground foundation."

Maya said, "Maggie, the fact that you took the time and energy to get to this remote location without being followed reinforces our judgment that you are truly committed to our long-term mission."

Tucker added, "When we met last year, we discussed the requirements for entrance into this secret foundation, so you know what's at stake. You know our mission, but what you don't know is who else are members of this foundation. Nor, for your protection, will the other members know you are a participant. You would recognize the other participants as, like you, almost all have been on a magazine cover at one time or another. There are only twenty-two of us in the world, excluding the team of people who provide our security and those who perform the work necessary to execute tactics.

"Our goal here today is to drill down and clearly define our broad mission to you, present our blueprint for success, discuss potential strategies, and clarify your specific involvement."

Maya said, "As you know, and have expressed yourself during your first get-together with Tucker, we must force a paradigm shift in the way we deal with the enemy—the liberal media. Hence, we have established an account in Belize. To protect you and every member with deniability, we will not share with you the specific tactics. Is that understood and acceptable to you?"

Margaret Mellon is portrayed by the gossip media as a shapely "dumb blonde" who won life's lottery, hid out in her luxurious Manhattan penthouse, watched TV all day eating chocolate, and drank thousand-dollar-per-bottle wine at night. The media depicted her as unintelligent, uninformed, and self-absorbed. The fact was, however, quite the opposite. The forty-eight-year-old type-B personality recluse received a Ph.D. in international economics from NYU and quadrupled her inheritance through investments in the stock market. She studied the market, developed her own quant algorithms, mastered option trading, studied blockchain technology, and out-performed alleged experts in the currency trading market. She is no dummy and hated the media's willingness to fabricate news about her.

She looked directly into Maya's penetrating blue eyes and said, "Before we go on, will we be breaking any laws? Specifically, did we have anything to do with last week's murder of the left-wing funder of the liberal media, Gabriel Lakatos? It seems a little coincidental that one of the staunchest liberal radicals and media manipulators is assassinated just before we convene to fight a war against our radical liberal enemies. I don't want to be associated with murder, torture, or anything ruthless."

Maya intentionally didn't answer the question but added, "Let us be clear. We are at war."

Maggie Mellon said, "My dear Maya, I'll repeat my question. Did this foundation or our secret society, have anything to do with the murder of Gabriel Lakatos?"

Maya Cherokee's response was a firm, "No." She continued, "We have some theories as to who may be responsible for the assassination of that troll, Lakatos, but it wasn't us. We are not sorry that he was killed, except for the martyrdom he received from his radical followers, but we did not authorize his demise. At this point, it is a mystery to us."

Tucker spoke up, "We did, however, learn tactics from him. We took advantage of his murder and contacted fifty-two decision-makers in the enemy's camp. We sent threatening messages to them and made it look like the messages were sent from North Korea."

The sophisticated and refined lady said, "I understand from news reports that he died instantly. It's too bad he didn't suffer. I wished more for him."

Tucker laughed and said, "Right on."

He looked down at his notes and said, "You understand our mission—that is to move the media from the Far Left to the right.

"Let's focus on strategy. The foundation will launch an attack on multiple war fronts. At this count, there are over twenty different fronts we intend to employ. We can't execute all the fronts in parallel—we just don't have the bandwidth, so we're going to attack in stages. Over the first 120 days, we intend to launch an offense on only four of the war fronts.

"The first order of business is to take control of a couple of old-school print media publications. We initiated activities to acquire control of *The New York*

Times and *The Washington Post*. This is a war front right out of the liberal playbook."

Maggie asked, "And if they won't sell?"

Tucker answered, "In time, I think they'll sell."

"I see. I don't want to know your methods, right?"

"It's for your own protection."

Maggie added, "OK, but more than eighty percent of Americans get some of their news and information through social media today. It's a tactical imperative, in my opinion, to execute a strategy to influence the young and uninformed. Print media and cable news is old school. You're focusing on the equivalent of addressing diode tubes and 45 vinyl records. We're missing the boat if that's our focus."

Tucker said, "We agree, you're dead on. But the Washington establishment still reacts to whatever Kool-Aid message the *Post* dribbles out.

"But to your point, our second war front leverages social media. The plan is to use the various social media formats and launch a firehose of fake news targeting the mainstream media. We have a team working that disinformation warfare angle.

"The third warfront targets cable news networks with the same voracity that our late nemesis Gabriel Lakatos and Media Matters attacked the Fox News Network. We'll go for their throat—their advertisers. We're targeting the news organizations that are barely surviving financially. Their existence won't be sustainable with fewer advertisers. Wouldn't you agree?"

Ms. Mellon said, "Hmm. Wasn't this tried before without much success?"

Maya said, "It might be easier than you think in today's politically volatile environment. People who follow the news closely still get most of their news on television. We're targeting the super-biased cable news networks before we try to tackle the big boys like ABC, CBS, and NBC.”

“Our last war front, which we intend to launch within 120 days, attacks Hollywood. We thought we’d start with infiltrating *Saturday Night Live* and other late-night comedy shows. Any thoughts?”

Ms. Mellon asked, “Are you saying we can influence its production to make fun of our enemies?”

“What a concept, eh?” Tucker added, “Although we have plans and approaches to sixteen other war fronts, we’ll hold off on them until the first four are well on their way.”

“What role,” Maggie finally asked, “are you asking me to play in this secret society or foundation?”

Tucker cleared his throat and said, “Maya is the organization’s treasurer. She’ll disburse the funds to the chief of operations, Tank, who’ll be responsible for executing the tactics necessary for successful completion of each war front. First, we’d like you to manage and invest our financial assets and make them grow.”

“Well, that is a lot of responsibility. You’re massaging my brain cells. Are you sure I’m the best selection for that role?”

Instead of answering the question, both Maya and Tucker looked over at their daughter, Star. Margaret had almost forgotten that the teenager was still in the cave.

Star had listened intently to every word spoken through the entire discussion. She looked into and through Maggie Mellon with an intensity that concerned—maybe even frightened—the banking heiress. Star didn’t smile, didn’t say a word, but did nod her head only slightly.

Maya said, “Yes, we’re sure you have the horsepower to get the job done.”

The expression on Maggie's face showed confusion. She started to say or ask something, but before she got it out, Tucker said, "What goes on here is secret."

Margaret Mellon stared for a few seconds into the eyes of Star who stared back unflinchingly. Star finally said, "No, Dr. Mellon, I have no say in what Mom and Dad decide to do. I just have a unique sense about who we can trust."

Maggie asked, "You know what I was thinking?"

Before Star answered the question, Maya said, "It was all over your face, your expression."

Maggie didn't buy the answer but said, "OK. How much money are we talking about investing?"

Tucker said, "We identified twenty-two very wealthy and influential members of the group who are as committed to this cause as you and we are. We collectively were able to raise a significant amount of money—money that we will return if unused."

Maya said, "Excluding what we need to keep liquid for operational purposes, around two billion US dollars."

Margaret Mellon was speechless.

"Dr. Mellon, you may be paid a visit by someone named Agatha Priest. Be sure to meet with her if she drops by to see you."

"Who is she?"

Maya answered, "Me. I won't call on you in person under my real name. We can never be seen together in public, and your staff can't know it's me. When I do call on you, it may be a request for you to get your hands a little dirty."

Maggie answered, "I fully understand. It's war."

Tucker looked at his watch. The next foundation member was due at the cave in thirty minutes.

CHAPTER 7

"When those prominent in the status quo turn and label you as an 'agitator' they are completely correct." – Saul Alinsky, 1909-1972, author of *"Rules for Radicals"*

Washington, DC - June 25th

Six uninterested D.C. Metropolitan Police officers observed thirty peaceful sign-carrying protestors on 'K' Street between 13th and 14th Street NW who chanted:

"The *Post* Sucks. Down with the *Post*."

A young George Washington University female student whose long dark eyelashes and mascara belied the green hijab she wore, carried a sign that read "Go home, Jorgensen!"

Another protestor held a sign that displayed "*Post* = Fake News" and repeatedly chanted "Fake news, fake news."

A rookie officer, right out of the academy, joked with a seasoned sergeant, "This is a first. I've never seen a protest by the right wing of our local society. Didn't even know there were any in the city, especially students."

"Fake news, fake news."

"The *Post* sucks."

The younger officer asked, "What's their beef? What started this?"

The sergeant answered, "I don't know and don't care. But here comes the first TV van. Things typically escalate from here, so be prepared."

"Fake news, fake news."

"The *Post* sucks."

"Go home, Jorgensen."

The well-dressed and made-up bubbleheaded blonde Channel Seven news reporter brought her microphone close to the protestors, spied the young lady in the green hijab, and asked, "What are you protesting about?"

The teenage student answered, "*The Washington Post* ran an editorial that accused white supremacists, the Republicans, and conservatives of the murder of Gabriel Lakatos with absolutely no evidence or proof. The pathetic media thinks that to claim editorial integrity, all they have to do is say it 'may' have occurred. We're tired of unfounded accusations that slander us conservatives. What if they ran an article on you saying you 'may' abuse animals or you 'may' be a pedophile? It would be unfair, right? It's bullshit and it has to stop."

A tall, long-legged man wearing a gray hoodie ran full speed out from the interior of the protest group carrying a 32-oz green ginger ale bottle and stopped abruptly. The sergeant said, "Oh, shit," just before the sprinter lit a gasolene soaked rag and threw the Molotov cocktail through the front door of *The Washington Post* headquarters. To the delight of the protestors, the flames spread across the tile floor of the empty, sterile lobby and ran up the building walls. The Channel Seven reporter was shocked and the six DC policemen who had watched the peaceful demonstrators for the past three hours were slow to react. The lobby's automatic sprinklers activated, and the local fire department was notified. Smoke poured out of the lobby into the faces of protestors, forcing them to retreat.

The student who threw the bomb, a college 220-meter track star, bolted into a side street while peeling off his hoodie, mask, and breakaway sweat pants and came out the other end in a Brooks Brother suit. He picked up a briefcase that was strategically placed next to a newsstand, and he casually walked into the rear entrance of the adjacent Hamilton Hotel.

The rookie and a female officer chased the bomber into the alley while the sergeant called for EMTs and backup. The track star was too fast and they lost him, but they discovered his removed clothing in the backstreet.

The man in the Brooks Brothers suit walked out of the hotel entrance, crossed the street, walked through Franklin Square, and eventually entered the McPherson Square Metro Station.

No one was hurt from the bombing event, firefighters were quick to limit the damage, but the impact of the violent protest resonated throughout the nation. People from all around the metropolitan area spontaneously mobilized to demonstrate and infuse new energy, new signs, and new slogans in support of the cause.

"Hey, hey, whatya say, no integrity here today."

College Park, Maryland

The Mitsubishi printing presses in the 324,000 square-foot facility adjacent to the University of Maryland pumped out the print version of *The Washington Post* reliably, partially because of the magnificent work of the production engineer and his maintenance crew.

Until today.

"Sir," said the shift supervisor, "the paper feeder on line number one is not responding."

The engineer answered, "Call in our troubleshooter, swap out the feeder on line one with the installed spare, and increase the speed on line number two."

"Yes, sir."

The production industrial engineer was a fifty-three-year-old who had won numerous awards from *The*

Washington Post for his exceptional work at keeping the presses operational.

"Sir," said the shift supervisor thirty minutes later, "we have a problem. None of the feeders are working. None of them are accepting paper. And I can't reach our troubleshooter."

Washington, DC

The CEO of *The Washington Post* received a call from his chief information officer. "Uh, sir. The unthinkable has happened. Someone hacked us. The current digital issue has a bogus article that we did not post. Someone has replaced an editorial we posted with a false article that was claimed to be written by one of our editorialists. Whoever did this is good."

The CEO said, "Jesus, we must be under attack. Our headquarters was bombed, College Park was sabotaged, and now this. Do you think this attack is domestic or of foreign interference? Do you think it is the Russians?"

"As I said, they're good. We followed the thread and determined that cyberattackers left a false flag from the North Koreans. But I don't think Pyongyang has the wherewithal to pull off a trick like this."

"Well pull down the fake article and replace it with the correct manuscript," he instructed.

"We've tried that five separate times. Each time we pulled it down, the wrong article popped right back up."

The CEO contemplated the new information for a few seconds and finally said, "Call Special Agent Rusty Winemiller over in the FBI Cybercrimes Division and inform him of the crime. See what the FBI can do to help. And by the way, what is the fake article about?"

"The false editorial was about Gabriel Lakatos. Instead of the piece we posted, which informed the readers about Lakatos's philanthropy, it talked about all the people hurt by him, all the harm he did, the lives he ruined, and his treachery. The editorial made him out to be a monster."

The CEO's face hardened, his eyes darkened, and teeth ground as he said, "So, it's domestic. It's those fucking right wingers."

Carlsbad, New Mexico

The Cherokees met separately and privately with seven Hall of Fame members of the clandestine foundation who each succeeded at traveling incognito. Alone in the caverns at the end of the day, Tucker watched Star apply makeup to her mother's face, help her put on the brown-colored contact lenses onto her blue eyes, pull her long black hair into a bun, place the blonde wig over it, and brush the mop so it looked unkempt. Satisfied with the way Maya looked, Star said, "It's perfect. You don't look anything like my mother."

Maya said to Star while making eye contact with Tucker, "How's your dad coming with his new look?"

Star glanced at Tucker and said as if he wasn't in the room, "He looks a little silly in a ten-gallon hat, but I think we can make it into the Trinity Hotel without anybody recognizing him. I'm sure glad I'm not as famous as my parents."

Maya said, "Fame, my beautiful daughter, is a double-edged sword."

They made it to their hotel room from Carlsbad Cavern without being identified. After pizza was delivered to the room, the Cherokee family watched the cable news coverage of the protests, bombing, and sabotage of *The Washington Post*.

Tucker said, "The first day of the war on the mainstream print media seems to have been a success with one exception."

Maya said, "Right, except for the bombing. We had nothing to do with that."

Maya's expression changed, a thought crossed her mind, and she asked, "Did we?"

"No. Unless Tank authorized it without our approval. It's not like him. An innocent person could have really been hurt."

Tucker picked up an encrypted satellite phone and said, "Tank, could you come up to our room for a couple of minutes?"

Maya stared at Tucker with eyes that could melt steel, "And we had nothing to do with Gabriel Lakatos's murder, did we?"

Although Tucker surrounded himself with people capable of pulling off the assassination, he was pissed that she would question him about it. He thought she knew him better than that.

Tucker said with a touch of anger in his voice, "No."

She responded, "Then someone else is out there attacking the same enemy we're focused on but with less restrictive rules of engagement. It won't be long now before our enemy knows the war they started years ago finally has consequences."

Star studied her parents, comprehended their distress, and said, "Don't worry, Mom. You and Dad know what you're doing."

Bang.

It sounded like an FBI assault team battered into the hotel room door. Star and Maya jumped with fright until they heard a familiar voice. It was just Tank knocking on the door.

Maya said, "Tank, can't you knock with less force? I thought there was a cosmic explosion. You scared the crap out of us!"

"Sorry, what's up?"

Tucker asked, "Have you seen your handiwork in front of the *Post*'s HQ? The paid protestors did a great job but . . ."

Tank interrupted and said, "The Molotov cocktail into *The Washington Post* office lobby was not in the script. I did not authorize that activity. What it means is that someone knew we were going to organize protestors today.

"Powers and I have racked our brains trying to figure out who has their nose under our tent."

CHAPTER 8

"Not every conspiracy is a theory."- James Badge Dale, actor

Wichita, Kansas - June 26th

The infamous Hurt brothers were both pilots and flew from their shared private ranch landing strip outside of Wichita to the Shoestring Ranch Airport in Organ, New Mexico. Their security detail accompanied them and rented a four-wheel-drive Jeep. The men were often required to travel incognito and became excellent at concealing their identities. In fact, they hired a costume designer to disguise them on this trip as camera-wielding Europeans. When they arrived at the rendezvous point in the parking lot of the national park, their four-man security detail surveyed their surroundings and scouted the premises. They observed a large man and three others standing in front of the meeting entrance.

"Boss," said the head of security for the brothers, "You're clear. Security at this meeting may be the best in the world."

The older brother, William, asked, "Why is that?"

"Have you ever heard of Tank Alvarez and Powers?"

"Yes, of course. We tried to hire their firm, White Knight Personal Security, to protect us at a fund-raiser, but they were backlogged at the time with other contracts."

"Well, we're looking at them."

The chemical industry entrepreneurs casually approached the entrance to the meeting when Tank stopped them. Tank shook hands with the Hurt brothers, introduced Powers and himself and said, "On behalf of the foundation, thanks for coming. It's an honor to finally meet you two."

Despite the cordial reception, Tank insisted that the brothers be swept for recording devices, cell phones, tablets, laptops, or other forms of electronics. Tank also demanded that he pat them down to make sure they were unarmed.

Tank said, "I'm sorry, sirs, but we cannot allow your security personnel past the entrance."

The younger brother, Nick, was a rangy, solid-looking Midwesterner who was used to giving orders, not taking them, and said, "I insist on having my security team with me through the entire meeting."

"Not going to happen, Mr. Hurt," answered Tank.

"May we speak with your employer?" asked the less-impetuous older brother.

"Not out in the open. You'll have to go in without security to speak with Tucker," responded Tank.

Nick said, "Let's blow this little get-together. We weren't sure we wanted to be a part of this anyway."

William said, "We've already made a significant financial contribution to the foundation's cause."

Nick Hurt looked at his head of security and said, "Talk some sense into these guys."

He said, "Sirs, I would entrust you under the protection of White Knight without reservation. You're safe. Go on in. You came this far and gave up that golf charity to be here."

The brothers grudgingly acquiesced to the meeting conditions and were escorted into the cavern without their personal security team to meet with Maya and Tucker.

Nick Hurt made an unsuccessful attempt to chest-bump Tank on his way in but only managed to bounce off him.

As they were led to the meeting area by Tank, the Hurt brothers could not help but observe the uniqueness of the caverns with their impressive stalactites and stalagmites.

Tucker greeted the men as they entered the meeting cave and said, "Maya and I are honored to have you as members of the foundation. The media has always accused you two of funding every activity the left doesn't agree with. After today, it might actually be true."

William took off his European fedora, exposed his thick mane of white hair, extended his hand to Maya, kissed her outstretched hand, and said, "I have been a big fan of yours. As Carl Sagan once said, 'The beauty of a living thing is not the atoms that go into it, but the way those atoms are put together.' I have a soft spot for women with both brains and beauty."

Maya's smile said it all.

Tucker and Maya briefed the men on the status of the foundation's mission and the details of each war front.

A thoughtful William Hurt asked, "Exactly who are we at war with? Are we attacking a specific group of people or individuals? It sounds to me as if we are attacking a mindset. You know, trillions of dollars have been wasted fighting unwinnable wars like the war on drugs, the war on poverty, and the war on crime. I've learned to pick my battles. Is the war against the dishonest media a winnable war?"

Tucker answered, "Excellent question. To some extent you are correct. It is a war against a mindset. Over a period of more than sixty years, our faceless enemy infiltrated our primary and secondary education system. Most parents trusted public education. They put their kids in the system at age five and went to work to provide for their families. By the time the children came out the pipeline at age eighteen, their belief system had been influenced, if not warped, by the rigged system. The children were taught a misguided sense of fairness and social justice instead of basic skills for reading, writing, and arithmetic."

Nick joked, "They even banned my favorite subject, dodgeball."

Maya added, "As Chris Plante says, 'What they don't want to ban, they want to make mandatory.'"

Tucker continued, "Over time, fewer and fewer hours were dedicated to teaching math and science while more and more effort was spent on social issues from the liberal point of view. History was either not taught or taught from books that revised history to satisfy the publisher's view of the world. Some parents were able to overcome the wrongheaded world view taught to their children; others were not."

Nick added, "And at the end of the pipeline, they were driven into the hands of batshit crazy liberal professors."

Maya said, "Exactly. The enemy is a philosophy. It was adopted by a cadre of people who have turned it into a religion, preached it for decades, and ingrained it into self-righteous writers of words who refer to themselves as journalists. It's a deadly war of words.

"Our war fronts are designed to neutralize the few who fund the larger enemy. Lakatos was one of them."

Tucker said, "To answer your question, the war is winnable if we define victory as reversing the current trend of media journalists who consider it more important to promote their political view than to report the news honestly. We win when conservative viewpoints reach parity with liberal perspectives. We win if we stop the progression of the move toward a one-world government and socialism."

Nick asked, "What is the timeline for accomplishing these objectives, and besides money, what do you need from us?"

Tucker answered, "Although we'll start the first four fronts in the first 120 days, the timeline to declare victory is likely to take years. Don't forget, the enemy is decades ahead of us. If you collected any information on the enemy that would be useful in developing tactics, it would be appreciated."

William smiled and said, "I think we can help with that."

Maya continued, "We will eventually address how higher education approaches the science of journalism, explore how intelligence agencies influence the reporting of news, and what international influences impact what we read. Later we'll investigate banks, the judicial conundrum, how to approach millennials, the military, law enforcement, Wall Street, and the United Nations. Our next meeting is in the Cheyenne Mountain Complex in Colorado Springs and is scheduled to occur at the end of the first 120 days. At that time, we'll discuss progress and any recommended change in strategy, but to provide you with continued deniability, we will not discuss tactics."

"I'm sorry," said William, "I didn't come all the way to Carlsbad, looking over my shoulder, hoping no one would recognize me in this foolish-looking costume for just this debrief. Nick and I didn't donate funds to the foundation's account for a passive role. We need to do more."

Tucker joked, "You could get me a margarita."

Tucker decided the brothers didn't have a sense of humor. William looked confused and continued, "What's your plan to affect future journalists?"

Tucker glanced over at Star, who nodded to Tucker imperceptibly—trust verified.

"OK," Tucker said, "here's how you can help. There are approximately ninety thousand journalists in the US. Members of our team have created and vetted an algorithm to grade all journalists against weighted criteria, including, among other parameters, the journalist's ideological predisposition based on the schools the journalist attended and the professors that mentored them. The software reviews every manuscript the writer has produced for honesty, not only for what they wrote but also against what they failed to include on the subject on which they wrote. The program judges the writer's proclivity to be influenced by his or her editor and publisher, his or her thoroughness, and the subject matters selected. Each journalist will be graded and evaluated for ethical conduct and things they've blogged on social media. We've beta-tested and assessed only 772 of the 90,000 journalists and made some adjustments to the algorithm based on some lessons learned. We're ready to launch but need a supercomputer and some leadership to complete the mission. It's going to require leaders with strategic patience."

Over the next forty-five minutes, the foundation conceived the mission of 'HonestMediaMatters.org.'

Seattle, Washington

Troy had to admire the spectacular sunset view of the estate on Puget Sound. From his elevated position in Discovery Park, the estate on Perkins Lane looked decadently amazing through his scope.

This was going to be the easiest and lowest risk contract he'd ever had. He didn't have to use his sharpshooting talents to kill anything. He was given the exact point on the estate to place his .50 caliber round. Because the target was 1,500 yards away, he had to position himself at precisely the right angle. Troy had all the time in the world to prepare and knew he could take multiple shots if necessary. Since no one was home at the residence that he was going to violate, his only concern was to escape the park unnoticed.

He waited. The sun reflected its aura over the sound and displayed a rainbow-like beauty over the water as it set. The night vision scope was state-of-the-art and zoomed in on the bull's-eye. Troy lay on his stomach for ten minutes, got into a mental zone that made him oblivious to his surroundings, tightened his fingertip on the trigger, and fired. The sound from his sniper rifle was loud enough to be heard miles away, but at least he didn't need a second shot. Troy was on the move.

The bullet blew through the north wall of the redwood siding on the third floor, through the drywall of the library, through the opposite-side bookshelf, into the master bedroom, through the bed's headboard, out the other side of the bedroom, through the master bath tile, out the south side of the estate, and finally into a fifty-year-old oak tree.

CHAPTER 9

"The third rule of the ethics of means and ends is that in war the end justifies almost any means." – Saul Alinsky, 1909-1972, author of *"Rules for Radicals"*

Malibu Beach, California - June 26th

The famous Oscar-winning actor was exhausted from the numerous takes he had to endure today on the $150 million movie for which he was the lead protagonist. But he had planned this cocktail party at his home in Malibu Beach weeks ago thinking he'd be through with his current engagement by now. So, he sucked it up and entertained his agent, seven producers, four directors, and their companions—who he knew were not necessarily their spouse. Unusual for him, he also invited a Hollywood reporter.

The 1980's era rock-and-roll band played Alan Parsons Project's "Damned if I Do" outside on the deck overlooking the Pacific Ocean as the two bars stayed busy serving mind-numbing drinks to the guests.

The actor grabbed the microphone to make an announcement, "Thank you all for coming. This is a celebration of an almost complete gig on my current engagement. Here is a toast to the producer, director, fellow actors and actresses, and special effects artists who will make it a box office smash."

"Hear, hear," was the universal response.

He continued, "And I want to toast to the fact that I've accepted a new contract as the lead actor in a new venture with a heretofore unknown producer with a script that is unique in our industry."

There was a smattering of applause and only one or two "hear, hears."

"I read the script and was offered the largest advance in my career. So, I accepted."

A few guests laughed; others waited for more information.

"I'm sworn to secrecy, so I can't elaborate anymore or provide details. Just know, there's a new sheriff in town. Enjoy yourself and look forward to announcements as things progress. Again, thank you for coming."

The band started back up and played a rendition of Kool and the Gang's "Celebration."

The actor wandered over to the table that catered his food and picked up an oyster on the half-shell. The sexy writer for the *Hollywood Reporter*, famous for her gossip column, was the first to approach him after his speech, as the remaining guests engaged in subdued and serious conversation. She wore a frilly-lace white blouse with a black bra underneath and asked, "So why did you invite me to this function?"

The actor was captivated by the aroma of her perfume, lost focus, but finally answered, "You hear about everything that goes on in this town."

She said, "I hope so; that's my job."

He asked, "What have you heard about a new production studio starting up?"

"If you're talking about Real America Productions, I've heard a lot."

The actor's agent stood close enough to the conversation to overhear the reporter ask, "Are they your new employer?"

The agent spoke up and said, "I'm sorry, but his contract doesn't allow him to answer that question."

She continued, "It's the buzz in the Writer's Guild. Many of the top writers, including the writers for

Saturday Night Live and *Comedy Central* are retained to pen stories that are completely distinctive in the industry. iiI heard that the writers' contracts include the production of hundreds of internet streaming comedy shows to appeal to the eighteen to twenty-nine age group. But I've also learned that the new production company provided guidelines that must be met and that they have final approval of the production."

The actor asked, "What do you mean by 'distinctive in the industry'?"

"I don't know exactly," she responded, "but if I read between the lines—pun intended—the writers have a message they must send to viewers. Based on rumors, they've also retained Clint Eastwood, Mel Gibson, Jon Voight, and Gary Sinise. Rumor has it that producers Dennis Michael Lynch, Dinesh D'Souza, and Julienne O'Kray are on their payroll.

"There may be more, but I guess that *Real America Productions* plans on flooding the market with new movies that have a less liberal agenda."

The actor said, "You're going to be busy the next few months because I suspect there is going to be an ugly backlash."

She said, "I can only hope. This is going to be fun."

New York City

Gabriel Lakatos's billions were hidden in offshore numbered accounts, shell corporations, trust funds, family member names, foundations, safe-deposit boxes, and gold coins. He awarded the responsibility of being his estate executor to his attorney, Levi Zimmerman. Levi thought Gabriel liked him until he learned he had to administer Lakatos's last will. Levi thought, "He must have hated me."

But in fact, Gabriel trusted Levi more than any person in his sphere of influence. Levi was a superb actor in his own right. He was, outwardly, unpretentious in appearance, exhibited a type-B personality, was laconic by nature, and small in stature. He appeared to be a threat to no one. But behind the façade was a brilliant—although immoral—strategist. He shared and, to some extent, influenced Gabriel Lakatos's world view.

Levi was the only person who knew where all the bodies were buried. He knew where every penny of Lakatos's fortune was tucked; he'd helped develop their tax evasion strategy; he knew what was in Lakatos's thirty-five different safe-deposit boxes; and, most importantly, he'd kept the billionaire's black extortion book for him.

He received a text from the Hollywood reporter: "You are correct." Levi put his phone down and contemplated his next move for a few minutes before he called the private investigation firm used by the Lakatos family of companies. As Zimmerman pulled out Lakatos's black book, he thought, "We'll put an end to Real America Productions in short order."

CHAPTER 10

"You can stand me up at the gates of hell, but I won't back down, gonna stand my ground…."—Tom Petty and The Heartbreakers, lyrics from the song *"I won't back down"*

Washington, DC – June 26th

In a private room at McCormick & Schmick's Seafood & Steaks on K Street, Jeff Jorgensen, the wealthiest person in the world and owner of *The Washington Post*, was enjoying the company of congressmen and women from the State of Washington. It was a fun time where they told each other off-color political jokes.

Until his cell phone barked. He looked down to see who had just sent him a text message.

It was from someone who called himself Judas. The text message read "It was not an accident that the shot penetrated your wife's side of the headboard."

The men and women around the table witnessed Jorgensen's face and shaved head turn red, a lump on his forehead throb, and the anger in his expression grow foul.

Then the same cell phone rang.

"Mr. Jorgensen?"

"Who's asking?"

"This is Detective Yamaguchi from the Seattle Police Department. I wanted to let you know that your residence in Seattle was, uh, vandalized. Do you have time for a few questions?"

Fort Chipewyan

Officer Doug Butterfield surfed through a myriad of web pages in the hope that one of them might help him figure out which helicopter models fit the rail impressions discovered in the grass in Wood Buffalo National Park. He narrowed the list down to nine and then tried to determine the range of each model. Then he drew a circle on a map with a radius of 200 miles, figuring the extraction helicopter had to make a round-trip.

"Hmm. . ." The list was small. Only Fort Smith, Fort McMurray, Yellowknife, Grande Prairie, Wabasca/Horizon Airport, and Northern Rockies Regional Airport were within range. He started to check with each of the airports to see whether a helicopter had registered a flight plan and refueled at their location during the timeframe in question when he heard a news report on the radio.

"One of Seattle's most famous residents fell victim to an attack on his home when it was vacant. Jeff Jorgensen, the founder of the world's most successful internet retailer and owner of *The Washington Post*, was away from his home with his family when a sniper shot a .50 caliber round through his mansion. No one has claimed responsibility, and there are no suspects at this time according to the Seattle Police Department. An investigation is ongoing. Now for the weather. . ."

Butterfield ran his fingers through his blond hair while contemplating the consequences of waking Nelson who'd gone to a motel to catch some Zs. Doug decided he was damned if he did and damned if he didn't. So, he called the motel.

"What is it, Butterfield? Did you figure out where the helicopter refueled?"

"Not yet," he answered, "but I have a thought I want to share with you. Someone placed a .50 caliber round into the home of Jeff Jorgensen in Seattle."

"So, what's the connection to our case?"

"I'm not a political junkie, but wouldn't Gabriel Lakatos and Jeff Jorgensen travel in the same circles? In fact, wouldn't Jorgensen be the heir apparent to Lakatos? I mean, if someone was going to fill a liberal billionaire activist's shoes, wouldn't the Seattle mogul fit the bill?"

Rod Nelson said, "You might make a good detective yet, Butterfield. I'll contact the Seattle police and see if they'll share any ballistic information with us. It will be a stroke of luck if they match. See if you can find a name for the case detective. And, Butterfield, keep working on the location of where the helicopter refueled."

CHAPTER 11

"I heard that, too, and it's a damn lie." – John Wayne, 1907-1979, actor, a line from the movie "*True Grit*"

Whites City, New Mexico – June 27th

The three-term US senator was scheduled to run a 10-K for a charity in Colorado Springs. But he never showed up. Instead, the senator caught a flight to the El Paso International / Juarez Airport. Upon arrival, he rented a car and drove northeast on Route 180 on Salt Flats; past Lake Linda; onto Route 62; past El Capitan; and on up to Whites City, New Mexico. He enjoyed the eventless two-and-a-half-hour drive from Nowhere, Texas, to Nowhere, New Mexico.

The senator got out of the car when he reached a national park, stretched, and looked around the nearly empty parking lot for his point-of-contact. As instructed, he texted the number he was given to notify the guy that he had arrived. A huge Hispanic man in an unmarked white van opened the van's passenger's-side door, got out, approached the senator, and asked, "Are you Peter Enya?"

"Yes, I'm Senator Enya. And you are . . ."

"My name is Tank. This German Shepherd here is my buddy Ram. He is a well-trained 100-pound military K-9. Be his friend. You don't want him to be your enemy. By the way, do you know, sir, that your latex mask is peeling around the back of your ears? You'll want to fix that before you enter the meeting."

Peter Enya responded, "My face is very recognizable. I had to hide it in order to not be identified while on my way or while here."

After Tank waved the wand around the senator and swept him for bugs and electronic devices, Tank escorted the senator into the Mescalero Cave.

After a respectful and deferential greeting, Maya and Tucker debriefed the senator in a manner similar to the way they briefed Margaret Mellon. Tucker was about to inform the senator about the details of the war fronts when he was distracted by Star who stood up abruptly from the back of the meeting cave and gave the universal sign for "time-out" with one hand vertical and the other horizontal. She nodded at her mother and father and slipped out of the meeting area where she saw Powers standing guard outside the cave. Powers looked into Star's eyes and knew immediately something was wrong. He leaned over and Star whispered something in his ear.

To delay the meeting with Peter Enya until they understood what Star was concerned about, Tucker said, "Senator, our next session will be fun. We're going to brainstorm methods and approaches to move the leftist media to the right. We want you to interact with us. Think about tactics and a strategic methodology for moving forward while I address a family matter."

Before Tucker and Maya left the meeting area, Powers entered the cave and approached his former colleague, Peter Enya.

Powers said, "How are you doing, Peter? You're wearing a great mask. I never would have recognized you. But, then again, that's how we assure secrecy, isn't it? Wow, you sure look fit. What's your secret?"

Senator Enya said coldly, "Look, Powers, I don't have a lot of time here. I need to finish my business with Tucker and Maya and be on my way."

Unfazed, Powers said, "Peter, do you remember the time we negotiated that law enforcement bill with Senator Wagner. That was quite an experience, wasn't it?"

Senator Enya smiled and said, "Yes, that was a hoot."

Powers placed his left hand on Senator Enya's shoulder, pinched a nerve that brought the senator to his knees, and ripped the latex mask off the man with his right hand to reveal someone twenty-five years younger than the real Senator Enya. Powers said, "You are not Senator Enya. Who the fuck are you, and where is Senator Enya?"

The imposter bolted to the cave exit only to find Tank and Ram standing in the doorway. Tank jammed the heel of his left hand into the man's chest forcing him to land flat on his back. Tank said, "Let's interview you here and now. Ram goes first. Ram, I think this man is bad."

Ram approached the fraud and bared his teeth, growled, and placed his snout in the man's face.

Tank said, "Whoever you are, know that Ram has killed other criminals at my direction. Think about that before you lie to me. I have photos with me of the autopsies of people who crossed Ram. Are we clear?"

The frightened deceiver nodded his head.

Powers asked, "OK, let's start with the basics. Who are you and what happened to the real Senator Peter Enya?"

Tucker caught up with the team and added, "I met with Senator Enya last year. You are not him."

The man hesitated too long before answering.

Tank directed his next question to Tucker, "Boss, is it OK if I turn this interview over to Ram?"

The fake senator said, "No! No, please! I'll tell you everything you want to know."

Tank turned to Tucker and asked, "I still think we should we let Ram impress upon him the need to be truthful?"

It was close, but the decision was to let him talk.

"My name is Clayton West III. I'm Senator Peter Enya's chief of staff. He desperately wanted to participate, but he couldn't be here, so we came up with this plan to gather data.

"I'm very sorry for this subterfuge and ashamed of our collective dishonesty."

Several pairs of eyes wandered over to Star, who had returned to the back of the cave. She shook her head only slightly.

Tank wanted to beat the truth out of the man but wasn't going to display the violence he felt toward the asshole—yet.

The silence only lasted a few seconds before Tucker said, "Mr. West, your presence here throws a dark cloud over the maiden voyage of this group. The patriots in this foundation will wonder how many other members are unreliable. These patriots are risking everything to right a wrong, and you have singlehandedly damaged its credibility and secrecy. Maybe that was your goal. If you keep the foundation from maturing, then the media status quo will continue.

"Tank, will you, Powers, and Ram escort Mr. West outside while Maya and I discuss our options. He might enjoy a walk through the caverns. He'd especially enjoy the Geronimo Cavern, don't you think?"

Tank had no idea what Tucker was talking about but played along and escorted Clayton West out of the Mescalero Cave and kept both Clayton and Ram on a short leash.

When the imposter and the security team left the cave, Tucker said, "Star, sweetheart, share with your mother and me what you know about Mr. West."

The young girl with curly auburn hair; bright crystal blue eyes; perfect teeth; and a perpetual smile sashayed down from the refreshment area in the back of the cave.

She hugged her mother and said, "Clayton West is very excited about the story he's going to share with his father-in-law, who is an editor for Lakatos-funded liberal web site MoveOn.org."

Tucker, concerned that the organization's secrecy had been compromised said, "This is ugly."

Maya objected and said, "Will you let her finish?"

Star continued, "He was feeling really bad about mixing some ipecac syrup into the real Senator Enya's lunch salad. He got so sick he had to stay in bed. Clayton not only lied to us, but he tricked his boss."

Maya asked, "Were you able to determine how he learned about Senator Enya's meeting with us? If the senator can't keep a secret from his chief of staff, then we need to cull him from the group."

"No, Mom, Mr. West didn't think about that."

Carlsbad Caverns National Park

Tank and Powers introduced Clayton West to a cave that contained the highest population of Mexican Freetail bats in Carlsbad. By the time Tucker caught up with them, West's face had lost all color.

"Ram," instructed Tank, "Hold!" Ram knew to force West in stay put while Tank left the cave to confer with Powers and Tucker.

Tucker asked, "So, what should we do with this guy?"

Tank answered, "I think the desert coyotes would enjoy a meal."

Powers said, "Do you think we could convince him that we abandoned our secret organization because he exposed us? That would appeal to his ego, and we could move on like nothing happened?"

Tank said, "I like the coyote solution better."

Tucker said, "Both ideas have merit, but I have another idea as to what we can do with him. Do you think the two of you and Ram could frighten him to the point where if he doesn't do as I tell him, he'll have to wrestle with Ram? Tell Clayton that Ram is undefeated so far."

Tucker looked at his watch. It was time for the arrival of the next foundation member.

Mescalero Cave

After dragging Clayton West up to parking lot and sending him on his way, Tank escorted a tall, sleek-looking, well-dressed, and well-maintained woman into the Mescalero Cave. Her weathered face, however, gave her the appearance of a woman older than her years. As she extended her hand, Tucker could smell the faint odor of cigarette smoke mixed with sweet perfume.

Julienne O'Kray lived in a closet forced upon her by the Hollywood culture. When she was approached by Maya to participate in the foundation, she jumped enthusiastically at the chance to do something for a cause she felt passionate about.

Tucker smiled and said, "Welcome, Julienne. You look great. Thanks for making the long, hard trip to get here; we promise to make your trip worth the effort. Can I get you anything?"

She shook her head.

Tucker asked, "Do you think you were able to travel without being noticed?"

Julienne said, "I'm not that well-known. I don't have the problem others in the foundation may have."

"Maya and I have several items we'd like to cover with you," Tucker said. "Let's talk about money first."

Julienne smiled with lips too large and puffy for her face and said, "I like people who dispense with social talk and get right to the point. You don't experience that in Hollywood."

Maya said, "As you know, we created *Real America Productions* and would like for you to be the producer of a movie entitled *Unsustainable*. The script is written, and contracts are signed with actors, actresses, special effects producers, and a marketing company. Your budget is one hundred million dollars."

Julienne interrupted, "You said you have already signed contracts with the cast. Who did you sign?"

Maya answered, "We were able to sign Mel Gibson, Angie Harmon, Jon Voight, and Gary Sinise."

Julienne's eyes widened and said, "You're kidding? That's great, but I'm not sure we'll be able to stay within budget with those four big-ticket stars."

Tucker said, "Don't worry. They were happy to have the opportunity to get on the ground floor of a conservative Hollywood production company."

"It will be my pleasure to produce Real America Productions' first movie. It's a lot of responsibility, and I'll take it seriously."

Tucker said, "You understand that you'll be ridiculed, treated with disdain, uninvited to social events, and, possibly, even in danger for producing a conservative-leaning box office smash. Don't expect an Oscar."

Julienne said, "I'm already treated that way. You mentioned that there were several items you wanted to cover."

Tucker asked, "Do you have the bandwidth to do more than produce *Unsustainable*? If we authorize the hiring of other junior level producers, could you provide oversight of the production of YouTube videos? We want to create a video every week that is entertaining and reaches the young while making fun of the mainstream media."

Julienne asked, "Would I get to select the young producers?"

Maya said, "Not only select them but mold them. We've also negotiated an arrangement with the Writer's Guild to help with scriptwriting. It could be fun."

Julienne O'Kray said, "I'm afraid to ask if there's anything else."

Tucker said, "We'd like you to facilitate a meeting between the producers of the Black Television News Channel and us. We assume you know your fair share of Hollywood producers and that you could make the introduction."

Julienne said, "Consider it done."

Carlsbad Caverns National Park

Maya and Tucker were not looking forward to meeting with the next member. They had no real strategy or plan to share with the person code-named Ben Fracking. Their fear was that Ben was going to be angry that he came all the way to Carlsbad in a costume to hide his too-well-known face for no good reason. They had no well-defined task for him.

Star registered her parents' distress and made an amazingly astute observation, "Maybe we need to drop this as one of the war fronts. If we don't have an idea what to do, then, maybe, we should drop it."

Tucker loved her use of the term "we."

Powers escorted the man into the meeting cave, patted the man on the back and said, "Good to see you again, Mr. Ambassador, I look forward to working with you."

Maya smiled at Ben and said, "Sir, you dyed your hair and mustache to get here unnoticed? Fantastic, it makes you look ten years younger. You should keep it that way."

Ben said, "In all my years, I've never before had to hide and be incognito. Actually, it was refreshing not to be recognized. People either hate me or love me—nothing in between."

Tucker said, "Well, we love you, especially for everything you had to go through to get here."

"And who is this young lady?"

Maya said with some pride, "This is our daughter, Star."

He held his hand out, and Star curtsied and said, "A pleasure to meet you, Mr. Ambassador."

He looked curiously at her and then at Maya, felt an unfamiliar sensation, but decided against expressing his thoughts.

They debriefed Ben like they had the other members and finally came to the moment of truth. Tucker said, "Rather than us, the foundation, sharing our strategy with you," he snuck a look over at Maya, "we thought we should wait and work with you on developing a strategy to alter the press coverage of the United Nations."

Ben jumped in and said, "There are 193 countries in the UN. I think 190 of them hate the United States. The press feeds on that hate and stokes the fire. We're the New York Yankees or New England Patriots of the world and everyone is tired of seeing America win. We're also the Vanderbilts, Morgans, and Rockefellers. Every shit-hole country hates us for having unfair and obscene wealth by their standards. We're not going to change how the leaders of these nations feel about America.

"What we have to do is prevent the raw animosity from metastasizing into control over our country by the other 192. We cannot capitulate to international law. We can't let bureaucrats in Brussels decide that the Second Amendment of our constitution is invalid. We can't let them determine our tax rates so that the UN can share our wealth unwillingly to the dictators and totalitarians in the UN. If we want to be charitable, that should be up to us. Hell, more than forty percent of the world population is still living in undemocratic countries. Do you think we should let them tell us how to run our lives?"

Tucker said, "You're preaching to the choir. So, what should we do about the trend to move away from our way of life to whatever or wherever the UN is trying to drag us?"

Ben said, "I'm of two minds. On the one hand, we could flood world news outlets with the fake news that the mood of the United States' electorate is tired of being fools who allow nations to bite the hand that feeds them. That we're getting out of the UN, that we are stopping our charity programs, eliminating all our State Department grants to nations that hate us, and turning isolationists. We could flood blogs, social media outlets, talk radio, and cable news, and we could interview on European Union outlets and get the word out.

"There might even be a popular groundswell to make it happen, but I doubt it."

Maya asked, "What is the other option?"

The Ambassador said, "The leaders of many nations of the world are laboring under disinformation provided to them over decades after World War II by the leftist-leaning media. We are not going to undo almost seventy years of lies overnight. But we can start to undo the Gordian knot now. It takes financial means, multilingual journalistic talent, and the world's most complete contact list of decision-makers.

"I have the list."

He waited.

Tucker asked, "Why doesn't our government do this?"

"Because our State Department is part of the problem. Half of them want the United States to be just another country, equal in all ways with the other 192. They agree that there ought to be a one-world government that abides by international law. And, of course, they're tied to the hip with the mainstream media. Anything they write will reinforce the media's negative world view of America."

Tucker said, "Depending on how much you need, we should be able to help with the means. And I have two institutions in mind to help with the journalism work."

Maya said, "I think we have a plan of action. Ambassador, do you have the time to direct the program?"

He said, "I'll make the time."

Ben Fracking stood up to leave and headed for the door, but then felt the sense of uneasiness again. He stopped, looked back, squinted his eyes at Star and said, "What?"

Star said, "Canada and Israel."

He nodded his head and left with an odd feeling about Star.

Adrenaline ran at Mach 3 through Tucker's veins. Over the next three days, he and Maya met with another fourteen people who made similar clandestine trips from locations around the country to arrive in southeast New Mexico. Each was briefed, and operational tactics were reviewed. The wealthy, the powerful, the religious, the brilliant, the influential, the principled, the loyal, and the best strategists in the world were secretly meeting to form a platform on which to declare war against the radical, liberal, mainstream media. Except for the Senator Enya imposter, they all passed muster with Star, The Media Transformation Foundation's final line of defense for establishing trust.

CHAPTER 12

"The definition of insanity is doing the same thing over and over again but expecting different results."—Albert Einstein, 1879-1955, theoretical physicist

Yellowknife, Northwest Territories, Canada – June 27th

"Damn it!" Doug Butterfield yelled at the phone, "Someone had to see that helicopter that lifted from Wood Buffalo National Park. Someone had to see it refuel." He'd called the Fort Smith, Fort McMurray, Grande Prairie, Wabasca/Horizon, and Northern Rockies Regional airports, and nobody claimed to have seen a helicopter land, take on fuel and supplies, and file a flight plan. Though it seemed highly unlikely that the chopper had flown north from the park, in frustration, Doug made the call.

"This is Napoleon Drygeese, Yellowknife Airport chief air traffic controller. Who is calling, and what do you want?"

The hostile attitude of the guy pissed Doug off, and he said, "This is Royal Canadian Mounted Police officer Douglas Butterfield. What I want, Mr. Drygeese, is information about a helicopter that may have refueled at Yellowknife last week on Wednesday, the nineteenth, between 13:00 to 15:00. Can you confirm that one refueled around that time?"

"I'll check my records about the exact time of the landing, but we don't get that many helicopters up here. I remember it. Let's see . . . it was a Bell 407GXP. It landed at 12:53, took off at 13:21, and filed a flight plan to Whitehorse."

"Whitehorse," asked Butterfield? "There's no way in hell it could reach that far without taking on more fuel."

"Don't shoot the messenger, boss. They had extra fuel tanks on the chopper. If they didn't make it to Whitehorse, they didn't make it, period."

Doug added, "Did you see anyone? Can you describe them?"

"I don't remember anything about their faces. They were white, not native. The one thing I do remember is that they carried themselves like military guys. You know, the way they walked, their self-confidence, and their bearing."

"How many of them were there?"

"I saw three, but I wasn't paying that much attention."

"Thank you, Mr. Drygeese, you've been helpful. I might come up and have a cup of coffee with you and ask around to see if anyone else saw or talked to them." Doug signed off.

Napoleon looked at his phone and thought, "Oh, no. I think I just shit in my mess kit."

He called his Cree Indian contact, Chuck, which was short for Kika Kisecawchuck, and who was the chief air traffic controller at the Wabasca/Horizon Airport.

"This is Napoleon. Look, I did what you asked me to do, but now I feel like I just made a big mistake. The Mounties are going to come up here and interview me and others. They'll learn that I lied to them, and they'll feed me to the grizzlies."

"I don't think they do that, Napoleon. What they'll discover is that no one remembers them but you. That doesn't make you guilty of anything. Don't forget, I'm holding that gift for you. With the scope and all, it's a

$12,000 rifle. All yours for remembering something maybe you dreamed about."

Napoleon Drygeese asked, "What's in it for you?"

"Oh, I get something out of it too."

Seattle

The detective was sitting in his cruiser thinking about his next step after interviewing neighbors on Perkins Lane when his cell phone rang. "This is Detective Yamaguchi from the Seattle Police Department. How can I help you?"

"Thank you for taking my call, detective. My name is Rod Nelson, a homicide detective for the Royal Canadian Mounted Police. And yes, I think you can help me. I'm investigating the death of Gabriel Lakatos, who was murdered up here in the province of Alberta. I was wondering if I could have a word with you?"

The Seattle detective said, "Oh, yes, I've heard about the murder of Gabe Lakatos. Good luck with that case; I believe he had more enemies than friends. I'd like to help you, but I don't see how with what I know so far."

Nelson said, "Are you aware of Lakatos's cause of death?"

"No, I'm not privy to the salient details."

"He was shot from long range with a high-caliber rifle. The type of rifle used may be similar to the rifle used in one of your cases."

Yamaguchi answered, "You mean Jorgensen's home?"

Rod Nelson said, "Yes, I heard it was a .50 caliber sniper rifle used to violate Jeff Jorgensen's home. I'd like to see the report on the recovered round; see if the striations match some of the rounds we recovered."

Yamaguchi said, "I'd love to cooperate fully with our Canadian friends in law enforcement, but it's no longer my case. The fucking FBI has claimed authority. You'll have to contact Agent Michael Roberts out of the Seattle field office. Here, I'll give you his number."

Rod Nelson paused before he finally asked, "How well do you know Roberts? Can I trust him?"

The Seattle detective laughed, "As I said, it's the fucking FBI."

CHAPTER 13

"Journalism is organized gossip." - Edward Eggleston, 1807-1932, American historian

Washington, DC – June 29th

"**H**ey, hey, whatya say, no integrity here today. Hey, hey, whatya say, no integrity here today."

The protests in front of *The Washington Post* headquarters on K Street grew over the past four days to include thousands of activists and began to resemble the yellow vest protestors in France. The organizers created their own Facebook page and turned the event into an upbeat social festival. The demonstrators were well organized in shifts so that different people from various occupations got a chance to protest while those that needed to bleed off and work were relieved by those who just got off work. Contests for the best sign and slogan attracted songwriters and poets.

"The Post: Science Fiction without Science."

People signed up to protest in front of Jorgensen's Kalorama home inn DC, as well as his home in Seattle. To the tune of James Taylor's song, "You've Got a Friend," hundreds of people sang, "You've Got No Friends."

Tents and bonfires populated the streets of Kalorama. Flyers and posters in neighborhoods east of the Anacostia River announced a party with free food and beer in Kalorama starting at ten o'clock p.m. each night for a week. Unfortunately, only one keg of beer was provided.

Riot time. What fun.

New York City

The dean of the School of Journalism at Columbia University opened the meeting on the school's curriculum for the upcoming year with, "I see we have one hundred percent attendance here today. Thank you, professors, for the good work that you do.

"I have two topics I want to cover before we launch into the revision to the classes which we offer this year. First, I want to talk about your safety. There are crazies out there that think we poison the minds of our students, punch writers out like cookie cutters, and create robots that only promote the party line for the Democrats."

The faculty laughed, clapped, and whistled.

"While that may be partially true, I'm serious about your safety. The Columbia School of Journalism has received threats of violence. We received four or five of them last year, but this year the intensity of the threats is frightening. We've informed NYPD, and they're going to increase the number of beat cops in the area, so, please, back off giving them grief."

One of the professors said, "Darn! You take all our fun away."

Another professor raised her hand and asked, "What is the nature of the threats?"

The dean answered, "I'm paraphrasing here and cleaning it up a bit, but many of the threats go something like this: 'Stop teaching lies, or we'll blow up Lerner Hall.' or 'If you don't teach honesty in journalism school, we'll infiltrate your digital program just like we did at *The Washington Post*.'

"I think the one most troubling to me was: 'We can hit a target from a distance of over one thousand yards. See Gabriel Lakatos for a reference.'

"So, stay vigilant and take the threats seriously.

"The second subject I want to discuss, which necessarily and naturally precedes a discussion on curriculum, is our long-term goals. What kind of journalists do we want to crank out of Columbia? It's true that the vast majority of journalists, writers, newscasters, radio hosts, political opinion writers, and school textbook authors that graduated from our School of Journalism have become mouthpieces for the Democratic or Socialist Parties. I maintain that we have held the bar too low.

"It's time for journalists to set the agenda for the political parties, not the other way around. The Democratic Party needs to be a mouthpiece for journalists. We need to graduate students who can make that happen. To do that, we need to rethink our curriculum. Next semester Columbia University will add the following classes: Corporate Greed 101, The Paradigm of Social Justice in the South 102, Social Benefits from Illegal Immigration 201, How to Hurl Labels 202, Use of One-liners 203, How to Phrase a Title to Conceal the Real Meaning 301, Protecting Non-Existing Sources 401, How and When to Employ Racism 402, Why the First Amendment is important and Why the Second Amendment is Not 403, and Code Word Insertion 404.

Thank you for attending. I will accept requests starting today for your preferences for which class you want to teach."

Little did the dean of the School of Journalism at Columbia University know that the auditorium in which he conducted his staff meeting was populated with listening devices.

CHAPTER 14

"I'm sorry, if you were right, I'd agree with you."—
Robin Williams, 1951-2014, actor and comedian.

Wiscasset, Maine – July 1st

Maya said, "It's not entirely our decision."

Tucker said, "Bullshit. It's still our job to make adult choices for Star. She is not quite mature enough to make decisions of this magnitude on her own. It's our job to protect her from herself."

Maya said, "Do you realize how much influence Miley Cyrus had on the youth in her prime? Star could have a positive influence rather than the counter-culture influence Miley Cyrus ultimately had."

"I'm sorry, Maya, I just don't want Star immersed in the cesspool of Hollywood. I'm surprised and disappointed that you would allow it."

Tucker knew he stepped in it with that comment, but he didn't want Star, at fourteen, going down the ugly Miley Cyrus path.

Star looked at Tucker and said, "Dad, I promise I won't display my body to the world on MTV. I won't perform suggestive acts, and I won't promote sexual promiscuity."

Tucker said, "That's a big word for a fourteen-year-old."

"Dad, you should trust that you and Mom taught me moral values. I won't let you down."

Tucker smiled and said, "Quit talking like you're an adult. I can't handle it."

Maya said with an edge to her voice, "Listen, Tucker, Julienne O'Kray told us that Star is perfect for the children's education fraction of the foundation's war front. To influence the young, we need an idol. Putting Star in front of kids as an idol would have a greater long-term influence than anything we could do with the written word. Let's put Star out there on YouTube, MTV, Pandora, and Google.

"We could start a wave of cultural change that turns into a tsunami of political revolution. Just think, if Julienne and Star produced a compelling video that was shown in classrooms around the country, well, it could be better than anything else we're working on to move the media to the right. You have to stop limiting yourself to linear thinking."

Tucker responded, "No, it's not going to happen. End of story. Maya, we agreed that something like this had to be unanimous between us. We each have veto power. I'm exercising my right to veto."

And with that, the two most important people in Tucker's world were not talking to him.

CHAPTER 15

"As law enforcement officers you have to put up with a lot of people bearing false witness against you. It seems to be the national pastime these days."- David Griffith, author, and editor of *POLICE Magazine*

Boston, Massachusetts – July 5th

Tank walked into Tucker's office at Entropy, LLC, for their scheduled twice a month meeting and sat down on an office chair Tucker had structurally reinforced to endure Tank's oversized frame.

Tank asked, "What's top on your list today?"

Tucker said, "I'm tired of the media bad-mouthing the police."

"Aren't we all."

Tucker said, "We need a strategy to turn it around— a strategy to get the media to write more fairly about the work the police do instead of writing headlines that make them out as the Gestapo."

Tank said, "You're the strategist; I'm the tactician."

Tucker continued, "Police were unfairly maligned after the Trayvon Martin, Ferguson, Missouri case. Misinformation; disinformation; fake news; and the racist, agenda-driven liberal media drove the reputation of law enforcement agencies down to the lowest level of confidence in history. Together with FBI political malpractice, the public needs a shot-in-the-arm from the media that law enforcement can be trusted.

"It has not been forthcoming.

"Instead, the police are instructed not to do their job without body cameras or proof when deadly force is used.

The National Police Research Platform claims that eight-in-ten police officers say the media generally treat the police unfairly. The long-term impact is that fewer and fewer able-bodied candidates will enter law enforcement as a career."

"The press is on the side of the criminal and not on the side of the victim. The left-leaning media considers the criminal to be the victim of police brutality and racial injustice. As a result, El Salvadorian Mara Salvatrucha gangs, MS-13, has gained a foothold in otherwise peaceful communities because police are restricted from pursuing minorities with the same freedom they would pursue others.

"ABC News stated that a new survey indicated that more than two-thirds of police officers believe that protests that typically follow high-profile police shootings are 'motivated to a great extent by anti-police bias'— one of several findings that appear to highlight deep divisions between law enforcement and the citizens they protect.

"To turn this around, we need to meet with some pro-law enforcement publications to effect a change."

Tank said, "I didn't know there were any pro-police journalists."

"I'd like for you to go to Torrance, California, to meet with the publisher of *POLICE Magazine*. Tell them that you have a customer who is willing to donate up to seven figures to the magazine and the National Law Enforcement Officers Memorial Fund with some conditions."

"Seven figures?"

"Maggie is doing a great job making our funds grow."

Tank asked, "What are your conditions?"

Tucker smiled and said, "You have any issues if I ask you to wear a body camera?"

Tank eyed Tucker and said, "You want me to ride with police?"

Tucker said, "I want the best possible video to use for our purposes. I want to compare what actually happened to what the media claims have happened."

Tank said, "That's likely to take a lot of time? I'll select a substitute for me."

"Tank, your intimidating size, security training, and minority background make you the perfect person to ride with a couple of police officers."

Tank asked, "Is that the only condition of the donation?"

"You know, Tank, some communities have media-supported gun-free zones."

Tank said, "You mean the zones that advertise for criminals?"

"I want *POLICE Magazine* to write an editorial lobbying for 'Police-free Zones' and a 'National Police-free Day' with a list of specific locations where police will not respond to crime. I've collected the names and addresses of anti-police journalists."

"Tucker, are you sure you want to do that? Police can't decide who'll they'll protect and who they won't"

"That's not the point. The point is that someone is out there promoting the idea and the police are 'considering' it."

CHAPTER 16

"You lie down with dogs, you get up with fleas."—Alan Parsons Project, musicians, a line from the album "*Eve*"

Washington, DC – July 8th

"**A**bigale! Abigale!" yelled the Democratic National Committee media manager, "I can't access the daily talking points file I uploaded into our secure website, and I only have five minutes before hundreds of people are expecting the information to be there. Can you fix this?"

Without saying a word, Abigale, the DNC administrator for the secure website, calmly finished what she was doing, pushed her rolling chair back, stood up, brushed her tight skirt with both hands, and strutted into the media manager's office. She leaned in next to him and asked, "May, I?"

He enjoyed smelling her perfume and said, "Sure. You drive." He handed her his mouse.

Abigale said condescendingly, "Now, you see where I've placed the cursor, right here on this icon, and click? It's the refresh button. And you see, the file you uploaded is there. Don't panic."

"It was always easier when you uploaded it for me."

She added, "By the way, have you approved the new people that want access to the talking points web address? The *Buffalo News* has a new editor that has requested access."

"Has Sean done a background check, yet? I didn't see it in my inbox."

"I'll confirm."

The media manager asked, "You going to the party at the Press Club tonight?"

She said, "No, I have a date this evening. And before you ask, he's no one you know, and I'm not going to give you his name so you can look under his kilt."

"You know I only check on these guys to protect you, right?"

Abigale ignored him and prepared herself for a date with the handsome Clayton West, whose life depended on his ability to steal access to the DNC secure website. It was clear to Clayton that if he failed, he'd incur the wrath of Ram.

Abigale was a slender, maybe bulimic, thirty-four-year-old divorcee with shoulder-length dirty-blonde hair. She walked like she was always on a runway modeling for an audience. She moved her narrow hips in a distorted sort of way. Her movements excited West, who otherwise found her personality a distraction.

At dinner, Abigale spoke in sexual innuendos, alluded to past indiscretions, and too often used her tongue to caress her upper and lower lips. Clayton didn't have to work hard to get her to join him for a nightcap.

She was so aggressive, Clayton was almost unsure about what he'd gotten himself into. She brought her own supply of condoms, lotions, and scents. She even pulled a DVD out of her pocketbook for them to watch as an added turn-on.

Uninhibitedly, she undressed and stood naked in front of him with her small breasts and oversized happy spot. She wasted no time and started to pull down Clayton's pants' zipper.

It was a night that turned into a week that he'd never forget. And the bonus was that he completed his mission and got access to the secret and secure DNC website.

With a gateway to the DNC daily talking points, the foundation could use the information against the liberal media.

Another baby step forward in the war.

Torrance, California

Tank flew into Long Beach, grabbed a cab, and arrived at the *POLICE Magazine* offices in Torrance ten minutes ahead of his scheduled meeting with the magazine publisher.

"Aren't you Tank Alvarez?" asked a police officer in the building. "You hire a lot of us former cops into White Knight Personnel Security, right?"

Tank said, "I'm glad you recognized me, and yes, we hire a lot of former police officers along with former military special operations talent."

"May I give you my resume? Are you recruiting in the area?"

Tank answered, "We're always looking for qualified talent."

The publisher of the magazine walked into the lobby donning multicolored hair and said, "Mr. Alvarez, thank you for coming all the way from Boston to meet with us. You know, I've never been to Boston."

Tank said, "You need a passport. We don't normally allow Californians through immigration control."

She laughed and said, "Come on back."

She sat behind her desk and offered Tank a seat. He assessed the chairs in her office and decided to remain standing.

She noticed his apprehension and said, "Here, sit on the edge of my desk. You dainty types have your issues, don't you?"

Tank didn't know how to respond to her statement and blustered on, "My customer, who will remain anonymous, recognizes the great job you are doing here at *POLICE Magazine* and would like to expand your operation, fund the hiring of more staff, and broaden your influence nationwide."

She said, "How wonderful! We certainly welcome the concept. What's the quid pro quo?"

Tank said, "You are a cynic and I can't blame you, but my customer would like to have an influence on your mission plan, your goals, and your operational objectives. We think the magazine could have a greater influence on the American public than it currently has."

She sat back, narrowed her eyes until her eyebrows touched, and said, "Like what?"

Tank said, "We think the magazine could be a vehicle for changing the public view of law enforcement if it had greater readership, was more visible and was discussed on a national scale.

"If you were able to hire an additional two hundred people who were tasked with blogging on hundreds of websites, you'd get greater exposure. We would want to propose something controversial to get mainstream media attention. We want the magazine to propose law-enforcement-free zones and a national law-enforcement-free day."

She said, "We can't afford to hire two hundred people. What are you talking about?"

Tank smiled and said, "My customer will advance you enough money to fund the recruiting and hiring of two hundred people, provided you give preference to retired military, police officers, civilian police officers, firefighters, veterans, and first responders.

"And one other thing: I want to ride with police officers in the most dangerous district in the country and videotape their activities."

87

Chapter 17

"Well, except for ABC, CBS, NBC, MSNBC, CNN, *The New York Times*, *The Washington Post* and about 100 other newspapers, I find little evidence of liberal bias in the media." – Rupert Murdock, 1931-present, Australian-born American media mogul.

Minneapolis, Minnesota – July 10th

"**M**r. Alvarez, if you're going to ride with us, you're going to have to wear body armor, and we don't have any here in your size."

Tank answered, "I brought my own. I was told I might need it."

"I know you run a security firm and that you were trained by a former special operations warfighter, so I assume you can handle yourself. We carry the new Remington 870 DM 12-gauge shotguns with six-round magazines. You ever used one?"

"No. Can I handle one before we get into the patrol car? Do you have a range here on-site?"

"No; you'll have to carry a side-arm though. What's your preference?"

"You have any Glock 19x's?"

The officer said, "We got you covered."

Tank said, "I understand we have the night shift in the Cedar Riverside 'No Go' zone, where Muslim Sharia Law prevails."

"Yes, we have the fun shift," the officer added sarcastically, "and we don't even get combat duty pay. But we do get a cool ride—an armored Hummer. I just wish it came with a mounted .50 caliber machine gun.

"Come on, hop in. It's time to patrol another world. I think I'd rather patrol Ferguson, Missouri."

While cruising on patrol, Tank asked, "What's the biggest problem in here?"

"The biggest problem is that the local community doesn't want us in here. We represent the infidel's law, not their own laws. They think this part of Minneapolis is no longer part of Minnesota.

"They have their own police to enforce their own laws. They target prostitutes, people drinking alcohol, couples who are holding hands, women they consider to be dressed immodestly, and people they perceive as gay. If they catch someone committing a crime against Islam, the Sharia patrol will throw them in a Muslim jail. Allah only knows what goes on in there."

Over the car radio, the driver heard the dispatcher call out: "Urgent! A 10-16, possible 10-32, in progress at the corner of Nineteenth Avenue South and South Sixth Street. The fifteen-year-old girl called 9-1-1. Possible honor killing. Lights and siren situation."

The driver said, "Copy, 10-76." Then he said, "We don't do sirens here. Might as well do a bugle call for the enemy. The Sharia police will be armed to the teeth in support of the honor killing and will defend Sharia Law if we give them enough warning."

His partner, riding shotgun, said, "She probably did something terrible like light up a cigarette or pet a dog."

The driver said to Tank, "You got the cameras rolling? We don't get many honor killings. This should be an Oscar winner."

"And, Alvarez, stay in the Hummer. We don't want the cameraman to get hurt."

With no lights and no siren, the Hummer was able to drive up Nineteenth Avenue to within thirty yards of where a crowd of eight people stood in a semicircle facing the side of a building. Two of them had bricks in their hands with three or four bricks at their feet. Two others had AK-47s pointing skyward while staring menacingly at the oncoming Hummer. They recognized the Minneapolis police vehicle, daring the cops to interfere.

The Minneapolis police officer who drove the Hummer called in for backup.

Tank watched a man throw a brick in the direction of the building wall. He was sure the target was the girl, but, as of yet, he hadn't seen her.

A couple more men appeared to join the implementation of their concept of justice.

The driver said to his partner, "Time to launch." Without saying a word, the cop lobbed a tear gas cannister into the middle of the group who were entertained by the prospect of watching a young girl get stoned to death.

The assault rifles held by the Sharia patrolmen cracked, though they remained pointed at the moon. The sound of gunfire would bring out hundreds of other Muslims incensed by the intrusion of police into the "No Go" zone.

One of the policemen pulled out a megaphone and said, "Go home. Break it up. Go home and no one will get hurt. This is the Minneapolis Police Department speaking. Go home."

Four of five observers coughed, choked, and ran blindly away from where the tear gas hovered. One of the armed Sharia patrolmen ran away from the conflict but continued to empty a magazine into the air.

It looked like twenty or more residents were running into the skirmish from their homes.

Tank finally saw the fifteen-year-old girl, crawling on her hands and knees on the concrete sidewalk, temporarily blind and coughing from inhaling the tear gas, blood dripping from her right ear. Tank watched as she was hit with another brick, this time on the back of the head—she slumped to the ground, unconscious.

Tank figured that in another thirty seconds, there would be twenty-five angry Muslims surrounding the police vehicle.

Backup had not yet reached Cedar Riverside.

The driver started up the Hummer and said, "Time to leave if we want to fight another day."

Tank said, "Fuck this."

He opened the back passenger's-side door, sprinted through the broken semicircle of brick throwers, grabbed the girl with one hand, lifted her onto his shoulder, and sprinted back to the Hummer. It took all of forty seconds.

In his wake, five men were knocked to the ground like bowling pins, one was stiff-armed, and one got a chop to the throat. Tank climbed in, placed the girl in the back seat of the vehicle and shut rear the door. But someone left a knife stuck in the back of Tank's left leg which he removed with a grimace.

Now he was really pissed. He lifted the shotgun, jammed the six-shell magazine into it, and . . .

"Please don't hurt anybody." The plea came from the brutalized teenager. Tank said to the driver, "Let's get her to the nearest hospital."

The next day, the Minneapolis *Star Tribune* covered the story:

"Four devout men who practice Islam and abide by Sharia Law were admitted to the University of Minnesota Hospital last night with injuries sustained from an altercation with a patrolling Minneapolis police unit. The brutality allegedly occurred after police hurled tear gas into an assembled crowd. Shots were fired. Witnesses at the scene claim the police kidnapped a fifteen-year-old girl right in front of her parents. As of this writing, the girl is unaccounted for."

Concord, California

At 0230 Pacific Daylight Time, Troy took aim from only 250 yards through his Armasight Vulcan 8x scope at the transformer that fed power to the transmission tower for California Media Group's KHZZ's TV station. He lay on the floor of the ubiquitous white van with the back door only slightly ajar and with the muzzle of the .50 caliber sniper rifle protruding into the still night air. He waited there for ninety minutes for the right moment when area traffic was light and no police cruisers were in the area. When a loud Peterbilt 579 diesel eighteen-wheeler cruised past the station, Troy fired hoping the truck would partially cover the sound of the rifle.

Troy closed the back doors to the van, hopped into the driver's seat, and headed for I-680 South. He didn't wait to see the sparks fly, the lights go black in the station control room, or the high school kids making out in a darkened car with fogged-up windows in a parking lot of an adjacent warehouse.

Troy pulled out his Apple 7 and called Tank to share with him the status of his task.

Tank thanked him for his update and advised him that his next target was KRPP in Bakersfield.

Mountain View, California

"Connect the fucking dots, Jeff," said Lawrence Slaughter. "First our friend Gabriel is murdered, every member of our private club is threatened with texts or emails, then your *Washington Post* is sabotaged, your home in Seattle is shot up, MSNBC is bombed, and my TV and radio stations are attacked. Tell me there is not some sort of a right-wing conspiracy going on here. Get one of your editorial writers to reveal what's happening and put pressure on the FBI. Do they have a clue as to who is directing these acts of domestic terrorism?"

"If you don't calm down, Larry, I'm going to hang up," responded Jeff Jorgensen. "If I want any shit from you, I'll squeeze your head."

No one talked to Lawrence Slaughter, the media mogul, that way. His silence was a warning to Jorgensen. Though Jorgensen was Slaughter's equal in many ways and his superior in net worth, Slaughter was the leader of their private club and demanded more respect. Like a mafia don, Slaughter always got even. Slaughter's empire controlled seventy-two percent of the nation's TV audience and a corresponding sixty-eight percent of the nation's radio-listening audience. Slaughter and Jorgensen conspired to create the world's largest wireless virtual multichannel video program distributorship. Jorgensen didn't want to blow the deal, so he capitulated to Slaughter.

Jeff spoke first, "I agree that this looks like a conspiracy. Here's what I know or don't know so far. Canadian law enforcement is on the trail of Lakatos's killers, although they have no suspects, yet. The Seattle police are checking the slug striations with the Royal Canadian Mounted Police to see if the same rifle was used to kill Gabriel. The DC police have determined that the protestors in front of *The Washington Post* were paid rioters. We have no clues yet as to who threw the Molotov cocktail, who sabotaged the printing presses, and who hacked into the digital version of the *Post*. The hackers appear to be foreign. I don't believe that, but that's where the thread led the cyber forensic experts. It could be a false flag. What about on your end; any clues?"

Slaughter said, "The California Bureau of Investigation identified one couple who said the transformer shooting in Concord originated from a white van that took off immediately after the shot was fired.

They weren't close enough to get a license plate number. No witnesses have come forward with information about the destruction of the high-voltage cable feed at KRPP in Bakersfield, the draining of the transformer in San Diego, or the arson that took place at the radio station in Fresno. But it's not a leap of logic to say that since all the attacks occurred at stations I own, there is collusion going on."

"Did I hear you say the protestors on K Street were paid? Who paid them?"

Jorgensen sighed and said, "You won't believe this. Somehow, they were paid out of an account owned by one of Gabriel Lakatos's 501(c) companies. How the hell could a right-wing group pull that off?"

Slaughter said, "I assume Levi is running Lakatos's companies. His idiot son couldn't do it. Levi needs to find out who stole from his trust fund."

"Agreed. And with Gabriel gone, we need to assemble a quorum and elect a new chairman. I'll nominate you. I sure as hell don't have the time."

CHAPTER 18

"The broad masses of a population are more amenable to the appeal of rhetoric than to any other force." - Adolph Hitler, 1889-1945, leader of the National Socialist German Worker's Party

Lynchburg, Virginia – July 11th

She poured over a topographical map, considered the rolling hills of southern Virginia, and asked, "Dad, what do they do in Lynchburg?"

Star was homeschooled, and Maya and Tucker took her education seriously. She accompanied Tucker on this trip to the beautiful, lush, green rolling hills of southern Virginia. On the flight from Wiscasset to Lynchburg in their Learjet, he gave Star geography and history lessons.

Tucker answered, "It may surprise you, but Lynchburg is home to some high-tech industries, such as the manufacturing of nuclear fuel for submarines and aircraft carriers, the operation and maintenance of national laboratories, and the design and construction of components for power plants. But it is mostly known for Liberty University, one of the few conservative higher education colleges in the nation.

"Now, let me ask you. What did you learn on our flight down here about the history of Lynchburg?"

Star gave Tucker a cold stare; she hated to be quizzed by him. Tucker suspected it was a daughter–father thing. His theory was that hormones, or some kind of anaerobic bacteria—both fairly likely— attack the brain of teenage girls and makes them want to prove their dads wrong. And she was still mad at him for not letting her audition for a Hollywood spot.

She answered, "I learned that the town was named after John Lynch, who operated a ferry that went across the James River."

"Very good."

"I learned that it used to be a tobacco-based economy and progressed to be a manufacturer with blast furnaces and railroads."

"Excellent. Now can you tell me a little history about Liberty University?"

Star shrugged her shoulders, cocked her head to one side, gave out a breath of exasperation and said, "It was founded by Jerry Falwell in 1971."

"Good start. We're going to meet with the provost and chief academic officer for Liberty University. Now buckle-up; we're about to land."

Tucker always enjoyed landing in regional airports where the hassle factor was low. Sometimes he could be at his ultimate destination in minutes after landing. It disturbed him that the terrorists had made American lives so fearful after the attacks of 911. At one point, travelers couldn't even carry toothpaste or mouthwash through security. Tucker hovered over the TSA guards when they patted down Star. It was a good thing the Cherokee family didn't go through security with Ram, or there would be fewer TSA agents around.

A limousine awaited them outside the terminal and swept Tucker and Star away, not to the university, but instead to Thomas Jefferson's Poplar Forest National Historic Landmark.

Assaulted by more shades of green than Crayola could muster, they sat outside at a round concrete table on uncomfortable concrete benches under a one-hundred-year-old crepe myrtle.

The provost said, "On behalf of Liberty University's sole member of The Media Transformation Foundation, thank you for what you're doing. It is long overdue and excellent service to our nation.

"We've received a contribution from an account in Belize in the name of The Media Transformation Foundation and a list of professors from accredited colleges and universities that will benefit our school of journalism. As you suggested, we will offer these famous professors salaries that far exceed their current salaries, offer to pay for their publications, and launch their careers on television. My concern is that professors from Columbia University; University of Virginia; and University of California, Berkeley; won't honor their commitment to Liberty University's journalistic standards.

"Do you really believe that our indoctrination program, or 'boot camp' as you call it, will alter their deeply held liberal ideology in the classroom?"

Tucker said, "No, I don't believe the professors will buy into it initially. But over time they'll learn to implement our curriculum or face the consequences. But if Liberty University is ever going to reach the pinnacle of journalism, you're going to have to attract renowned professors.

"Equally important is that these professors are removed from schools that, if left unchecked, will continue to contaminate and corrupt the thought process of young students. Let's remove them from their altar of wrongheadedness and use them for good."

The provost asked, "How else can we help your honorable cause?"

Tucker asked, "How's your language program? Could you translate articles written by others into fourteen different languages?"

"It depends on the fourteen languages, of course, but I think we can get that done using our graduate students."

"Good. A man named Ben Fracking will contact you. He'll send you the manuscripts and ask you to make the translations. I need to warn you in advance that the frequency of the requests may exceed your capacity to respond. If or when you reach that point, let me know, and we'll spread the burden to another institution."

"What's the purpose of the translations?"

Tucker just smiled, and said, "It's for a good cause."

On the way back to the airport, Tucker asked Star, "Can we trust him?"

Raising a teenage daughter had taught Tucker that teenagers were more likely to use body language to express themselves than their adult counterparts. It was like they wore their emotions on their face, posture, and breathing habits. Noticing Star's familiar signs of distress, Tucker immediately sensed that they couldn't trust the provost. He waited for her observation.

She screwed up her face like she just sucked on a lemon and said, "He's jealous."

"Jealous of what?"

"He'd like to be paid as much as you're offering. . . Dad, is it OK for me to say the bad words that he was thinking?"

Tucker said, "OK, I guess."

"He'd like to be paid as much as he's offering these godless liberal assholes."

"Anything else?"

"He wishes Jerry Falwell was alive. He'd love what we're doing."

Tucker thought, "Someone has to do it."

CHAPTER 19

"He who fears corruption fears life." – Saul Alinsky, 1909-1972, author of *"Rules for Radicals"*

New York City, New York – July 15th

"**M**s. Mellon," asked Jonathan, her overly protective butler, "were you expecting a guest? There is a woman in the lobby waiting to see you. She says that you know her and that it is important."

"Who? What's her name?"

The butler answered, "Agatha Priest. Do you know her?"

"Oh! Uh, yes. Please show her in—quickly."

Maggie Mellon was confused and flustered. She feared that if Maya was observed in her building that it would somehow compromise the secrecy of their new-found foundation. But Maya was already in the lobby— she needed to minimize the exposure of her well-known face in public. The longer Maya was down there, the more likely it was that she would be recognized. Maggie nervously waited for the butler to escort Maya into her study.

If it were not for her exotic-looking eyes, Maggie would not have known it was Maya who flowed into the room. They stared at each other for a long time. Finally, Ms. Mellon said, "Thank you, Jonathan, please close the door and let us old friends have a private discussion." Jonathan was hesitant to leave his employer alone. He sensed that they were not really "old friends." But he did as he was instructed.

When they were alone, Maya removed her burqa headdress and said, "I don't know how women tolerate this clothing. I felt smothered."

Maggie said, "But it is a good costume. I'm sure no one recognized you in the lobby. That's a relief. To what do I owe the honor of your visit?"

"How well-known is it in the Mellon family that you are staunchly irritated with the liberal media? If you assert yourself in Mellon business, would anyone suspect the assertion to be ideological?"

"Where are you going with this, Maya?"

Maya's smile was as brilliant as the idea she shared with Maggie.

Rockefeller Center, New York City

Tucker set the DVD to record the program. He thought, "This is going to be great entertainment."

This evening, the eyes of the evening news reporter on MSNBC belied the disingenuous and forced smile painted on her face. The makeup didn't cover up the blemish of her disposition and the elevated blood pressure that pulsed in the veins of her neck. The anchor appeared much less attractive today than yesterday as she said, "Competing cable news networks have announced that the parent company of MSNBC is considering a major network shake-up in response to seven coordinated, but unfounded and baseless, lawsuits filed against MSNBC earlier today.

"Let it be known that these conservative network accusations of a shake-up have no basis in fact. As to the seven lawsuits for one billion dollars each in damages filed in New York Southern district court this morning, well, consider the source. Well-known Republican-leaning groups filed all seven lawsuits."

Tucker noticed that the network reporter clenched her jaw as she continued. The producer segued to a video of the lawyers leaving district court; all of them were handsome, well-dressed men and women with broad smiles on their faces. The video was quickly pulled to prevent the audience from empathizing with the lawyers and replaced the video with an uncomplimentary shot of the allegedly unpopular Republican president leaving the White House.

"These lawsuits claim that MSNBC is derelict in its responsibility for honest news reporting and that we compromise facts with editorial information that intentionally misleads viewers.

"The lawsuits also claim that the network has violated FCC regulations by presenting uncorroborated information as news. The lawsuits allege that MSNBC fabricated stories, libeled conservative political candidates, distorted information to attract viewers, and lied about 'unnamed sources.'"

Barely able to maintain her composure, the news anchor said, "I'm pleased to announce that we have in our studio a former civil defense attorney to opine about the merits of the lawsuit."

"Thank you for inviting me to speak on this subject," said the guest. "Unless the discovery process discloses intent to deceive viewers, the claims will be very hard to prove. However, I read two of the legal claims before coming on here tonight, and they are well written. The judge in one of the cases has demanded that all of the network's internal correspondence must be preserved for discovery. No e-mail, memorandums, faxes, policy statements, or electronic communication can be deleted or destroyed until the case is closed.

"One claim not mentioned in your opening remarks is the claim that MSNBC intentionally failed to report information pertinent to the subject event. The claim is that the news network does not report news that doesn't fit its overriding agenda. In other words, the claim is that the most egregious thing a reporting entity like MSNBC can do is selectively leave out relevant information that it doesn't want to report. That is not a claim, in my opinion, that is provable."

Tucker stopped the recording. He was a believer in celebrating even small victories. Exposing MSNBC's journalistic malpractice, at least, was worth a drink.

Eleventh Avenue, New York City

"What do you mean, Mellon Bank has pulled its advertisement on MSNBC for damage to the bank's business," growled the president of Obsidian Advertising Agency, "I personally negotiated that contract. They will violate the terms of our agreement unless they continue for two more years."

"Uh, not true," responded the Obsidian corporate lawyer. "There is a clause that allows them to cancel the contract for cause."

"That's my point—there is no cause."

"Mellon thinks the claims of the lawsuits provides them with a basis for cause."

"Bullshit. Countersue them."

The corporate lawyer's cell phone pinged.

He looked at his boss and asked, "May I?"

The president of the ad agency nodded his head.

The attorney pulled his smartphone out of his suitcoat pocket, opened the call, and listed to the caller.

"Oh." The lawyer's eyes widened, and his expression changed to one of shock. "Apparently, things are escalating rapidly. Three more advertisers are pulling their support."

"Shit."

The lawyer continued, "And seven lawsuits of one billion dollars each were filed against CNN."

Harpers Ferry, West Virginia

A low decibel alarm sounded which was just barely audible to the room's occupant. He looked at the fifteen screens on five monitors to determine whether the detector was just picking up a deer or something more threatening tripped the intrusion detector.

A second alarm rang, this time louder and from something closer to the shack. Again, Jimmy Ma searched the monitors of the pan-tilt-zoom closed-circuit tv cameras for a sighting of what set off the alarms.

Protocol required Jimmy to shut down power to the computers and destroy all data on hard drives and servers by initiating a program he had created.

Jimmy heard footsteps on the wired front porch. He waited for the pressure-sensitive plates under the steps to trigger the explosives. Nothing happened. Then he heard a familiar voice say, "Jimmy, stand down."

"Tank, you crazy asshole," reacted Jimmy Ma. "You have no idea how close I came to destroy a year's worth of collected data. It would have set us back months."

"Bullshit," said Tank, "I don't know how or where, but I'm confident only you could find the source of the backup."

Ma said, "Damn, am I that transparent?"

"Yes."

"What are you doing here, Tank?" asked Jimmy.

"Besides testing the security system, I installed, I'm here to give you a new assignment. You hacked *The New York Times*, *The Washington Post*, and Lakatos's 501(c) company so well, we thought you needed a new challenge."

Jimmy said, "I like a challenge."

"You're a 'follow-the-money' kind of guy, right?"

"Right."

"We want you to tie Mrs. Jeff Jorgensen to something financially shady. We'll leave the details to you. And, Jimmy, send Jeff a text message from Lawrence Slaughter. Make it threatening. Piss him off."

"And what's my special reward for this new assignment?"

"A visit to Chinatown in New York. I'll stand guard while you cheat at 'Go.'"

"I don't cheat. I'm just good."

"Either way, I'll stand guard."

CHAPTER 20

"What goes around, comes around." – Paul Crump, 1930-2002, death row inmate and author of "*Burn, Killer, Burn*"

New York City, New York – July 18th

NEWSFLASH: "Arnold Goldberger, Publisher of *The New York Times*, has provided financial support to the North Korean Great Leader, Kim Jong-un, according to an unnamed source.

"*The Associated Press, Fox News Network, Wall Street Journal, Drudge Report,* and *London Time* received the breaking news from Drake Pasqua, editor in chief of *The New York Times*, according to a reliable informer within the British Broadcast Corporation.

"Drake Pasqua is blowing the whistle and exposing his publisher's anti-American crimes, according to an unnamed source." This information was confirmed and posted on Drake Pasqua's Twitter page."

"*The Washington Times* reported that "a fake news article showed up in the digital version of *The Washington Post* providing photoshopped proof of Mia Jorgensen's charitable contributions to the National Rifle Association, the Hell's Angels, and the Ku Klux Klan. A fake audio surfaced of her yelling racial epithets. Mia Jorgensen is the wife of Jeff Jorgensen, owner of *The Washington Post*."

New York City

They sat across a wide table in the boardroom of *The New York Times* Company. "Drake," said Arnold Goldberger, "as they say, you have some 'splain'n to do."

"Sir," said Drake Pasqua, "you know me better than this. I would never make such unfounded claims. Someone hacked into my Twitter account and made totally untrue statements. I know you trust me and don't believe the shit that was reported."

Both men picked up on the irony that they, promoters of fake news and uncorroborated reporting, were now victims of their own making. Neither men embellished the subject.

Goldberger said, "I used to. I don't know what to believe anymore."

Timing is everything.

At just that moment, Goldberger's cell phone pinged with a text message. The message: "Fake news. What's good for the goose is good for the gander. Check out *Breitbart*."

Arnold took a deep breath after showing Drake the text message, turned to his computer, and opened the web browser to *Breitbart News*.

"We have it on good authority from an anonymous source that the rift between *The New York Times* Publisher Arnold Goldberger and Editor in Chief Drake Pasqua is nothing more than a lovers' quarrel. Don't expect a shake-up in *The New York Times*. This too will pass.

"On a similar note, the stock value of The New York Times Company has dropped almost twenty percent in the last three weeks. Rumors have it that shares of the stock are being picked up by hostile activist investors."

Drake Pasqua said calmly, "Well now you know what it's like to be on the wrong side of bad reporting and fake news. This is exactly why we must continue to verify and validate all our sources before we go to print and provide honest news reporting."

Arnold stared at Pasqua for a few seconds with an expression of incredulity.

Tears started to form in the publisher's eyes, his face screwed up into an ugly contorted expression resembling a medieval gargoyle. Drake tried to hold back his emotions but eventually broke down.

It was Arnold who first let a snicker out. It was the trigger for the unleashing of contagious laughter. Drake couldn't contain himself; he let go with a short giggle and burst out laughing.

Together, they laughed hysterically, tears running down their cheeks. The laughter would slow down until they made eye contact and burst out laughing again.

After several minutes of uncontrollable laughter, they both slowed down, caught deep breathes, coughed, and gradually stopped. Finally, Drake said, "You know, all kidding aside, this is really some serious shit."

And it was on—uncontrolled laughter.

The Hamptons, Long Island, New York

Levi Zimmerman folded the editorial section of *The New York Times* in half before he threw it into the fireplace. He thought, "That's a true metaphor. The *Times* is in ashes." He stomped around the great room in his mansion, formulating a strategy to stop whatever was going on out there. He hated having no control of the fake news situation.

Levi looked like his shorts had too much starch in them as he walked to the wall where a clock hung and lifted it off its hanger. Behind the clock was a safe. He dialed the combination, opened the safe door, reached in, and pulled out a satellite phone. He punched in the number he knew by heart.

But Lawrence Slaughter, an old friend of Gabriel Lakatos, a business associate of Jeff Jorgensen, and owner of California Media Group didn't answer.

CHAPTER 21

"If they didn't have double standards, they'd have no standards at all."—Chris Plante, radio talk-show host, 1959-present, host of *"The Chris Plante Show"*

Washington, DC – July 19th

Special Agent Rusty Winemiller, FBI Cybercrimes Division, didn't particularly enjoy the brutal ride from Quantico to the headquarters in downtown DC. But when duty calls, you do what's expected of you. He felt like it was a punishment to show up at a Hoover Building meeting where, invariably, his superiors would focus on what he hadn't yet done instead of what he had accomplished.

It wasn't his handicap that made the trip so unpleasant; it was the superior attitude projected by people who didn't have a clue. If he could stand, he would be six feet, three inches tall. He was rail thin, but his upper body was powerful-looking. The van stopped on Pennsylvania Avenue where it used the designated van lift to drop him to street level.

The deputy assistant director was already sitting in the conference room even though Agent Winemiller had arrived twenty minutes early. He said, "Good to see you made it early, Rusty. I have a couple of things I wanted to cover with you before the rest of the meeting attendees arrive."

Winemiller didn't like the sound of that and gave a tentative, "OK, sir."

"The director ordered us to make the subject of the meeting our number one priority. That means the other important projects you're working on will have to take a back seat."

Rusty said, "People have short memories. Can I get these new priorities in writing?"

"Don't be a smart-ass, though I agree with your concern. We both know what it is like when the big dogs have convenient recollections of history."

Winemiller asked, "What's the subject?"

The deputy assistant director, a political appointee, sighed and said, "It looks to the director like we're losing the cyberwar. When hackers can replace articles in *The Washington Post*, when totally fake news about the publisher of *The New York Times* can hit the BBC and the AP, and when doing so they can leave false flags in North Korea's lap, then we've lost control. Rusty, how sophisticated are the Northcoms? Can they hack into a nuclear power plant control room? Can they hack into a chemical plant and release toxic gasses? Can they hack into the Pentagon and fire ballistic missiles? Can they hack artificial intelligence? Just how far behind are we?"

Before Rusty could address the questions raised by the deputy assistant director, the director of the FBI walked into the conference room with the vice president of the United States at his side. The deputy assistant director stood up in respect for the VP—Winemiller was unable to rise to the occasion.

The FBI director addressed the deputy assistant director and asked, "Is Special Agent Winemiller fully briefed on the subject at hand."

"No, he only has a high-level view of the subject."

"Special Agent Winemiller, you have a new assignment. Find out who is hacking into *The New York Times* and *The Washington Post* and what level of sophistication they are using. Though we're glad they are revealing their talents and tools on relatively unimportant private sector areas of concern, we're fearful they, whoever 'they' are, will invade more critical items of national security."

The vice president said, "Special Agent Winemiller, I've heard good things about you and your leadership of the Cybercrimes Division. But there is something bigger going on here. Are the cybercrimes related in some way to a more insidious attack on the United States? Please find out who is committing these crimes, how they are doing it, and what do we need in order to stop it from flowing over into the control of our military operations.

"If Vladimir Putin gets a text message from our president, how can he be sure it's the real deal? If Tokyo gets correspondence from Kim Jong-un threatening to send a nuclear-armed missile at Japan, and it's a false message, what are the consequences?"

"No pressure," said the FBI director. "Only the safety of a billion or so people depend on your leadership."

Rusty looked at the three bureaucrats and said, "I assume you know that the North Koreans have six teams of fifteen hundred hackers each? I think you know that the People's Republic of China uses five thousand cyber experts for a single project. The Russians and the Czechs have comparable armies of state-sponsored cybercriminals. Collectively, they grow more sophisticated daily.

"I'll need more resources than are currently allocated to the problem in Quantico. I'll require some specifically unique subcontractors. Tell me that I won't be resource limited."

The director and the deputy assistant director looked over at the vice president for confirmation. The VP said, "You tell me what you need, and I'll make sure you get it."

Rusty Winemiller said, "Thank you, sir."

Little did the VP know that Special Agent Winemiller already knew who committed the cybercrime. Rusty, after all, was one of the twenty-two members of The Media Transformation Foundation.

Brooklyn, New York

The Bentley Flying Spur W12S was driven clockwise around Pratt Institute on Willoughby Avenue, to Classon Avenue, to DeKalb Avenue, to Hall Street, and back to Willoughby Avenue. The driver was told to continue the route until his boss flagged him down at the Ryerson Walk Gate.

A professor in the School of Fine Arts who specialized in photography sat in the cafeteria waiting for her guest who, as usual, was already fifteen minutes late. She read the *The National Enquirer*, sipped on her bottled water, and nibbled on some carrot sticks she brought with her in a recyclable container. Under the cafeteria table was a Macy's shopping bag—the kind with handles— with a gift-wrapped, shoe-box-sized carton inside.

"Traffic was awful."

She heard him from behind her before she saw him.

"I'm sorry for being late, love." He leaned over, kissed her on the forehead, and asked, "How much time do we have before your next class?"

She answered, "About thirty minutes."

He said, "Not enough time for me to take you to lunch at my favorite restaurant. What do you say I come back and take you to dinner tonight?"

"Sounds good to me." She added, "Listen, a student from Columbia University came all the way here to give me a gift from him to you. What's the occasion and why would he give it to me?"

The man said, "Because I asked him to. It gave me an excuse to see you, and I didn't want to talk to him. He's a little weird and starts into conspiracy theories when I meet with him. The gift is a book he wrote about what really happened with the downing of the Malaysian Airlines Flight 370."

"Who is the student, and how do you know him?"

He said, "Let's not talk about him; let's talk about us. I want to know if you would fly to Bermuda with me this weekend."

"This weekend?"

He said, "I like to be impromptu; I'm an impulsive type of guy."

"Oh, Craig, I'd love to. That sounds so exciting."

"We'll talk more about it over dinner tonight. Pick you up after your last class. Seven thirty OK?"

She just nodded her head, handed him the shopping bag, and kissed him on the lips.

He walked out of the cafeteria and walked a block to the preselected meeting point and waited three minutes before he saw the Bentley.

After he climbed into the back seat, the driver asked, "Where to, sir?"

"30 Rockefeller Plaza."

Wiscasset

Maya sat in her favorite outdoor chair in the screened-in porch overlooking the pool and the river while Star swam laps. Her laptop was on a glass table before her. She searched on Edge to learn about the background of journalism school professors.

She opened a new window when the news popped up about a bomb exploding in Rockefeller Center. She quickly clicked on the top story icon and then clicked on a live video link to see chaos filmed from a network helicopter—fire trucks, ambulances, people still pouring out of Rockefeller Center, police cruisers, traffic blockaded, smoke billowing out of upper floors, and water sprayed out of firehoses from extended ladders. Maya felt a sense of déjà vu with memories of 9/11. She read the rest of the article on the website:

"No organization has taken credit or posted an explanation for the bombing. Neither the New York City Fire Department nor the New York City Bomb Squad has released their initial findings, but an unnamed source suggested that the device was a homemade, low-yield bomb.

"MSNBC, a tenant in Rockefeller Center, is the defendant of a highly visible, billion-dollar lawsuit for malpractice by several right-wing organizations. An unnamed source close to the case speculates that the lawsuits triggered right wing activists to take the law into their own hands."

CHAPTER 22

"War is the remedy that our enemy has chosen."- General William Tecumseh Sherman, 1820-1891, Civil War general for the Union Army

Butler, New Jersey – July 25th

Tony Vinci was only four feet, ten inches tall with dwarf-like legs—although his upper body was all muscle.

Tony was a genius. By the age of thirty-two, he had seventy-six patents either awarded outright, pending or applied for. As chief scientist for Entropy, LLC, he spent most of his time in their Boston office, but Tony had a home office in his ninety-year-old, white, three-story Victorian home with a wraparound porch.

Tucker got out of his rented car and started up the concrete walkway. He observed two separate CCTV cameras panning over him as he advanced up three steps and approached the front door.

He rang the doorbell and heard a ringtone that sounded like a tune from Santana's "Black Magic Woman." The door opened, and a large man with a military bearing and who openly carried a Beretta answered the door. Tucker never looked at the man—his glance was locked on the gun. The bodyguard and butler spoke first, "Hi Mr. Cherokee, we were expecting you. Pinot Grigio?"

Tucker was surprised that the intimidating guard knew his wine preference but answered, "Yes, thank you."

Tony watched the exchange on his forty-eight-inch monitor. In his deep baritone voice, Tony said, "Come on in, boss. Make yourself at home, I know we've got a lot of territory to cover. Harold, are those hors d'oeuvres Tucker likes ready?"

Harold answered, "Of course."

Tucker noticed that the inside of the house was a study in contrast. The furniture was stark, 1920 vintage construction, upholstered in fabric patterns not seen in decades. A metal grating where the heat from a coal furnace once provided warmth for the house was still in place. The stairway to the upper level was narrow, with a beautiful, highly polished, refinished, hand-carved banister.

He marveled at the diversity of tools and electronics that littered the house. There must be a hundred unfinished projects going on. In the dining room on the other side of the old coal grate was a metal shop with lathes, drill presses, welding machines, metal saws, toolboxes, container after container of fasteners, electrical connectors, dumbbells, and wiring materials.

Standing in the adjacent kitchen was Tony Vinci with his right hand out to shake hands, and his left hand stroking his goatee. Tucker didn't shake Tony's hand. He made that mistake once. No one shook hands with the bone-crusher twice.

Tony said, "I'm glad you came. I have something I can't wait to show you. You're going to go nuts when you watch this video."

Tony waddled to his computer control center, typed in a few commands, and said, "This video was taken in the home of a newspaper reporter in Alexandria, Virginia."

Tony pushed 'play' on his remote: Waylon Trout pounded away on his keyboard, writing an editorial piece about the need to control federal spending. It was scheduled to go into the following day's conservative regional newspaper, *The Washington Times*. His doorbell rang, which was unusual at 8:10 p.m. Waylon cautiously looked through the peephole to see two Alexandria police officers standing at his townhouse doorstep.

The writer opened the front door and let the officers into his well-furnished living room with a floor-to-ceiling bookshelf filled with vintage hardbacks. "What can I do for you gentlemen?"

The first officer pulled out his nightstick and hit Waylon on the thigh. Trout grimaced in pain and yelled, "You can't do this! What's the matter with you two?" The second officer used plastic ties to bind his wrists, pulled a washrag out of his pocket and stuffed it in the writer's mouth, then ran duct tape around his head to keep him from spitting it out.

"Mr. Trout," said the first officer, "we only hit your thigh. Though it will hurt for quite a while and leave an ugly bruise, you'll recover. If you don't stop writing your anti-government bullshit, we'll be back, but next time, it will be your knees. Do you understand?"

Tony stopped the video.

Tucker said, "We always wondered if that sort of strong-arm tactic was used by the left. That's a very interesting video, Tony. Why in the world did you deploy one of your nanodevices with cameras in Trout's home?"

"Wasn't it you," answered Tony Vinci, "that asked me to launch, fly, and locate the nanodevice—nano-drone-camera-bug—in as many homes and offices of the people in the mainstream media as possible to see if we could get something on them?"

Tucker said, "I didn't figure *The Washington Times* met the criteria for 'mainstream.' How many of these nanodevices do you have out there?"

"I don't know."

"What do you mean you don't know?"

"I lost count. Maybe a little over two thousand."

"Holy shit, Tony. And each one records everything that goes on in each target's home?"

"No, some are located in their offices. That is what you wanted," said Tony.

Tucker eyed Tony with a stare that could dissolve granite.

"No, sir," said Tony, "I don't have a nanodevice in your home."

Tucker growled, "If I discover one in my home…"

Tony said, "If I placed one in your home, you'd never know."

"OK . . . for now," Tucker said. "The two policemen in Trout's house: what did you learn about them?"

"They aren't cops; they wore fake badge numbers and stolen uniforms." Tony continued, "So, I ran their faces through my proprietary facial recognition software and compared it against a database I hacked into. They are hired, thugs. Anyone could have hired them."

Tucker waited.

Tony said, "Here are their names and addresses. They're out of Baltimore. I figured Powers and Tank might want to interview them to determine who hired them."

"Are there any other videos or audio in the homes of the mainstream media that will be interesting to our team?"

"I can't view them all, so I'm writing an algorithm where I only have to see the ones that have a potential for use. They'll be categorized by type of use like sexual, illegal, bribery, pedophilia, illicit drugs, and violence."

Tucker added, "Don't forget to listen for conspiracies. Do you have any more nanodevices?"

"Does a bear shit in the woods?"

"Good, I want you to listen in on the next Writers Guild conference in San Diego."

"Have any of the people you're monitoring discovered one of these devices?"

"They aren't picked up by normal electronic sweepers because everything is made with carbon fiber and transmitted in a microwave frequency. A couple of units were mistaken for insects and were crushed, but no one has suspected them for what they are. Yet."

Tucker said, "All this is interesting, but that is not why I came today."

Tony sat erect and said, "Did I do something wrong, boss?"

"Probably. I just haven't caught you at it yet. Did you watch the protests in front of *The Washington Post* on the news?"

"It was hard to avoid. It was on every channel for a while."

Tucker said, "Has Tank talked to you about it?"

"No."

"The Molotov cocktail was not in the plan."

Tony responded, "It's what got all the news."

"True, but it means someone knew we organized a protest in advance and took advantage of the opportunity. How could that happen, Tony?"

"Boss, you're not accusing me of leaking information, are you?"

"No, it was a real question: how could someone know about it in advance with enough time to put together a getaway plan? A pretty good one, I might add."

Tony said, "You've heard of the dark web, right?"

"I've heard of it, but I can't say I know anything about it."

"Tank asked me to contact the protestors by using the same account liberals use—it's funded by one of Gabriel Lakatos's nonprofit companies. I did that using the dark web. So, it was out there."

"Is anybody taking credit for it on dark web blogs?"

"I'll check Onion, Tor, and others to see what I can find."

"While you're at it, check to see if anyone on the dark web is taking credit for the murder of Gabriel Lakatos. And, Tony, you realize you stole money from Lakatos's estate to pay for the hired protestors, and you violated a whole bunch of laws planting these nanodevices all over the place? I'll bring you cookies when you go to jail."

Tony smiled and said, "To quote my boss, 'This is war.'"

Washington, DC

Senator Peter Enya listened intently to the closely guarded WebEx conversation as he sat behind the closed door in his Hart Building office. He used the laptop and hotspot router Tucker gave him, which was configured by Tony Vinci, to be secure from discovery. Peter was near an emotional fault line when he learned from Tucker that his chief of staff, Clayton West, had betrayed him. Half serious, Enya asked if he could borrow Ram for ten minutes.

Tucker had to pull Peter back from the edge of violence and revenge. He convinced Enya that it turned out to be a good thing to have a spy in their midst and a significant advantage for the foundation's cause. Since the gutless and unprincipled West secured for them access to the call, Tucker asked Peter if he would be the single person in the foundation to listen every morning to the daily Democratic National Committee talking points. He also asked the senator to keep his reptilian chief of staff on so that they could use him to pass on disinformation to the enemy.

That turned out to be "a bridge too far" for Senator Enya, but he did agree to drop any charges he intended to file against Clayton West "at this time."

The daily talking points WebEx started:

Arnold Goldberger, *The New York Times*: "The fake news story about me and Drake Pasqua, which was fabricated by someone with the the ability to have the article replaced in digital news publications, was effective at showing the public how powerful misinformation and fake news stories can be. All news organizations lost a little credibility as a result. We need to fight back and destroy the credibility of whomever or whatever organization is behind this travesty."

The chairperson of the Democratic National Committee: "Do we know who is behind the fake news attack on you?"

Arnold Goldberger, *The New York Times*: "Not yet."

Levi Zimmerman, Lakatos Foundations: "We'll assign a team of private investigators to the task."

Executive Producer of CNN: "So, what are today's talking points?"

The chairperson of the Democratic National Committee: "The illegal fake news story put out by our ideologically flawed white supremacist Republicans may be prosecuted under hate crime laws."

Editor of the *San Francisco Chronicle*: "I love the concept, but how do we make that stick?"

Arnold Goldberger, *The New York Times*: "Note that the fake news story had two villains, me and the North Koreans. I'm Jewish, and the North Koreans are, well, not white. The good guy in the fake news story, Pasqua here, is white."

President of MoveOn.org: "Let me get this straight: the illegal fake news article that may have been planted by a white supremacist group is another example of the continued racist actions of the Republican Party members."

The chairperson of the Democratic National Committee: "OK, I think we got it. We'll talk again tomorrow. Same time."

Peter Enya thought, "So that's how it works."

Mountain View

"Jeff," said Lawrence Slaughter, "I had a visitor. She was Israeli. I'm unsure exactly who she represented, but she extended her sympathy to you and me for the loss of our friend Gabriel Lakatos. That was creepy enough and came across almost like a threat, but then she added that she wanted me to pass a message on to you."

Jeff said, "You've got some big cajones calling me after you threatened me and my family. I've sent a copy of your text to Detective Yamaguchi in Seattle. Expect a visit from him to arrest you for life endangerment. What the fuck is the matter with you?"

"Whoa, my friend. What are you talking about?"

"You sent me a text threatening me and my family if I didn't help fund the private investigation into the death of Gabriel Lakatos. You admitted you hired the sniper that shot into my Seattle residence. All you had to do Larry is ask me for money."

"Jeff," said Slaughter, "I never sent you a text message and I did not hire the sniper."

Silence.

Lawrence added, "You don't suppose the people who sent us that threatening text after Gabriel was murdered are the same people who posted fake information in you're *The Washington Post*, could also send you fake texts from me?"

Silence.

Finally, Jeff said, "How did Israeli woman connect you and me to Gabriel?"

"Don't know. I asked, but the woman didn't give me an answer. I got the feeling she was maybe Mossad."

"What was the message?"

"She said she represented a company that is willing to buy *The Washington Post* for 750 million dollars if you agree in principle by close-of-business tomorrow. She says the offer drops to 500 million dollars by the end of next week and 250 million dollars by the end of the month."

Jeff said, "That's bullshit. I don't believe it. Why did she contact you and not go through normal channels or contact me directly?"

"Call her bluff. Take the $750 million. I know you don't need the money, but God knows it's surely a pain in your ass."

Jeff asked, "What are the terms?"

CHAPTER 23

"I love it when a plan comes together." – Col. John Hannibal Smith, The A Team, 1983 - 1986

Washington, DC – August 1st

As quickly as it started, the protestors in front of *The Washington Post* headquarters on K Street and the demonstrators in front of Jorgensen's homes in Seattle and Kalorama disappeared. The printing presses in College Park operated smoothly, and the cyberwarfare against the digital version of the *Post* stopped, as did attacks on Lawrence Slaughter's TV and radio empire.

The front page of the next issue of *The Washington Post* announced: "A Bahamian shell corporation called The Cedar Umbrella, LLC, acquired both Jeff Jorgensen's ownership of *The Washington Post* and controlling interest of *The Washington Times*. The two will be merged effective immediately. The current management of *The Washington Times* will run both newspapers. The new slogan for the merged newspapers is 'The Truth and Nothing but the Truth, So Help Us God.'"

Mountain View

Slaughter asked, "When do I get paid the ten million dollars you promised for brokering the deal with Jeff Jorgensen?"

The woman looked more like someone from Sweden than Israel. She didn't smile and didn't answer the question. Instead, she said, "You're seventy-five years old, right?"

"What's that got to do with anything?"

"Your ungrateful children are all multimillionaires, thanks to you, right?"

He asked, "Is there a point to this line of questioning?"

"Take a look at this dossier on you. Read it carefully." She handed him a leather satchel.

Slaughter said, "Listen, woman, I don't need to read the report. What the fuck do you want?"

"I want you to hire someone as president of your media empire. You do that, and you get the money I promised, and I won't release this dossier to the new management of *The Washington Post*. You'll get the added benefit of staying out of prison for the rest of your life. Deal?"

"Who do you want me to hire?"

She said, "The man is currently the senior vice president of communications and editor in chief of the *Daily Signal* for the Heritage Foundation."

"Fuck you." Slaughter pushed a button on his desk to summon his security team.

No one answered his emergency call.

She said, "Have it your way." She stood up and started out the door. "You'll find your security team at the bottom of a well in San Jose. They're alive. We're not quite as ruthless as you are.

"Yet.

"Things will get worse for you and your family from here on."

Slaughter stammered, "OK, OK. It's a deal."

The petite woman didn't even crack a smile at her negotiating success when she said, "The money will be in your Latvian offshore account by 0900 Pacific time tomorrow. Your new president will take control by close-of-business two days from now. Any change of heart on your part will result in disclosure of the report, which, in turn, will assure your incarceration. Are you sure you don't want to read the dossier first? There is nothing in it we can't prove."

He asked, "Who the hell are you?"

She answered, "Your worst nightmare if you ever find out."

Oklahoma City, Oklahoma

The Israeli woman caught a chartered flight from San Francisco to Oklahoma City where she agreed to meet her father at the memorial site of the Oklahoma City bombing. Sonja McLeod was a petite blonde who grew up in Israel with stepparents. She became one of Mossad's most feared snipers. Her stepmother had left Sonja an envelope after she died informing her of who her real father was. Powers did not know he had a daughter until Sonja showed up at his doorstep five years ago. They bonded and had watched each other's back ever since.

He watched her roam the memorial grounds for a couple of minutes. She reminded him so much of his deceased wife. Sonja smiled when she saw him, and it was difficult for both not to hug each other. But this was a clandestine meeting. He sat on a concrete bench next to a sign describing the event of the tragic Timothy McVeigh bombing. As she pretended to read, he asked, "How'd it go?"

She answered, "I don't trust him."

He said, "With good reason. But we have a few more tricks in our bag if he bolts or tries to renege."

"Was everything in the report true?"

"Yep."

She looked around to make sure no one was within earshot and asked, "Let me guess: Jimmy Ma and Tony

Vinci gathered the information no one else could find? They should work for the FBI or Mossad. Anyway, will you need me for any other assignments?"

"Yep. Any excuse to see you is a good one."

CHAPTER 24

"It's just a job. Grass grows, birds fly, waves pound the sand. I beat people up." – Muhammad Ali, 1942-2016, professional boxer

Stony Brook, Long Island, New York – August 11th

Homicide detective Roger Sheppard walked out of the nasty weather—what seemed to him to be the constant drizzle of Long Island—into the estate's entranceway, wearing a bright yellow, lightweight, hooded fisherman's rain jacket over his short-sleeve golf shirt, jeans, and hiking boots. He was a man with an attitude and not someone you'd put on your list to have lunch with. He was not an abrasive, intolerant, crusty old man—he was an abrasive, intolerant, crusty thirty-two-year-old with a chip on his shoulder about the size of Long Island.

The local Suffolk County police officer on the scene placed the yellow and black police barricade tape back into place. Sheppard asked, "Is the forensic investigator done? I want to see the crime scene before the victim is hauled off to the lab."

"No, sir, he's still on the premises."

"Where can I sit without contaminating the crime scene?"

"Uh, you might want to go back to your car, sir, and stay until he's done."

Without saying a word, the detective narrowed his eyes, considered the officer's comments, and returned the way he'd come in, back through the entranceway into the unpleasant weather. Outside, he wandered the perimeter with his head swiveling in constant movement, looking for anything out of place. He sloshed down the driveway to a detached mother-in-law suite over a four-car garage. His instincts drew him to climb the stairs on the outside of the building up to the second level. About halfway up the stairs, he observed that the door to the suite was cracked.

Sheppard pulled his 9mm Walther PPQ and cautiously climbed the remaining stairs, but he stopped short before reaching the landing. He yelled, "Police. Come out with your hands where I can see them."

The rain was just hard enough to dampen the sound of any movement in the suite. He waited fifteen seconds before he followed with, "Throw any weapons you may have on the floor. If you're holding a weapon when I come in there, I'll shoot, so keep your hands out and drop your weapon."

Still nothing.

With his back to the wall, he reached up with his right hand and opened the door farther while remaining out of the potential line of fire.

A dim light, forty-watts or less, emanated from within the suite. Sheppard turkey-peaked around the door and into the room. In the half-second he looked, into what he guessed was a family room about twenty-feet square, he was sure he saw a body lying on the 1970-vintage shag carpet. The detective pulled his radio and called for backup.

Two minutes later, the county police officer he'd met in the estate entranceway earlier came up the steps behind him, his Glock 17 held firmly by both hands, and momentarily slipped onto a knee on the wet steps.

The detective hand-signaled to the cop for his flashlight. Sheppard placed the high-beam flashlight over his Walther, looked over at the police officer, and mouthed the words, "One . . . two . . . three!"

Sheppard barged into the suite's family room and swept the room quickly. The county officer followed closely behind him and swung a full 360-degrees with his Glock at the ready.

Sheppard said, "You check the kitchen area, and I'll check the bedroom."

Thirty seconds later, Sheppard heard, "Clear."

The suite was empty except for the body in the middle of the family room.

Sheppard pulled out a set of latex gloves from his jacket and forced them over his wet hands. He said, "This is a little weird, don't you think?"

They were looking at the head of a mannequin, and the body was covered with pasted newspapers.

The police officer holstered his gun and said, "Do you think this has anything to do with the murder in the main house of the estate?"

Sheppard said, "I don't know. We'll see if forensics can pull a print or anything else that might tie this bizarre find to the murder. Get some more barricade tape and place it across the doorway. And ask the forensic investigator to come up here."

As Roger Sheppard waited for the cop to return with tape and for the medical examiner to arrive, he scanned the odd discovery for a clue of some sort. He read a few lines on the paper wrapped around the mannequin's torso.

From a voice behind him that Sheppard recognized, a man said, "So, what has my favorite homicide detective found that may shed light on this case?"

Sheppard said, "Maybe something that will lead us to a motive, Doc. My gut tells me this . . ." he hesitated to find the right word, "this is a statement—a message of some sort."

Dr. Maverik Patton pulled a polyester cloth out of his back pocket, wiped the droplets of water off his trifocals, and said, "There are plenty of messages left downstairs at the murder scene. They'll make your asshole pucker. Let's see if this message is consistent with the other statements made by a very sick perp."

Sheppard said, "The mannequin seems to be completely covered with the editorial pages of *The New York Times*. Further, though I haven't turned the mannequin over, all the articles appear to be written by the editor. Look here, Maverik, this article was circled with a pen."

Maverik asked, "You know who the murder victim was, right?"

"No, I wasn't informed before I arrived. The dispatcher just gave me an address. So, who is the victim, what is the cause of death, and what messages were left by the killer?"

"Well, aren't we a little demanding?" Dr. Patton had very few pleasures in his life but pulling the always-unpleasant homicide detective's chain was one of them.

Mav waited fifteen seconds in silence before Roger exploded. "Are we on the same team or not? Why are you fucking with me?"

The forensic investigator smiled, enjoyed his ability to spin the detective up, and said, "The cause of death is from intracranial hemorrhaging from penetrating trauma. The weapons were No. 2 pencils forced through the labyrinth and cochlea of the inner ear. The trauma was not postmortem. Nor was the computer mouse shoved down his throat and the thumb drive forced into his anus."

The detective said, "Yeah, that sounds like a message. What's on the thumb drive?"

"Don't know yet. I want to take it back to the lab, check it for prints, try to figure if it has some unique markings to help you keep your win rate up."

Roger gave Maverick a disapproving look for his snide comment and asked, "Who is the victim?"

"Drake Pasqua, editor in chief of the *Times*. Maybe the pen isn't mightier than the sword after all."

CHAPTER 25

"Lies sound like facts to those who've been conditioned to mis-recognize the truth." — DaShanne Stokes, sociologist, author, speaker, and pundit.

Wichita, Kansas – August 21st

The president of Wichita State University enthusiastically shook hands with two of the university's most important benefactors, William and Nick Hurt. The Hurt brothers had contributed many millions of dollars to the university over the years, including funds that built a state-of-the-art cybersecurity research center.

William spoke first, "The university does a wonderful job at producing very talented graduates who are heavily recruited by industry. Wichita State has the potential to lead the nation, not only in cybersecurity but in blockchain technology and artificial intelligence."

Nick tag-teamed with, "We want to award scholarships and co-op jobs to your top fifty masters students. They can stay on campus when they work for us but must sign secrecy agreements. For WSU's agreement, we'll fund the building of a campus radio station and transmission tower."

The university president looked suspiciously at the two famous businessmen and responded, "Your offer is generous, but I must understand what is expected of our students and why you think we need a radio station."

William Hurt added, "We want to grant to the university HonestMediaMatters.org. The organization is only six weeks old, but it already has fifteen million members who have contributed an average of twenty-five dollars to the cause. That's $62.5 million per week, which could become university funds."

The university president noticeably salivated but said, "I'm sorry, but I don't understand the organization's cause."

William continued, "It's an honorable cause. The founders want to encourage the media to be honest in their reporting. Is that too much to ask?"

Nick added, "Most professions achieve quality and aspire to high standards through self-regulation. Medical doctors can lose their right to practice if they violate AMA ethical standards. Lawyers can be disbarred. Engineers and architects can lose their licenses. But reporters, publishers, editorialists, and writers can write whatever they fucking want and claim they are protecting a source, with impunity. The Organization of News Ombudsmen has failed in its purpose to achieve and maintain high ethical standards in news reporting. It's failed the institutions it represents. The credibility that journalists once had may have fallen below that of used car salesmen. HonestMediaMatters.org was formed to protect readers from media bullies who are clearly unrestrained from writing fiction. Wichita State has the opportunity to leverage this organization and, in time, become the most respected journalism school in the nation. Not to mention the increase in the school's endowment fund."

The president of the university asked, "How do we proceed?"

Nick Hurt opened his briefcase, pulled out a letter-of-intent and the framework of a legal agreement. He put on his reading glasses and scanned the first two pages before he looked up and asked, "Why are you requesting an increase in the number of campus police and why must they be trained in the use of lethal weapons?"

William answered, "That's in case the university becomes a target from the violent left-leaning media who think it is a hate crime to require them to be honest."

Wichita

Four hours later, in a private, soundproof room in the back of Chester's Chophouse and Wine Bar, Tucker enjoyed a glass of Italy's famed Santa Margherita Pinot Grigio while the Hurt brothers sipped on drinks of Glenfiddich Private Vintage Single Malt Scotch Whisky.

They chatted about football, politics, business, and the stock market before they got down to the real purpose of their meeting. But before it began, Tucker held up his hand, palm out, and reached down into his Halliburton briefcase. He pulled out a noisemaker that would generate sound in a frequency that would jam anyone trying to overhear their conversation.

He said, "Just an added precaution. So, how'd it go?"

William stated, "We think the university's board will buy off on the program. It will, after all, bring a new dimension to the university and maybe some notoriety."

Nick added, "Not to mention a lot of badly needed money to support their growing aerospace program."

Tucker said, "Great. If we pull this off like I think is possible, we'll create a new standard for journalism. Once you have all the hardware installed, the high-speed connection established, the building secured with physical security systems, around-the-clock protection from White Knight Personal Security officers, and the background check on the students completed, we'll send Jimmy Ma to install the algorithm and database. He'll train the staff and whomever you want to supervise the operation to mine the information. I think HonestMediaMatters.edu will be better known than any other conservative website, blog, talk radio program, or cable TV show. We are going to grade the media, list the lies, expose the villains, destroy a few careers, embarrass the unembarrassable, and create a following of people who have longed for knowing who to trust. In phase two, we'll launch our own talk radio show and stream a video program right here in the heartland of America, and no one will know that our foundation is responsible.

"But there will be a backlash. We'll have to find a way to protect the safety of our honest media soldiers. Plan for the worst."

Washington, DC

Sitting before the Vice President of the United States in the stately if not gaudy office of his residence at Number One Observatory Circle mansion located on the northeast grounds of the U.S. Naval Observatory in Washington, DC, Rusty Winemiller anticipated a thorough chewing out at his failure to identify the hackers that violated *The Washington Post* and threatened national security. Agent Winemiller sat adjacent to his director who he was sure not there to protect him but rather to join in on his castigation.

"Winemiller," the VP said, "up until now you have been a rising star in the FBI. You've been extremely effective at identifying cyber criminals and helping the country bring them to justice."

The VP took a deep breath and said, "I agreed to provide you with all the funds you needed to uncover the source of the cybercrimes committed by who-knows-who against *The Washington Post*—crimes I fear are a "canary in the coal mine" that is merely a prequel to what is coming. It's been over a month and we haven't heard a peep from you as to the progress you've made. What gives?"

Rusty had rehearsed his response and said, "Mr. Vice President," he looked over to his boss and added, "and Director, as I hope you've been informed, there are over ten million cyber attacks on the Pentagon alone—ten million. Some are domestic but most are from international sources including China, Russia, Turkey, North Korea, Romania, Brazil, India, and Taiwan. They attackers use a variety of techniques that sometimes reveal the geographic origin.

"I can't say yet with certainty, but our cyber team gives it a 45% probability that the source is domestic and a 30% probability that the cyber criminals are from India.

"Sirs, I regret that your expectations were that we could locate the criminals with specificity within a month. If I gave you that impression, I'm sorry."

The VP asked, "How much longer do you think you need?"

Rusty said, "With the use of the supercomputer you ensured we had access to, I'd give it another sixty days."

"Not good enough, son. See that you do better than that. With that, you may go, but do a better job of keeping the director here informed."

Winemiller motored out of the VP's residence, caught the waiting van to take him back to Quantico, and proceeded to call Jimmy Ma on an encrypted phone.

Jimmy answered, "Genius here."

"Jimmy, this is Rusty Winemiller. Is your phone secure?"

"Always."

"The hack job you did on *The Washington Post*, can you do it again but make sure the source looks like it came from India?"

Jimmy asked, "Anyone in particular in India you want to frame?"

"Actually, yes. There's a company in Calcutta that is very close to being able to hack into US artificial intelligent manufacturing."

"OK, but clear this with my bosses. How soon do you need this done and what's my reward?"

CHAPTER 26

"There are things we don't know we don't know." - Donald Rumsfeld, - 1932 to present, former Secretary of Defense

Butler, New Jersey – August 27th

Two guests in matching, but expensive, wool coats exited the back seat of an inconspicuous white Ford Edge, walked thirty feet up to the ninety-year-old brick steps, and onto the wraparound porch. They didn't have to ring the doorbell. Harold's eyes looked out with shock and amazement at the beauty of the unexpected visitors and stuttered into the microphone, "B-Boss, were you expecting any special guests today that you forgot to mention to me?"

Tony Vinci turned on his CCTV monitor to see Maya and Star Cherokee standing at his front door.

The visitors heard Tony on the porch speakers ask, "My God, why are you here? What happened?"

Harold regained his composure and said, "Please, come in. May I take your coats? Can I offer you anything to drink?"

Tony reiterated, "Really, Maya, why are you here?"

"Calm down, Tony; there is no emergency. I just have something important I need to discuss with you. As you know, we can't discuss our business over the phone or on the internet, nor can I let you know my itinerary for fear that someone may be monitoring the airwaves."

Harold said, "It's an honor to meet you and Star in person. I've heard so much about you. Do you want me to park your Ford behind Tony's Jaguar? We can't leave it where it is parked out in the street."

Maya said, "The driver will stay in the car. It's no ordinary Ford. It'll be just fine there."

Maya said to Tony, "Shall we?"

Maya knew that Tony had a room in the basement designed to meet Department of Defense's Sensitive Compartmented Information Facility, or SCIF, requirements, where they could talk without fear of their conversation being overheard or recorded. He rode his electric cart to the door of the elevator and gestured to Star that she should enter first. Tony said to Star, "Since you can read my thoughts, you know you are safe."

Maya said, "Don't worry. We trust you, Tony. That is, as much as we can trust anyone."

The three of them rode the elevator down into the old coal boiler room in Tony's basement. Tony leaned in, scanned his eye, which opened a key pad. Tony punched in four digits and opened the sealed door to the secret compartmentalized information facility.

Tony waved his two visitors into the secret compartment and asked Star, "So what were the four digits I punched into the key pad?"

Star answered, "7-3-1-1."

Tony said to Maya, "You know, I'll have to change it after you leave."

She said, "Just don't think about your new pin."

Tony eyed Star with concern, admiration, and a little fear.

Star said, "You don't have to worry. We're on the same side. You're one of the good guys. Right, Mom?"

"Right, sweetheart."

Tony closed the door, turned the door wheel and said, "OK, Maya. We're in a secure environment. What do you want to discuss?"

"Tucker reported to us the progress you've made planting nanodevices around the world. He tells me you record and analyze relevant discussions between our ideological enemies."

Tony brushed his fingers through his graying hair and said, "I promise you, Maya, I have no nanodevices on your personal premises." Sweat beaded on Tony's forehead.

Maya narrowed her eyes, furrowed her brow, and said, "Until now, I never considered that you would." She looked over at Star to see whether she uncovered anything new in Tony's thoughts but was disappointed to learn nothing from her daughter.

Maya continued, "Tony, do you monitor journalism schools' classrooms?"

"I continuously monitor classrooms taught by Professor Erika Dell at Columbia University; Professor Jose Orwell at the University of California, Berkeley; Professor Paul Diamontopolis from University of Virginia; and Professor Siva Karamchandani at the University of Missouri."

"Tony," Maya continued, "for our foundation to have any long-term effect on the quality of the media, we must find a way to penetrate the teachings at journalism schools. Young minds are twisted and warped by foolish professors who want the young idealists to promote their ideology. They aren't interested in teaching journalists to present honest news; they're only interested in promoting their distorted concept of universal social justice.

"So, Tony," Maya said pleadingly, "which classrooms do I need to view to get the best perspective as to what they're teaching our future journalists?"

"Maya, I have millions of hours of recordings from thousands of nanodevices placed around the country. I can't possibly listen to them all, so I've developed a program whereby I can input key words and listen to discussions around the input. Let me see, here. OK. I've keyed in the words, 'politically correct' journalism. I see we have over eight thousand hits, but the most recent lecture on the subject was by Jose Orwell at Cal-Berkeley. Here, let me pull it up."

"I'd like a show of hands of those of you who consider yourself sensitive. Ah, good, almost all of you. OK, how many of you have written something that offended others? Come on now, be honest. Once again, nearly all of you. If you're going to be a journalist whose writing has any chance whatsoever to be impactful, you'll have to offend a class of people. You don't want to offend the downtrodden, weak, minority, or undocumented. Go for the easy target: the greedy, the racist, the capitalist, the bosses, the homophobes, the mercenaries, the womanizers, the NASCAR hunters, the polluters, the global-warming deniers, the evangelical Christians, and the ruling party. You can do this with impunity. Your next assignment is to write a one-thousand-word op-ed manuscript that is offensive to corporate executives but sensitive to the people under the thumbs of these same oppressors.

"All good journalism is anti-conservative in the sense of challenging existing authorities. There are many forces that constrain what journalism really ought to be, and American journalism, far from being the orgy of liberalism that some conservatives think it is, is actually deferential and timid in its approach to power and the general ignorance of large sections of the American public."

Tony said, "Young journalists are taught from day-one to attack conservatives. The professors teach students that all conservatives are ignorant, greedy, and racist. Journalism schools teach that bigotry against conservatives is honorable."

Maya said, "We have to understand the root cause of why professors teach this garbage before we can implement a plan to stop this cycle of hate."

Tony smiled and said tongue-in-cheek', "If you can do that, you're a better man than me."

Maya leaned back, shook her head such that her silky waste-length jet-black hair flowed like it was alive and said, "I see you've learned a thing or two from these journalism professors, but you'll have to do better than that if you're going to offend me.

"Tony," Maya continued, "Dig up some personal information on Jose Orwell. He may need a visit from Tank."

"OK. Will you two stay for dinner? Harold's a pretty good chef."

"That's kind of you. Yes, we'll stay because I have another subject I want to cover with you."

Tony said, "I expected you had another reason to come all the way here. How can I help you?"

"Tucker visited you on the subject of the dark web. He gave you a couple of assignments. I'd like a status report on the assignments."

Tony responded, "There are two or three very active far-right organizations on the dark web, or darknet, that promote violence as a solution to ending what they call 'government-sponsored dishonest news.' One of them extolled the great success that right wing organizations have achieved based on the murders of Gabriel Lakatos and Drake Pasqua. They also praised the bombing of *The Washington Post* lobby and the sniper attack on Jorgensen's Seattle home.

"The group named itself, newsvigilantes.org on the web, and its leader's tag is #MrCraig. If he doesn't already know about this organization, I'd share this with the foundation member who is responsible for the FBI's cybersecurity efforts."

Maya said, "Can you tell how well funded they are? I'm concerned that when we start publishing our journalist rankings, this violent organization may start taking them out one by one."

"Not yet, but I'll keep working on it. What I can tell you is that *Soldier of Fortune Magazine* advertised for former military snipers using code. There may be a connection." And with that, Tony abruptly changed the subject. "Are we ready for dinner? Harold has prepared Veal Parmesan and opened a bottle of our top Chianti."

Star stared Tony down.

Tony said, "What?"

Star said, "You should tell Mom everything."

Maya's beautiful eyes took on a menacing look. She asked, "What are you holding back, Tony?"

Tony said, "Star, I haven't verified my suspicion. I don't want to lead you all down a path I haven't confirmed, but since you have cornered me, I'll tell you my theory. #MrCraig is Gabriel Lakatos's son, Craig Lakatos."

CHAPTER 27

"No good deed goes unpunished."—Clare Boothe Luce, 1903-1987, American Dramatist

Colorado Springs, Colorado – September 18th

The pilot brought the Bombardier Challenger 350 to a stop on the Colorado Springs Airport tarmac, where Tank and Powers awaited the Cherokee family arrival. Though a little cool and windy, Maya, Star, and Tucker deplaned to cloudless, sunny, and dry weather.

Tank was not one for mindless courtesy speak. He didn't ask how their flight was or how well they felt. Instead, he said, "The commander of the 721st Mission Support Group wants to speak with you before he assigns an escort for us to enter the mountain. He doesn't have a pleasant disposition, so prepare yourself for a hostile meeting. You must have gone over his head at the Pentagon to get special privileges here. I don't think he's happy about it."

Overhearing the discussion between Tank and Tucker, the pilot approached and asked Tucker, "Do I need to stay in the pilot's cafeteria in case you need to return sooner than expected?"

"No. Go ahead to the hotel. We'll spend the night here either way. If our meeting with the commander goes south, we'll return in the morning."

Tank said, "Did I mention that he is waiting?"

"By all means, take me to your leader. And, Powers, would you be kind enough to escort Maya, Star, and Ram to the hotel while I smooth down some of the commander's ruffled feathers?"

Peterson Air Force Base

It took thirty minutes for Tank and Tucker to get through security to see Commander Blackstone. He was a humorless kind of guy—all business, no fun. He asked Tank to stay in the waiting room and Tucker to follow him to a private meeting room. When they got to the entrance of the room, he asked Tucker to lock up his cell phone in a safe before they entered a SCIF.

When the two were alone in the four-hundred-square-foot SCIF, Blackstone broke out into a wide grin, and they shook hands enthusiastically. Wes Blackstone was one of the twenty-two members of The Media Transformation Foundation.

The tall, hawk-nosed commander said, "Tucker, I won't detain you long, but, because I can't be seen with you in the mountain, I need to give you a status report on my task for the mission."

He handed Tucker a notepad and a cheap ballpoint pen and said, "I can't give you a disk or thumb drive in here, so you'll have to take notes."

Wes proceeded to dictate from memory the names of four high-ranking military officers he had reason to suspect had ties to Lakatos, Jorgensen, Zimmerman, and Slaughter. He added, "I guess that if you have your crack cyberteam chase down correspondence between this list of officers and Lakatos's organization, you'll discover that at least one is linked to an international entity. The international influencers of world press editorials push for a one-world-government, which would necessitate a one-world military. Hence, the secret motivation of these four arrogant Pentagon officials."

Tucker said, "Great job, Wes. I'm not going to ask you how you got these names. But I am going to ask you to take the next step. We need to know how big and how deep into the military the Lakatos movement has penetrated. What do you need from us to help you?"

"When do you need this information?"

"Three months from today."

Wes responded, "That may be difficult without some help. What kind of help can you offer?"

It was difficult for Tucker to compartmentalize everything and not disclose information to a foundation member that could be beneficial to the completion of their assignment if it compromised information provided to him by another member.

Tucker finally answered Wes's question with another question, "In addition to the names you just disclosed, is there anyone else you'd like for me to eavesdrop on and surveille?"

Wes answered, "Yes."

CHAPTER 28

"The mainstream media is really the key, the gatekeeper. It effectively ensures that truth stays in the dark and lies and distractions remain in the bright lights of public interest."—Justin Steckbaue, Founder of Lifestyleofpeace.com.

Cheyenne Mountain Complex, Colorado Springs, Colorado – September 19th

The Cheyenne Mountain Complex is an underground city operated by the Air Force designed to be the "nerve center" for North American Aerospace Defense Command (NORAD). It was built to deflect a nuclear detonation, with eleven multiple-story buildings standing on coil springs to absorb the shock of a blast. It was designed so that up to eight hundred people could survive the fallout from a nuclear bomb. The buildings were encased in steel and surrounded by granite, and the facility was constructed behind twenty-five-ton blast-proof doors, as well as a tunnel and portal structures designed to deflect a nuclear detonation. The complex was set up to shield the interior against an electromagnetic pulse, which fries most electronics.

It wasn't Tucker's first trip into Cheyenne Mountain, so he knew what to expect to get through security. Commander Blackstone made it harder than it had to be to get the entire foundation team through security. He threw administrative roadblocks and bureaucratic speedbumps in front of Tucker's group to make it look like he resented Tucker's presence in the Cheyenne Mountain Complex. However, the private conference room Wes had set aside for the two-day retreat was perfect.

Although Maya's and Tucker's security clearances had expired, Powers and Tank both had active top-secret clearances. They couldn't get Star cleared to enter the complex, so she stayed in the hotel guarded by Ram and two of Tank's most trusted White Knight employees.

Ten minutes after they got settled, the first foundation member was escorted into the meeting room by an Air Force major who was handpicked by the commander to support the foundation. At the conference room entrance, she was passed like a baton over to Tank. If Tucker hadn't known in advance who the first member to arrive was, he would have never recognized her. Margaret Mellon looked like her name should be Mark Mellon. She wore a gray wool suit under a classic trench coat, men's dress shoes, a white shirt with a red striped tie, and a gray vest. Her hair was tucked up under a fedora hat. The makeup she wore made her appear like she hadn't shaved this morning.

Powers said to Margaret, "Well, I bet you avoided the paparazzi with that getup."

The diva said, "Yes, I should do this more often. No one gave me a second look. It saved having to call you to the rescue again, though it wasn't nearly as exciting as the last time we met."

Margaret turned to face Maya and Tucker, "Speaking of exciting, I can't wait to tell you two what's happening. I'm really having a lot of fun in this new, how should I say, experience."

Tucker said, "Ok, let's get to it. I asked you to be the first member to meet with us today because I wanted to be able to report to the other members the status of our war chest. They'll all ask."

"Remember," Maggie said, "you asked me to report to the treasurer, so, Maya, consider this my first quarterly report."

Tucker could tell based on her body language that she was pleased with herself and was about to brag about her handling of the foundation's money.

"As you know, I didn't have to be a financial genius to do well in the stock market over the last three months. The Dow-Jones and S&P rose an average of three and a half percent, or fourteen percent on an annual basis.

"We did better than that with most of our investments and much better than that with the some of it. I took five percent of our funds and invested in marijuana stocks and ETFs. I took another five percent and invested in energy futures. I took five percent more and bought palladium bars and five percent in cryptocurrencies and other blockchain-related stocks. Although we were in and out of the crypto-craze, we did well. The bottom line is that we invested $1.6 billion conservatively, which grew 4.2 percent, or $67 million in three months. The $400 million we invested aggressively grew by 100 percent to $800 million."

Maya said, "You've got to be kidding me! So, we now have a war chest of over $2 billion, $467 million?"

Maggie said, "Our operational costs were modest by comparison. Tank used only $42 million in the first quarter, most of that on lawyers, paid protestors, and our crack cyberteam.

"I took the liberty to invest $750,000 that I think will pay future dividends into a firm to provide investment advice."

Tucker looked at Maya, who seemed as surprised as he was. Why would Maggie need outside investment advice?

Margaret Mellon smiled and said, "We now have a list of all MSNBC, CNN, *New York Times*, *LA Times*, *Chicago Tribune*, Google, Yahoo, and *The Washington Post* advertisers, the names of each advertising decision-maker executive's families, their indiscretions, and their breaking points."

Maggie looked around the room at mouths agape and said, "Hey, you said I might have to get my hands dirty."

Maya asked, "You got that for only $750,000? Are you sure it's accurate and reliable?"

Ms. Mellon winked in the direction of Powers and said, "I told the company about Tank, Powers, and Ram without mentioning their names. They got the message."

Tucker said, "That brings us to the next subject: what is the status of the pulled advertisements and lawsuits against MSNBC and CNN?"

"Before we go on," Maggie interrupted, "I have one more surprise for you."

Maya said, "OK."

"We have raised an additional $75 million from members. So, our current account totals $2.5 billion."

Maya said, "This is fantastic news. But next time, meet with Tank before you spend any operations funds."

Maggie said, "Maya, our protocols and rules of engagement for communications are onerous. I can't contact anyone by phone, e-mail, or text. To be honest, I didn't know how to move on this time-sensitive opportunity. We need another way to reach each other than face-to-face every three months in caves or inside mountains."

Tucker knew this, of course, and had already taken the initiative to assign the task of solving that problem to Tony Vinci.

He said, "Let's get back to the subject of the lawsuits and advertisement pullback on MSNBC and CNN."

That's when the pounding on the door to the conference room changed everything.

Tank opened the door and thought he was looking into a full-length mirror. The man who pounded on the door was the same size, same age, and same apparent ancestry as Tank.

The man, equally surprised to be looking eye-to-eye with someone of his stature said, "I am Military Police officer Major Javier Castro."

Everyone in the room was wide-eyed, waiting for the next shoe to drop.

He continued, "I am here to apprehend Tucker Cherokee and turn him over to the Colorado Springs police who are waiting outside security to take him to the police station for questioning."

Colorado Springs Police Station

Tucker sat across the table from MP Major Castro, along with an Air Force lieutenant commander, and a young JAG. The case officer in the room was Colorado Springs Police Detective Slick White. The lieutenant commander acted agitated, nervous, shifty—wired a little too tight. Tucker sensed the commander was struggling to contain the anger he vectored in Tucker's direction. The almost obese baby JAG who Castro dragged into the interview had eyebrows that touched over his nose, a deviated septum, an ugly cold sore he didn't try to hide, acne on his neck, a pointed chin, and greasy black hair. Compared to his caustic personality, he was a handsome man. If Tucker had any violent tendencies, just being in this guy's presence would have brought them out.

Castro asked, "Mr. Cherokee when was the last time you saw Commander Blackstone?"

Tucker immediately thought the question implied something happened to Wes. Tucker answered, "Late yesterday afternoon, in his office at Peterson AFB."

"Did you meet in his office or in one of NORAD's SCIFs where secrets are discussed?"

Tucker answered, "He asked me to join him in a SCIF. I assumed he had the authority to extend me the invitation."

The JAG said in an accusatory tone, "Why would he agree to speak with you in a SCIF? He should never have allowed an uncleared civilian in a NORAD SCIF. What did you discuss in there?"

"You should ask him, not me. To my knowledge, nothing classified was discussed."

Major Castro said, "Commander Blackstone is dead. As best we can tell, you were the last person to see him alive."

Tucker tried to look like his shock was genuine, but it wasn't. He tried earlier to assess what was going on here and thought Wes might be in the middle of the issue.

"What happened to him?"

The JAG said, "We'll ask the questions, here."

Tucker asked, "Am I under arrest for the suspicion of his murder?"

"We never said anything about murder."

"Then why am I here?"

Since Tucker was a civilian, he was not subject to the military justice system. Hence, it was why they were sitting in the Colorado Springs Police Department's interrogation room rather than somewhere in Peterson Air Force Base. Whatever the charges they intended to file against Tucker, this was the police detective's case.

Yet, the detective only listened and took notes. He said nothing. His silence made Tucker nervous.

"You are under arrest for the unauthorized use of government property. Do you have written authorization from Commander Blackstone to occupy a conference room in Cheyenne Mountain?"

"Actually, I do." Tucker presented the paperwork. "Now, what do you mean, I'm the last person to see him alive?"

The JAG sternly repeated, "We'll ask the questions, here. What did you two talk about inside the SCIF?"

"If he didn't want it to be private, he probably would have discussed it in his office conference room. I think it is time for me to ask my attorney to be present. I'm a civilian. I'm not subject to a military trial."

The JAG said, "Unless we invoke a terrorism statute."

"What the fuck are you talking about?"

The lieutenant commander finally erupted, "Here are photographs of the remains of Commander Blackstone, you son of a bitch, along with photos of you and Jorge Alvarez at Peterson yesterday with Blackstone. We received these photos anonymously accompanied with a letter claiming that the commander was blackmailing you."

Tucker responded, "Let me get this straight. You think I met with Blackstone in full view of anyone looking, killed him, and then hung around here as if nothing happened. Do I have this right?"

The lieutenant commander's face was bright red. He looked like he was about to have a coronary. Tucker said, "Did it occur to you that maybe the author of the anonymous letter might be a person of interest and that maybe he or she was trying to frame me to put you on a false trail? Is this your first murder case?"

The lieutenant commander crossed his emotional fault line, bolted out of the chair, ran around the table with his fists clenched, and took a round-house swing at Tucker. But Tucker ducked his head to the left and the commander missed. Tucker badly wanted to counterpunch but controlled his anger. Instead, Javier grabbed the lieutenant commander and muscled him to submission.

Tucker said, "Listen, drop the ridiculous drummed-up charges against me, and I'll cooperate fully. I'll even support your investigation with some of my own people. You must know my background, who Tank and Powers are, and our capability to help with the investigation."

The JAG said, "Why were you in a NORAD SCIF?"

Castro held up his huge hand to the young JAG and gave him a look that made him shut up immediately. The MP asked, "Do you have any idea who would want to murder Commander Blackstone?"

Though the answer was "yes," Tucker was afraid to say so. It could lead to the disclosure of the secret foundation. But his hesitation gave Tucker away, so he said, "Possibly."

The Colorado Springs detective finally spoke, "There are no charges against you, Mr. Cherokee, but you will remain a person of interest until our investigation is complete."

CHAPTER 29

"If there are no dogs in Heaven, then when I die I want to go where they went." - Will Rogers, 1879-1935, journalist, humorist, and actor

Colorado Springs, Colorado – September 20th

Tank stood at the gate of a home on Vine Cliff Heights in the exclusive Trail Ridge community and spoke into the security speakerphone, "Hello, my name is Jorge Alvarez. I provide security for a customer with whom Michelle Mallard has a meeting scheduled for later today in Cheyenne Mountain. I need to speak directly to her."

A few seconds passed before a man's voice responded, "Hold for a moment."

Two minutes passed before Tank heard the gate lock click and the gates swing open. The speaker crackled before the man said, "Please, come to the front door."

The cobblestone driveway was 150 yards long, with healthy red, pink, and yellow rose bushes bordering both sides. The driveway turned into a circle with a four-car garage on one side of the circle and a magnificent stone entranceway on the other.

Standing in the open front double-doors was talk show queen Michelle Mallard, with her arms spread wide but with an expression of concern on her famous face. She said, "Hello, Tank, this is a surprise. I hope everything is alright."

Tank had never met the franchised prime-time radio voice with over fifteen million regular listeners. He'd seen her on a couple of cable news channels and was surprised to see that she seemed older in person. He wondered why she knew who he was—he'd explore that question later.

"I'm sorry to barge in on you uninvited, but we have a situation. Would it be possible to either reschedule your meeting with the foundation? Or would it be better if someone met with you out here on your home field?"

"It would be convenient for me to have the discussion here, but I understood there were privacy, secrecy, and anti-eavesdropping reasons for conducting the discussion in the mountain."

"Well, that's no longer possible. We were ejected from Cheyenne Mountain, but we still want to complete our planning strategy sessions over the next two days. Others are arriving from distant points around the country.

"You have a soundproof studio here, correct?"

Michelle nodded.

"With your permission, I'd like to do a short security walk-through. If it passes muster, I'll bring Maya Cherokee and Powers back here for the meeting."

Ms. Mallard took a step back, looked angry, and said defensively, "Maya? What happened to Tucker? It is with him that I agreed to participate. Why am I relegated to the second tier?"

"Have you heard anything about the death of the commander of the 721st Mission Support Group?"

Michelle's expressive face showed confusion. "Yes, but what's that have to do with anything?"

"Apparently, Tucker was the last person to see the commander alive. He's being interviewed by authorities. Out of respect for you, he wanted to make sure we received your input, that you were properly informed of our mission status, and that the task he had assigned to you was fully vetted."

Michelle said, "I understand. I'm sorry for my initial reaction. Go ahead and conduct your security walk-through. It would be an honor to have both Maya and Powers in my home. I have to confess, though . . ." she looked down in the direction of her feet, "Tucker seems like a regular guy, easy to talk to. Maya is intimidating, and Powers scares the hell out of me. Will you be able to join the meeting?"

Tank said, "I was supposed to meet with the next foundation member and straighten out logistics for the meeting after yours but let me see what I can do."

"Meet with the next member here. In fact," she said, "why don't we have all the sessions you were going to have in Cheyenne Mountain, right here?"

Colorado Springs

Powers drove Maya and Star to the Mallard Estate along with White Knight security officer Lucas Justice and Ram. Tank explained to Michelle that Lucas and Ram would walk the perimeter while the meeting was conducted in her studio.

Maya said, "Ms. Mallard, it is gracious of you to offer your home to conduct these very important foundation meetings. Thank you very much. I hope it is OK with you that I brought our daughter, Star. She won't be any trouble."

Star looked into Michelle's eyes and smiled. Michelle sensed that Star looked right into her soul. Star remained silent which added to her discomfort.

Tank and Powers made sure no recording or transmitting devices remained in the soundproof studio before they started discussing any sensitive information.

Maya said, "OK, let's get started. First, we are so grateful to have someone of your stature on our team. I've listened to your talk show for years. You articulate the issues associated with the abuse of the First Amendment better than anyone else I know. We know you're passionate about the subject, and we know you represent millions of Americans that rely on you to reinforce their opinions.

"We have also heard you express anger about the need to monitor the advanced aggregating and analytical modeling techniques used by entities that conduct polls, such as Rasmussen, Nielsen, and Reuters."

That seemed to flip Michelle's switch. "The polls are no longer tools to ascertain public opinion, which would help honest politicians and true civil servants to make policy. Instead, polling has devolved with insidious and intentional systematic errors designed to influence the general public to agree with a specific polling company's ideology.

"Polls are currently flawed in the way they collect data. Polling data is not reflective of the larger voting population. Some polls intentionally poll categories of people who usually don't vote.

"It's a garbage-in-garbage-out situation. The poll collectors apply no lessons learned from inaccuracies because they want the public to believe their misleading poll. In the last presidential election, the polls conducted by Nate Silver's 538, the Princeton Election Consortium, *The New York Times*, ABC News, and CNN were wrong by a staggering percentage.

"Something needs to be done about it."

Maya said, "I love your passion. Our off-the-radar foundation has accumulated funds to ***do*** something about it. We want you to direct the effort to change the way polls are conducted. We'll not only assign funds to this war front; we'll also support you with cyberexperts to help modify polling algorithms to more accurately reflect what the voting public truly prefers."

"Maya," asked Michelle, "what is our plan to gain access to said algorithms?"

Maya said, "The tactic for this war front is to gradually acquire controlling interest in Nielsen Holdings, which also owns Harris Polling. The Nielsen's publishing arm also owns several publications, including the *Hollywood Reporter* and *Billboard Magazine*. This should give us some additional influence over media honesty.

"After Nielsen, we intend to acquire a controlling interest in Rasmussen, which was a pioneer in the use of flawed automated telephone polling techniques. We intend to fix these intentional flaws and reveal the truth.

"Ms. Mallard, you are the nucleus for this effort, and we look forward to hearing your progress report four months from now. You should know we authorized the gradual acquisition of Nielson and Rasmussen this morning."

Vine Cliff Heights

Lucas Justice was a dangerous, rugged-looking guy with visible scars that were hard to hide. Although he was short and weighed 225 pounds, there was not an ounce of fat on him. He had thick blond eyelashes, and his eyelids covered the upper half of his powder-blue eyes. Lucas always maintained a three- or four-day growth of blond hair on his face.

At thirty-two, he'd already experienced too much of the dark side of human nature. Lucas rarely smiled, never joked, and did not appear to enjoy life. His humorless disposition reflected his history. He had witnessed some pretty ugly things and was responsible for some of them. He was one of seven "unofficial" SEALS in black operations sent into Africa to eliminate the leader of an ethnic-cleansing civil war. The unspeakable horror of what some of the rebel soldiers did to women and children converted him into an anti-evil zealot. He had a personal mission to confront evil head-on.

Lucas had no confidence in humankind. At first meeting, he suspected a person to have a black heart—guilty until proven innocent. After leaving the navy, Lucas did a stint with the private contractor Triple Canopy, where he successfully protected dignitaries for the State Department in Iraq. He wasn't someone a sane person would want to screw with.

A group of twelve young students from the University of Colorado stopped their vans and piled out to protest Michelle Mallard's talk show.

Lucas yelled from inside the security gate for them to leave.

The students ignored Lucas, pulled out all kinds of protest tools from the vans: spray paint cans, crowbars, bolt cutters, baseball bats, three full cans of gasoline, galvanized pipe, urine and feces filled mason jars, and prepared signs with anti-radio talk show slogans.

Lucas followed protocol and fired off a quick text warning to Tank and Powers, who were in the studio with Maya and Michelle.

One of the students who wore a ski mask tried to use a crowbar and bolt cutter to open the gate mechanism. Lucas reached through the wrought iron opening in the gate and grabbed the kid's wrist. The power in Lucas's hand paralyzed the student. The protestor screamed as if he were hurt but Lucas was not going to break the viselike grip. Two of the young man's compatriots came to his rescue—one with a baseball bat. Five others started climbing over the eight-foot fence with intent to overwhelm Lucas.

Lucas warned the students, "Do not climb over the fence. By my side is a very dangerous military-trained German Shepherd."

The young men ignored Lucas's warning and continued their climb. Lucas noticed that each of the five was carrying something. He first thought the items were cell phones. Instead, he understood their misplaced confidence—they were carrying stun guns.

Six other protestors started throwing the disgusting mason jars. The first missed and hit the ski mask student who could not break Lucas's wrist lock.

Another van drove up Vine Cliff Heights. On top of the van was a satellite dish—the local Colorado Springs TV news van had arrived.

Five protestors now stood inside security boundaries. Lucas let go of Ram's leash and said, "Bad." Ram bared his teeth. All five students took a step back.

A student on the outside of the fence with a baseball bat tried to hit Lucas by swinging vertically between the iron struts. The University of Colorado's star second baseman brought the bat up and began his swing down on Lucas's head but found he couldn't swing. Someone grabbed the bat from behind. The kid turned around to face Tank, who took the bat away from him and landed a line-drive quality swing onto the kid's right thigh.

Tank grabbed the bolt cutter from the young man Lucas still controlled and threatened to remove body parts if he didn't give up. Lucas was now able to address the five protestors inside the fence.

The local TV station had its cameras rolling. Lucas said, "Place the stun guns on the ground. Put your hands up, in view, and whatever you do, do not act aggressively toward the dog."

Two female protestors carried gasoline in the direction of Tank with obvious intent to pour it on him and set him on fire. Powers had grabbed a six-foot-long piece of pipe brought to the scene by the students and was within seconds of taking out the gasoline-carrying ladies when the first firearm announced itself.

Everyone stopped. No one moved. Michelle Mallard held the barrel of her 9mm Walther PPQ vertically and said, "Go home. Go back to Boulder. Get out of here before someone gets hurt."

Colorado Springs Police Station

After a long day with the military police and that nerve grading JAG, Tucker was exhausted. He wondered whether attorneys are taught how to be jerks in law school or it's some kind of character flaw indigenous to the type of people who pursue the profession. He gave a little, and they took a lot. Tucker gave up two of the five names in the Pentagon that he suspected had a motive to murder the commander based on the information he shared with Tucker in the Peterson AFB SCIF. The steroid-using MP, Javier Castro, let Tucker retire for the evening but assured him that the MP wasn't through with him. He called for a military escort to take Tucker to his hotel.

Tucker knew he couldn't reach Maya because she was supposed to be in a room where cell phones don't work. As he rode in the back seat of the vehicle, Tucker thought about his friend and foundation member, Wes. "Was he really murdered by someone in the Pentagon?" he thought. "Did Wes unintentionally leave a thread that the murderer followed? Will that thread lead to the disclosure of the foundation and its mission?"

CHAPTER 30

"Three may keep a secret if two of them are dead." -
- Benjamin Franklin, 1706-1790, one of the Founding
Fathers of the United States

Colorado Springs, Colorado – September 21st

Ten people crammed into Michelle Mallard's studio, which was designed to hold no more than five. It wouldn't take long before the stuffiness, elevated temperature, and body odor would drive the meeting to a close. Too much hot air. Tucker loved and respected the people in the room but not this much. There is something called a bad breath radius. Tucker prayed that he could contain the burrito he'd had for lunch.

Tucker used an empty coffee cup as a gavel, hit the table hard with it and called the meeting to order.

"Maya and I tried to keep each member of *The Media Transformation Foundation* a secret from other members. We didn't want associates to know each other in order to protect each individual's anonymity. My apologies to each of you who may feel that we've violated your trust by holding a meeting where you get to meet each other. If any of you here today want to resign your participation in the foundation because you are now exposed to some of the other foundation members, please, let me know right after this meeting, and we'll arrange to return any funds you may have contributed.

"This is the third day of the second meeting of The Media Transformation Foundation. Our first order of business today is to revise our protocols for communication. To maintain utmost secrecy, we've established a process whereby we communicate only in face-to-face meetings. The protocol was excellent to maintain secrecy but is no longer practical. For that reason, each of you will be given a tablet that communicates encrypted messages via satellite. The tablet is biometrically programmed to open based on your thumbprint. Once opened, pick the person you want to communicate with, type your note, and it sends an encrypted message. Each of you has a call name. In the event a tablet falls into the wrong hands, they will not know who the call names belong to. To the best of our knowledge, even the NSA can't recover our messages. Is that correct, Blackbeard?"

Blackbeard was the call name assigned to Rusty Winemiller, the special agent in charge of cybersecurity for the FBI. No other member in the room knew who Rusty was or what his profession was.

Blackbeard activated his motorized wheelchair and said, "I was briefed earlier by one of your cyberwizards, and he convinced me of the elevated level of security the tablets offered. So, yes, that's correct."

Tucker asked, "Do any of you have a question?"

Michelle Mallard asked, "Where do I find the list of call names?"

Maya answered, "The list in embedded in your tablet's contact list."

Tucker said, "Let's move to the second order of business. We need to discuss the elephant in the room. Who wants to go first?"

Maya raised her hand and said, "The days are numbered before the foundation's mission is discovered by our enemies. Between *The New York Times*'s conspiracy piece, the investigation into the murder of Commander Blackstone, and the televised circus here last night, it won't be long. Someone is going to connect the dots if they haven't already and apply some sort of chaos theory."

Tucker looked around at heads nodding in agreement.

He asked, "The question before us is: what do we do about it? Do we pull back, keep a low profile, and reemerge months from now?

"Or do we move full speed ahead, chin up, and announce The Media Transformation Foundation's intentions openly and with pride? Just remember, when everything is a crisis, nothing is."

Senator Enya raised his hand and said, "I suggest we do a head fake. Split the foundation into two entities—the disclosed version and an undisclosed version. We can call the undisclosed version, the false flag, by another name. The foundation will shield the new entity from what we're really doing behind-the-scenes. Leak the name of the foundation to the press while the new entity clandestinely does what we wanted the foundation to do in the first place."

William Hurt looked over at Nick Hurt and asked, "I think I like it depending on the details. What do you think?"

Nick Hurt said, "I'm OK with it as long as we are not part of the disclosed foundation. We need to be part of the new entity."

"Same here," interjected Blackbeard.

Michelle Mallard said, "It's too late for me to duck out of the foundation, but I still want to contribute to the new entity."

Margaret Mellon said, "Let's call the secret entity, 'The Amberdelic Group.' It is a made-up word and has no meaning. The people who would like to do us harm will have trouble finding a way to interpret it in a negative light. As far as I know, there is only one reference to the word. A jazz group called one of its tunes by that name."

Potential Amberdelic member and conservative Hollywood actress/producer, Julienne O'Kray, spoke up for the first time, "Sounds like an interesting name for a screenplay."

"OK, do we all agree? The Media Transformation Foundation will be the public side of the house, and *The* Amberdelic Group will be the undisclosed side of the house. Any objections?"

No objections were voiced.

"Maya and I will have a series of meetings with you. First, we'll meet with Blackbeard, followed by a joint meeting with the rest of you."

Rusty Winemiller, FBI special agent, Cybercrimes Division, sat in his wheelchair and looked at Tucker over his glasses. Tucker asked, "Will you agree to be a member of Amberdelic? I'll understand if you bail on us. You are probably the person with the most to lose if you're discovered to be a part of a 'conspiracy' to improve the honesty of journalists."

"Tucker, my motive for supporting you two is not just because I'm ashamed of the current state of dishonest journalism; I'm ashamed of the FBI's role in supporting the depravity. There was a time when the FBI was respected in this country as the one institution with unassailable integrity. Today, half the US population distrusts us. They think 'fucking' is a word which always proceeds FBI. I'd gladly sacrifice my career to reverse the current trend.

"But, Tucker, you've got to get better control of keeping things secret. We can't afford another screw up. On that subject, what's the status of the investigation of the murder of Commander Wes Blackstone?"

"I gave them the names of a couple people in the Pentagon who Wes claims were lieutenants of Lakatos. Can you believe officers in the Pentagon think it's viable to form a one-world government?"

Winemiller shocked Tucker by revealing that he knew their names. He said, "I know them. We've monitored them for years. We've not moved on them because we want to see where it leads. They were careful with their cyber protection but not careful enough. But I've not seen them on the dark web where you'd think they might go to find a mercenary hit man."

Tucker said, "If I give you the other three names, can you do a background on them for me?"

"Yes, and I'll do better than that. I'll give you a name to investigate: Rocky Watters. He's not associated with the Pentagon, but you'll want to check him out. He works for a guy named Levi Zimmerman—a behind-the-scenes type but Lakatos's former right-hand man."

"You never fail to surprise me, Rusty."

Maya asked, "Changing the subject on you, is your team vigorously investigating the cybercrimes associated with the substitution of articles in the electronic version of *The Washington Post*? Do we need to be concerned? How close is the FBI to learn how it was done and who was responsible?"

Rusty gave Maya a knowing smile and said, "Yes, we are investigating the cybercrime. I've delegated it to one of my subordinates. He's a clueless newbie forced on me. He's the son of a Vermont congressman, and, frankly, I have no idea how he passed the entrance exam. I guess that someone else took the test for him. He doesn't know his ass from first base."

Tucker said, "So, they're nowhere."

"At least for now. Until I'm forced to assign someone competent to lead the effort. The vice president and director are on my ass to make more progress. My plan is to identify a Russian and frame him for the crime."

Maya added, "Are you close to the murder investigation of Gabriel Lakatos?"

"No, Special Agent Michael Roberts oversees the case for the FBI out of the Seattle field office."

Maya added, "You might want to check out '#MrCraig's' organization called newsvigilante.org and share your findings with him."

Winemiller wanted to ask Maya where she got the hashtag name but decided against it.

CHAPTER 31

"Death is the solution to all problems. No man – no problem."—Joseph Stalin, 1878-1953, ruled the Soviet Union from the mid-1920s until his death

Yellowknife, Northwest Territories, Canada – September 22nd

Because Napoleon Drygeese was the chief air traffic controller for the Yellowknife Airport, he knew that a Learjet 70 was landing from Calgary. He also knew by the tail number that it was owned and operated by the Royal Canadian Mounted Police. His day of reckoning was here. For weeks, he'd thought about how he would handle the interrogation by the police and decided that he had to face it head-on. There was no future in running.

Twenty minutes later, an airport security officer contacted Drygeese and advised him, with obvious stress in his voice, that he had visitors.

"They'll have to wait until my shift is over. I can't leave my post, and I can't be distracted while on duty."

The airport security officer said, "You might want to reconsider that, Napoleon. These three guys are serious-looking people. One of them is wearing a suit. The other two are obviously Mounties. Piss them off at your own risk."

"Tell them I'll be out when my shift ends. I don't care if it pisses them off. Have them wait in the cafeteria."

Two hours later, Napoleon took a deep breath before he entered the cafeteria. Wearing khaki workpants, a red-checkered flannel shirt, and a trapper hat, the contrast with his visitors was almost comical. He spotted them immediately and walked to their table. They hadn't eaten but looked like they were on their second pot of coffee.

Both Douglas Butterfield and Rod Nelson wore Canadian Royal Mounted Police dress uniforms, complete with scarlet tunic, Stetson hat, Strathcona boot, and brown pistol-holder containing a semiautomatic 9mm Smith & Wesson. Rod looked comfortable in his outfit, but Doug looked awkward, clumsy, and unnatural as if his uniform were overly starched and painful to wear.

The third person wore a dark gray wool suit under a full-length wool trench coat, white shirt with cufflinks, and an expensive-looking red silk tie. His matching felt fedora was hanging on the chair next to him. His hair and eyebrows were platinum-blond, his eyes were an ocean blue, and his prominent nose dominated his hairless face. His mouth didn't seem to move when he spoke.

"Mr. Drygeese, the US Federal Bureau of Investigation is cooperating with the Canadian Royal Mounted Police in the investigation of a homicide case involving an American citizen. I am Special Agent Michael Roberts out of the Seattle field office. These gentlemen are Rod Nelson and Douglas Butterfield with whom I believe you spoke earlier."

Rod Nelson said, "Butterfield here said you told him that three months ago on the twentieth, a Bell 407GXP landed at 12:53, took off at 13:21, and filed a flight plan to Whitehorse. Is that correct?"

"Yes, that's correct."

Agent Roberts asked, "Is that still your story, or do you remember it differently today?"

Drygeese knew it was a defining moment for him. He chose to tell the truth.

"I was paid to tell you the story about the Bell. They didn't file a flight plan to Whitehorse. They filed a flight plan to Medicine Hat, Alberta."

Rod Nelson asked, "How did Kika Kisecawchuck pay you for the disinformation?"

Napoleon was surprised that the police already knew who'd paid him. "How did you know it was Chuck?"

"Because you made a phone call to him seconds after you hung up on Officer Butterfield."

"Chuck gave me a hunting rifle."

The three law enforcement officers exchanged glances. They may have just had a breakthrough.

Special Agent Roberts asked, "What model hunting rifle?

"An M82 Barrett. It'll take down moose from long range."

"I bet," said Rod Nelson. "We'll need to take custody of the rifle. Although you were cooperative, if this weapon turns out to be the murder weapon, you could be in big trouble."

Napoleon Drygeese added, "I will fully cooperate. You should know, Agent Roberts, you are not the first American up here asking questions about the Bell helicopter."

Wabasca, Alberta, Canada

Kika Kisecawchuck, or Chuck, as everyone called him, thought of himself as a damn good part-time aircraft mechanic. In a storage barn seven miles from his home, he was babying his newly acquired Bell 407GXP. Because he had his earphones in listening to country music, he didn't hear the vehicle pull up.

A pockmarked middle-aged face got right in Chuck's. He could smell the cigarette odor on his clothes and the even more offensive body language of a cop.

Chuck looked into the eyes that looked like they belonged to a greyhound and asked, "Who the hell are you and what are you doing here?"

The man said, "I know what you did, Chuck. Your friend up in Yellowknife gave you up to save himself a little pain."

Chuck concealed carried and pulled his Ruger from his belt holster. But the man anticipated the move and tackled Chuck before he could get the gun completely out of its holster. In the struggle, it discharged into Chuck's thigh. He screamed in pain while the big man stripped him of the weapon.

Chuck grabbed the only thing within arm's reach and swatted the unwelcome visitor with a wrench. The man went down, holding the side of his head, feeling the blood flow into his hands. He'd dropped the Ruger in the process. Chuck crawled toward the gun but didn't make it before he heard the unmistakable click of a bullet entering a chamber.

Chuck froze.

The man said, "Touch that gun and I'll put a hole in your face."

The man kicked the Ruger out of Chuck's reach, then proceeded to kick him in the head with his steel-toed boot.

When Chuck awoke, he was chained to his workbench. The trespasser was sitting on a stool, smoking a cigarette, and holding a drill in his right hand.

Chuck said, "My leg. I'm bleeding. Let me put a tourniquet on it before I bleed out."

The man said, "Yes, you are bleeding. Before I help you, I want two things from you. First, I want a confession in your handwriting that the killers of Gabriel Lakatos paid you to mislead authorities as to their escape route and that the two guilty of the crime were Tank Alvarez and his partner, Powers."

Chuck looked confused and said, "Who?"

The man pulled the trigger on the drill. It whirred menacingly. The man said, "Just write what I tell you to write or brace for impact. The pad and pen are located at your feet. They're within your reach."

Chuck picked up the pad and pen and wrote what was dictated to him.

The man said, "OK, now sign it."

Chuck did.

The man threw a dirty rag at Chuck and said, "Use that to stop the bleeding."

Chuck pressed the rag against his thigh wound and asked, "What's the second thing you wanted?"

"The truth. Who really gave you that helicopter to cover up the escape route for the assassination of Gabriel Lakatos?"

Chuck said, "I don't know. I never met anyone. Someone spoke to me on the phone using one of those weird electronic sounding voice-over things. They told me if I agreed, they'd leave the copter and the rifle here in this barn. I promise on Cree honor that I'm telling you the truth."

Rocky Watters said, "That's too bad."

CHAPTER 32

"Objective journalism and an opinion column are about as similar as the Bible and Playboy magazine." - Walter Cronkite, 1916-2009, journalist and news anchorman

Colorado Springs, Colorado – September 22nd

Star's presence in the room confused the members who had not yet met her. Margaret Mellon said loudly enough for Star to hear, "Don't worry. You can trust her. She's trying to determine if she can trust you."

Maya asked, "Tucker, should we re-start the meeting?"

He said, "Let's start with the Hurt brothers. Progress on HonestMediaMatters.edu?"

Nick opened with, "Wichita State University does not require additional funding from us. It is not only self-sustaining but is providing positive income to the university. Membership has grown to eighteen million. The last three million contributed an average of $27.50 each. Our only issue continues to be one of security. Protestors from outside WSU constantly harass the students that enter or exit the building. Thank God you suggested that White Knight Personal Security protect us."

William added, "You should know that WSU negotiated the use of Virginia Tech's supercomputer at a favorable rate, and, as a result, we have now graded 4,575 of the 90,000 journalists using Jimmy Ma's algorithm. He did a great job in training our staff."

Tucker asked, "When will we be able to start posting the grades for the journalists who have been assessed?"

"Anytime you want."

"I need to introduce you to one of the members whose identity we will try to keep secret. His call name is 'Hashtag,' and he is a social media founder and closet conservative. He's the world's number one expert on social media data mining and information cascading."

Julienne said, "Can I meet Hashtag? We share a common affliction?"

Tucker answered, "I'll discuss it with him.

"Anyway, Hashtag will advise you as to other ways for us to reach the people that get their news and information only off the web."

William Hurt asked, "How else can we help?"

To Tucker's surprise, Star rose her hand for permission to speak. This was unscripted. She knows the rules—she shares her thoughts with only her parents and in private.

Star said, "You are a target. Stay safe."

Both William and Nick took Star's warning seriously—they had grown to respect Star's "special" talent.

Maya said, "Star, please explain yourself."

Star said, "Blackbeard thinks the Hurt brothers need to worry about their safety."

Though William was very shaken up about Star's revelation, he pretended to cavalier and said, "We'll take that under advisement, young lady, and be extra diligent."

Tucker said, "OK, let's move on. Julienne, how's *Real America Productions* progressing?"

"Not as well as I had hoped. Writers are being intimidated. One writer I previously hired admitted to me that his family was threatened."

"By whom?"

"He wouldn't say."

Maya asked, "How's the first movie coming along? So far, we've invested twenty-five million dollars into it. Is that correct, Maggie?"

"Yes, but we've reserved one hundred million dollars for it."

Ms. O'Kray answered, "I'd say we're a third of the way through but a little behind on the special effects required for the movie, *Unsustainable*, which I think is going to be a box office hit."

Tucker asked, "What do you need from us?"

Julienne answered, "Help me find out who is intimidating the writers and put an end to it."

Tucker answered, "We'll assign Tank to the problem."

"Margaret, how's the MSNBC and CNN war front coming? How badly are they suffering from poor advertising commitments, and how are the lawsuits against them for dishonest reporting coming?"

Margaret Mellon said, "Advertising for MSNBC is down, but CNN is unchanged. I've reorganized the approach to CNN and am in discussion with Obsidium Advertising Agency to reassess their position.

"The lawsuits are having their intended effect. We've uncovered some truly nefarious conduct through the discovery process. The more we dig, the more crap we find. It's fun to watch their attorneys squirm."

The ten in the room jumped reflexively when it sounded like a battering ram smashed into Michelle Mallard's studio door. Either that or Tank had knocked on the door. An interruption of the meeting was unlikely to be good news.

Tucker had a concealed carry permit and put one hand on his short-barreled 9mm gun. He opened the door to confirm, with relief, that it was Tank. His relief was short lived because he could see in Tank's eyes that trouble brewed.

Tank asked, "Michelle, I noticed earlier that there is a TV in the studio. Could you turn it on and tune it to CNN?"

Michelle pulled a remote out of one of her desk drawers and pushed the "on" button. The program anchor was interviewing a *New York Times* reporter: "So, what do you think this means?"

The reporter said, "It means our suspicions are confirmed. A Far-Right wing group killed Gabriel Lakatos, the patriarch of the progressive agenda. The fact that former Republican Senator Powers and his partner, Jorge Alvarez, killed Lakatos is as much evidence as we need. Alvarez is tied to the hip with billionaires Tucker and Maya Cherokee. It wouldn't surprise me if they funded the hit on Lakatos. You may remember that Maya Cherokee was the science advisor to the prior Republican administration. The dots are connecting."

Michelle turned the TV off. Tank said, "Someone leaked a signed confession saying that he helped Powers and I hide the murder weapon and escape by helicopter. This is fake news at its best. It is pure bullshit. The confession was signed by a Cree Indian in Alberta, Canada. Both the helicopter and the murder weapon were recovered. The Cree is nowhere to be found. My guess is he's in a deep lake somewhere in Canada after being forced to write the bogus confession."

Tucker asked, "Where's Powers?"

"On the phone with the director of the FBI. We both have solid alibis, but the damage is done. We're too exposed. Reporters are going to haunt us like flies on shit for a while. Every move you make, Tucker, is going to be scrutinized."

Tucker was not one to sit on his ass and let things happen—he made things happen. So, he convened a strategy meeting with his favorite team: Maya, Tank, Powers, and Star. Star's presence always forced Tank and Powers to say whatever was on their minds and hold nothing back.

Tucker asked, "Who has the motive to frame you two for the death of Lakatos?"

Powers said, "At least a hundred people I can think of."

"Let me rephrase the question. Who would go to the trouble to force someone to write a confession that you killed Lakatos and then make the accuser disappear?"

Maya answered, "The real killer."

Tank said, "Whoever is trying to stop us, that is, whoever is trying to stop the foundation."

Powers said, "The media."

Tucker said, "Lawrence Slaughter, CEO of California Media Group."

Maya added, "Jeff Jorgensen, former owner of *The Washington Post*."

Tank said, "*The New York Times*."

Star said, "The people that killed Commander Blackstone."

Maya and Tucker exchanged a glance. Star was growing into more than just a mind reader.

Tucker moved the strategy session in another direction. "How are we going to convert this disaster into a victory? How are we going to turn this sow's ear into a silk purse?"

Maya said, "Prove that the information was bad journalism; this is a classic example of abuse of the press and their failure to apply their own alleged code of ethics—that the media attacked Tank and Powers because they're conservatives."

Tucker said, "Excellent idea." He smiled.

"Uh, oh," said Powers, "I feel it coming. I sense a speeding steamroller in my path."

Tucker said, "Powers, you are the best there is in an interview. You need to show up on the Sunday morning talk shows. I'll make it happen."

Tucker continued, "Tank, what is Lucas' next assignment. I know Jolene, your better half, is running White Knight while you're on assignment with me, but do you know what his next project is?"

"Jolene was going to assign him to protect the daughter of an Arab oil billionaire, but we can assign someone else to that if you think we need him."

Tucker said, "We need to learn who forced the Cree Indian to falsely accuse you of murdering Gabriel Lakatos. Who better than Lucas?"

Tank said, "What are you going to do? I know you're not going to just observe from a distance."

Maya said, "Knowing Tucker, he's headed to Arlington, Virginia."

Powers cleared his throat, smiled, and said, "Tucker, you're a devious bastard."

Tucker said, "Well, Powers, you were going to be in DC anyway for the talk shows. It's just a stone's throw, or should I say silver dollar's throw, to the Pentagon."

CHAPTER 33

"I am as innocent regarding any conspiracy as any of you gentlemen in the room." - Jack Ruby, 1911 – 1967, killed Lee Harvey Oswald

New York City, New York – September 22nd

In the editorial section of *The New York Times*, the following piece was posted:

"There are numerous conspiracy theories about the death of JFK, the massacre in Las Vegas, and the missing Malaysian airline. We all have a right to express our suspicions and arguments, as long as we don't claim them as fact.

"Throughout the blogosphere, millions of conspiratorialists have expressed theories as to who murdered Gabriel Lakatos. We at the Times feel compelled to present facts surrounding the death of the mega billionaire liberal philanthropist and let you manufacture your own theory.

"Fact number one: His death immediately preceded the onslaught of attacks on *The Washington Post* and *The New York Times*.

"Fact number two: Anti-media protests began only days after his assassination.

"Fact number three: whoever orchestrated the murder must have had substantial financial backing.

"Fact number four: An unauthorized article appeared in the virtual version of *The Washington Post* smearing Gabriel Lakatos as a monster instead of as the supporter of causes to promote freedom of speech.

"Fact number five: Acts of intimidation of owners of TV, radio, and print media occurred immediately after his death.

Fact number six: *The Washington Post* was acquired by a right-wing organization and merged with a conservative competitor.

"Fact number seven: Fake news reports were promulgated to intimidate the editor and publisher of this newspaper by what apparently are racists.

Fact number eight: *The New York Times* editor, Drake Pasqua, was murdered.

"Fact number nine: *Saturday Night Live* began making fun of liberal news organizations.

"Fact number ten: The FBI and the Royal Canadian Mounted Police have disclosed no leads on who assassinated Lakatos.

"Fact number eleven: MSNBC's headquarters was bombed.

"We at *The New York Times* smell a rat. Could Gabriel Lakatos's murder be just the first step by a group of anti-free press, racially motivated, right wing activists? What's their next step? What's your theory?"

The Hamptons

Zimmerman finished reading the editorial page of *The New York Times*. He found the conspiracy piece humorous and hopefully thought-provoking for those who didn't have the facts. Levi had his own theories about who murdered his mentor. He was contemplating calling his contacts at the FBI when he got a call from that asshole Slaughter. Though they worked together for a common cause, he found the man obnoxious.

"Levi," Slaughter said, "thanks for taking my call. Have you watched any recent TV news coverage of the incident in Colorado Springs?"

"No, I haven't turned the TV on."

"Well," Lawrence said excitedly, "I think we just discovered evidence of the right-wing conspiracy we always feared existed."

Zimmerman said, "You're not buying in on the conspiracy theories the *Times* is sponsoring, are you?"

"Listen to me, Levi. Former Senator Powers and that big guy who provides personal security services, Tank Alvarez, were just caught on TV breaking up a protest at the home of that right-wing talk show bitch, Michelle Mallard. Mallard was actually caught firing a weapon at the protestors on TV.

"Tell me it's not true that they're part of the group that intimidated me into hiring a new president of operations. Levi, I'd check it out if I were you. They may be behind your boss's assassination."

Levi Zimmerman knew that one of Lakatos's foundations sponsored protests conducted by University of Colorado students. He said, "You might be on to something, Lawrence. I'll engage our private investigation firm and see what we can find out. God knows we can't wait for the FBI to do their job."

Chicago, Illinois

Fifteen years on the force was enough. Rocky Watters looked back and wondered why he wasted his life as a Chicago Police Department detective. He concluded that after all those years, he'd have something to show for it. What Rocky got out of it was two divorces, two alimony payments, and child support for three kids who didn't like him. He barely had enough left out of his paycheck to cover his two-bedroom rent in a shabby neighborhood and a six-pack. He didn't want to live like that for another five to ten years, so he took the plunge, quit the force, and started his own private investigation company.

As an entrepreneur, he was a great detective. He was a terrible businessman. He didn't plan very well and missed a couple child support payments before he got his first customer. He brought her evidence of her husband's indiscretions. She couldn't pay. Watters failed to make two alimony payments and was on the way to bankruptcy. That was before he got a call from someone named Zimmerman.

That was seven years ago. Now, Rocky lived in a lakefront condominium, had a reserve account large enough to invest in stocks, and had three kids who thought he was the best dad in the world.

Money is the great equalizer.

So, when Zimmerman called, Rocky jumped.

Investigator Watters answered the phone immediately when he noticed it was Zimmerman's cell phone. "Yes, sir."

"Rocky, how are you today? How's your backlog of business?"

"Great, thanks to you. I've staffed up to eight investigators."

Zimmerman said, "You may need to add a couple more after this phone call."

Rocky was beaming from ear to ear but tried not to make it too noticeable in his voice. "OK."

Levi said, "Your first job is to investigate the death of my boss, Lakatos. I've lost confidence in the FBI's ability to promptly close this case. I have no knowledge, one way or the other, about the Canadians' crime investigating skills. Find out what the fuck is going on.

"The second job is to investigate a new Hollywood production company call Real America Productions and a producer, Julienne O'Kray. I want to run them out of town.

The third job requires you to investigate who is running these cyberattacks on *The New York Times*. If you have access to people in the cyber universe, retain them.

"Before I tell you about the last job, are you familiar with ex-senator Powers and his colleague Tank Alvarez?"

"Very much so. I interviewed with Tank to join his company before you retained me, but it didn't work out."

Zimmerman said, "I suspect they're up to no good and may even be linked to your first assignment. Your goal is to be my source whereby I can leak something to the press. Do I make myself clear? They're about to walk into a shit storm.

"Check your account. I've already wired you an advance. Don't let me down."

Flyover Country, USA

Tucker sipped his A&W Root Beer while Powers accessed the White Knight database nursing a Scotch on the rocks. He was upset with Tucker because he was too successful—successful at getting him on four straight Sunday morning TV talk shows starting with Fox and ending with NBC.

Tucker's new tablet buzzed. Tony Vinci needed to talk. Powers asked Tucker to put Tony on speaker.

Tony asked, "You in the air?"

Tucker said, "Yes, I'd say somewhere over Tennessee. What's up?"

"Do you want to know what the brigadier general said on the phone last night before you meet with him at the Pentagon?"

"You mean you had one of your nanodevices spying on him? Jesus, Tony, you're going to get us all imprisoned."

"Prison? If we got caught, we'd never make it that far. Anyway, I was only able to hear one side of the conversation with a counterpart at NATO in Brussels. They spoke cryptically, but the gist of the conversation was that the project was successful and that the carpenters expected to get paid immediately. That's code for the "hit" was successful, time to pay the assassins.

"And guess what? They're paying in bitcoins. Oh, this modern world."

Tucker asked, "Could you determine if the NATO compatriot was American or European?"

"I'd say he was French unless it's common to say, 'Au Revoir' when ending the conversation."

Powers asked, "Tony, do you have the two other Pentagon suspects under observation?"

"Of course."

Tucker ran his fingers through his jet-black hair, rubbed his hairless chin, and said, "You're sure no one can pick up this encrypted conversation?"

"Yes."

"Not even the NSA?"

"Pretty sure."

"Ugh." Tucker disconnected the call.

CHAPTER 34

"Politics is the art of looking for trouble, finding it everywhere, diagnosing it incorrectly and applying the wrong remedies." - Groucho Marx, 1890-1977, comedian

Medicine Hat, Alberta, Canada – September 26th

The name "Medicine Hat" is a Blackfoot word meaning the "eagle tail feather headdress worn by medicine men." The 60,000-plus populated town in southeast Alberta should be called "spookville" because it has a higher concentration of former CIA case officers and operatives than any other town in the world. Most of the retirees work freelance for various private investigation firms. Others are subcontractors to foreign nations and some work for less than honorable crime syndicates.

Gary Chung Lee had retired from the agency seven years ago with a full pension and bought a log home along the South Saskatchewan River where he spent his time fishing. Well . . . *most* of his time. Being an intelligence agent isn't something you just walk away from.

So, when a Canadian Security Intelligence Service agent acquaintance of his sat down in front of him at a breakfast table at the Stardust Restaurant, it didn't surprise Gary.

What did surprise him was what the agent said: "You have visitors on the way. Don't run. My advice to you is to tell them the truth." The agent left with no explanation.

Gary Chung Lee had done many things in his life that could come back to haunt him. It was impossible for him to speculate what the visitors wanted. He refilled his coffee from the carafe provided by the waitress and continued devouring his strawberry waffles.

He sensed it before he heard it. It was a change in pressure or vibration, but he knew they were here. Other patrons in the restaurant looked up, squinted their eyes, creased their foreheads as they tried to understand the sound they were hearing.

The small four-passenger helicopter hovered overhead, looking for a place to sit down where no power lines or light poles were in the way. The center of a mostly empty parking lot satisfied the pilot's criteria.

Former case officer Lee finished his breakfast as if nothing unusual was happening as the others in the Stardust were magnetically drawn to the restaurant's front windows unable to resist the excitement.

The first man out of the helicopter wore faded jeans, a buckskin coat, a cowboy hat, and hiking boots. The second person to exit the aircraft wore a dark gray, full-length Andrew Fezza Italian cashmere-blend coat; a matching fedora; expensive fur-lined black gloves; and black wingtips. The men didn't look like they were together, but they were.

The two amigos entered the front door to the Stardust and immediately located Gary Chung Lee sitting alone, eating his breakfast, and pretending to be uninterested in the newest diners.

The visitors walked to Lee's table, and before either of them spoke, Gary said, "Why don't you Feds just carry a neon sign around with you? It would have to be more comfortable. You're going to bust your ass walking around here with those slick city shoes.

"Who is the local you're dragging around with you— a Mountie?"

Rod Nelson responded, "Yes, I'm here to arrest you for exceeding the toxic content limit for persons with shitty attitudes."

Lee considered Nelson more seriously and said, "Ah, I know you. You're the high-profile homicide detective for the RC. Maybe I have it backwards. Maybe you're dragging the FBI agent around with you."

"Special Agent in Charge," said Michael Roberts. "And thank you for inviting us to join you for breakfast. What's good here?"

Lee answered, "The Belgian waffles are good. In charge of what?"

"Actually, Detective Nelson here is in charge of investigating a murder that occurred up in Wood Buffalo National Park. Because the man was an American, the FBI is cooperating with the Royal Canadian Mounted Police."

Roberts removed his hat, hung it on a hat rack, removed his coat, spread it across a chair of an adjacent unoccupied table, pulled out a chair across from Lee, and sat. Nelson waved at a waitress to take their order.

Gary Chung Lee asked, "Why are you talking to me? What lead in your investigation of Gabriel Lakatos's murder brought you to my dining table?"

Both Roberts and Nelson ordered breakfast before either responded. They saw that Lee was carrying. Lee also noticed that both men were armed.

Nelson asked, "Can I see your concealed carry permit?"

Lee stared menacingly at Rod Nelson before he acquiesced to the request and said, "I'm reaching for my wallet." He showed Nelson his Alberta permit and Roberts his Utah permit.

Special Agent Michael Roberts dragged his fingers across his thinning blond hair and said, "Rumor has it that you know everything that goes on in Medicine Hat."

"Where did you hear that?"

Without answering the question, Nelson asked, "A Bell 407GXP dropped some people off here and headed back to Wabasca. Someone had to arrange their egress to their final destination. Since Medicine Hat is a safe haven for former spooks, it isn't a giant leap of logic to suspect one of your buddies is embroiled in the operation. Maybe they didn't know its purpose. Maybe they did. Either way, can you tell us anything?"

Gary Chung Lee said, "Be at my place around seven o'clock tonight. Bring some cash."

Nelson and Roberts looked at each other trying to decide how to react to the shakedown. Nelson said, "I'm not authorized to buy information, Lee. I am authorized to charge you for bribery and drag your ass into the interrogation room at the police station with your lawyer and ask questions for hours."

Lee said without smiling, "We have a scheduled poker game tonight with six of my buddies as you referred to them. What's the matter? Don't you play Texas Hold'em? You could learn a lot at the game. Bring cash."

Fort Chipewyan

Officer Douglas Butterfield was alone in the office tediously reviewing passport information on people in and out of Alberta from the five days before to the five days after the murder of Gabriel Lakatos. Although he thought it was a waste of his time to analyze thousands of leads, Rod Nelson demanded that he do it. If the unsubs were non-Canadian, they most likely entered and exited Canada during that ten-day period. His job was to narrow down the list of visitors that the police should check out.

He was deep in concentration when someone pounded on the front door to the Fort Chipewyan Detachment.

Butterfield was glad to be distracted from the boring assignment. He opened the front door and stared at a short man with blond eyebrows and a three- or four-day growth of blond hair, wearing an unbuttoned black leather jacket. Doug started to speak but stopped when he made eye contact. The coldness in the man's blue eyes made him look away—in the direction of his loaded 12 gauge.

"My name is Lucas Justice. I'm a private investigator with White Knight Personal Security out of the United States. May I come in?"

Douglas let Lucas in. Before he could ask to look at his PI license, Lucas flipped open his credentials and said, "Our license includes doing business here in all Canadian provinces."

The officer moved to within arm's reach of the shotgun, just in case the man who claimed to be legit, wasn't.

Butterfield asked, "What brings you all the way up here from the states?"

"I hear you won first prize for the right to track down Gabriel Lakatos's killer."

"Actually, the lead detective for the investigation is Rod Nelson out of Calgary. I have been relegated to a supporting role."

Lucas said, "I'm here to give you a heads-up. I'm going to do my own investigation. I'll not interfere with your case and I will share anything of value with you.

"I know the .50-caliber slug dug out of the oak tree on Jorgensen's property in Seattle didn't match the slugs found in Wood Buffalo State Park after they passed through the victims. But the slugs did match the rifle given to Napoleon Drygeese by Kika Kisecawchuck."

Doug was shocked that this guy could know this information and said, "I can neither confirm or deny that information."

Lucas gave an understanding nod and asked, "Have you tracked the ownership and registration information of the M82 Barret sniper rifle Drygeese turned over to you guys?"

Doug said, "Who are you and from whom did you collect the information you are claiming as fact?"

"I already told you who I am. Are we going to share information or not?"

"Not. Can't do it. It's against the rules."

Lucas said, "Have it your way."

He handed Doug a card and said, "This is my contact information."

Lucas headed out the door, looked over his shoulder at Doug and said, "And by the way, the M82 was stolen off a dead American sniper killed by the Taliban in Afghanistan in 2007. It hadn't been seen or heard from since."

Lucas left Doug with the officer's mouth open wide enough that you could park a dump truck in. Lucas thought, "I love Jimmy Ma and Tony Vinci."

Butterfield called Rod Nelson before Lucas was out the detachment driveway and shared his encounter with Lucas Justice with him.

Nelson said, "White Knight Personal Security, eh? Doug, you know the principals of White Knight are persons of interest in the murder of Lakatos, right?"

Rod could feel the heat of Butterfield's embarrassment through the phone. It was apparent to Nelson that his junior investigator hadn't connected Lucas with the two Americans accused by Chuck to be the real murderers of Gabriel Lakatos, but despite his flaming red ears, Butterfield recovered and responded, "That's why I called you right away."

Nelson let it go and said, "Don't share any information with Lucas Justice, but check him out and keep an eye on him."

Nelson decided not to share the new development with the FBI.

CHAPTER 35

"We have the bubble-headed-blonde who comes on at five. She can tell you 'bout the plane crash with a gleam in her eye. It's interesting when people die. Give us your dirty laundry."—Don Henley, 1947-present, musician, lyrics from the song "*Dirty Laundry*"

New York City, New York – September 27th

The courtroom clerk said in a loud and authoritative voice, "The next case is the Heritage Foundation, Fox News Network, Forbes Media, National Review, Accuracy in Media, *The Washington Times*, The Republican Party National Committee, The American Conservative, PEW Research Center, *The American Spectator*, NewsMax, Rolling Thunder, *The Christian Science Monitor*, Liberty University, Accuracy in Academia, The Conservative Caucus, Texas A&M University, Freedom's Watch, the American Conservative Union, the Tea Party Organization, *Judicial Watch*, Cato Institute, Eagle Forum, *Washington Free Beacon*, Hoover Institute, Media Research Center, *POLICE Magazine*, and Hillsdale College as plaintiff versus MSNBC, the defendant."

Judge Michael Levine looked over his spectacles at the attorneys representing both the plaintiff and the defendant. Judge Levine was well-known for being apolitical, fair, and humorous, but impatient. He had no tolerance for frivolous lawsuits or cases that turned into circuses. The tall, handsome, well-dressed, imposing, silver-haired senior partner for one of the most famous law firms in New York was pitted against a tie-less, nationally known, charismatic defense attorney who spent more time opining on television talk shows than in court.

The judge said, "Will the lead counsels for the litigants please approach the bench."

Both men approached the bench respectfully. Judge Levine first looked the plaintiff's lawyer in the eye and said, "You've come before me on other cases. You know I have no patience for wasting the court's time. Before we drag the jury in here for what is choreographed to be a very long trial, I ask that you try to settle the matter before us out of court or choose an arbitrator."

Judge Levine then turned and looked the defendant's attorney in the eye; the attorney reflexively looked down. The judge said, "Look me in the eye, counsel, not down at your shoes. They aren't that special."

The famous attorney looked up. The judge continued, "I won't tolerate showmanship in my court. You are not in Hollywood, nor are you participating in a reality TV show. I'm not going to allow cameras in the courtroom. You turn this into a spectacle, and I'll throw you out of here before you can call Uber. Do you understand? And show some respect for the court—wear a tie. You two have two weeks before I'll hear your opening arguments. Tell your clients to figure out a better way to resolve your political differences than here in civil court."

Baltimore, Maryland

On a cold, cloudy, and windy day, two men walked their dog north on Stiles Street away from the inner harbor. They reached South Exeter Street, where they separated. One of the men continued north while the other walked kitty-corner with his dog toward a two-story brick building painted white.

Tank kept Ram on a short leash, pulled his Smith & Wesson M&P9 and pushed the button on the frame of the front door. He didn't hear a buzzer, chime, or bell and wondered whether the doorbell worked. The green and white striped canopy over the entranceway reduced the glare off the glass storm door, but he still couldn't see whether someone was peering through the peephole. Tank knocked on the aluminum frame. Cars passing by and other constant city noise kept Tank from hearing any movement inside the old structure.

Ram growled.

Tank stepped to the side and pulled Ram next to him just in case a person was on the other side of the door with a weapon.

Curiously, Ram wagged his tail just before Powers opened the interior door. He said, "Welcome to this house of sin. The current resident tried to bolt out the back door. I considered that to be an invitation by him into his home."

Tank, Powers, and Ram walked through the house, stepping around empty pizza boxes and Budweiser cans, toward the kitchen, where a man lay unconscious, face down on the floor with plastic ties around his ankles and wrists.

Powers added, "I found a side-arm on him, a knife in his boot, and his cell phone. He'll wake up in a couple of minutes."

Tank looked down at Ram and said, "Clear." Ram ran around the first-floor sniffing. He returned and looked up at Tank.

Tank said, "Go." Ram went up to the steps to the second floor. They could hear him rummaging around until he barked. Tank nodded at Powers, pulled his S&W, and with his weapon held with both hands in a close-combat position, slowly negotiated the stairs until he stood next to Ram. A door to one of the rooms was closed. Tank shouted, "Come out with your hands up."

There was no response. Tank found the door unlocked and with his body away from the door center, pushed the door open. Ram charged through the opening. After a few seconds, Ram returned. Tank went inside to find the room empty of people but full of electronic equipment. He yelled down to Powers, "All clear."

By the time Tank and Ram returned to the kitchen, the runner was stirring and groaning. He opened his eyes, rolled over on to his back, and tried to move his hands to pull his gun but discovered he couldn't move.

The man said, "What do you want? Why are you here?"

Powers answered, "I find it interesting that you didn't ask who we are."

He looked in the direction of Tank and said, "Your face is all over the news. You're the guy who killed Gabriel Lakatos. What do you want with me?"

Tank said, "Allegedly killed Lakatos. Don't tell me you believe everything you hear on the news."

Tank picked up the man, who weighed about 210 pounds, as if he was a child, dragged him into the dining area, and sat him on a chair. The man was rock hard and rough looking; he wore jeans and a black leather Harley-Davidson jacket.

Powers said, "You look a little different when you're not wearing a fake police uniform. You don't look as intimidating all tied up and helpless. I bet if we look around the house, we'll find the nightstick that you used to hit Waylon Trout, *The Washington Times* reporter."

The hired thug's eyes showed recognition. The expression on his face went from one of being pissed off to one of fear.

Tank said, "Tell us who paid you to threaten Wayland Trout, and we'll leave here with no further confrontation. You will tell us eventually, so don't think there is a way out. Ram here can be a very persuasive puppy. Save yourself some pain or worse. Who paid you?"

The man answered, "I don't know who paid me. I get wire transferred funds from an offshore numbered account."

Power looked at Tank and said, "Should you tell him?"

"Yeah, I guess he deserves to know."

The man said, "Know what?"

"We have special commands to manage Ram's effectiveness. One command we use instructs him to go directly to the throat. That's merciful; death is quick. Another command we use is more torturous for his victim. That's the command where he rips your balls off. It usually takes less than five seconds for him to get through a pair of jeans." Then Tank looked at Ram, pointed at the man, and said, "Bad."

Ram charged the man, growled like he was about to rip his throat off, bared his teeth, and placed his snout inches from the man's face.

The man soiled his Levi's.

Tank said, "Down."

Ram stopped, returned to Tank's side, and sat awaiting his next command.

Powers said, "Tell me where I can find the deposit information from the numbered account."

The man hesitated.

Powers said, "You know that after Ram rips your manhood off and you lay bleeding out, we'll take all the electronics upstairs and find this information anyway. Whomever you're protecting, I hope it will be worth it to you."

The man was considering his options when Powers nodded in Tank's direction.

The man panicked, "No, please, I'll tell you everything I know."

Tank and Powers listened to his story. Afterwards, Powers confiscated his cell phone and gun while Tank went upstairs and grabbed his laptop and a tablet.

Powers said, "Before we leave, I have one other question for you. How many other reporters, journalists, editors, or publishers have you threatened or intimidated?"

The man shrugged his shoulders and said, "I don't know, maybe a dozen or so."

Powers and Tank left him on the dining room chair with his wrists and ankles still bound.

Tucker waited outside in a rented Jeep while Tank and Powers interviewed the fake cop. He saw that Powers carried a shopping bag while Tank held Ram's leash. Tucker started the black Wrangler, flipped the lights on, and unlocked the doors to allow the three of them to jump in.

Ram licked the back of Tucker's neck. It felt slimy and nasty to him, but for some reason he always loved it. Better to be Ram's good buddy than not.

Tucker didn't ask questions. His experience with the two White Knight employees was to wait until they were ready to talk.

Tucker hated driving in the city, but Baltimore was especially bad with the trolley cars sometimes coming out of nowhere.

Powers spoke first, "We need to get this hardware to Jimmy Ma. I bet it won't take him ten minutes to figure out who owns an offshore numbered account. This guy says he gets paid from one of Gabriel Lakatos's shell companies."

Tank said, "I bet it's one of Lakatos's companies that sounds respectable like Children Charity, or Free Speech Institute, or Medicine for the Poor Foundation, when, in fact, it's an anarchist organization."

Tucker asked, "Rather than give this to Jimmy, why don't we share it with the person we're meeting next."

Tank said, "I thought we were headed to the other fake cop that intimidated Waylon Trout?"

Tucker said, "No, we're headed to Quantico."

Quantico

Tucker drove the Jeep down I-95 South from Baltimore, around Washington, DC, and into northern Virginia. Traffic, as always, was awful, but at least they took advantage of the HOV-3 lanes since Tank and Powers were in the vehicle with him. Ram should count, but the people who made the rules had never met him.

They got to the Quantico exit and resisted the temptation to visit the National Museum of the Marine Corps. When they got to the gate, a serious-minded young marine asked, "What is your business here, and may I see your identification?"

The three of them handed him their driver's licenses.

The marine looked at each of their IDs, and suddenly he stiffened to a marine-straight posture and said, "Powers, please exit the vehicle."

Powers did as he was told, opened the back door of the Jeep, and stood before the marine. The security officer pulled out his camera and took a digital photo of Powers. He proceeded to the guard gate, entered the digital photo into the database, and waited.

A green light came on, which confirmed that this person was, in fact, Powers."

The marine said, "Sorry, sir. I had to confirm that it was you. Please proceed to your destination. Special Agent Winemiller's office is awaiting your visit. Sir, it's an honor to meet you. You are a legend."

They followed the narrow road surrounded by the lush green landscape offered by northern Virginia until they reached a nondescript, unnamed building ostensibly occupied by the FBI Cybercrimes Unit.

They parked, cracked the windows of the Jeep, provided water and food for Ram, and walked in the direction of the FBI building. Before they entered the building, an FBI agent stopped them and asked the men to sit at a picnic table fifty yards from the FBI building. Tank returned to the Jeep and let Ram out to sit with them.

Five minutes later, Rusty Winemiller exited the FBI building and wheeled his chair to the picnic table. Rusty became a paraplegic as a young man when he took a dare and dove off a bridge into shallow waters.

Winemiller asked, "Why are you here? We should never be seen together in public. We're outside to avoid recorders. Let's make this quick."

Tucker said, "Here's a laptop with data on it that I'm sure provides information useful to the FBI to identify criminal activities by allegedly charitable organizations. What you'll find is a group that intimidates conservative journalists. Free speech is dead if we can't stop this kind of activity. We provide this to you as a service from American citizens. Anyone that sees us together should see nothing else unless they are conspiracy theorists. What you'll want to discover is who funds the intimidators.

"On another subject, Rusty, how are you coming with your investigation of the entity that managed to supplant articles in the electronic version of *The Washington Post*?"

Winemiller answered, "The pressure to learn the identity of the perpetrators has lessened since the merger of *The Washington Post* with *The Washington Times*. However, the vice president and my directory truly fear that our nation is at risk with the kind of cyber talent out there as demonstrated by the attack on *The Washington Post* and *The New York Times*.

Tucker said, "What the FBI needs to do is figure out who funds all these anarchist-based, anti-American, liberal websites." He handed Rusty a list. "This list should help and is given to you by American-loving citizens."

Tucker, Tank, and Powers left Quantico knowing full well that Agent Rusty Winemiller, one of The Media Transformation Foundation's most important members, would get to the bottom of who funded the intimidation of conservative journalists and who encouraged leftist violence.

Tucker said to Tank and Powers as they climbed back into the Jeep, "I suspect both the intimidators and violent leftists are funded by the same organization."

CHAPTER 36

"Everyone appreciates your honesty until you are honest with them. Then you're an asshole."—George Carlin, 1937-2008, comedian

Medicine Hat, Alberta, Canada – September 28th

It was Michael Roberts's turn to deal. He said, "It's time to play real poker, none of these girly luck games." He picked up the deck of cards and placed it on his right, and a player he didn't know split it.

"Five-card draw, nothing wild. Ten-dollar ante." He dealt cards to the five others at the table. The man on his left looked at his hand and said, "Pass."

The second man said, "I'll raise five dollars."

The next guy said, "I'll see your five and raise another five."

Roberts said to the fourth man, "That's ten dollars to you." He said, "I fold."

Roberts looked at the man on his right, the same man that cut the cards, and said, "You?"

He threw ten dollars into the pot, as did Roberts and the man to his left. The original better threw in five dollars and the pot was good. Without looking at the player to his left, Roberts asked, "How many?"

"Three."

The next guy said, "Three."

"Two."

"One."

A player at the table said, "Drawing to a straight, eh?"

While Roberts was dealing at his table, he heard someone at the other table, where Rod Nelson sat, yell. "You son of a bitch. Damn you."

He heard Rod say, "Hey, I didn't deal this hand. I'd rather be lucky than good. Does anybody need another drink? I'll buy."

Nelson pulled in his winning, rose from his chair, went to the bar, and returned with a half-full quart bottle of Wild Turkey and poured it into the glass of each player at his table.

At the table that Roberts and Gary Chung Lee sat, the second round of betting began.

"Pass."

"Five dollars."

"I'll see your five."

"Five plus two hundred."

They all looked at the guy who'd bet two hundred dollars. Gary was next and said, "You aren't trying to buy the pot, are you? I think you're bluffing."

The man said, "You can call my bluff."

Gary thought for a moment and said, "No, I'll fold."

As did everyone at the table.

Gary said, "Time to refresh our drinks." He went to the bar in his man-cave and brought out an unopened quart bottle of Wild Turkey 101 bourbon.

Most of the players were well on their way to inebriation and la-la land. They talked trash, shared off-color jokes, cursed, and smoked cigars. By the end of the third hour of poker, the players started telling stories about missions and operations they were engaged in the past. Some were obviously bullshit, but others were credible.

The big-gambler at the table talked about a case he ran in Berlin involving a former-Soviet counterpart. Another talked about how he missed working a case in Colombia where he captured a cocaine king. A third man said, "If you still want action, I know where you can play."

Without looking up, Gary Chung Lee said, "I'd like a little action. You know who's buying?"

"I might be able to introduce you to someone."

Gary asked, "Is it legal work? I'm not interested in spending any time in the shower with Big Willie."

The man slurred, "As legal as all the work you did for the agency."

Agent Roberts said, "I heard the heroes that took out that asshole Lakatos escaped through here. Now, that's the kind of work I'd like to find—help eliminate scum like that. Where did those guys go from here?"

The man took another sip of bourbon, spilled a little on the table, and said, "That's what God makes Humvees for. Don't need to pass through immigration. There's no wall between Alberta and Montana."

The game broke up around 12:30 a.m. Only the host, Gary Chung Lee, and the two law officers remained at the table. Special Agent Roberts said, "At least five of the players had no business getting in a car and driving home. They could kill someone in their state of inebriation."

Gary said, "Take a look outside. Flood lights are still on."

Both Rod and Michael opened the front door to see six vehicles in various positions either on the main road or parked on the lawn.

Gary said, "We have a driver show up at midnight every Friday night with his Suburban. It's Medicine Hat's version of Uber."

Rod said, "Now you tell me. I could have had a better time tonight."

Roberts said, "Sounded to me like you cleaned their clock over at your table. How much better time could you have had?"

"Good point."

Michael Roberts said, "Can we help you clean up before we leave."

Gary answered, "You weren't going to leave without asking a few questions, so, sure you can help clean up while I answer your questions."

"Where's the trash can so I can start dumping the garbage?"

Gary pointed at a closet and said, "The table cloths are disposable."

Rod found a broom in the same closet and started sweeping around the card table and asked, "I noticed one of the vehicles outside is a Humvee. Any chance it belonged to the guy that implied the unsubs crossed the border in a Humvee?"

"That would be his."

Michael asked, "What's his name?"

"He goes by the name of CJ, but most of the people at the table leave their real names behind and use aliases. It's safer that way."

Rod said, "Is Gary Chung Lee an alias?"

"Of course. I don't want some damn terrorist hunting me down because of something I did as an agent."

Michael asked, "Where can we find CJ?"

The host said, "See the phone number behind the refrigerator magnet? The one that says 'driver.' He'll know where he lives."

CHAPTER 37

"I have, indeed, no abhorrence of danger, except in its absolute effect - in terror."—Edgar Allan Poe, 1809-1849, American poet, critic, short story writer, and author

Medicine Hat, Alberta Canada – September 29th

Early the next morning, before breakfast, Rod banged on the front door of a double-wide trailer seven miles out of Medicine Hat and a quarter of a mile off a paved road. The deep storm water ruts in the driveway looked like they were intentionally unmaintained to discourage unwanted visitors. Stacks of split wood populated the grounds and smoke billowed out of an aluminum chimney.

Michael Roberts pointed out two cameras on the way in. Two, maybe three, large-sounding dogs were barking ferociously in the back yard. Both lawmen were hoping CJ hadn't gone out the back and unleashed the hounds.

Agent Roberts readied his firearm. He hoped he didn't have to shoot the dogs. He said, "My guess is his alarm has already gone off and is armed."

"CJ," Rod yelled, "open up. It's two of your poker buddies."

The front door opened. A disheveled-looking woman wearing a bathrobe opened the door holding a shotgun pointing in their direction. She was in her late thirties or early forties and was shapely in an athletic way; she had high cheekbones and a serious-looking scar on the side of her neck.

The woman raised the barrel of the 12-gauge and pointed it at the sky when she saw Rod Nelson wearing his Royal Canadian Mounted Police uniform.

She yelled back into the trailer and said, "Stand down." She looked Detective Nelson in the eye and said, "Before I invite you in, what's your business? Has CJ done something? And why is a Fed here with you?"

Nelson said, "We're here to give CJ a ride back to his Humvee. He wisely left it where we were playing poker last night."

She eyed them suspiciously. She said, "He's not feeling so hot. Maybe you should come back later when he gets his head out of the toilet." When she gestured with the shotgun to head in the direction of their Jeep, her bathrobe opened just enough to see that she wore no clothes under the robe. She quickly recovered and tied the sash.

But Michael wasn't looking at the woman. He was looking at the reflection off the half-opened storm door. He saw CJ or some other man holding an assault rifle—maybe an AR-15.

Michael said, "OK, tell CJ we hope he feels better. We'll see him around."

They turned, climbed into the Jeep, and backed out of the driveway until they could find a place to turn around. Once they were back on pavement, Rod asked, "What was that all about?"

Agent Roberts said, "Do you remember that she yelled back into the house and said, 'stand down'?"

"Yeah."

"Well, someone was standing right behind the door holding an assault rifle. Whatever shit they're into, she's a part of it. She may be the brains behind it—who knows? I thought we might want to regroup, do a little research, and call for backup before we go back there."

Roberts thought for a moment and then continued, "How much pull do you have in the RCMP?"

"Enough. What's on your mind?"

"Can you authorize a transmitter to be placed on his Humvee still sitting on Gary's property?"

Rod answered, "Does a moose shit in the woods?"

Roberts said, "I sure as hell hope so."

Wiscasset

Maya clicked off the TV and said, "The taped episode of last week's *Saturday Night Live* skit produced by Real America Productions wasn't great, but it's a start. I'd give it a C+. Let's just say that there were no atoms smashed on the show last week. It's a good thing Julienne is taking over production of the show this week."

Tucker said, "It will get better. We didn't have access to the top comedy writers in the business to help with the script. However, the arrangement we just negotiated with the Writers Guild will change all that. I think you'll notice a change in all late-night comedy."

"You know, Tucker, there really is a lot of material to work with. Most of it would be hysterically funny if it were not so sad. We could do a show just on how the liberal media uses soundbites and headlines instead of detailed explanations of complicated issues.

"The liberal media uses anti-conservative clichés that can be refuted, but the explanations are too long to respond in a headline fashion. I have images of Dennis Miller standing up and saying," Maya changed her posture, lowered her voice, and tried to imitate Dennis Miller, "if I don't want a thirty-two-ounce drink, I don't buy one. If he or she or the transgender liberal journalist doesn't want a thirty-two-ounce drink, the lib expects the federal government to ban them.

"Or, you know you're a liberal reporter if you insist that all assumptions must be questioned . . . except for their assumptions. Questioning those are a hate crime.

"Or, you know that if your idea of a classic car is a 1997 Prius, you just might be a liberal author.

"Or," Dennis might say, "If I don't like a talk show host, I switch stations. Liberals demand that the host is tossed off the air.

"Or, what did the Democratic National Committee say to Russia? We are going to build a Great Firewall and make the hackers pay for it."

Maya bowed.

Tucker said, "Maybe we need to put you on the stage."

CHAPTER 38

"It should be remembered that you can threaten the enemy and get away with it. You can insult and annoy him, but the one thing that is unforgivable and that is certain to get him to react is to laugh at him. This causes irrational anger." – Saul Alinsky, 1909-1972, author of *"Rules for Radicals"*

New York City, New York – September 30th

The tried and true antics on the traditional late-night comedy shows continued to mock anyone who did not share Broadway's and Hollywood's disdain for conservative values until Real America Productions bought one hundred percent of the advertisement time for the *Saturday Night Live* time-slot. At four times the going rate, the contract allowed the advertisers to have a say in the show's production and the selection of the lead comedian.

Real America Productions' philosophy was that the repetitive scorn and ridicule on SNL's favorite victims—replayed on the following mainstream Sunday morning talk-show panels where all projected a sense of superiority while they tried to ratchet scorn and ridicule—wore thin with viewers. The public's willing consumption of the dribble and poison thought process would sustain itself until an alternative comedy show emerged.

Only months after Real America Productions directed its first late night comedy show segment, the truth began to resonate: same message, different target. The conservative citizens had heard all this before when it was directed toward them. Now the tables were turned, but there was a sense of exhaustion by viewers over the continuous barrage and insults, despite the new targets—liberals. Glee for SNL-type shows devolved into something between idle curiosity and apathy. Real America Productions sent Julienne O'Kray to New York City to produce a new show to keep The Media Transformation Foundation's gains intact and to influence those still on the fence. A truth emerged. Disparaging the dishonest media with one-liners had a shelf life. Having leftist comedy writers reveal their idiocy through direct observation became the course correction.

Julienne worked tirelessly to shock the audience and surprise viewers. Real America Productions had to generate sustainable enthusiasm and engagement from its inaugural production. She understood that a new approach was clearly needed. And so, it began.

O'Kray told the writers and director that she'd hired Charles Barkley to moderate the new comedy show. She said, "In 2017, *People Magazine* readers voted him 'the person I'd most prefer to have with me on a desert island.' Of course, Victoria's Secret models were disqualified from that vote. He brings a rich mix of timing, comfort in front of the camera, and values to this new role as moderator. Back in his basketball star days, he famously said, 'I am not a role model.' Many took that as his rationalization for his edgy behavior both on and off the court. As he became better known as a person, the public realized that his message was for youth not to emulate or get their ethics and values from celebrities or sports stars.

"As Johnny Carson was the Tonight Show, Barkley will be the *Andrew Jackson College Bowl* replacement for SNL. His presence, combined with the unpredictable content, will make the show perfect for both the video and radio/audio medium."

One of the twenty-something writers asked, "What are you talking about? A college bowl pits two winning football teams against each other."

O'Kray answered, "Put it in a search engine, see what comes up. Despite the fact that the original *College Bowl* became the equivalent of the Harlem Globetrotters vs. the Washington Generals, the public was hooked on the program back in the sixties and seventies. The video on demand, the trending Tweets, the new Facebook likes, could make this the most viewed and heard production in media history."

Julienne said with a sly smile, "This new version of the *College Bowl* pits a team of snowflakes from the University of California, Santa Cruz, against a squad from Auburn University, Barkley's alma mater."

"Originally, the matchup was to be UC Berkeley against Hillsdale College but that didn't work out. But, UC Santa Cruz students, with their Banana Slug mascot, are just as clueless as their Berkeley cohorts. Most UCSC students sought degrees in 'Entitlement and Victimization.'"

O'Kray said, "The group from Auburn should show well, their students were well-informed critical thinkers who supported, and in some cases, enabled, the new order.

"This will make for great sport. The format involves two teams of three players each. The moderator, Barkley, asks a question and the team that hits their buzzer first get a chance to answer. A correct answer generates points; incorrect answers allow the other side to respond.

"There are two significant reasons why this segment of the show, renamed the *Andrew Jackson College Bowl*, will be a spectacular success. First, the format provides a stark contrast to today's two divergent worldviews. Instead of humor in the form of sarcasm and irony, this is reality TV. No buildup to a punch line, no hyperbole, no fictional accounts, no piped-in laughter. This is pure observation and easy conclusions.

"The second reason for the *AJCB*'s popularity will be the profound selection of the host. We had seen enough of vapid pretty boys (and girls) as well as toothless barking Chihuahuas. The moderator position calls for someone with gravitas, credibility, and an ability to deploy the nonverbal cues that make for great comedy. We reviewed archival films of Jackie Gleason, Jonathan Winters, Lewis Black, and other greats. The perfect host would draw from them all. The smirk, the cocked eyebrow, the rolling of eyes, and the drawn-out sigh were keys to comedic success for these icons.

"These are the traits needed for a successful host, plus an imposing physical presence—someone who could not be intimidated by the minority of the audience who still hold liberal beliefs. He was an Auburn graduate, sportscaster, and NBA Hall of Famer.

"Remember one of Saul Alinsky's famous quotes, 'The most important weapons known to man are satire and ridicule.' Is everyone ready? Let's do a dry run."

Darrell Hammond announced, "Live from New York City, it's *Andrew Jackson College Bowl* with special guest Charles Barkley hosting the modern version of the College Bowl popular in the 1970s."

Big Charles walked onto the stage and waved his hands over his head to the audience. Offscreen, someone threw him a basketball; he caught it and passed it into the audience.

Barkley did his best impersonation of Elvis Presley and said, "Thank you. Thank you very much.

"Is the team from the University of California, Santa Cruz, ready?"

"Yeah!"

Barkley: "Is the team from Auburn University ready?"

"Yes."

Barkley: "For twenty points, what organization was created in 1913 at Jekyll Island, Georgia? It had a profound impact on our economy."

UCSC: Buzz. "Charles, it was the National Football League. We support freedom and kneel for our incarcerated brothers, despite their alleged felonies."

Barkley: "No, take it, Auburn."

Auburn: "The Federal Reserve, an entity owned by international bankers, designed to siphon wealth from Americans to their banker families."

Barkley: "Yes, twenty points for Auburn. Next question. Who was the enemy in the War on Terror?"

UCSC: Buzz. "The enemy is people who made us feel bad and unsafe."

Barkley: "Close. Care to elaborate?"

UCSC: "Yes, they were people who refused to use appropriate pronouns when referring to LGBTQ EIEIO people."

Barkley: "No, you Zir fool. Take it Auburn."

Auburn: "The enemy included radicalized followers of Mohammed, a child molesting, goat romancing, eleventh century gangster who founded a political system posing as a religion."

Barkley: "Correct. And they agreed that **I** shouldn't be a role model. Easy on the goats. Twenty more points for Auburn. Next question. This one is somewhat personal. Who is responsible for generational welfare families and underachievement in urban communities?"

UCSC: Buzz. "White people, Asian people, Indian smartasses, climate change, poor cell coverage for our Obama phones, attendance rules for graduation, lack of respect for rapper artistry, discrimination of people with traditional African names like D'Vagina and L'Dipshitta, police brutality against the sainted Trayvon Martin and Freddie Gray, cheap hos."

Barkley: "Let me know when you're finished. Nothing against cheap hos."

Barkley: "Time for a short profit time-out."

COMING TO THEATRES NEAR YOU.

Real America Productions releases *Unsustainable*, a movie about terrorists who burn California into bankruptcy and drive the nation into its second civil war. Starring Mel Gibson, Jon Voight, Angie Harmon, and Gary Sinise.

Barkley: "We're back. Are you multiple-gendered geniuses at UCSC ready to come from behind and win? Ah, there was no intended sexual reference to the question. Repeating the question because I know you brilliant students at UCSC have pot-induced short-term memory problems, who is responsible for generational welfare families and underachievement in urban communities?"

UCSC: "Did we mention white people? Black History Month is the shortest month, disrespect of Maxine Waters, no jobs for African studies graduates, the myth of black on black crime. Are we getting close?"

Barkley: "No, in fact, you are missing it entirely. I warned you about role models. Take it, Auburn."

Auburn: "Government subsidy and social acceptance and embracing of ghetto culture. Lyndon Johnson's Great Society."

Barkley: "Yeah, we voted Democrat for sixty years. Lyndon was forty short in his estimate. Points go to Auburn. That's it for tonight, please tune in next week. Good night and God Bless America."

Off camera, Charles said to the UCSC team: "Quit whining, you bitches!"

Washington, DC

The Washington Times headline: "California Media Group Freed to Report the News"

"A trend by media outlets to report news and events without an ideological spin is emerging. Is the timing coincidental that since *The Washington Times* acquired the Post, the California Media Group has restructured its TV and radio lineup to include both progressive and conservative shows? CEO Lawrence Slaughter hired the former editor in chief of the Heritage Foundation's newspaper, the *Daily Signal*, as president of the group. Shortly after that, the new management negotiated a contract with conservative radio talk show host Michelle Mallard. The new president of the largest US radio broadcaster stated that the new approach was also intended to reverse a steady loss of listeners to new platforms and sluggish sales.

"Slaughter announced in the Wall Street Journal that California Media Group's earnings increased over the previous quarter primarily due to the addition of new advertisers, including fast food sponsor Chick-fil-A.

"This trend could stave off the damaged reputation of the media environment, which has struggled with truth and credibility. A recent poll published by HonestMediaMatters.edu ranked the honesty of journalists and reporters for the mainstream media below used car salespeople, class-action suit lawyers, and politicians. Have we in the media hit bottom? Is the trend finally up? We hope so.

"Editor, *The Washington Times*. The Truth and Nothing but the Truth, So Help Us, God."

Senate Hart Building

Senator Peter Enya threw his stocking feet up on a hassock and listened to the next day's WebEx conversation sponsored by the Democratic National Committee.

Arnold Goldberger, *The New York Times*: "I think the talking point today should be that the one-percenters are suppressing free speech."

The chairperson of the Democratic National Committee: Arnold, aren't you a one percenter?

Arnold Goldberger, *The New York Times*: "Think about it. Jorgensen sells *The Washington Post* after a sniper puts a bullet through his bedroom headboard. Our editor is brutally murdered by some right-wing kook, Slaughter hires a conservative leader for his media empire, and don't forget: Gabriel Lakatos was killed. Someone is trying to suppress the progressive message."

President of MoveOn.org: "Arnold, can you confirm that there is pressure on *The New York Times* to sell to the same group that owns *The Washington Times?*"

Arnold Goldberger, *The New York Times*: "I cannot say."

Publisher, *Chicago Tribune*: "What proof do we have that a group of conservative one-percenters is suppressing free speech? Your logic holds up, but we need more evidence.*"*

Vice president, ABC News: "Aren't the people accused of murdering Lakatos, you know, former Senator Powers and his partner, evidence of some sort of collusion to suppress free speech?"

The chairperson of the Democratic National Committee: "Good point. OK. Today's talking point: Conservative one-percenters are suppressing free speech through abuse of financial power and intimidation."

CHAPTER 39

"Journalism is what we need to make democracy work." - Walter Cronkite, 1916-2009, journalist and news anchorman

Medicine Hat, Alberta – October 1st

FBI Special Agent Michael Roberts put his cell phone down and filled his coffee cup for the fifth time.

Rod Nelson said, "They don't live at the place we visited. It's owned by a couple in Calgary. It's the owner's getaway, a place they escape to once or twice a year. CJ and the lady 'borrowed' it. Ten cents on the dollar, they'll take their dogs and be out of there before the end of the day."

Roberts said, "I just got off the phone with our facial recognition gurus. CJ's real name is Winston Albert Davidson, terminated for cause by the Central Intelligence Agency."

Nelson said, "When did you get a photo of CJ?" Roberts said, "Hey, I wasn't just playing poker like you were. That's why I lost money; I wasn't concentrating on the game.

"Do CIA agents get to live if you're dishonorably discharged from the agency?"

Roberts said, "You do if no one finds you. Did you get a transmitter placed on the Humvee?"

"Do you know that Apple even has an app for that? It's still sitting at Gary Chung Lee's home?

"By the way, what's Gary's real name? I assume you also checked him out."

Agent Roberts looked at Rod Nelson like his feelings were hurt. "No, I didn't learn his real name. Has your detective in Fort Chipewyan or your forensic expert in Calgary made any progress?"

"Butterfield said some American private investigator was snooping around, trying to find out what we know. I figure it was a reporter trying to get a lead on the story. As you know, the forensic expert confirmed that the sniper rifle given to Napoleon Drygeese was the murder weapon. Nothing else, I've got Officer Butterfield researching passports in and out of Canada during a ten-day period. It may be a wild Canadian goose chase."

Rod Nelson jumped. He checked his iPhone and said, "Humvee's on the move."

Roberts asked, "What's the range on that thing?"

"Around twenty-five kilometers."

"We better get moving."

Los Angeles, California

Officer Angela Garcia reviewed the LAPD website and oversaw four assistants who were responsible for responding to website comments from concerned citizens of LA. The vast majority of the comments focused on LAPD's non-responsiveness to neighbors playing music too loudly, cases of suspected domestic violence, and the failure of the local cable company to show a Lakers game.

Maria Rodriguez reviewed a comment sent by #MrCraig: "C-4 under the globe. Stop Fake News."

Maria said, "Angela, we may have something."

"What?"

"We have a bomb threat."

Angela asked, "Any reason to suspect it's credible?"

"Not really. But easy to check out. LAPD has sniffers across the street from the LA Times building, right?"

"Right. The safe thing to do is notify the bomb squad. Do it."

Maria called the LAPD bomb squad and spoke with Officer Clint Womack for the tenth time this month. "Officer, we got another threat. Claims to have C-4 under the globe. Thought you'd want to check it out."

Clint said, "Only if we can share a drink after work."

She said, "Works for me. Call me when you clear the threat."

Sammy sat lazily at Clint's feet. He said, "Get up Lazi-Wan Kenobi. We have work to do." The coonhound lifted his head with his ten-pound ears dragging on the floor and stood at the door waiting for his master.

Officer Womack put a leash on Sammy, opened the office door, and sashayed across the street to the *Times* Building. The Globe Lobby was adorned with ten-foot-high murals and historical exhibits showcasing the first one hundred years of the *Times*. But the architectural highlight in the lobby was the roped-off, huge world globe sitting on a pedestal.

Sammy ran under the ropes, placed his snout in the space between the pedestal and Antarctica, and howled like he'd just cornered a fox. Clint saw the C-4 and backed out as fast as he could.

He ran to the nearest fire alarm and pulled it to evacuate the building while he alerted his cohorts in the bomb squad.

Yellowknife, Northwest Territories

The mosquitos drove him nuts this time of year. He'd tried all sorts of repellents, but insects seemed to develop a resistance to the stuff. The electric zapper killed hundreds of them every couple of minutes. For every mosquito electrocuted, two more were attracted to the light. Napoleon Drygeese relit one of ten citronella candles, which he kept burning constantly. The benefits the candles offered were marginal, but every little bit helped. Besides, his woman would nag him when she got home if he didn't keep them lit. It pissed him off that when the weather finally warmed and was at least tolerable enough in Yellowknife to venture outside, he had to be assaulted by these hordes of insects.

He waved the burning match out, turned, and damned near had a heart attack. No more than six inches from him, nose-to-nose, was an unsmiling blond man built like a fire hydrant.

Drygeese grabbed his chest, took a step back, and said, "Damn, you scared the shit out of me. Where did you come from? Normally I can hear someone approaching from a quarter mile up the road. Who are you?"

"My name is Lucas Justice. I'm following up on the murder of your friend, Chuck."

"Are you a Mountie?"

"Nope, I'm an American private investigator.

"Chuck, or Kika Kisecawchuck, gave you the rifle— the murder weapon—that killed Gabriel Lakatos. All you had to do was misled authorities, send them on a wild goose chase. Who did you tell this to?"

"The Royal Canadian Mounted Police Detective Rod Nelson, Officer Butterfield, and an FBI agent. I think his name was Roberts. That's all."

"Do you believe any of those three killed Kika Kisecawchuck?"

"No."

"Then you must have told someone else. Who came by here and threatened you? Let me guess, the perp threatened your family if you told anyone his name? Or maybe you never learned his real name."

Napoleon stated dryly, "I told no one. Now, leave my property."

"You understand that you are a loose end, right? The guy that killed Chuck is going to come back and eliminate the potential risk you pose. He let you live, not because he was soft, but because if you lied to him, he wanted to return to torture the truth out of you. If I walk away from here with nothing, if I don't find this guy, you'll be looking over your shoulder for the rest of your life, which could be only days.

"What did he look like? Was he tall, was he young, was he Caucasian or Asian or African-American? Was the killer a woman?"

"I'm not just a traffic controller at the airport. I'm more than that—I'm an artist."

Unsure where this was going, Lucas waited for him to continue.

"I work with chalk and graphite pencils. Would you like to see some of my artwork? Wait right here, and I'll show you my latest masterpiece." Napoleon turned and started toward the front door to his home. Lucas suspected that Drygeese was going to grab a weapon if he could get close enough to one.

"No. I won't fall for that trick. I didn't come all the way here to Bumfuck, Egypt, to be conned." Drygeese turned back to face a 9mm Wilson Combat 1911. "Know that I never miss in close quarters. I'll follow you in but keep your hands where I can see them."

The first thing Lucas noticed when he entered Drygeese's modest home was a 12-gauge Mossberg semiautomatic shotgun by the door. The second thing he noticed was all the artwork hanging on the walls. They looked professional. But Lucas didn't let his guard down and watched his host's movement carefully.

Napoleon asked, "May I reach down to pick up the sketch that I wanted to show you?"

Lucas nodded, still holding his weapon with both hands. Napoleon displayed his artwork for Lucas to see. Lucas finally understood. It was a sketch of the man who had killed Chuck.

Tucker took the call immediately—on the first ring.

Lucas said, "I'm about to send you a scanned sketch of the guy who, I'm pretty sure, is the guy who forced Chuck to write a confession letter claiming that Tank murdered Gabriel Lakatos. I'm hoping you know someone with a facial recognition database. I'm staying at the Trout Rock Lodge up here. I'll wait here until I hear back from you in case this guy is local."

Tucker said, "Good work. I'll get this to Jimmy Ma, and we'll know within hours. Then I'll give the name to Tony Vinci, who'll learn everything about the guy down to a pimple on his ass. Before you move on the guy, we'll provide you some backup."

Lucas said, "If you mean Tank, I don't think that's a good idea. I don't want to have to pick up body parts strewn over a square mile of his last-known location after Tank learns who set him up for murder."

CHAPTER 40

"Aggressive suppression of the truth is a critical feature of American higher education." – Professor Amy L. Wax, University of Pennsylvania

San Francisco, California – October 2nd

Professor Orwell rode down the elevator from his luxury suite in 181 Fremont in downtown San Francisco into the pristine glassed-in lobby with its twenty-five-foot ceiling. He walked out through security into the fog and walked in the direction of the Bay Area Rapid Transit or BART to catch a train to Berkeley.

He didn't make it to class.

When he awoke, startled, in a private room in the San Francisco General Hospital, he had an IV running into his left arm and he was hooked up to a monitoring system which digitally displayed his blood pressure and other vital information.

"What happened? Why am I in a hospital? I don't remember anything."

A large man he didn't recognize sat in the private room with him. The giant said, "Hi, I'm the man that caught you when you passed out. I just happened to be behind you. I brought you to the ER, and they were unable to return you to consciousness, so I stayed with you even after they admitted you to the hospital. Now that you are awake and recovering, I'll leave you to the good doctors and nurses here in the hospital."

Tank started to rise when Professor Orwell said, "Wait a minute. How can I repay you for your kindness? What's your name?"

"My name is Jorge Alvarez. No need to repay me. I did what any concerned citizen would do for another human being. But thank you for wanting to repay me. I'm quite well-off in my own right. I didn't save you for a reward. It was just the right thing to do."

Professor Jose Orwell said, "You're Hispanic, like me."

"True."

"What's your heritage?"

"I'm an American from western North Carolina. How about you?"

"My mother was from Spain, my father British. I hated the bastard."

Tank said nothing, waiting for Orwell to shed more light on his malignant thought process.

"He was stinking rich, exploited the labor of Asian Indians to produce rubber from his five thousand-acre plantation. He made millions off the backs of the poor."

Tank calibrated the man's anger and could imagine his vitriol in his journalism classroom.

Orwell asked, "Jorge, how did you achieve your well-off status?"

Tank said, "I earned it. I worked hard for it."

"What do you do?"

"I'm the chief executive officer of the leading personal security and private investigation firm in the United States. I protect people. I use force if necessary. In fact, I'm carrying as we speak. While you were unconscious and laid up in your hospital bed, I did a little research on you. After all, it's who I am. You teach journalism at the University of California, Berkeley.

Congratulations on achieving the status of professor. You were educated at Columbia University with funds contributed to the school from the father you hate. The very one that employed six thousand people in India that had jobs that provided for their families. A little research showed that he paid more than the prevailing wages in the community he employed. In fact, he was loved by the people who worked for him, and they gave him honorary gifts.

"You, on the other hand, hypocritically live in a three-million-dollar condominium in downtown San Francisco off your father's inheritance while railing against successful entrepreneurs like your father and me. You teach impressionable students that I'm the problem and to hate people like me. You teach them to write about the evil of success instead of encouraging them to write about the truth.

"I'm not sorry that I may have saved your life. I am sorry to discover that you are so wrongheaded and are able to compel young minds to follow your lies as truth. I'm sitting here thinking about your background, the root cause of your fact-less ideology. I propose the following: allow me to come in as a guest speaker and present a different vision to your students once a month. What do you say?"

Professor Orwell studied Tank for a moment and said, "I'm not in this hospital by accident, am I? You staged this whole thing, didn't you?"

Tank said, "Professor Orwell, it is a systemic problem you have that once you discovered that I was a CEO you lost trust. I'm not your father. Seek medical help for the foundation of your hatred. I hope you recover, and I'll be back here thirty days from now. I'll enjoy speaking to your students."

Tank left the professor in the hospital room with Orwell wondering what had happened to him to put him there. Tank caught a taxi to the airport and dumped the syringe in a public dumpster.

Concord, California

The pretty blue-eyed, blonde-haired anchor for California Media Group's KHZZ's TV reported on the Six O'clock News, "Wichita State University announced today that its first honesty/integrity ranking of journalists will be released on its HonestMediaMatters website. WSU collaborated with Liberty University to develop an algorithm that ranked over two thousand journalists, editors, publishers, and reporters based on their job description and position in their media entity. Their work was then checked or cross-referenced with FactCheck.org. Publishers around the country claim the report is itself dishonest and funded by right wing activists.

"In a statement released by Wichita State University, their HonestMediaMatters.edu website received over twenty million hits in the first six hours from the release of the free report. The honesty/integrity ratings are categorized by type of publication and whether the journalist is a news reporter or an editorial page contributor. The *Los Angeles Times* announced that it was pleased to learn that no writer from that publication made the top fifty 'dishonest and/or lacking in integrity' journalists on the WSU report.

"In other news . . ." Lawrence Slaughter muted his TV and called the newly hired president of California Media Group. He was irritated that he had to go through the president's assistant before reaching his top executive. Finally, Slaughter said, "I just listened in on KHZZ. What are you doing? Do you think our viewing and listening audience gives a flying fuck what Wichita State does? You're going to drive our advertisers away. Our audience wants to hear about local news, shootings, racial conflicts, and Hollywood gossip. Quit reporting that shit."

The president of California Media Group was formerly senior vice president of communications and editor in chief of the *Daily Signal* for the Heritage Foundation. He'd expected this call and said, "First, Chairman Slaughter, you should know that our income from advertisers has increased since I joined the firm and updated the program.

"Secondly, our viewing and listening audience has increased according to the latest survey. We performed a detailed demographic study in KHZZ's range and polled the potential audience. As a result, we modified the program and were able to increase the going price per minute for advertisers.

"And thirdly, I think you grossly underestimate the intelligence of your listening audience. Until we separated ourselves from the pack and modified our program, our audience had nowhere to go to get the real news.

"Sir, we should be proud that we are not high on the Wichita State list of dishonest media producers."

Slaughter said, "As I said, I don't care what WSU thinks. One of us is completely out-of-touch with our audience."

"Yes sir, I agree."

CHAPTER 41

"Life is fraught with opportunities to keep your mouth shut." – Winston Churchill, 1874-1965, Prime Minister of the United Kingdom during World War II

Medicine Hat, Alberta, Canada - October 2nd

The Humvee pulled a trailer carrying three rottweilers south down Crowsnest Highway away from Medicine Hat. The shotgun-bearing bathrobe-lady drove, now dressed in Gloria Vanderbilt jeans, expensive leather Dingo boots, a western shirt, a Rifleman leather jacket, and a felt rhinestone western hat.

And she packed heat.

CJ rode shotgun with his Colt AR-15 within reach and two thirty-round magazines under his seat.

CJ's woman had prepared for the inevitable discovery of their presence in Medicine Hat. She'd identified four different unoccupied residences for them to use in an emergency if and when they had to run. They headed to an extremely remote hunting cabin on Onion Lake. The two of them loaded the trailer with fuel for the portable generator, two weeks' worth of food, dog food, household items, and ammunition.

FBI Special Agent Michael Roberts said, "I'm impressed with your pull with the Royal Canadian Mounted Police hierarchy. You not only got us a warrant to search their Humvee, but you got us an Airbus AS-350 helicopter to track them and you achieved unheard of cooperation between Canadian and US law enforcement agencies."

Rod Nelson bantered, "I thought my poker playing skills were what impressed you." To both Roberts and the pilot, Nelson said, "We'll stay five miles back until they reach their destination."

He continued, "What's the timeline for dispatching an FBI SWAT team if we need them?"

SAC Roberts answered, "It won't be the FBI SWAT team. The CIA wants to clean up its own mess. The CIA is sending its Special Activities Division's Special Operations Group operators. They are referred to as Ground Branch and are a deniable asset for these type missions. They will be positioned in Great Falls, Montana, within the next hour. An armed Apache helicopter is ready to transport them across the border when we make the request."

Nelson said, "I hope it doesn't come to that and we don't need them. I don't know about you, but I don't want to be involved in a Ruby Ridge type fiasco."

"If you have a better idea, now would be a good time to share it with me."

Nelson said, "You Yanks always choose overwhelming power over finesse. The FBI and CIA would use a sledgehammer to crack a peanut. These two we're chasing are small potatoes in the scheme of things, eh?"

Agent Roberts bristled and said, "Overwhelming force sends a message to any other federal law enforcement agent that the consequences for betrayal are terminal. Besides, I'm concerned that wherever their last-resort hideout is, that it may contain a stockpile of weapons. Hopefully, nothing that could bring down a chopper. Now, do you have a better plan or not?"

Detective Nelson said, "These two US federal law enforcement fugitives are on the run, desperate, and have nowhere to go once they know we're on to them. They may even try to run through or around the blockade I set up about twenty kilometers from here."

Roberts exploded, "You did what? I thought we were working together? You realize that if they open fire on your officers and try to run the blockade, they'll be killed and the trail to solving this case will turn cold? I thought you wanted to avoid a blood bath. You just fucking guaranteed one."

Undeterred, Nelson calmly said, "Agent Roberts."

"Special Agent in Charge Roberts."

Rod Nelson resisted a smile and said, "Do I need to remind you that you are in Canada and that I'm in charge of this case, not the FBI? We appreciate your support, and we welcome the opportunity to work together, but, the quote, 'fucking FBI,' unquote is not in charge. Now, it's time you listen to how we're going to handle this operation."

Roberts's face turned bright red; he seethed and gritted his teeth but remained silent.

Nelson continued, "We're going to talk to them and give them an opportunity to save their collective asses." The RCMP detective displayed a satellite phone and pushed a button while continuing his calm explanation to SAC Roberts, "It will take them a few minutes to discover where the unexpected ring is coming from. You see, when we placed the transmitter in their Humvee, we also placed a small satellite telephone in the springs under the passenger side seat. It's about the size of a half-dollar, but it's making quite a racket right now. It's playing the Canadian national anthem. I guess that CJ and the woman are pulling over to the side of the road to find the source of the noise."

Roberts asked, "You sure they didn't find it before they left Medicine Hat?"

Nelson answered, "I thought I was wrong once, but I was wrong."

Then they heard CJ ask, "What the fuck is this?"

Nelson smiled and said into the satellite phone, "This is Royal Canadian Mounted Police Detective Nelson. How are you two doing on this lovely day? We see you are taking a little joyride through the plains of Alberta. Unless you want to go like Butch Cassidy and the Sundance Kid, you need to surrender. There is a blockade up ahead on Crowsnest Highway. They will take you out before you get within range with your AR-15.

"Your former employer has dispatched an armed Apache helicopter with orders to release Hellfires on your position. It would be a shame to kill your dogs like that, but it's your choice.

"We're a couple of minutes behind you watching your every move. So, here's the deal: throw your weapons on the ground, put your hands out where we can see them, and stand next to your trailer with the dogs. If you follow those directions, we'll call and tell the Apache to stand down. We'll land near your position in our chopper, approach with overwhelming force, cuff you, and ask a few questions. If you cooperate, we'll haul you back to Medicine Hat to stand trial. If you don't cooperate, we'll transfer custody of you to the FBI on behalf of the CIA.

"Your chance to live longer is much higher in the Medicine Hat detention center than back in the states, probably in Leavenworth where you'll stand trial for treason, if not murder.

"You have thirty seconds to decide."

Ten seconds of silence passed before they heard a woman say, "OK, it's a deal."

"I want to hear CJ, or should I say, Winston Albert Davidson, agree."

Ten more seconds passed before he asked, "How can you protect me from a CIA assassin in jail? I'm dead either way."

Nelson answered, "Your sense of self-worth is highly inflated. Based on our research, you aren't that important. The CIA isn't going to waste an asset on you. You have five seconds left. Is today the day you die or not?"

CJ answered, "OK. OK."

Nelson instructed Roberts, "Go ahead and tell the Apache to proceed across the border, intimidate the fugitives with their presence, but not to arm the Hellfires."

Detective Nelson then contacted the officer in charge of the blockade and said, "Move up within two hundred meters of the parked Humvee and set up. It should take you, what, fifteen minutes? And let me know when Officer Sawyer is in position, locked and ready."

They could hear a muffled argument between the lady and CJ but couldn't hear distinct words, just tone and a blast of anxiety.

The pilot the landed the Airbus AS-350 helicopter gently in the field adjacent to Crowsnest Highway to within five hundred meters of the Humvee, and spoke into the satellite phone, "Hang tight, you two. We'll be approaching your position on foot. But you need to know we'll have the Apache within range and an excellent sniper is positioned with you in his crosshair. You can't blame us for not trusting you completely." He terminated the call and made another call to his team in Medicine Hat.

He said, "Stop all traffic coming south on Crowsnest until further notice."

Unfortunately, an eighteen-wheeler carrying hogs to slaughter was already on the highway before the northern end of Crowsnest Highway was barricaded.

SAC Roberts said, "There's something you need to know."

"Don't say it. I know you love me."

"It's about the woman."

"You held back information crucial to the case?"

Roberts continued, "Her name is Yelizaveta Vasilyevna, known in the intelligence world as the 'Man-eater'—she chews up men and spits them out. CJ here, or Winston, is her latest victim. She is GRU, the foreign military intelligence agency of the General Staff of the Armed Forces of the Russian Federation. The woman crossed a high-ranking GRU operative and disobeyed a direct order to terminate CJ. She is at greater risk for assassination than CJ. She's not likely to surrender easily."

Rod Nelson scowled and said, "Good to know."

Fifteen minutes later, the Apache was in view, the northern blockade was in place, and the sharpshooter viewed the forehead of Winston Davidson through his scope. Although the wind was brisk, west to east, he felt confident that he could take out CJ with one shot, if instructed.

Detective Nelson viewed the fugitives through binoculars and saw that the woman was on the roadside of the Humvee in the back of the trailer, both hands within view, talking to the rottweilers. CJ was on the field side of the trailer, both hands resting on the top of his head, and speaking into the miniature radio, "Let's get this over with."

Nelson nodded at Roberts. Roberts had his Glock 19M with its flared magazine well and no finger grooves on the front of the grip. He held it in the ready position as they walked the last fifty yards. Nelson held his chambered Beretta by his side.

They heard it coming: a Peterbilt traveling at high-speed alone on the highway. So did the Man-eater. The driver of the eighteen-wheeler pumped his brakes when he saw the Humvee on the side of the road and the flashing lights from the police roadblock a kilometer away. As the truck passed by the Humvee, the woman opened the rottweiler cages, jumped to clutch onto the grab handle with one hand, landed on the battery cover, pulled a Ruger from her concealed carry holster, and aimed it at the driver's head, all in one fluid motion.

The truck driver ignored the threat until the woman blew out the passenger side window. Shards of broken glass cut into her face and blinded her vision from her left eye. She yelled over the loud diesel engine and wind to say, "Next shot is through your skull if you don't blow through the police barricade. Now pick up speed."

Winston Davidson ran toward the Peterbilt screaming, "No, my love, no!"

Nelson spoke into his phone, "Don't shoot CJ. If you get a clean shot, take out the woman." But the sharpshooter was more preoccupied with saving his own life than refocusing on a new target, as he was in the line of destruction from the runaway eighteen-wheeler.

Shots were fired from the officers in the blockade—many of them in an attempt to stop the out-of-control 550-horsepower truck by shredding its tires, but it was too late. The momentum of the sixty-five-thousand-pound tractor-trailer plowed into and through two parked Ford Tauruses as if they weren't there. When the truck finally came to a stop about 150 meters later, it lay on its side, with the police cruisers totaled nearby and hogs running around aimlessly.

CJ was laying on his side, screaming for medical help with a 9mm bullet in his thigh.

No Royal Canadian Mounted Police officers were hurt. The truck driver was in serious condition, but alive. The woman was shot in six different places from multiple weapons, but it was probably the Peterbilt cab atop her that was her cause of death.

New York City

The chief executive officer of *World Publishing House* dove into his western omelet as he listened to his marketing manager debrief him on the status of textbook acceptance by the state of Indiana. At the same time every week, at a private table reserved for the publishing company, the CEO met with at least one of his executives for breakfast. It was well-known by the insiders that the two-hour breakfast meeting was where most decisions for the publishing company were made.

The vetted waiter refilled the coffee cups while the marketing manager detailed his discussion with the state's head of the department of education.

The waiter cleared his throat.

Both men went silent at the break in protocol and glared at the waiter.

"My apologies for the interruption, but there are two ladies waiting in the next room who want to meet with you. Here is the card for one of them."

The CEO pulled his glasses up over his nose and looked down at the business card like it was contaminated with anthrax.

"You've got to be kidding me. The reclusive Margaret Mellon?"

The CEO looked at the marketing manager for a moment and said, "Stay with me. I may need you to listen to this discussion. It might be good for us to have a relationship with the Mellon Bank."

Addressing the waiter, the CEO said, "Thank you, show them in."

Two women entered the corporate breakfast room, and neither looked like Margaret Mellon. The two men stood up to greet the ladies but were slightly confused as to who they were.

Maggie removed the brunette wig, the hat that partially blocked the view of her face, and the padded-body London Fog coat that made her look overweight.

Maya removed her veiled sun hat; tilted her head back; shook her long, silky, black hair; and said, "I hate having to wear a costume."

The marketing manager said in an octave higher than he intended, "Dr. Cherokee?"

Margaret said, "Thank you, gentlemen, for seeing us. I know we just barged in here on you, but you are quite gracious for accommodating us. I guess I don't need to introduce you to Maya."

The CEO asked, "How did you know we were here? Is it that well-known in the business community that we conduct business in this restaurant?"

Maya said half-jokingly, "We have this room bugged." She wondered whether it was true, knowing Tony Vinci had his nanodevices everywhere.

The startled CEO started to say something, but Maggie interrupted him and said, "No, we don't have this room bugged, but it is fairly well-known that you meet here for breakfast regularly. I would occasionally sweep this place for listening devices if I were you."

Maggie continued, "The reason we are here is that we would like to make an offer to World Publishing House for a small fraction of your publishing empire."

The CEO said, "Who is 'we'?"

"The Media Transformation Foundation."

The marketing manager leaned over and whispered, "You mean it is real? I've read about it in a conspiratorial context, but no one ever confirmed its existence. The two of you are part of it? Amazing."

The CEO regained control of the conversation and asked, "What part of our operation are you proposing to acquire and why? We have no reason to divest any sector of our publications."

Maya smiled, her radiant blue eyes mesmerized the marketing manager, but the CEO maintained focus when she opened her purse and pulled out a Post-It note with writing already on it. She said, "Check out this website. It contains a link to a report prepared by Wichita State University, fact-checked by Liberty University, and peer-reviewed by the Media Research Center, the Heritage Foundation, and Hillsdale College.

"The conclusion of the report, yet unpublished, is that textbooks published by World Publishing House contain numerous inaccuracies."

She stopped, let the message sink in, and then added, "The inaccuracies are in textbooks published to educate our children."

Margaret Mellon said, "It is not our intent to damage the reputation of World Publishing House. We just want to fix a problem. The easiest way to fix this problem is to buy the sector that needs to be fixed and republish textbooks."

The marketing manager said, "The publication of textbooks is one of our largest business units. It is unlikely that The Media Transformation Foundation could afford to buy out the entire sector."

Maggie answered, "The inaccuracies we speak of are limited to American history. The Educational Research Analysts' biased interpretation of American history reflects an ideological intent to rewrite history.

As an example, twice as many soldiers (most of them white) died fighting to free the slaves in the civil war than died fighting in Vietnam. If you read your history book, you would get the idea all white men were slave owners. The administration in charge of freeing the slaves was Republican. Your text books paint republicans as racist.

Democrats fought to keep blacks in slavery and passed the discriminatory Black Codes and Jim Crow laws. Democrats started the Ku Klux Klan to lynch and terrorize blacks. Democrats fought to prevent the passage of every civil rights law beginning with the civil rights laws of the 1860s and continuing with the civil rights laws of the 1950s and 1960s. It was Republican President Dwight Eisenhower who pushed to pass the Civil Rights Act of 1957 and sent troops to Arkansas to desegregate schools.

Your text books conveniently fail to cover that part of American history. As a result, we'd like to make an offer to acquire your American history textbook business—not the entire textbook business line."

"No," the CEO answered.

"Sir," said Maya, "you haven't heard our offer. It may be to the company's and your stockholders' advantage."

"No. We're not interested. Now, if you will leave, I have other business to attend to."

On the way out, Maya said, "Be sure to read the information on the website I just gave you. Have a good day, gentlemen."

The following day, an article appeared in the *Wall Street Journal,* Fox Business News' digital site, *The Washington Times, Barons, Market Watch,* and *Financial Times*: FALSE INFORMATION PUBLISHED IN TEXTBOOKS

"New York City—A recent report prepared jointly by multiple American universities identifies misinformation and disinformation inserted in textbooks used by more than sixty percent of American school systems. A reliable source claims that textbooks published by World Publishing House may have intentionally inserted incorrect information to rewrite history and advance the publisher's ideology. The report notes that World Publishing House exercised little, if any, quality control or journalistic integrity—the publisher was more concerned about social responsibility than facts."

Later, the same day, radio, television, and digital outlets covered the subject of the posted polarizing article.

The value of *World Publishing House* stock dropped sixteen percent on the first day the news hit the stands.

On Maya's flight back to Wiscasset, she surfed the financial news outlets to see the impact of the article on the publisher's stock value. She thought, "This is what conservatives have endured for years. Now, the 'foe is on the other shoot.'"

CHAPTER 42

"I don't make jokes. I just watch the government and report the facts."—Will Rogers, 1879-1935, journalist, humorist, and actor

Philadelphia, Pennsylvania – October 6th

They looked out the windows at the passing of the back side of life—laundry pinned to lines on back porches, rusted washing machines leaning against chain-link fences, trailers backed up to loading docks, trash littering empty parking lots, and broken windows in abandoned textile factories. Tucker, Maya, and Star rode Amtrak from Boston to Washington, DC. Tucker wore a brown fedora pulled down low. Maya wore a blonde wig and a wide brim hat. They hoped no one would recognize them.

On the train ride down, Star received geography and history lessons. She learned not only about the rich history of Philadelphia but also about the history of the railroad, its significance in the advancement of humankind, and the science behind the development of coal-fired steam, diesel, and electric engines. She learned that locomotives with as much as four thousand horsepower could pull twenty thousand tons. Star was a fact sponge.

Star asked, "Why are we stopping in Philadelphia?"

Tucker said, "What would happen if you discovered that all the facts you just learned about the history of Philadelphia and the railroad were false?"

Star answered, "I'd be angry that you and Mom taught me things that were wrong?"

Maya added, "And you'd lose confidence that anything we told you would be accurate. Facts shouldn't be malleable. It is a fact that gravity exists. It is not a fact why it exists. It is a fact that the earth rotates on its axis. Hence, the sun rises from the east every day. It is not a fact that the world will end because people burn coal to stay warm.

"We're getting off Amtrak in Philadelphia to visit an organization that was created to make sure that statements made by people, or facts published by journalists, are correct. Someone has to do it."

Tucker wanted to push the kill switch when he heard pundits quote "facts" that were not facts. He said, "Who controls what is fact and what is not fact? I liked the concept of fact-checking websites until I learned that fact-checking was funded by Gabriel Lakatos. I'm afraid he may have influenced the fact-checkers to publish what he 'wanted' the fact to be.

"We're here to check on the fact-checkers."

They arrived at the Philadelphia Thirtieth Street Train Station and, rather than grab a taxi, they decided to walk to the Annenberg Public Policy Center on Thirty-sixth Street—home of FactCheck.org. They stopped on their way and ordered a famous Philly cheesesteak which they split between the three of them, for lunch.

They arrived at the office and were greeted by a delightful receptionist. "Villanova" was spread across her ample chest on her sweatshirt. The Cherokee family was escorted to a small but efficient office of the director of the not-for-profit organization.

Tucker made the appointment as a potential donor without identifying himself. The director expected a visitor but didn't plan to meet with three people. Nor did she expect to see the Cherokee family.

The director's eyes widened, and her jaw dropped when she recognized Maya. Maya Li Cherokee was appointed the science advisor to the former president of the United States. Maya was exceptionally photogenic and was frequently invited to participate in the TV network Sunday morning talk shows. The director stood up, shook Maya's hand, and said, "Dr. Cherokee, what an honor."

Maya smiled and said, "This is my husband, Tucker, and our daughter, Star." Upon meeting the director, Tucker appraised the woman's self-inflicted unattractive appearance and thought, "Some people shouldn't wear tights." Tucker let Maya take the lead since she, more than he, would receive cooperation.

The director said, "What can we do for you?"

With a serious expression on her face, Maya said, "We support the concept of FactCheck.org and are here to donate to the Annenberg Public Policy Center. There is a need for honest reporting, which, sadly, is harder and harder to find. I, personally, have found that it is difficult to identify a source of honest reporting. We'd like to explore your process, your methodology, and your staff, along with their background, their ideology, and their journalistic credentials."

The director was shocked by Maya's inquiry and said, "Dr. Cherokee, you are the first potential donor to request this level of due diligence. I'm afraid we will not be able to grant you the privilege of interviewing our staff."

Maya said, "There is no way FactCheck.org can support the workload required with just interns and undergraduates. You are understaffed. The number of facts that need scrutiny is overwhelming. Last year you received less than one million dollars in contributions for an operation that requires ten times that to do the mission justice. We will donate ten million dollars today to your operation if you meet our conditions for the grant. The funds will be subject to our right to terminate anyone who doesn't comply with our standards and on the condition that you retain ten employees selected by me. And finally, we require our daughter to be interned with the staff for a month each year for the next three years.

"Director, this grant will sustain you for more than a decade at your current burn rate. What do you say?"

The director said, "I don't have the authority to authorize this agreement. I must call the board of directors together with the director emeritus for approval. It will take me a few hours to get confirmation.

"Please, enjoy Philadelphia, and we'll get back to you as soon as possible."

Maya said, "We're taking the next Amtrak down to Union Station in DC. If you want to talk further, call me, and we'll stop on our way back to Boston. Good day, director."

Maya stood, extended her hand to the director, turned, and walked out the door. Tucker followed like a dutiful husband with Star by his side.

They were a block away before they could laugh. Tucker said, "You played her like a cello. I'm pretty sure we just took control of the left-leaning FactCheck.org. What do you think, Star? What was going through the director's head?"

Star said, "She saw job stability and a pay increase coming out of it. She'll lobby hard to meet Mom's conditions. I'm proud of you Mom. You were great."

Maya said, "Thank you, sweetheart. Let's see if we can be equally successful at the Pentagon."

Philadelphia to Washington, DC

The ride from Philadelphia to Union Station in Washington, DC, offered Tucker and Maya an opportunity to strategize.

Tucker said, "You know, Maya, the fake news story we posted in *The New York Times* ended tragically with the murder of the editor by some wacko. I wonder how many fake news stories posted by the mainstream media have damaged lives. Editorial misconduct could be career threatening, if not life-threatening.

"What do you think about establishing a division of FactCheck.org that chases down the damage done when fake news is published? We should hire a real investigative reporter to follow up when dishonest articles are written for the sole reason of advancing an agenda."

Instead of Maya answering, Star interjected, "We could start with the fake news story about Tank and Powers killing Gabriel Lakatos."

Tucker loved her use of the term "we."

Maya said, "Certainly that isn't going to end well for somebody. I think your idea is good, but I'd also like to write fake news stories about the people who write fake news stories. Eventually, these so-called journalists will think twice before they fabricate news."

"Hmmm," Tucker said, "Sounds like a task for the Wichita State University School of Journalism. I'll contact the Hurts."

Arlington, Virginia

The Cherokee family departed the train, walked down the platform, and wondered into the grand vaulted spaces that Washington, DC's Union Station was famous for. Star looked in awe at the ceiling heights of up to ninety-six feet above the floor and the expensive marble, gold leaf details, and white granite used to construct the station back in 1907.

Powers thought it was too risky for Maya and Tucker to take the metro—someone would identify them. So, Powers advised Tucker that someone would wait in a Tesla outside Union Station to escort them to the Pentagon.

Tucker spotted the Model X waiting outside and waved. It pulled up. Star was jumping up and down with excitement, which he found odd until Tucker realized who was driving—Sonja McLeod, Powers' daughter. Star played a role in Powers learning that he had a daughter and in Sonja's bonding with Powers after that. Sonja was a big sister to Star, and they got along very well.

Tucker said, "What a pleasant surprise, Sonja, to get to see you on this trip."

Sonja, all business and conscientiously looking around, said, "Get in, this is not the place to exchange greetings."

The three of them climbed into the back seat. Sonja accelerated and said, "Hi, Star, I have a surprise for you if your parents agree."

Concerned, Maya said, "Agree with what?"

"I'd like to drop you two off at the Pentagon and take Star to the Pentagon City Mall. I know neither of you can take her there because someone will recognize you. Star will enjoy walking the mall like a normal teenager. And you know she is well-protected with me by her side."

Tucker said, "True. Only a fool would threaten Star with you around to protect her. Maya, what do you think? It would be good for Star."

Star begged, "Please, please, please."

Maya asked, "Don't we need her with us at the Pentagon?"

Tucker said, "Maybe at our second meeting. We should be able to do without her mind-reading skills at this first meeting."

Maya nodded, and Star screamed with joy.

Tucker and Maya taught Star on the way down from Philadelphia that the Pentagon construction started on September 11, 1941, during World War II. The "coincidence" of 9/11 was not lost on Star. They taught her that the Pentagon was one of the most massive office buildings in the world with six million square feet and twenty-three thousand employees. What Star didn't realize was that the location was once swampland and that many tons of soil had to be brought in to stabilize the foundation.

Sonja dropped Tucker and Maya off at the Potomac River side of the Pentagon near the metro exit. Tucker felt the hair on the back of his neck raise. He sensed that they were being followed. Tucker looked around but saw no one that appeared to be too interested in them. He could tell the difference between a stare at Maya by men that admired her beauty and men that were observing her to keep track of her whereabouts.

Halfway up the stairs to the north entrance, Tucker was grabbed from behind. His instincts and training caused him to drop low, grab the man's wrists, lift straight up, and force the attacker to fall to the ground.

Only it didn't work. Although Tucker weighed over 210 pounds, his move had no impact on the aggressor. He felt like a child trying to out-muscle his father.

The man said, "Whoa there, Tucker, I don't want to have to hurt you."

Military Police officer Major Javier Castro stood behind Tucker with two other MPs who were equally intimidating. One of them restrained Maya, who had started into a defensive move only to have her excellent hand-to-hand combat skills mitigated.

Tucker said, "Major Castro, what are you doing here?"

He answered, "I could ask you the same question. You wouldn't impede a federal investigation, would you? You wouldn't be here to investigate Blackstone's murder on your own, would you? The investigation of Commander Blackstone's murder is not your job. If I find out you've been trying to get involved in my investigation, I'll have your ass thrown in jail. Do you understand?"

Tucker answered, "I don't trust the military to clean up its own internal mess. I'm sure you're competent, major, but you're only a major. You must take orders from people that outrank you, which, by the way, represents most of the people in this building. I trust you, but I don't trust orders you may be given to sweeping this incident under the rug. I'll share with you everything I learn, but I won't be shut down. I am a civilian, and you have no authority over me."

The two intimidating MPs stood next to Tucker and Maya. People stared at the confrontation between Major Castro and Tucker but didn't stop or want to get involved.

Castro said, "I understand you have an appointment with Brigadier General Ronald Zax. What the hell do you expect to gain by alerting him that you even know who he is? You walk in there with a former advisor to the president, and his antenna is going to pick up vibrations. He's going to vector out of here before we gather enough evidence to interrogate him, much less convict him."

Tucker pulled in close to the major and whispered, "Fair enough. Maya will stay behind, and I'll go in alone, but with a device that allows you to not only listen but view everything that goes on while I'm in there. I promise you, Major, I'll ask him nothing that alarms him and nothing that will make him suspicious. The primary reason for my visit is to leave the device behind. Here, take my mini-pad. Maya will show you how to access the audio and video feed."

Major Castro said, "Wait, just one minute. You're talking about leaving a bug in the general's office in the Pentagon. You must be out of your fucking mind. Do you know how many laws we'd break?"

Tucker said, "Major if we're right, General Zax is guilty of the murder of a military officer and treason. This bug would be placed in his office by a citizen 'without your knowledge.' Whatever information we get out of the use of this device will never become exposed and could never hold up in military court. But we'll know of his guilt or innocence. What happens after that will be up to you. Commander Blackstone was my friend. I owe him this."

Maya intentionally interrupted, "Where can I find a good cup of coffee in the Pentagon, Major Castro? I understand there's a Starbucks in there somewhere."

Tucker followed Maya's lead and didn't give Castro a chance to think about it. He turned, walked up the steps to the entrance, and shuffled to the security desk.

"I have an appointment with Brigadier General Ronald Zax. Would you let him know I am here in the lobby?"

A tall, athletic-looking woman dressed in crisp military dress came down to the lobby and asked, "Are you, Mr. Cherokee?" He nodded and extended his hand, which she dutifully shook.

She said, "Follow me." He followed her to the security checkpoint, placed his briefcase on the conveyor belt, removed all objects from his pockets, put his wallet and watch in a tray, and walked through the full-body scanner. He hoped like hell that Tony Vinci was right and that the device in his briefcase would not be noticed going through the x-ray and explosive detection systems.

Once through security, Tucker followed the twenty-something Air Force lieutenant for what seemed to be miles until they arrived at the windowless office of General Zax.

The lieutenant saluted a small man barely visible behind his over-sized desk. His loud, deep, baritone voice, however, sounded like it belonged to a man twice his size, "Thank you, Lieutenant, that will be all."

He looked Tucker directly in the eye and said, "Why are you here, Mr. Cherokee?"

"General, are you familiar with Entropy, LLC.? We're a contractor that specializes in commercializing unclassified defense-related research. Here, let me show you a brochure."

Tucker reached into his briefcase and pulled out a couple of flyers. He left his briefcase open for the nanodevice—controlled by Tony Vinci—to escape.

"Mr. Cherokee, I did a little background check on you before you arrived. With all due respect, you're not here to drop off a couple of brochures.

"Why *are* you here? A man in your position and with your connections has no reason to waste time introducing your company to me. You have the influence to have a private meeting with the SecDef. I repeat, why are you here?"

Tony Vinci had the nanodevice operational in time for Major Castro to watch and listen to the interaction between General Zax and Tucker. Castro groaned when he heard Zax challenge Tucker.

Most of the time, Tucker was quick on his feet with an ability to extemporaneously come up with a story. He responded, "You're right. But I did a little research on you too."

Major Castro watched the interview go south and his case fall apart.

Tucker continued, "What I hear is that you are likely to be promoted to run all of the Department of Defense communications and press releases worldwide. You will be responsible for flag officer and general officer announcements, Defense TV, Defense Department social media accounts, press advisories, DOD live blogs, speeches, special reports, RSS, the Defense Visual Information Distribution Service, newswire alerts, and advertising, including the sponsoring of NASCAR drivers.

"I wanted to make sure you knew who Entropy is before you get too busy with the enormous job ahead of you."

The general asked, "From whom did you hear this?"

Tucker smiled and said, "As you said, I'm well connected."

Peterson AFB, Colorado

Major Castro could have delegated the onerous and boring task of listening for days to General Zax's private discussions in his Pentagon office, but he didn't want anyone to know what he was doing. He knew he was overstepping legal boundaries.

What he didn't know was that Tony Vinci also had a nanodevice in Zax's home.

CHAPTER 43

"The threat is usually more terrifying than the thing itself." –Saul Alinsky, 1909-1972, author of *"Rules for Radicals"*

Pentagon City Mall, Arlington, Virginia – October 6th

Star was not interested in shopping in the Pentagon City Mall, but she was enjoying the freedom of walking around, people watching, and seeing other kids her age wandering floors. But most of all, she enjoyed being with Sonja.

Sonja asked, "Do you get away from your parents much?"

Star said, "No, they're a little overprotective. They're always afraid someone is going to kidnap me."

Sonja said, "Well, Star, can you blame them? Someone did try to kidnap you when you were six years old. Do you have friends at school?"

"Nah, they pulled me out of school and decided to home-school me."

The two of them walked through Nordstrom's upper level, looked at girls' clothing, strolled to the store escalator to a lower level, and continued talking.

Sonja asked, "Why did they pull you out of the private school you were in?

"It was my fault."

"What do you mean?"

"I came home every day and told Mom or Dad that someone in class or a teacher had serious problems. I told them that two friends of mine and a teacher were abused at home. I told them that a teacher in school had ugly thoughts about sex with kids. Mom and Dad would always want to do something about it."

"Does that mean you don't have any friends?"

Star answered, "You're my friend, aren't you?"

Sonja felt sad for Star and remembered too late about Star's uniqueness.

Star said, "You don't need to be sad for me, Sonja, I'm OK."

They visited the Apple store, Things Remembered, Calvin Klein, GAP, and American Eagle Outfitters, where Sonja bought a black lace-up T-shirt.

Sonja asked, "Are you OK with your parents taking you to their business meetings for the sole purpose of using your skill to decide whether they can trust their business associates?"

Star's laugh was genuine and natural, a child's giggle, "They don't want me to go to the meetings with them. They argue about it all the time. Dad thinks they are exposing me to danger. He feels like I'm being used and am missing my childhood. But I want to be a detective when I grow up. I've got this talent no one else has. I might as well make use of it as my grandfather did. He made a gazillion dollars at the poker table with this skill that skips a generation.

"Mom agrees with Dad except that I want to 'learn' how to use it. By going with Mom and Dad to these meetings, I help them, and they help me learn."

Sonja said, "It never occurred to me that it was your idea."

Star smiled a knowing smile and said, "I know.

"Can we go to the food court, that's where all the other kids are."

"Sure."

Sonja and Star walked casually around the food court floor until Star stiffened.

Sonja asked, "Star, what is it?"

A child of about ten sat at a table by herself. No food or drinks were spread on the table top.

Star approached the little girl and said, "Hi, I'm Star. What's your name?"

The little girl did not answer and looked away. She was a thin African-American with a cute red bow in her curly jet-black hair. She wore a dress with flowers patterns, frilly white socks, and black vinyl shoes.

Star asked, "Are your mom and dad here with you?"

The girl didn't answer.

Her eyes widened and stared at Star incredulously when Star said, "Amber, it's OK. What would you like to eat?"

Sonja asked, "Star, what's going on?"

Star asked the little girl, "How long have your mom and dad been gone?"

The little girl shrugged her tiny shoulders.

Sonja repeated, "Star?"

Star said, "I think her parents are in trouble. Amber thinks two men forced them into the parking garage to answer questions. Her mom said she'd be right back, but that was a long time ago. She's hungry; let's get her something to eat."

Sonja looked around the food court. Nothing seemed out of order. They bought Amber a McDonald's happy meal and sat with her while she ate. Sonja noticed that

Amber kept turning to look at a specific mall exit to the garage. A man was standing just inside the entranceway talking on his cell phone—or pretending to be talking.

Sonja asked, "Is that the direction your mom and dad went with the men?"

She nodded her head as she stuffed French fries into her mouth. Sonja wanted to check it out but would not let Star out of her sight.

Sonja said, "Amber, Star and I are going to see if we can find your mom and dad. We'll be right back."

Amber spoke for the first time, "No, please, please, stay with me. I'm scared."

Sonja noticed that a man twenty yards away kept sneaking glances in their direction as he spoke on his cell phone. She looked around to see whether any other man resembled the first man who was also on a cell phone. There were about six of them; too many to tie to the first man.

Sonja thought that the food court was way too busy for someone to grab a child without being noticed by people with cell phone cameras. If the man was a threat to this child, he was waiting for something. Then it dawned on her: the restrooms were near the same entranceway. He was waiting for her to go to the bathroom. Sonja kept her observation to herself until she could confirm the threat.

Star talked to the little girl about where she lived, where she went to school, and what she did for fun for about fifteen minutes. The man did not move, though he quit talking on the phone. He concentrated on texting or appearing to be texting.

Amber started to slide off her chair and said, "Excuse me, I have to go to the bathroom."

Star said, "Let me go with you."

Sonja said, "No, you stay here. Let her go by herself."

Star frowned, stared into Sonja's eyes, and nodded. She got it.

Sonja looked around to see whether anyone nearby could be a threat to Star, who was her first priority. Then she walked casually away from Star in front of Amber in the direction of the lady's room.

The man shifted on his feet, stopped working his cell phone, and slipped a hand in the side pocket of his sports coat.

Sonja was still unsure whether the man was after Amber or she was just being paranoid.

He brought a handkerchief from his pocket and took a step in the direction of the rest room. Still, there was no evidence he was guilty of anything.

Amber suddenly stopped, her face contorted, her hands brought to her mouth—she recognized him as one of the men who had asked her mom to go with him. He took another step in Amber's direction when Sonja said, "Scream, Amber! Scream!"

The man turned to look at Sonja just in time to see the heel of her boot.

Amber screamed, Sonja yelled, and Star screamed. The commotion caused others to scream in fear. "What's going on?"

Two Pentagon City security officers were on-site in thirty seconds to find a man lying face down on the floor with his arms behind him and flex-cuffed.

Arlington City police arrived five minutes later.

Sonja told the police that if they checked his handkerchief, they'd find chloroform on it. She explained the child's story and said she and Star would gladly cooperate with the police investigation.

Sonja called Maya and explained the situation. Maya arrived six minutes later, grabbed Star, and embraced her with a tight heartfelt hug.

Sonja said, "Maya, Star was never in danger."

Star said, "Mom, I couldn't just ignore the girl. She needed our help. I know you want me to stop it, but I'm just like you and Dad, I want to fix things that are broken."

CHAPTER 44

"Everything is funny, as long as it's happening to somebody else." –Will Rogers, 1879-1935, journalist, humorist, and actor.

Wiscasset, Maine – October 8th

Tucker was back in his home office directing activities for Entropy, his day job, when he received a call from Major Castro.

The major asked, "Is this a good time to talk?"

Tucker asked, "How secure is your line? Mine is secure."

"The same."

"Shoot."

"I think the general is clean. While under surveillance, no inappropriate or compromising discussions were overheard that provide evidence against him in our case. Do you have anything?"

Tucker asked, "Are you recording our conversation?"

"No, it would only incriminate me."

Tucker continued "Zax is trying to gather information as to who killed Commander Blackstone. That would imply he didn't have an active role in the commander's murder and is attempting to solve the crime on his own. To date, he's not found a lead."

"How do you know this?"

Tucker didn't answer his question but added, "There is one more person on Blackstone's list who we haven't investigated."

"The civilian?"

"Yes, she is a TS-cleared person who provides IT support—a geek—to the Pentagon. She probably knows secrets that transcend different departments. I understand she also participates in antiwar rallies and is an active member of Code Pink."

Major Castro asked, "How does she keep her TS clearance?"

"I don't know, but my guess is her employer is unaware of her activities."

"How did you come across this information?"

Tucker sounded exasperated when he said, "Major, I told you back in Colorado Springs that I could help your investigation. Her name is Eboni Williamson. When I get more, I'll pass it along. In the meantime, maybe we need to keep the Colorado Springs homicide detective informed. Someone should interview her. I'd ask him if he has anything. As far as I know, I'm still his only person of interest."

Major Castro said, "I spoke to him yesterday. If he has anything, he's keeping it close to the vest."

They hung up, and Tucker called Tony. "Have you placed a nanodevice in the home of Eboni Williamson yet?"

"Of course. She lives in Prince George County in Maryland."

"And?"

"I take it you need me to run the data through my algorithm?"

"Call me if you get a hit."

Hours later, Tucker had accumulated relevant facts that he believed were important to Castro's case.

"Major, this is Tucker Cherokee."

"Yes, Tucker, what do you have?"

"I have a recorded a conversation with a low-level Code Pink officer if that's what you call them. The conversation basically says that if there is a one-world government, there would be no need for a military, and world peace would follow."

Castro said, "OK, but that doesn't make her a suspect in the killing of Blackstone."

Tucker said, "True, but she mentioned Commander Blackstone's name in the conversation. Said that they hurdled one roadblock."

Major Castro said, "She is unlikely to be the killer, but she may know who is and who ordered it. Someone at Peterson Air Force Base had to take the photos of you with Blackstone and write the note. Do you have the wherewithal to find out if a telephone call to the base was made by Williamson?"

"Does a monkey have a climbing gear? Anything on your side?"

Castro answered, "The medical examiner completed the autopsy. Cause of death was head trauma. We're looking for a baseball bat or something similar as the murder weapon. It doesn't look like a professional hit. And I don't mean a 'hit' in baseball."

CHAPTER 45

"Power is not only what you have but what the enemy thinks you have." - Saul Alinsky, 1909-1972, author of "*Rules for Radicals*"

Washington, DC – October 8th

George Stephanopoulos knew in advance that he would have his hands full interviewing former Senator Powers on ABC's *This Week* Sunday morning talk show. He'd seen Senator Powers in action during a prior hearing. The ABC staff had assembled a long list of questions to ask him with the sole purpose of trying to bring Powers to a boil—something that could be replayed several times during the following week. It would make great theatre. George's strategy was to throw Powers a few softballs to soften him up and then zing him with a hardball, close and inside.

Three, two, one, "Good morning. Today we have a special guest, the former senator from Maine, the colorful no-nonsense, straight-talking Powers." George looked over at Powers and continued, "We're glad to have you on the set today. You've been absent from the spotlight for a couple of years. How's civilian life?"

Powers said, "George, you didn't ask me here to talk about my private life, and I doubt anyone watching your show cares. Let's talk about why I agreed to surrender my usually pleasant Sunday morning routine to be here with you. Hell, I even wore a tie just for your audience. I'm not generally this pretty."

Stephanopoulos laughed disingenuously and said, "OK, then let's get down to it. You are a partner in the largest, most successful personal security company in the nation, White Knight Personal Security, LLC. You protect dignitaries, families of billionaires, and performers. You provide security for special events and heads of states. To thwart attacks, you must be well-armed. No doubt, some of your work is offensive and not just defensive in nature. With that background, what is your stand on gun control?"

Powers half expected this question and was prepared. "First, thank you for the free advertisement. That was perfect. Are we done?"

Stephanopoulos gave a nervous laugh and said, "Back to gun control."

Powers said, "I'm in favor of it. Let's pass a law that keeps guns out of the hands of criminals. Maybe we should outlaw murder."

"Seriously, Powers, don't you think we need stronger background checks to keep guns out of the hands of the mentally ill? And why should a person need an AR-15 assault weapon?"

Powers said with a straight face, "I think liberals and progressives are mentally ill and we need to keep guns out of their hands."

George Stephanopoulos twisted in his seat and said, "You just insulted the watching audience."

Powers ignored the comment and said, "My point is, once we go down that road, it becomes a slippery slope. Whose judgment prevails? For example, Senator Feinstein of California thinks anyone that served in the military is mentally ill. And by the way, she is for gun control as long as she is protected by people with guns.

"Now that I think about it, I think *she* is mentally ill. Why do you liberals ignore the fact that the cities with the strongest gun control laws have the nation's highest murder rates? Cities like Chicago and Baltimore.

"As a practical matter, American civilians have 270 million guns. Good luck taking them away from the owners. Blaming the gun is like blaming the car for death by DUI.

"To answer an earlier question, the reason to have an AR-15 is to use them when the government comes and tries to take their guns away."

It was time for Stephanopoulos to throw a fast ball. "Have you ever killed someone?"

"George, I would have been a pathetic Army Special Forces operative if I had never killed someone. You want me to demonstrate?"

Stephanopoulos smiled and said, "It's time for a commercial break."

During the commercial, George said to Powers, "Kids are dying in school shootings because mentally ill boys are allowed access to assault weapons. I'm going to ask you what we should do about it. Be prepared."

The commercial timeline filled, and the green light let Stephanopoulos know they were live. "We're here with the outspoken, straight-talking former senator from Maine, Mr. Powers.

"Senator, your partner, the CEO of White Knight Personal Security, Tank Alvarez, is a person of interest in the murder of the philanthropist, Gabriel Lakatos. In fact, I understand there is a note signed by a Canadian that confessed to his role in the assassination. And, as I understand it, he named your partner as being complicit in the crime. It's not a leap of logic for those watching today's show that if, in fact, your partner is culpable, you must have known something about the murder. Given the business that you're in, it seems quite possible that to protect one of your clients, it was necessary to terminate the billionaire. What do you have to say about the accusation?"

Powers wanted to reach out and grab Stephanopoulos by the throat and squeeze until his eyes bulged. An attack on Tank like this with hundreds of thousands, if not millions, of people watching was unconscionable. Instead, he responded, "Your watching audience probably understands that you're grandstanding question is strictly for ratings. They know that there is a lot of pressure on you to attract more advertisers than Fox News Sunday.

"The reason my partner is not indicted is that he is innocent of the charge. His alibi is airtight. What will be interesting is whether you'll invite me back here when the truth of who is trying to frame him is revealed. I also think your listening audience is offended by your blatant character assassination of my partner. Whatever happened to the 'innocent until proven guilty' sense of justice? Your ideological nearsightedness prevents your listening audience from receiving the truth."

The coloring on Stephanopoulos's face changed, but he maintained composure. "Finally, I'd like to ask you what we should do to keep assault weapons out of the hands of teenagers hell-bent on killing students and teachers in schools?"

Powers' body language expressed frustration. The lines in his face grew more pronounced, he grit his teeth, and his dark eyes narrowed. He said, "If I were still in the Senate, I'd support a law giving local communities the right to protect themselves against the very small number of batshit crazies that want to kill fellow students. I'd guess that millions of retired military personnel would love to support their community by providing armed protection for their grandchildren in public schools. I guarantee you that a retired Ranger or SEAL would be honored to serve their community and education system as security volunteers. A punk with an AR-15 would be no match for a volunteer retired SEAL.

"And finally, I reach out to your listening audience and say to you, take responsibility for your child. If he or she needs mental health help, make sure they get it."

"Thank you, retired Senator Powers, for coming here today. You are a fascinating guest. Now from our sponsors."

George Stephanopoulos addressed Powers during the break, "You'll never be invited back to ABC's *This Week* again. I'll make sure of that."

Powers said, "Facts are important, George. Try to get them straight."

Wiscasset, Maine

The Washington Times: *Arlington, Virginia* – "Pentagon City Security with support from Arlington police apprehended a man attempting to kidnap a ten-year-old child in the food court at Pentagon City Mall. The alleged kidnapper, twenty-eight-year old Marko Kovac, led detectives to a site near the mall where the parents of the child were held captive and interrogated by Serbian illegal immigrants. As of this writing, the purpose of the criminal activity is unknown. The parents are reunited with their daughter and are residing in a safehouse until more information is gathered."

Tucker said to Star, "Well, Sweetheart, you and Sonja did good and helped little Amber live another day and be reunited with her parents."

Star's eyes revealed a touch of sparkle, and her face showed that she had something to say.

"What is it?"

"The jerk was going to torture Amber in front of her parents to get them to talk."

"Do you know what they wanted to learn from her parents?"

Star hesitated to answer but finally asked, "Where is Serbia?"

"Serbia is in eastern Europe, northwest of Greece, why?"

"Why would his brother be in jail in Virginia?"

Tucker asked, "What are you saying—they wanted to find out where a brother was, what jail he was in?"

Star said, "I think so."

Tucker got on the phone and called the Arlington Police Department and eventually reached the case officer.

"Detective, my daughter was on the scene when the Serbian was apprehended. She heard him say that he was trying to free his brother in prison. I thought that information would be useful to your investigation."

Tucker hung up before he could ask him any questions.

CHAPTER 46

"Print is the sharpest and the strongest weapon of our party." – Joseph Stalin, 1878-1953, ruled the Soviet Union from the mid-1920s until his death

New York City, New York – October 10th

The courthouse was always busy, but today it was a zoo. The zookeepers, in the form of security, denied Tucker access to the courtroom unless he surrendered his satellite phone, cell phone, encrypted mini-pad, digital camera, and any other electronic device he carried in his suitcase. Unwilling to give them up, Tucker fought his way back out the courthouse hallway, through a clogged stairwell, and into the parking lot. Crowds like this gave Tucker the creeps. The press corps was bad enough, but the looky-loos and protestors added to a Mardi Gras-type atmosphere. He wouldn't have been surprised if KISS was out there somewhere.

Tucker wished he had one of Tony Vinci's undetectable nanodevices or had instructed him to insert one in the courtroom, but he hadn't. Tucker placed all of his electronic devices in the truck of his rental car.

He had an uncomfortable feeling like his fly was down, or he locked his keys in the car, or his wallet wasn't in his back trouser pocket. Sensing queasiness, he thought maybe he was coming down with something.

Tucker pushed his way through the crowd, noticing that almost everyone was either speaking on their phone, texting, sending emails or playing a game. He realized his unidentified "feeling" was that he felt naked without his iPhone.

The throng outside the courthouse grew with additional reporters, vans with satellite dishes, and hundreds of people carrying signs and megaphones. New York's finest collected around the area, directed traffic and intermingled with the crowd.

He knew what was coming.

Tucker passed through security and found a place to sit in the back of the courtroom trying to look like just another courthouse lawyer. He wore a navy-blue Brooks Brother suit, a red and blue striped tie, a white shirt, and recently shined wingtips. He carried a leather clipboard and appeared to be prepared to duteously take notes.

"Everyone, please rise for the Honorable Judge Michael Levine." The judge walked briskly in his long black robe and pushed his glasses up from low on his nose with his middle finger. He had thick gray hair and wore an expression that resembled a smile but was actually a genetic misplacement of bone structure. He sat down, slammed down the gavel, and said, "The court is in session. Will both the plaintiff and defendant's attorneys please approach the bench."

They both knew they were going to get their asses chewed.

"Obviously," said Judge Levine, "you two are determined to waste the court's time." He looked over his Ben Franklin spectacles directly into the green eyes of the plaintiff's attorney and said, "If I have even a tiny bit of suspicion that your claims are exaggerated and frivolous, I'll stop you in midsentence and shut these proceedings down."

He turned his head to the attorney for the defendant and said, "If I detect grandstanding on your part and a deliberate attempt to extend the duration of this trial for the drama, there will be profound consequences for your client."

Judge Levine raise his voice to the court assistant and said, "The jury may now join us."

Tucker observed the jury makeup as they glided into the jury box. Half of the jurors were senior citizens, four older women, and two grumpy-looking old men. He wondered how they'd gotten through the jury selection process. The women seemed excited, sneaking looks at the handsome and famous defense attorney with his long silver hair, deerskin sports jacket, and turquoise bolo tie.

The first of the two old men looked like he couldn't stay awake while walking past the judge to the juror's box. Tucker had no doubt that the old man would nod off during opening arguments. The other geriatric man was the antithesis of the first; he seemed wired, looking from side-to-side, observing everything until he fixed his gaze on Tucker. The man recognized him.

What Tucker noticed about the younger six jurors was their attire. Walmart polyester made-in-China specials. One wore a New York Giants sweatshirt and dirty tennis shoes. He thought, "There needs to be a dress code for jurors."

Judge Levine addressed the assembled jury. "Ladies and gentlemen, thank you in advance for your service to the judicial system. This case is a civil case. Your job is to determine whether the preponderance of the evidence justifies that the defendant, in this case, MSNBC, should be held legally responsible for the damages alleged by the plaintiff, the extensive list of organizations, institutions, competitors, magazines, schools, research centers, and other entities. You will also be charged with the task of determining the size of the plaintiff's damages if, in fact, there are any real damages. From time to time during this trial, I'll provide you with instructions and an opportunity to ask the court questions.

"Is that clear?"

It appeared to Tucker that at least four of the jurors had no idea what the judge had just said."

Tucker knew it was coming and it came. He could hear the crowd outside starting to make a fuss.

Judge Levine ordered, "Counselor, please proceed with your opening statements."

The senior partner in the famous New York law firm stood well over six feet tall and wore a five-thousand-dollar suit. He flashed a brilliant smile at the jurors, spread his arms wide, palms visible, and said, "MSNBC lied to the public, intentionally misreported the news, abrogated its responsibility for journalistic integrity, failed to self-regulate, fabricated fake news, colluded to misinform its viewers, heavy handedly smothered news it didn't want its audience to hear, lacked ethics, and desecrated the First Amendment of the Constitution.

"Ladies and gentlemen, the list of damaged entities that could pile into this class-action claim against MSNBC could include almost half of the population of the United States. This claim against MSNBC is to penalize them for lying to us. There must be some sort of penalty for a trusted news agency to lie to its viewing audience to support its narrative.

"This case is a critical case. You are burdened with the responsibility of holding journalists, reporters, editors, and publishers to a standard of integrity and honesty. You have a chance to reinstate truthfulness to the news reporting industry. Hundreds of millions of people will thank you for bringing trust back to a profession that devolved into arms of political parties. You jurors are important to our future. Let's put an end to 'fictitious facts' and fake news. Find in favor of the plaintiff. Thank you."

The noise outside the courthouse increased in volume. Tucker wondered whether the protestors could stop the trial.

The judge continued, "Will the defense proceed?"

The flamboyant defense attorney stood up, ran his fingers through his thick, silver-gray hair, strutted in the direction of the jury box, and said with a booming Texas-accented baritone voice, "Thank you, judge.

"The plaintiff said that MSNBC lied to the public, intentionally misreported the news, abrogated its responsibility for journalistic integrity, failed to self-regulate, fabricated fake news, colluded to misinform its viewers, heavy handedly smothered news it didn't want its audience to hear, lacked ethics, and desecrated the First Amendment of the Constitution.

"Wow," he emphasized, "that sounds like something a politician would do, doesn't it?"

A couple of the jurors laughed.

"At the end of this trial, you have to ask yourself three questions. First, how was the plaintiff damaged? Second, as Judge Levine explained, does the preponderance of the evidence justify that MSNBC should be held legally responsible for the damages alleged by the plaintiff? Third, what was the motive for the alleged intentional misrepresentation?

"The plaintiff will tell you that the motive was ideological, that MSNBC is merely an arm of a liberal agenda, and that promoting a progressive belief system outweighed its obligation to report the news."

He waited a couple of seconds before he said, "We will prove that to be patently false.

"We will prove that the plaintiff is not damaged and that the plaintiff will not be able to provide a preponderance of the evidence that MSNBC is responsible for the imagined damage. If there is no damage, there is no case here. You'll find in favor of my client. Thank you."

Tucker thought, "I wish I had a deerskin jacket like that." He was sure some of the jurors were thinking the same thing instead of listening to his opening comments.

"Plaintiff, please state your case."

"Your honor, we call to the stand as our first witness Mr. Tucker Cherokee."

Tucker stood up in the back of the courtroom, feeling a little self-conscious, with all twelve jurors staring at him—the old man with a smile on his face. Tucker was glad the judge denied media coverage of the trial and wondered whether the courtroom artist made him more handsome than he really was or more sinister looking to promote the media narrative. Tucker took his seat and swore on a bible to "tell the truth and nothing but the truth, so help me God."

The plaintiff's attorney stood before Tucker and said, "Mr. Cherokee, you are not listed as one of the plaintiffs, yet we learned through the discovery process," he looked at the defense attorney when he said this, "that you are contributing funds to the plaintiff for this civil suit against MSNBC. You are well-known in some circles as an American hero. You facilitated an agreement between our nation and the People's Republic of China to reduce our national debt by trillions of dollars after you discovered a means to make electricity without fuel. You saved every man, woman, and child in the country tax dollars in doing so."

"Objection, your honor, there was no question asked of the witness and no known relevance to the case."

"Your honor, I am establishing the credibility of the witness for the jury."

Judge Levine said, "Sustained. Get to the point."

"Mr. Cherokee, why are you contributing funds to the plaintiff to try this case in civil court?"

Tucker said, "Because I miss my country."

"Would you elaborate for the jury?"

Tucker continued, "Our divinely inspired forefathers drafted the First Amendment to the Constitution to—"

"Objection, your honor. The witness has no idea if our forefathers were divinely inspired or not."

"Your honor, we asked Mr. Cherokee why he is supporting the plaintiff. He is answering the question, which may include his opinion."

"Overruled. Let Mr. Cherokee answer the question. The attorney for the defendant needs to stop grandstanding. My patience is growing thin. Continue."

Tucker looked directly in the eye of the attorney for the defendant and said, "If I'm allowed to continue my First Amendment right to free speech, I will answer the question honestly. My honest opinion is that at some point during the last decade or so, MSNBC and several other news organizations stopped reporting the news honestly and started reporting a narrative they believed their niche audience wanted to hear. The promoters, producers, and editors began twisting or ignoring facts to suit their target audience. They were successful and unchallenged. Emboldened, they stopped just twisting facts and moved on to fabricating news."

The defense attorney stood, but the judge held his hand up and glared at the man. He sat back down.

The judge said, "The jury is reminded that this is Mr. Cherokee's opinion and his reason for supporting the plaintiff and should not be confused with evidence of damages. You may continue."

Tucker said, "The First Amendment gives us free speech. It does not prevent news organizations from lying or distorting and fabricating news. The defendant has that constitutional right. In theory, a person has the constitutional right to yell 'fire' in a crowded movie theatre, but it's not right, so laws were passed to restrict that right to free speech. It is my hope that this case will force news agencies to reflect on their greed and return to the time-honored purpose of reporting the news."

"Nancy Pelosi, Speaker of the House, and liberal democrat explained, as captured on C-SPAN, how the democratic party works with news media cooperation. She stated that one of the party tactics is to implement a 'wrap-up smear.' Quote: "You smear somebody with falsehoods and then you merchandize it. You [the press] write [about the smear] and then we say, 'see, its reported in the press and we have validation. ' MSNBC is a willing participant in that tactic."

"The symbiotic relationship between the ideological left and the press is used continuously. Examples include the smear of Brent Kavanagh, police with the "hands up, don't shoot" falsehood, the Covington Catholic school kid, the Duke lacrosse team, the Trump dossier, and the Wisconsin Nazi salute fiasco."

Outside, protestors began yelling through megaphones and chanting. The jurors could hear the commotion and started to squirm in their seats. The importance of their decisions dawned on them—it showed in their discomfort.

Down with MSNBC. Down with MSNBC

Tucker continued, "The defendant will claim that there are no damages to the plaintiff.

"That's like a man admitting to assaulting an officer but claiming innocence because the assault didn't hurt the cop. A verdict in favor of the plaintiff could force the news agencies to police themselves. In theory they have ombudsmen, but, apparently, they are either ineffective or overruled by the producers who want to attract an audience, and, therefore, advertisers, who want to hear and believe these fabricated stories. It's all about money.

"Another result of a favorable outcome to this case could be that these news agencies drop the premise that they are reporting the news and start referring to themselves as entertainment channels.

"The damage MSNBC is currently causing is two-fold. The first damage is that the uninformed audience who tunes in to hear the news and believes the garbage they're fed causes unnecessary anxiety. In the worst case, the second damage is from viewers who learn that they can no longer trust the news from any source, which, in turn, damages the honest news reporting entities like those represented by the plaintiff. A result of a recent poll conducted by Monmouth University is that more than 3-in-4 Americans believe that traditional major TV and newspaper media outlets report "fake news."

"Hey, hey, whatya say, no integrity here today.

"This is an extremely important case, and I'm supporting the plaintiff in hopes that all Americans have access to honest reporting."

The plaintiff's attorney said, "Your honor, I'd like to present as Exhibit 'A' a video copy of a report aired on MSNBC that is an example of misreporting the news."

"Objection, your honor. The defendant has not seen the video. It was not presented during discovery."

Judge Levine asked, "Is that true?"

"They did not ask for video examples. If they had asked, the plaintiff would have gladly provided the defendant with a copy."

"Down with MSNBC. Down with MSNBC."

The judge said, "This case is adjourned. I expect the defendant to have seen a copy of Exhibit A before we reconvene. Mr. Cherokee, you may step down."

"Hey, hey, whatya say, no integrity here today."

CHAPTER 47

"I always lose the election in the polls, and I always win it on election day." - Benjamin Netanyahu, 1949-present, Prime Minister of Israel

Colorado Springs, Colorado – October 12th

"**H**ello out there in conservative land, flyover country, heterosexualville, and my born-again friends, this is the Michelle Mallard radio talk show. I'm your host, and it's my honor to take your calls. Today I want to talk about polls, and I'm not talking about people from Poland. Do you trust polls? Do you believe they are honest? Do you wonder about the process used to develop these poll results? We're talking about Rasmussen, Gallop, Nielson, Reuters, CNN, Fox, Nate Silver, ABC, and Harris Polling. I look forward to hearing your opinion.

"Do you trust them? Do you pay attention to them? Do you give a . . . darn?

"Dawn in Manassas, Virginia, what's your opinion?"

"Did any of the polls you mentioned predict the outcome of the last presidential election correctly? I think not. Therefore, the poll methodology is corrupt. So, no, I have no confidence in poll numbers. They're skewed in the direction of the polling company's ideological owners or controllers."

"Well said, Dawn from Manassas. How about you, Erik from Charlotte, North Carolina?"

"Poll algorithms do not use universal data sets that represent outlying parametrics and, therefore, are improperly bounded."

"I'm good with whatever you just said, Erik. Colleen in Charleston, South Carolina, go."

"I trust the polls. Poll takers are like weather forcasterss, they try hard even if they're not always accurate."

Michelle Mallard announced, "Ladies and gentlemen in the listening audience—notice I didn't mention all the new gender options—I'm here to tell you something you won't hear on MSNBC or CNN. I mean beside the truth. Rasmussen, Reuters, and Nielson are under new ownership. The new owners intend to review the poll methodology with the intent to improve accuracy.

"As an example, all Rasmussen Reports' survey questions are digitally recorded and fed to a calling program that determines question order, branching options, and other factors. Calls are placed to randomly-selected phone numbers through a process that ensures appropriate geographic representation.

"Rasmussen Reports determines its partisan weighting targets through a dynamic weighting system that considers the state's voting history, national trends, and recent polling in a particular state or geographic area.

"OK. It's time to take the next caller. David from Greeley, Colorado. What say you? Do you trust the polls?"

"I will trust the polls less now that you right wing neo-Nazis have control of them. Watch your back and tell your buddies that what happened to Commander Blackstone could happen to all of you in your secret society."

Michelle Mallard said, "Uh-oh, is this another right-wing conspiracy call? Is this Hillary Clinton in disguise?

David or whatever your real name is, why would I, a minority, be involved with a neo-Nazi group?"

David said, "It's all about money. You'd sell your mother for money."

"You got your free speech time in. You're out of here."

She continued and said, "I hope the future of science will be able to take DNA and predict who is mentally unstable.

"Next caller, Darlene from Knoxville, Tennessee."

"I was going to talk about polls, but after the last caller, I worry about your safety. I think he meant it. Be careful. Is there a poll on the number of Americans that are crazy like your last caller?"

"Good question. We should start a poll today. I'll start asking callers their opinion as to the percentage of the population that is mentally ill. What's your opinion, Darlene?"

"Hmmm, let me think. I'd say around five percent."

Michelle said, "Let's do the math. There are around 330 million legal citizens. Ten percent would be thirty-three million, so it's half of that or sixteen and a half million crazies out there. That sounds about right.

"Next caller. Sam from Statesville, North Carolina. Do you trust the polls and how many crazies are out there?"

"No, I don't trust the polls. If you poll heavily in Democratic-leaning zip codes, you get a left-leaning answer. If that's the answer the polling company wants, they publish it."

"As far as the mentally ill out there, I think Darlene's estimate is way low. There are over one hundred million liberals and progressives out there, and they are all mentally ill."

"Great answer, Sam, and that's it for today. I'm hunkering down, batting down the hatches, and fortifying my studio to protect myself from the likes of David in Greeley. Talk to you again tomorrow."

The Colorado Springs Homicide Detective Slick White listened to Michelle Mallard's talk radio show. He immediately picked up the phone and called Major Javier Castro. The phone rang five times before Castro picked up.

"Major Castro here."

"Major, I just listened to someone call in to Michelle Mallard's show who threatened her and referenced the murder of Commander Blackstone. He said the same thing might happen to her."

Castro said, "Yes, I was just on the phone when someone else called to share that news with me. I understand he called from Greeley."

"Or so he said. To your knowledge, did Blackstone belong to an outside organization? Is there some connection between him and Mallard?"

"I haven't investigated that angle."

"I'm going to pay a visit to Michelle Mallard. You're welcome to join me."

Vine Cliff Heights

Detective White pushed the security speakerphone button at the gate of Michelle Mallard's estate and waited. Major Castro pointed at two separate video cameras strategically located too high for someone to spray paint the lens.

They waited.

White pushed the button again. A minute later a man's voice came through the speaker. "Yes, how can I help you, officers?"

White spoke into the security speakerphone, "This is Colorado Springs Detective White with Military Police officer Major Javier Castro. We'd like to speak with Michelle Mallard."

"You don't have an appointment with Ms. Mallard. Why do you need to speak with her?"

Slick White was getting a little impatient and said, "Is she home or not? This is police business. I don't have to explain to you what I'm going to discuss with her. What is your name? And why are you obstructing justice?"

"My name is not relevant; I'm head of security and take my job seriously. Please display your badge on the video camera. Both of you."

They did as they were instructed.

"I'm going to take a few minutes to verify your credentials. Please be patient."

Ten minutes passed before they heard the gate lock click and the gates open.

They walked the same 150-yard-long cobblestone driveway with its healthy red, pink, and yellow rose bushes as Tank Alvarez did weeks earlier. Again, standing in the open front double-doors was talk show host, Michelle Mallard.

She said, "Gentlemen, I'm sorry for the inconvenience my security may have caused you, but I can't be too careful. Please come in."

Big Castro had to duck his head down to enter Mallard's home. Both men remained standing in the entrance hall when Michelle asked, "How can I help you?"

White said, "We're investigating the murder of Commander Blackstone and have a few questions for you."

Michelle narrowed her eyes and asked, "Why do you think I might be able to help with your investigation?"

White continued, "You were threatened today by a caller that referenced the murder of Blackstone. The implication of what he said was that you are also a target. Our first question is why did the caller connect you to Blackstone?"

Mallard answered, "Good question. I never met him. Detectives, I get threats almost every day—most via blogs and emails. That's why I have 'immoral' gates and security around my home. It comes with the job as a conservative talk radio host."

Major Castro said, "But he made an accusation that the two of you belong to a secret society? Is that true?"

Michelle hesitated, looked down, and took too long to answer the question.

"Ms. Mallard," said White, "we're trying to solve a murder, not investigate the secret society you and Commander Blackstone belonged to. And your life might be in danger. It's in your best interest to answer the question. It is not a crime to belong to a secret society. It *is* a crime to obstruct justice and perjure yourself if the question is asked of you under oath."

Michelle said, "We're getting close to where I invoke my right to an attorney. But to aid your investigation, I can tell you that Commander Blackstone was a member of one of the same organizations I participate in. Not all members know each other. I did not know him and never spoke to him."

"Are Tank Alvarez and his partner, Powers, members of this organization? Is Tucker Cherokee?"

The question surprised her but she quickly realized that it shouldn't have and said, "I see where you're going with this. You think the same guy that threatened me today may be the same guy who killed Commander Blackstone, left a note accusing Tucker Cherokee of the crime, and framed Tank Alvarez and Powers of the murder of Gabriel Lakatos. Do you think the same guy organized the student assault on my home when Tank and Powers were here?"

White said in an accusatory tone, "Attending a secret society meeting?"

Michelle gave no response.

"By the way, Ms. Mallard, I'm glad you had a permit for that gun you discharged here that night. I see you also have a Utah concealed carry permit. Based on what we've learned here today, I recommend you continue to carry.

"Good evening, Ms. Mallard. Thank you for your cooperation."

CHAPTER 48

"A lie cannot live." – Martin Luther King, 1929-1968, Baptist Minister and a leader of the civil rights movement

Chicago, Illinois – October 15th

Lucas picked up Tank and Powers in a rented black Ford Expedition in front of the United Airlines baggage claim at O'Hare. He'd learned to rent the largest vehicle Avis had for his oversized boss. Before Tank got in, he always moved the seat as far back as it would go. Powers climbed in behind Lucas on the driver's side.

Tank asked, "What's the plan?"

Lucas answered, "First, my plan is to keep you away from Watters. We need hard evidence as to who hired him and proof of your innocence. Then, if you want to beat the pulp out of him, go for it. But he's more likely to speak clearly with all his teeth."

"It's not his teeth I plan to remove."

"Yeah, boss, I get it."

"According to Tony, the guy's name is Rochester Brevard Watters, known by the Chicago police force as Rocky. He retired after twenty and became a private investigator. He struggled financially for months and couldn't get a gig with one of the insurance companies to investigate fraud.

"Now he lives in an expensive condominium on the North Shore overlooking the lake. I'm a better PI than he is. How come you don't pay me the kind of money Rocky must make?"

Tank said, "Because crime pays."

Powers spoke up from the back seat, "You know that our FBI cybercrimes friend, Blackbeard, gave Tucker the same name in connection with a guy named Zimmerman, one of Lakatos's right-hand men?"

Tank and Powers said in unison, "There are no coincidences."

Lucas said, "Jimmy Ma told me that Rocky Watters received a $150,000 wire-transfer from a Cayman Island account two days after the murder of the Cree Indian Kika Kisecawchuck. Jimmy claims the account is tied to the estate of Gabriel Lakatos."

Tank said, "Let me guess: the Lakatos estate is managed by this Zimmerman guy?"

Lucas said, "Bingo."

Powers said, "We should pay a visit to Zimmerman rather than waste our time with Watters. We could turn everything we know over to the Chicago police and let them handle him."

Lucas said, "It would be nice to know what other instructions he has from Zimmerman. Maybe his next assignment is us."

Powers added, "Or Tucker."

"Back to my original question," Tank asked, "what's the plan?"

"Watters knows what both of you look like. Hell, now everyone knows what you look like. Your faces are burned into most Americans' TV screens. You've been on national TV ever since these clowns tried to frame you for the murder of Gabriel Lakatos.

"Rocky's got a little office he keeps about five blocks from his condo. He walks to it every morning, rain or shine or snow. I figure that we have enough room in this Expedition to take him for a ride. I'll approach him coming from the opposite direction about the time you drive up."

Tank said, "We're going to kidnap him in broad daylight? I don't think so. We need a backup plan. What else did you learn about him from Jimmy?"

Lucas said, "He has kids, is twice divorced, shoots at a range twice a week, and is a regular at the Bar Louie adjacent to his condo."

Powers said, "I think I need a drink. I didn't want to wait until morning anyway. Let's get this over with."

Bar Louie

Tank and Powers stayed in the Expedition, parked in a garage a half-block away but within range of their radios. Lucas sat at the bar drinking a dark beer, pretending to be playing a game on his iPhone.

Over coms, Lucas said, "He's here carrying on a conversation with another patron."

Tank said, "Wait for a few. We don't want to rush things."

Rocky was explaining to his bar friend why the Chicago Bears were not Super Bowl contenders and what needed to be done about it. Drinkers at an adjacent table took issue with Rocky's assessment. The conversation got heated, and Rocky chest bumped his adversary. It went downhill from there. Lucas left his stool at the bar to break up the fight before it started. One look at Lucas sobered up even the most inebriated supporter of the Bears.

Lucas said to Rocky, "Hold on big fella. Even if you're right, it's not worth a night in the pen."

Rocky slurred his words. His breath smelled like rotting seaweed as he asked, "Who the fuck are you?"

"Someone who is trying to keep you from committing assault and battery on another patron of this bar. Someone who is keeping you out of jail. Keep your cool. Can I buy you another drink?"

That was code to Tank and Powers to pull up in front of the bar.

Rocky said, "Sure."

Lucas threw a twenty on the bar and said, "First, we're going to get a little fresh air."

Lucas said as he eased him out the front door, "You know, Rocky, you're right about the Bears. The management is the problem."

Rocky slurred, "Damn right it is."

Lucas slapped Rocky on the back, put his right hand around the back of his neck, and squeezed the pressure points he was so well trained to apply.

When Rocky woke up, he was in the back seat of the Expedition, Lucas by his side.

Rocky blinked a few times and tried to gain clarity, but his buzz interfered. He looked over at Lucas and asked, "Who are you again?"

"I'm the guy that kept you from beating an innocent person to a pulp over nothing. I'm the guy that kept you out of jail tonight."

"Where are you taking me, and who are your friends in the front seats."

"My, my, my, aren't we the one needing answers. Rocky, you're very close to the needle. Is that the way you want to go out?"

"What are you talking about?"

Lucas said, "What we're talking about is you being found guilty of the murder of Kika Kisecawchuck, who went by the nickname, Chuck."

Rocky considered his situation as best he could in his inebriated state.

Tank pulled the Expedition over to the side of the road, turned around, and said to Rocky, "I promised your protector in the back seat with you that I won't beat you to death. It's getting harder to keep that promise. I'm not known as a patient man, and my partner here, who is trained in the art of torture, is even less patient than I am. So, fucking sober up and tell us who paid you to kill Chuck and frame us for the murder of Gabriel Lakatos. I'm not going to play rope-a-dope with you."

Rocky sobered up instantly when he realized who was in the front seat and reconsidered his situation. He tried to open the door to roll out of the SUV and run, but the door was child-locked. Rocky had a concealed carry permit and carried a short Sig Sauer. He reached for it only to discover his holster was empty. Lucas held it up in front of him with the magazine removed, and said, "The dainty man in the front seat has a short fuse. Now is a good time to answer his question."

Rocky looked at his three captors and decided he didn't have a chance against them.

He said, "Levi Zimmerman."

The Hamptons, Long Island, New York

Tank, Powers, and Lucas caught a flight from O'Hare to LaGuardia. Tank and Powers flew first class, and Lucas was relegated to coach. Lucas rented a GMC Yukon while Tank and Powers retrieved their luggage.

The drive from the airport to the Hamptons was consumed with strategizing and tactical discussions as to how they should approach Levi Zimmerman, Gabriel Lakatos's number two man. They spoke with Tony Vinci, who performed a detailed background search on the man's business history. Tank's idea was to use overwhelming power—scare the shit out of him, make him believe his life was at risk.

Powers thought that would make Tank look guiltier and would be counterproductive. Powers wanted to attack him at his greatest vulnerability—his financial freedom. So, as they drove east on I-495, they talked on the phone with Jimmy Ma.

Tank asked, "Jimmy, just how good are you?"

"Uh-oh. You're going to challenge me, aren't you? What impossible thing are you going to ask me to do this time?"

"Have you looked into Levi Zimmerman's financials?"

"Yeah, Tucker asked me to do that earlier."

"How difficult would it be to find out how much money he's paid Rocky Watters out of Chicago over the years, if he's transferred any funds to someone in the Colorado Springs area, and whether he has funded Code Pink?"

Ma let out a sigh and said, "Whew, I thought you were going to challenge me. Do you want me to limit the search to just Zimmerman's account or include the Lakatos estate that he currently manages?"

Tank chuckled and said, "Both. How long will this take you?"

"Give me ninety minutes."

"Call as soon as you have something."

Tank hung up from Jimmy and called Tony Vinci again.

"Tony, do you have a nanodevice in Levi Zimmerman's home?"

"Are you asking me to check it while we're on the phone?"

"Could you?"

"Give me a couple of minutes."

"While you're pulling that up, can you tell me anything about his security?"

Tony said, "State-of-the-art with pan, zoom, and tilt video; intrusion detection; and an electrified fence."

"Can you cut the power?"

"Won't do any good; he has UPS backup."

Tank asked, "How many people in his security detail?"

"Two around the clock. Wow, the nanodevice is up. Zimmerman's with a woman. She's going down on him. She's really good. Wonder if I could get her phone number."

"Tony, stay with us. How would you penetrate his security?"

No answer.

"Earth to Tony."

"Sorry, I was distracted."

Tank repeated, "How would you penetrate his security?"

"I'd come in from the beach side. Levi doesn't have water-side security."

"Thanks, Tony. You can go watch the Zimmerman porn show now."

"Too late: it's over already." They hung up.

Powers said, "We don't have equipment or suits for an operation like that."

Lucas said, "Maybe we should wait until he leaves—stop him out on the road."

Tank's phone rang. His caller ID displayed a Colorado Springs area code. He answered, "Tank here."

"This is Colorado Springs Detective White with Military Police officer Major Javier Castro. As you know, we're investigating the murder of Commander Blackstone and would like to talk to you. I can tell that you are in a vehicle. Please pull over, open your laptop or tablet, and use Facetime with us. Now, if possible."

"Sir, I want to cooperate with you. I want to know who killed Blackstone myself and will do anything in my power to help. But this is not a good time."

"Too bad. Pull over, now."

Tank didn't want to use his phone for the interview and instructed Lucas to pull off the interstate, find a place where they could pull up his laptop, find access to Wi-Fi they could use, and wait for Detective White to initiate the call. He asked Lucas, "Do you know how to Facetime? I've never used it before."

They parked in a Starbucks parking lot and answered the Facetime call from the detective, who conducted the interview with Tank.

White started by asking, "When you were with Tucker Cherokee on Peterson Air Force Base meeting with Commander Blackstone, did you notice anything or anyone paying a little too much attention to you?"

Tank answered, "No. I racked my brain trying to relive the visit, but I come up empty."

"What was the meeting about?"

"It was private between the commander and Tucker. I was not present during their discussion."

"Did it have anything to do with a secret society?"

Tank said, "What? Could you repeat that?"

"You heard me, Tank. I spoke with Michelle Mallard today. She was threatened by someone who called in to her show and said she was likely to receive the same fate as Commander Blackstone. I asked her if she and Blackstone belonged to a secret society. She didn't deny it. Connecting the dots, I remembered that you and your partner, Powers, were at Michelle's place when a group of University of Colorado students tried to overrun her security. Add to that that the killer tried to implicate Tucker Cherokee for the murder of Blackstone. So, it's not a leap of logic to figure that someone is aware of your secret society, is threatened by it, and wants to eliminate its members one by one. Maybe this person even has something to do with you being allegedly framed for the death of Gabriel Lakatos.

"Tank, without disclosing the secret society, what its purpose is, or who its members are, can you think of anyone that may know of its existence and want to harm its members?"

Tank said, "Three names come to mind: Levi Zimmerman, who was Gabriel Lakatos's right-hand man; Lawrence Slaughter, CEO of California Media Group; and Clayton West, Senator Enya's chief of staff."

"One last question: what is Tucker Cherokee's involvement in all this? What was his relationship with Commander Blackstone?"

Tank said, "He was Wes' friend. They shared a world view. He would never do anything to hurt him."

"I mean what's his role in this secret society?"

Tank said, "Alleged secret society."

Tank disconnected the call.

They got back on I-495 east. No one spoke. All three were deep in thought. Finally, Powers said, "Do you really think that weasel Clayton West is still poisoning our well and disclosing information to someone who would try to kill us? I didn't think he had the gonads to do that after we dealt with him in Carlsbad."

Tank said, "We need to inform Tucker about these developments."

Before they could call Tucker, Jimmy Ma called back.

"As I had already informed Lucas, Zimmerman recently transferred $150,000 to an account in Chicago in the name of Rocky Watters. He didn't even try to hide it. Over a period of two years, he's paid Watters a total of $800,000. He also transferred $70,000 to an account in Pueblo, Colorado, to a nonprofit organization in the name of OWG. I did some research and discovered that OWG is solely managed by an army captain who works at the Pueblo Chemical Weapons Destruction Facility."

"Do you have a name?"

"Yes, Captain William West."

Powers, Lucas, and Tank looked at each other. Powers said, "Could it be?"

Jimmy said, "What? Does that name mean something to you guys?"

Tank said, "Work with Tony and find out if he's related to Clayton West, who works in Senator Enya's office."

Jimmy said, "OK. One more thing. Zimmerman has not contributed funds to Code Pink. However, the Lakatos Foundation contributed $500,000 a year over the past five years to them."

"Thanks, Jimmy. You're the best."

Jimmy said, "I know," and disconnected.

Wiscasset

Tank, Powers, and Lucas debriefed Tucker and Maya by phone. Tucker sat in his office chair waiting for an epiphany or something to inspire him about what to do next.

Nothing came, so Tucker contacted Senator Enya.

"Peter, this is Tucker Cherokee. Can you talk freely?"

Peter Enya said, "No. Give me ten minutes, and I'll return your call on a secure line."

Maya sat in the office with Tucker and said, "If our cover is blown, if our foundation cannot maintain secrecy, we're going to have to regroup. It's getting too dangerous. We're going to find ourselves a target again. Jeez, Tucker, this is déjà vu. We must protect Star. Clayton West knows about her and he operates in an unknown wavelength. She's the one who outed him."

"Agreed. Tony has a nanodevice in his office, his home, and his car. We'll neutralize him soon."

Maya said, "Can't be soon enough. Ram needs to pay him another visit."

Senator Peter Enya returned the call and said, "What's up, Tucker? You don't call unless it's important."

Tucker said, "Clayton is a bad boy. He feeds the enemy information, some of which has resulted in murder. He's neck deep in counterespionage. We have to neutralize him, but we must do it by the book. You're going to get a visit from Colorado Springs homicide detective Slick White. He's going to ask you some questions. Burn Clayton. Implicate him. Tell the truth, even if you must disclose our secret foundation. We need Clayton out of the picture. Incarceration is in his future, but we need to learn who he is passing information to. We think we already know, but if you can participate in the interview, it may be useful."

Peter said, "Tucker, I'm sorry my assistant has caused us so much grief. I'm embarrassed and ashamed. I thought we could control him. My bad."

"Understood."

The Washington Times: *Arlington, Virginia* – 'The mayor of Arlington, Virginia, gave a joint press conference with the chief of police of the Arlington Police

Department to announce that the Arlington police SWAT team penetrated and eliminated a terrorist cell of Serbian fighters here in the United States illegally. The group attempted to free a high-ranking officer in the terrorist group from incarceration in a previously undisclosed high-security penitentiary.

The group held the prosecuting attorney captive to learn the whereabouts of the imprisoned Serbian leader. The leader's brother, twenty-eight-year-old Marko Kovac, attempted to kidnap the prosecuting attorney's ten-year-old daughter at Pentagon City Mall to force the attorney to reveal the leader's location. Fast response by the mall security team and the Arlington Police Department foiled the attempted kidnap."

Once again, Tucker asked himself the enigmatic and unanswerable questions: *Why are we here? What's the purpose of our lives? Do we really have free will or do we have a destiny?*

More and more Tucker thought that Star had a destiny. Time and time again, she'd used her unique skills to save lives and stop crime. She had a good heart and a quick mind. Maya and Tucker needed to decide on the best course for Star's future.

Little did Star appreciate that her life had a destiny and that destiny was not just a philosophical theory.

CHAPTER 49

"You are not only responsible for what you say, but what you don't say." – Martin Luther King, 1929-1968, Baptist Minister and a leader of the civil rights movement

Calgary, Alberta – October 16th

CJ's court-appointed attorney was two years out of the University of Alberta in Edmonton. He was young and eager to represent his client with vigor—after all, he had a reputation to build. Representing a rogue American CIA agent seemed like just the kind of high-profile case he'd dreamed about. He wasn't going to blow this opportunity.

He said to his client, Winston Davidson, "CJ, answer no questions unless I give you permission to do so. They want something from you. They're not interested in prosecuting you as much as they want information from you. Maybe we can get you a deal that greatly reduces the duration of your incarceration."

Winston, "CJ," Davison smirked; gave a short, sarcastic laugh; and said, "Are you suggesting that you can reduce my three consecutive life sentences in half?"

"You won't get that harsh a sentence. You didn't kill anyone, rape anyone, or deal in drugs. Be quiet now; I hear them coming."

The interview room was a classic. It was three meters by three meters; the thermostat was intentionally set so the room was much too hot; and it had a one-way mirror/window, one table, uncomfortable chairs, no lamps or appurtenances that could be used as weapons, and bright overhead fluorescent lights.

Three people entered the locked room while an armed police officer waited just outside the door. Along with the case lead, Royal Canadian Mounted Police Detective Rod Nelson and FBI Special Agent in Charge Michael Roberts, the crown prosecutor for the Province of Alberta entered and sat down directly opposite the court-appointed attorney. The young attorney knew who the crown prosecutor was and was instantly intimidated by her. She had a reputation for ripping inexperienced defenders a new one.

Nelson looked at Davidson and spoke first, "Special Agent Roberts here wants to extradite you to the US to stand trial for treason. He explained to me that there is a high probability that you will get the death penalty if we agree. Indeed, it would be a lot easier on us to pack you up and send you on your way with an FBI escort.

"But you're charged with numerous crimes against the Queen here in our constitutional monarchy. We may try you here, first, before we respond to the American request for your extradition."

The crown prosecutor added, "I've reviewed your case, and we're going to charge you with second-degree murder, attempted murder of an RCMP officer, aiding and abetting the escape of felons, leaving the scene of the crime, violating Canadian immigration laws, possessing illegal and unregistered firearms, the unlawful occupation of property . . . "

Before she could continue, the court-appointed attorney interrupted to ask, "Second-degree murder? Of whom?"

She answered, "Gabriel Lakatos. We believe your client was a participant in his assassination by helping in the escape of the killers."

The young attorney said, "You're trying to pin the murder on my client? What a joke. I know there is a lot a pressure on the RCMP to charge someone, but Winston Davidson is not the killer." Looking Rod Nelson straight in the eye, he said, "He had an airtight alibi until you killed her. How convenient. My client is lucky to be alive after you shot him too."

The crown prosecutor said, "I've reviewed the evidence and can assure you: it's damaging. Your client's failure to cooperate with law enforcement in both countries will contribute to his ultimate harsh sentence."

Despite the warning not to speak without his attorney's approval, Winston "CJ" Davidson scratched the three-day stubble on his chin and said, "I'll cooperate."

Agent Roberts jumped in and asked, "Who'd you rent the Humvee to? Where did they go?"

The defense attorney said, "Hold on, there, Winston, don't answer that question."

The crown prosecutor said, "Let me get this straight: not only has your client failed to cooperate until this moment but as his attorney, you're advising him not to cooperate? Your client may suffer from said actions."

"I'll cooperate," Winston repeated.

"Who paid you?" Roberts asked.

Davidson's attorney stood up and said, "This interview is over until I have a private discussion with my client."

CJ blurted, "I don't know who paid me. I was promised 150 Canadian Maple Leaf gold coins if I would help three men cross the border into Montana without going through a checkpoint."

The young attorney leaned down and whispered something into Winston's ear, who then nodded at his lawyer and immediately clammed up.

The defense lawyer sat back down and said, "I think everyone at the table knows that Mr. Davidson did not kill Gabriel Lakatos and did not knowingly aid and abet the killers.

"I think everyone also knows that my client did not attempt to murder anyone in law enforcement. I understand he never even fired a round—he was the one shot." The attorney glared at Rod Nelson.

"We don't want to waste the court's time trying to prove the unprovable. If you drop the charges of second-degree murder and attempted murder and decline extradition to the United States, he'll turn evidence over to the RCMP against the killers of Gabriel Lakatos. He'll agree to tell you everything he knows."

Rod Nelson looked directly at CJ and asked, "Do you know who killed Lakatos?"

CJ asked, "Do we have a deal?"

Both Nelson and the prosecutor looked over at Agent Roberts. Roberts said, "I don't have the authority to make that decision on behalf of the US attorney general, but I have a lot of influence and will promise to recommend dropping the request for extradition."

The crown prosecutor said, "I'll prepare the proper documentation for this plea deal while you guys talk."

CJ shuffled in his seat, used his open hand to rub the perspiration off his forehead and said, "They came to my place in Medicine Hat to exchange a key to a post office box that contained the gold coins for a key to the Humvee. This was all prearranged by code in plain site on Craigslist.

"I don't know who they were or their names."

Rod Nelson said, "I hope there's more than that. What did they look like? You know, height, weight, nationality, race, gender, all that stuff."

"We had two trail cameras on the trailer site," CJ responded." One was pointed down the driveway, the other at the front door. The cameras got full face views of all three of them. I figure it will take the FBI about fifteen minutes to figure out who they are once you guys view the thirty-two gigabyte memory cards."

"Where are the memory cards now?"

CJ said, "I'll give you the cards after the deal is signed."

"How'd you get the Humvee back after the mercenaries crossed the border? Why didn't they just leave it and make you pick it up?"

CJ said, "If they left it stranded in Montana, the probability would be high that authorities would tag it and run it down to the owner, me. They thought that if it were returned to me, nobody would be the wiser. No record of the transport, no passport stamp, no rental car receipt, no trace."

"How'd you get it back?"

"A couple of nineteen-year-old college kids returned it. One cowgirl-type studying to be a vet and her boyfriend, who lost his athletic scholarship."

Roberts asked, "Even though we'll eventually see the video, describe the men you rented your Humvee to."

"One of them was in his late twenties—wiry thin, no chin, and sandy hair. A second one was maybe in his early thirties, a rugby-player-type, mouthy, looking for a fight with an Aussie accent. The third guy was older, never said a word, followed the other two, timid, scared, not in charge."

Calgary

Nelson, Roberts, and the crown prosecutor viewed the video on a wide-screen TV. Rod Nelson said, "I guess that the Australian rugby-type guy is the sniper. I bet he is former military."

Agent Roberts said, "We'll run all three through the FBI and Interpol facial recognition databases."

The prosecutor asked Nelson, "Don't we have access to the Australian Criminal Court System database? We should be able to get information on the shooter immediately from the Federal Police."

Rod Nelson called Doug Butterfield, who'd remained in Fort Chipewyan, and said, "I'm going to send you a video feed. We think it's the Lakatos sniper team. I want you to search all known facial recognition databases, including the Australian ACCS. Call me back as soon as you have anything."

Butterfield said, "Alright, that's fantastic. I'll run the program. I have some other news for you."

"What is it?

"We got a call from the Chicago Police Department. They sent us a package about a guy they have reason to believe is the bag man for Chuck. You know, the Cree Indian, Kika Kisecawchuck? He's tied to this case."

Nelson said, "Send me and the crown prosecutor a copy of the package down here in Calgary. Sounds like we caught a break."

Special Agent in Charge Michael Roberts overheard the conversation and asked, "Did I hear correctly that you received something from the Chicago PD?"

"Yes, they provided us a lead on the murder of the guy who was paid handsomely to help the hit team."

The Crown Prosecutor said, "While we are waiting to hear back from our data search team, can we take inventory as to where we are? Who paid this hit team? How did they know to be within rifle shot of Lakatos? Money was no object. They could afford to dump a $3.6 million helicopter as part of their plan. Do you have any reason to think the guys that killed Lakatos also murdered Chuck? Who benefits financially from Lakatos's death. Do we need to talk with Gabriel's estate attorney?"

Nelson and Roberts smiled at each other as if sharing a joke. Nelson answered, "All good questions."

CHAPTER 50

"If we like it or not, we will have a One World Government. The question is if it will be achieved through consent or through conquest." - J. Warburg, 1896-1969, Illuminati

The Hamptons, Long Island, New York – October 16th

"No Craig, you'll have to wait until probate is complete. There is an enormous lien on the estate. It's going to take a year to clear. The largest lien is with the IRS, which is, as you know, problematic. I can't lawyer my way around it. Also, there are fifteen pending lawsuits, two of them by the largest financial advisors in the nation. I can't rush it."

Levi listened impatiently as Craig Lakatos responded on the other end of the phone with a rant. Finally, Zimmerman said, "Go blow off some steam somewhere else. I don't have to listen to your shit. You have plenty of money to survive for a year in accounts set up in your name. Quit sounding like a selfish, greedy asshole."

Levi hung up. He was looking out his office window at the Hudson River, counting to twenty, taking deep breaths, and regulating his pulse when he was interrupted.

"Mr. Zimmerman, an FBI agent is here to see you."

Suddenly, his pulse raced, his heart fluttered, and he had trouble breathing.

"Send him in."

Zimmerman's assistant opened the double door to the executive suite, and Rusty Winemiller motored in.

"Thank you, Mr. Zimmerman, for seeing me on short notice."

"But, of course. Can I offer you anything? Water, coffee, or tea maybe?"

"No, thank you. I'd like to get right down to business if I may. I'm in the Cybercrimes Division, which supports multiple cases simultaneously. Two cases have curiously intersected, and I was hoping you could clear up some inconsistencies.

"The first case involves the death of Gabriel Lakatos. I understand that he was your boss and you are the executor of his last will?"

Levi asked, "Is there a cybercrime involved with this inquiry?"

"Be patient, Mr. Zimmerman. Would you say that you are the most knowledgeable about his financial situation?"

Zimmerman nodded.

"Who, to the best to your knowledge, had the most to gain financially from his death?"

"Agent Winemiller, I can only give you ballpark estimates. I honestly don't know, and no one can until probate is complete. We must settle with the IRS, there are lawsuits to contend with, and who knows what claims will come out of the woodwork. But what I *can* tell you is that he intended to leave $500 million and his Manhattan properties to his only son, Craig."

Rusty said, "I understood Gabriel was worth billions."

"He was, but he transferred $18 billion to his primary philanthropic foundation just before he was murdered. He left the bulk of his remaining estate, $1.5 billion, to secondary activist groups like Black Lives Matter,

UnidosUS, Antifa, Color of Change, Planned Parenthood, and Center for Media and Democracy. Lakatos funded over one hundred organizations in more than sixty countries."

Winemiller asked, "Anyone else in his will?"

"He left $5 million to share equally with the fifteen people in his service staff, maid service, chefs, guards, and drivers. He left the contents of his safe-deposit box to me and the balance of his estate to an offshore bank account. I have no idea who has access to the account. I just followed his instructions."

"What was in the safe-deposit box?"

"I choose not to share that with you."

Winemiller reached into his travel bag attached to the wheelchair and said, "I have a warrant."

"It contained a key to another safe. Does the warrant cover that too?"

Winemiller ignored the toxic attitude and asked, "Where are the offshore accounts and how many of them are there?"

"I'm certain the warrant doesn't cover that information."

"So, Gabriel had no spouse, ex-wife, or other family members?"

"No."

"So, who manages the $19.5 billion in his charities and nonprofit organizations."

"I do."

Rusty Winemiller already knew this, but he wanted to hear Zimmerman say it.

"You just moved into the number one spot for who benefits most from Gabriel Lakatos's death. What private investigative service did you receive for the $150,000 you paid Rocky Watters?"

The question sent a jolt through Levi. He knew he'd given away something to the FBI agent but was caught off guard. His breathing became labored and perspiration formed on his forehead.

Zimmerman recovered and said, "I asked him to investigate a new Hollywood movie production company called Real America Productions."

"Why?" Rusty wanted to keep him talking.

"For investment purposes."

"I see. I have a geography headache. Why would Watters get his passport stamped crossing into Canada to get to Hollywood?"

Zimmerman said, "I'm sure he has other clients. He could have gone to Canada for them."

Winemiller knew Levi was lying to him.

Rusty followed up with, "The second case I intended to discuss with you involved the cybercrimes committed against *The New York Times* and *The Washington Post,* but we'll have that discussion another time.

"Thank you for your time, Mr. Zimmerman. You were very helpful."

Calgary, Alberta

Officer Douglas Butterfield was first to report in. He said, "Detective, the name of the Australian is Daniel Murphy, thirty-one years old. He's a former sharpshooter with the Australian Army, charged with selling army weapons to gunrunners, dishonorably discharged, served five years, and is suspected to live somewhere in the United States. Nothing yet on the other two guys."

"Good job, Butterfield." They disconnected.

Agent Roberts called the Seattle field office and provided them with the new information. While on the phone he said, "See if you can find this Murphy guy's bank account and who made a large deposit into it recently. I've got to go; I've got an incoming call from the New York field office.

"Hello, this is SAC Roberts."

"Roberts, this is Agent Rusty Winemiller calling from the New York field office, though assigned to the Quantico Cybercrimes Division. I completed an interview with a man named Levi Zimmerman. He's the executor in charge of Gabriel Lakatos's will and currently runs the operations of the Lakatos Foundation. I thought you should know my findings. They are relevant to your case."

Roberts said, "I'm in Calgary, Alberta, with the Royal Canadian Mounted Police Lead Investigator Rod Nelson. May I put you on speaker?"

"Sure."

"OK. Let it rip."

Winemiller said, "Zimmerman has the most to gain from Lakatos's murder. If he isn't, he should be top on your list of persons of interest. I also think he had something to do with the murder of Kika Kisecawchuck in Wabasca. He paid a Chicago PI six figures around the time the PI entered Canada, which also coincided with the time when Chuck was murdered. Roberts, this guy stinks with guilt.

"The other person of interest is Lakatos's son, Craig, for no other reason than he inherits around $500 million. A lot of people would knock off their old man for that kind of money."

"Thanks, Rusty. We'll keep you posted but hang on the call for a little bit longer."

Michael Roberts said to Nelson, "So, it's Zimmerman that paid Rocky Watters. We need to look up Levi's skirt. This guy is looking good for the murder of Gabriel Lakatos. Let's find out if any money has passed between Zimmerman and the Australian, Murphy."

"Agent Winemiller," asked Roberts, "can you investigate the transfer of funds from Levi Zimmerman and the Lakatos Foundation to an account owned by Daniel Murphy, an Australian immigrant?"

Winemiller answered, "Not without a warrant. I'll see if I can get one. Do you have an account number for this Murphy guy?"

Roberts answered, "No, but I can send you his Australian military ID and a photo. I'd first check for a California driver's license."

They disconnected, and Agent Winemiller immediately punched in a secure phone number he knew by heart.

Tucker's caller ID displayed "Quantico."

He answered, "Blackbeard?"

"Yes, we have a development. The special agent in charge of the investigation into the murder of Gabriel Lakatos asked us to track the transfer of money from Levi Zimmerman to a former Australian who turned out to be an army sniper living in the United States. Tucker, I don't have enough evidence to get a warrant. We don't even have a bank account for the Australian. We can't legally get this information. I need your help."

Tucker said, "I think we can help. Send me what you can. Is the Australian a person of interest in a crime?"

"Yes, we suspect he's the shooter in the death of Gabriel Lakatos and that Zimmerman paid for the hit. Tucker, time is of the essence. You might be able to come up with the connection before I can get a warrant and maybe before the shooter leaves the country."

After terminating the encrypted call with Winemiller, Tucker contacted Tony Vinci. "I'm about to forward you the name of an Australian suspected to be living in California and who is a person of interest for the murder of Gabriel Lakatos. See if you can find him and his bank account number. Forward the information to Jimmy and copy me. Tony, we need this yesterday."

Tony never said a word and hung up.

The Seattle field office forwarded SAC Roberts the identification of the other two people who escaped Canada into Montana with Daniel Murphy:

"Beau Meyers, Alaskan Airlines pilot, based out of Long Beach, California, 32 years old, sandy hair, green eyes, 145 pounds, former US Air Force helicopter pilot, wife, and three children, no priors, missing, did not report to work.

"Dale Ford, 47, San Jose, California, a veteran of Desert Storm, suffers from PTSD, currently, a paid employee for Black Lives Matter. Formerly employed by California Media Group."

Roberts shared the information with Nelson and said, "It rounds out the team. Meyers is the helicopter pilot, and Ford is the spotter. Where have I heard of California Media Group? Do I remember correctly that the company has a connection with Lakatos?"

Nelson said, "Let me check with Butterfield." Rod punched in the call number for Doug.

"Doug, Nelson here. Is there a connection between California Media Group and Gabriel Lakatos?"

Officer Butterfield said, "Yes. Maybe you forgot, but a sniper shot out transformers that fed the California Media Group's TV and radio stations in multiple locations. The CEO is Lawrence Slaughter, who was a close friend of Lakatos and *The Washington Post's* prior owner, Jeff Jorgensen."

Butterfield continued, "Oh, by the way, I got your warrant."

"What warrant?"

"The warrant you asked me to get to find out what was in Gabriel Lakatos's safe-deposit box."

"I don't remember asking you to do that. How can a Canadian get a warrant for a US bank safe-deposit box?"

"I'm resourceful."

"Doug?"

"Actually, the warrant was applied for by the Seattle Police Department. You remember Yamaguchi, right?"

"Where's the box?"

"It's in a Mellon Bank in Pittsburgh, Pennsylvania."

CHAPTER 51

"It is only the dead that have seen the end of war." –
Plato, ancient Greek philosopher

The Hamptons, Long Island, New York – October 17th

At 07:00 the gates to Levi Zimmerman's estate in the Hamptons opened. A chauffeur drove his armored Lincoln limousine with mobile Wi-Fi, satellite television, an espresso maker, full HDMI integration with a thirty-two-inch LED flat screen TV and four captain's chairs. His virtual boardroom on wheels allowed him to conduct business on the long drive to the city. But it only got one hundred yards away from his estate before the driver had to stop. A barricade was placed across the street.

Sensing danger, the driver tried to back up, but he found a GMC Yukon had pulled up behind him. The armed chauffeur reached his Sig Sauer from his holster, but before he could pull it free, he was looking into the barrel of a rifle. The windows were bullet-proof but not from a rifle loaded with high-velocity rounds. Two or three blasts from the rifle would shatter the window and blow his face into another dimension.

Zimmerman called 911 before the doors to the limo opened.

Tank said, "You know who I am, right? So, then you know what I'm capable of. Get out and get into the Yukon."

Lucas invited the chauffer out and placed plastic ties on him and sat him in the passenger seat. Lucas drove the limo back to the estate and parked in the driveway leaving the chauffeur zip-tied.

Powers sat in the back seat of the Yukon with a Taser in his right hand. He asked Levi, "You ever been Tased?"

Zimmerman shook his head.

"Have you ever had to endure pain?" Powers asked. "It's not fun.

"You need to know that I have an internal bullshit meter. I know when I'm being bullshitted. I'll use this Taser only when that meter pegs. Do you understand, Levi?"

He nodded his head.

We're driving you to a remote location where we'll ask you questions. We've already changed plates so don't think the local police will find us before we have a little talk with you.

"We know you paid Rocky Watters to frame Tank and me for the murder of Gabriel Lakatos. What we don't know is why."

"Now, it's your turn to talk. Don't forget I have an internal bullshit meter. Unless you'd like a permanent change to your nasal passage, I'd answer the questions honestly."

Zimmerman looked into Powers's cold, dark eyes and saw a man that meant what he said. He hesitated for a few minutes but eventually capitulated. He saw no way out of his predicament.

Levi said, "I've spent my entire life trying to influence Gabriel Lakatos to do the right thing and fund efforts to move America and other nations toward socialism and a one-world government where the people of all nations have access to the world's resources. The US is still a tribal nation where artificial borders prevent the unfortunate and downtrodden people access to water and power, and a standard of living worth staying alive for. You and your misguided soldiers of capitalism and democracy are trying to reverse all the progress we've made over the past decades. We took control of the education system, the media, Hollywood, and the judicial system. Do you know how long and how hard that was? It's taken over sixty years. You idiots want to reverse it all. You started with killing Gabriel, and you've formed a group to destroy everything we've accomplished. I had no confidence that the FBI and the Canadian law enforcement agencies would discover the truth, so I helped it along and led them to you."

Powers said, "First of all, you appointed yourself judge, jury, and executioner. Secondly, we didn't kill Gabriel Lakatos."

Zimmerman said, "It makes no difference. Removing you and Tank from the secret society mix weakened your hateful right-wing organization and if it wasn't you, then it was people just like you."

Powers asked, "You referred to a secret society. What are you talking about? Why do you think one exists?"

"It's called The Media Transformation Foundation. It's led by Tucker Cherokee and operated by you and Tank. You have twenty or so members and a large war chest. Your purpose is to change the media's left-leaning ideology to the right. Good luck with that."

"How do you know all this?"

"You have a leak. His name is Clayton West."

Powers said, "So far, I've not detected bullshit. Keep it up. Why did you have Commander Blackstone murdered? What was his crime?"

"I had nothing to do with that."

"Uh-oh, the needle just pegged at maximum bullshit."

Powers pulled the Taser close to Zimmerman's neck when Levi said, "Hold on. I'll tell you what I know."

Powers pulled the weapon back.

"Money is power. Gabriel had lots of money and used it to leverage power. We funded many different organizations, each with the long-term goal of moving the electorate to the left. A one-world socialist government is unachievable as long as the United States remains a capitalist nation.

"Though we funded many nonprofit organizations with a common goal, we didn't have individual control. Yes, we supported anti-military groups like Code Pink and OWG, but we didn't direct their actions."

"Who murdered Commander Blackstone and why?"

Levi said, "There is no history of violence from the nonviolent Code Pink, so I guess that OWG committed the crime after receiving information shared from Code Pink. As to why, that's also a guess, but the commander was active in stopping the internal military news from moving left. It was a hard-fought battle to get liberal journalists engaged in the production of military news. Commander Blackstone tried to reverse the progress we've made over the past five decades."

Tank asked, "Who do you suspect murdered Gabriel Lakatos?"

"A right wing group. I thought your group was as likely a group as any. You had means, motive, and opportunity. Look for an organization similar to yours."

Tank asked, "What's your relationship with Lawrence Slaughter? Could he have directed the murders of Blackstone or Lakatos?"

"We are generals on the same side of the war against the ideological far-right. We share information, tactics, and make sure we don't step on each other's anatomy. Lawrence is more of a follower of Saul Alinsky than either Gabriel or I and believes the ends justify the means.

He was a strong believer that to be a journalist is to pursue questions, and usually, that leads you into conflict with faith, mythology, or authority. If we define conservatism as respect for authority, then the journalism profession is, by definition, a force against conservatism."

Powers said, "Damn, and I really wanted to Taser you, but you didn't give a reason."

Lucas said, "Boss, may I ask a question?"

Tank said, "Sure, go for it."

"Why don't you practice what you preach?"

Powers jumped in to say, "You, Lakatos, and Slaughter were or are successful capitalists. Lakatos was famous for not paying his fair share of taxes. He believed federal income tax was a form of forced charity and that it was not charity if it was demanded from you. In a socialist one-world government, ten families would move into your estate with you and mooch off you. If that is what you want, why don't you offer your home to the downtrodden now?"

Zimmerman said with condescendence, "We can't fight the good fight without money. We set ourselves up as examples of the abuse of capitalism."

Lucas said, "How convenient. One last question— what's your lady-friend's phone number?"

"What?"

"Never mind."

Tank said, "Lucas, stop the car. Let Levi out. He can find his own way home."

Lucas pulled into a parking lot of an elementary school to let the old man out. Before Levi was allowed out, Tank asked, "Are you aware or have you ordered any other actions against us or our foundation members?"

Zimmerman looked away, hesitated, and then said, "No."

Powers said, "It looks like I'm going to get the chance to use this Taser after all."

"OK, OK. I instructed Rocky to stop the progress of Real America Productions in Hollywood."

Long Island

The GMC Yukon pulled out, and Tank said, "Get Tony on the line." Powers did so while Lucas drove.

"Tony, I need you to drop everything and work on this assignment. I'm going to send you an mp3 on an interview with Levi Zimmerman. I want you to edit out parts of it that incriminate us and then forward it to the following: Homicide Detective White in Colorado Springs, Major Javier Castro at Peterson Air Force Base, Detective Rod Nelson with the Royal Canadian Mounted Police, FBI Special Agent Michael Roberts, Suffolk County Detective Roger Sheppard, Agent Rusty Winemiller, and Lawrence Slaughter."

Powers added, "And don't forget to send a copy to Tucker."

Lucas said, "Lawrence Slaughter?"

Powers said, "I assume that's our next scheduled interview? Tank, is it OK if Sonja meets us there? He's already scared shitless of her."

Tank answered, "I think we better visit Julienne O'Kray in Hollywood first."

Pittsburgh, Pennsylvania

Special Agent in Charge Michael Roberts handed the bank president a warrant to review the contents of five separate safe-deposit boxes. Roberts brought with him two people: Royal Canadian Mounted Police Detective

Rod Nelson and a local FBI contractor to drill out the locks to the safe-deposit boxes.

After the lock on box number one was drilled out, the bank president watched as Roberts tried to pull out the box, but it was too heavy. Rod Nelson and the FBI contractor helped Roberts remove the box, which was filled with Canadian Maple Leaf gold coins.

Nelson said, "Probably no coincidence that CJ was paid in gold coins."

Roberts said, "Ironic that the person that murdered Lakatos was paid with Gabriel's own gold coins. I'm correct, am I not, that besides Gabriel Lakatos, only Zimmerman had access to the safe-deposit box?"

Boxes two and three were also filled with the same, but box number four was filled with American Eagle gold coins.

Box number five was different; it was not heavy. Inside were documents and thirty other safe-deposit box keys. The document contained a list of names, contact information, and titles. The keys were to banks all over the world.

The names were for people who belonged to a cabal to form a one-world government. Roberts was not surprised to read the top four names:

Czar – Gabriel Lakatos

Premier – Lawrence Slaughter

President – Jeff Jorgensen

Vice President and Treasurer – Levi Zimmerman

There were roughly fifty other names on the list, including national leaders. With the list was a manifesto outlining the goals, objectives, strategy, and group tactics. Included with the tactics were names of mercenaries. Daniel Murphy of Australia was on the list. The final document in the box contained a list of offshore accounts numbers, user names, and passwords.

Nelson said, "It's not a jump in logic that the safe-deposit box keys fit boxes in banks that match the banks for the offshore accounts."

Agent Roberts said, "It's time to arrest Zimmerman. I'll issue the arrest warrant. You want to join me in the takedown?"

Nelson said, "I wouldn't miss it. But I must tell you: I have new information that leads me in another direction."

"What? You're just now telling me this?"

"Doug Butterfield discovered that the Bell helicopter was registered to a company owned by Gabriel Lakatos."

"You've got to be kidding. You're telling me that the helicopter used to kill Lakatos was owned by the victim. My head hurts thinking about it. The killers might have been paid in gold owned by Lakatos and killed from a helicopter he owned. To me, Zimmerman looks more and more like the most likely perpetrator. "Except . . ."

"Except what?"

"Except the company owned by Gabriel Lakatos was run by his son, Craig."

CHAPTER 52

"Political correctness to me is just intellectual terrorism."—Mel Gibson, 1956-present, actor and producer

Hollywood, California – October 19th

It looked like the entire world was on fire. The dry underbrush and debris acted like kindling and fueled the rapid spread of the blaze. The forty-mile-per-hour Santa Ana winds caused the fire to jump from one evergreen to another. Firefighters were exposed to unbearable heat, which made it too difficult for them to get precious water close enough to contain the blaze. The wind made it impossible for the DC-10 tankers to drop the firefighting chemicals, foam, gels, and water necessary to contain the conflagration.

Julienne O'Kray reviewed the videos of real-life California forest fires with her special effects producer for *Real America Productions*' first full-length movie release, *Unsustainable.* She said to the special effects producer, "I like the videos you selected. We'll go with them. What's the status of the scene in which the dam fails?"

He said, "We're in the middle of creating them. Give me three more days, and I'll bring them by for you to review."

She said, "It's just as well. I couldn't have reviewed them now anyway. I'm late for a meeting with the attorneys. See you in three days."

Waiting in the studio conference room to speak with Julienne were two attorneys retained by *Real America Productions*. Julienne enjoyed producing movies, reviewing special effects options, editing scripts, and negotiating scenes with directors. But she hated the time she spent with lawyers. She felt it was counterproductive.

Julienne walked over to the studio conference room with slumped shoulders, opened the conference room door, and found that the well-dressed lawyers were conducting business and talking to other clients on separate cell phones. Both quickly terminated their calls and deferentially shook Julienne O'Kray's hand.

Julienne said, "Thank you for coming. We asked your law firm to perform a risk analysis and determine the upper end of our liabilities and to determine the probability of the risk. We need that information before we can secure liability insurance. What's the bottom line?"

The senior attorney spoke slowly, carefully enunciating each word with a deep and calm voice, "The risk with the highest consequence is the risk that the movie will inspire terrorists to employ the ideas presented in *Unsustainable*'s story line. The consequence is that the liability exceeds a trillion US dollars, which, of course, is uninsurable."

"And the probability of this risk?"

The second younger lawyer said, "Higher than you might think. We estimate a five percent probability."

O'Kray responded, "What's your basis for that number? Have other Hollywood studios lost suits for stimulating ideas for terrorism?"

Before either lawyer could answer the questions, Julienne's assistant knocked on the door and ducked her head in, eyes wide, looking a little concerned. "I'm sorry to bother you but three, uh, very intimidating-looking men insist on seeing you, now."

Julienne looked over at the lawyers and said, "Would you stay in this room with me in case these men are a problem?"

The two lawyers nodded in agreement.

Through the doors walked Tank, Powers, and Lucas.

Julienne was relieved to see it was them and the two lawyers smiled and shook hands with the three of them as they also provided the legal support to White Knight Personal Security.

Julienne said, "Well, I'm glad you all know each other. Let me guess, you're also Tucker Cherokee's attorneys?"

"Yes, ma'am."

She turned her attention to Tank and Powers. Her face showed stress as she searched for a pack of cigarettes. Julienne said, "It scares me that you are here and that my assistant said it was urgent. What's up?"

Tank answered, "The stated urgency was because we didn't know who was in the conference room with you. It could have been the person we are after. Sorry. We're here to protect you."

"Why do I need protection, and why would it take the three of you? You're really scaring me now."

Powers said, "You have a right to be scared. There may be a hit out on you. We're here to stop it."

The two lawyers and Julienne said in unison, "A hit?"

Tank said, "We know who ordered the hit and who the hit man is; we just don't know when he plans to complete his assignment. You'll get around-the-clock protection from us until he is captured. Until then, as unpleasant as it may be, we want you to wear body armor under your regular clothing.

"Lucas will take the first shift as your bodyguard. Please, Julienne, take this seriously. Lucas must be with you every moment until one of us takes his place. In the meantime, Powers and I are going to upgrade the studio's physical security system."

Powers added, "We've sent a couple security officers to survey the area around your home. Maybe we'll catch the bastard there."

Julienne asked, "Why does someone want to kill me?"

"Let's just say someone doesn't think it's a good idea for *Real America Productions* to be successful."

Julienne asked, "Does that mean my director, actors, actresses, and screenwriters are at risk?"

Tank said, "Possibly. Could you call an all-cast, all-hands meeting? I think we need to inform them of the problem. Who knows what the killer will do to put an end to Real America Productions?"

One of the attorneys said to Julienne, "You may want to stop production until he is apprehended."

Powers said, "That's good legal advice, but then he'll know we're on to him and that will make it more difficult for us to apprehend him. If so, he may change tactics and go after his targets off the set."

The other attorney said, "Tank, have you informed local law enforcement?"

"Yes, and we've posted his photo with the Hollywood Division of LAPD and the California Highway Patrol."

Hollywood

Actors Mel Gibson, Jon Voight, and Gary Sinise all laughed at a joke shared between them. They sat on director chairs impatiently thumbing their iPhones when Tank and Powers walked in with Julienne O'Kray.

Gary Sinise stopped texting, stood up, extended his hand and said, "Senator Powers, it's great to see you. I truly enjoyed your dismemberment of Stephanopolis. We miss you on the Senate floor watching you on C-SPAN. There's nobody left that honestly says what they mean or is as entertaining. I loved your straight talk and disdain for political correctness. It was great entertainment. Speaking of someone with no respect for PC, have you ever met my cohorts here, Mel and Jon?"

Gibson said, "Yes, I'm Mr. PC. I'm offended by how easily others are offended."

Powers shook hands with both men, introduced Tank and Lucas and said to Gibson, "I have watched with pleasure every movie you've ever made, I'm a big fan of yours. But you're just not as good looking as that lady over there."

He nodded in the direction of the actress, Angie Harmon who smiled back radiantly, flipped him a wave, and returned to her conversation with Kelsey Grammar.

Fifteen other people who supported the production of *Unsustainable* milled around until Julienne O'Kray raised her voice to say, "May I have your attention, please. The shorter we make this meeting, the sooner you can get back to whatever you were doing before I called this impromptu get-together."

The staff conversations came to a stop.

"This big man standing next to me is Jorge Alvarez, known to everyone as Tank. Call him Jorge at your own risk."

Everyone laughed when Jon Voight said, "Mel, you try it first. I'll watch."

Tank said, "The producer of *Unsustainable* hired White Knight Personal Security because we have reason to believe that Julienne is at risk from a life-threatening attack by a mercenary paid by people who don't want Real America Productions to succeed in Hollywood. You all know more than I that Hollywood is a monolithic society of liberals, progressives, socialists, and even communists who don't want this conservative-leaning production to be a blockbuster."

Kelsey Grammar said, "So, what's new?"

"What's new is this guy." Tank held up a photo while Lucas handed out photocopies of Rocky Watters.

"This man's task is to stop the production of this movie using any means possible. If you see anything out of line or identify this guy in or around the studio, please inform either Lucas—please raise your hand, Lucas—Powers, or me."

Angie Harman asked, "What should we look for? What do you mean 'out of line'?"

Tank said, "Much like TSA encourages you to let them know if a package is left unattended, make sure you do the same around here.

"Also, if someone you don't know shows up acting as they belong in the studio, please, inform us. Any other questions?"

Gary Sinise raised his hand and asked, "Do we know who hired this hit man, is law enforcement informed, and why don't we shut down production until this criminal is apprehended?"

"Yes, yes, and that's up to Real America Productions. Stay vigilant. Back to you, Julienne."

"Thank you, Tank. The reason we don't want to shut down production is because that tips our hand to the thug that we're on to him. If we do that, he'll not come around—he'll more likely come to our homes."

One of the scriptwriters in the back yelled out, "We should make a movie about this!"

Mel Gibson said, "Yeah, I'd get to play myself."

Another person said, "We could call it 'Getting Even with Mad Max.'"

Julienne said, "OK, everyone, back to work."

Rocky laid on the rooftop of a Chinese Restaurant two blocks away from the Real American Productions studio peering through his high-powered binoculars. He saw Tank go in and out of the main entrance directing a contractor as to where they should locate CCTV cameras. No doubt, he thought, they'd also install an intrusion detection system and insist that the studio issue access control keys.

He thought, "Going to Plan B."

Real America Productions, Hollywood

It was 02:30 PDT and only one light was on in the central office—a digital artist was on a creative roll to depict the destruction of California's primary water aqueduct.

The artist's creative juices were fading, so he decided to get a jolt of caffeine in the cafeteria. He pulled out a Keurig K-cup, Emeril's Big Easy Bold; placed it in the coffee maker; and waited for it to fill his Real America Productions coffee cup.

He sniffed. He smelled something out of place, like rotten eggs or someone's fart. It had a sulfur smell. He wondered where he had experienced it before. He couldn't quite place it.

He never did.

The explosion overpressure blew the artist fifteen feet into the cafeteria wall; his head whipped onto cinderblock seconds before the fireball engulfed him. The flames reached thirty-five feet in height, but the sprinkler system dampened the structure enough to contain the fire until the firefighters and police arrived.

At 03:10, Tank walked up to an LAPD officer who was having a conversation with the fire chief and said, "I'm the head of security for Real America Productions. What happened here?"

The cop assessed Tank and decided he wasn't part of the press corps and said, "Apparently there was a leak in a line that provided natural gas to this studio." He looked at the fire chief and added, "The explosion took the life of an occupant of the studio. He or she is not yet identified."

Tank asked, "Were you aware that there was a threat against this studio? Could this be arson?"

The fire chief said, "The fire marshal investigating the scene has not ruled out arson."

Tank pulled a piece of paper out of his back pocket and said, "This is a photo of the person who threatened this studio. Have you observed anyone looking like this guy hanging around, maybe watching his handiwork?"

The fire chief shook his head, but the police officer studied it a little longer. He said, "Chief, isn't he one of yours?"

The fire chief shook his head and said, "He's not from Station 35."

The officer said, "I could have sworn I saw someone resembling this guy in a fireman's suit."

Tank asked, "Where and how long ago?"

The cop pointed in the direction of the security fence and said, "Maybe ten minutes ago. His uniform was clean. It's what drew my attention to him."

Tank ran off in the direction the officer pointed with his high luminous flashlight to find a firefighter not doing his job. What he found seventy-five yards later was a pile of firefighting equipment, boots, a suit, and gloves.

Tank yelled a series of foul words in Aztec.

Los Angeles

The *Hollywood Reporter*: "It is rumored in Hollywood circles that the production of a conservative movie by Real America Productions is suspended indefinitely after a fire broke out in the studio overnight.

The cast of Unsustainable was unhurt in the fire although the expected B-rated movie special effects producer remains in critical condition at Hollywood Presbyterian Medical Center. Arson has not been ruled out by the Hollywood Fire Department."

CHAPTER 53

"If you want to change the world, pick up your pen and write." – Martin Luther King, 1929-1968, Baptist Minister and a leader of the civil rights movement

Philadelphia, Pennsylvania – October 21st

The Annenberg Public Policy Center increased the size of its staff at FactCheck.org to cover the ever-increasing number of claims made by politicians, historians, cable news pundits, editorialists, scientists, and academics. Each new hire was interviewed via webcam by Maya Cherokee. The rejection rate was high, so it took the director of the nonprofit organization much longer than the director had hoped.

Two of the new hires were consumed with the plethora of facts emanating from Wichita State University's HonestMediaMatters.edu and Liberty University's School of Journalism website.

They were busy checking facts like: What countries have the highest per capita homicide rates? Honduras, Venezuela, Belize, El Salvador, Guatemala, and Jamaica. Facts like: NASA reports that ocean water levels fell for the past two years. Facts like: Seventy-nine percent of guns used in crimes were owned by someone else other than the gun owner. Facts like: The USA, New Zealand, and Canada have the highest rate of charitable donations as a percentage gross domestic product in the world.

Wiscasset

Some men have man-caves where they party, watch sports, play pool and foosball, and stock a bar. Other men have woodworking shops where they neatly display their tools and make birdhouses. Tucker had a laboratory where he and Maya performed experiments. They enjoyed testing theories involving physics and chemistry. The lab also provided learning experiences as part of Star's home schooling.

It was rare for Tucker to get out on his own. He decided to drive down to the city of Bath to pick up the latest in underwater drone technology and a few other items at a hobby shop. The owner of the shop, Steve, knew Tucker by sight and loved to share his most recent scientific discoveries with him.

Out of habit and training, Tucker always tried to keep his back against a wall. He tried to stay vigilant and not let his guard down. It was a good thing because two hard-looking men wearing unseasonably heavy outerwear entered the hobby shop while the owner showed Tucker a GPS with greater range than previously available.

One of the men looked in Tucker's direction while the other stood by the door. Tucker asked the owner, "Do you recognize these men? Are they regular customers?"

He shook his head and casually wandered over to the checkout counter. The owner knew Tucker's history.

Tucker had a concealed carry permit and had his Sig Sauer with a bullet chambered. But he wasn't quick enough when the man pulled a Colt 1911 and said, "Freeze, or I'll shoot. Put your hands on your head."

Tucker assessed the situation and decided to obey the attacker's instruction.

The man said, "Walk out the front door with your hands on your head, and no one will get hurt."

The owner pulled a 12-gauge shotgun out from under the counter and said to the stranger, "Drop your weapon, or I'll blow your face off."

The man turned to look at the owner. Big mistake.

Tucker dropped to the floor while he pulled his Sig. The man turned in reaction to Tucker's movement and fired his pistol in Tucker's direction.

As promised, the attacker's face was removed. The second man charged into the shop, his 9mm Glock outstretched, fired, and hit the owner in the right shoulder. Tucker fired three shots from his Sig Sauer; one landed in the attacker's chest, one hit the man's stomach, and one missed and embedded in the door frame.

Glock-man was down but not out. He rolled on the floor and aimed his gun in Tucker's direction. But before he got a round off, he was hit by a second blast from the owner's semiautomatic Mossberg.

Tucker couldn't tell whether he was deaf from the gunfire, or the silence meant the battle was over. He tried to stand to check on the shooter but couldn't. Tucker was hit.

He called out to the owner, "You OK?"

He said, "No, he got me."

Tucker pulled out his cell phone and called 9-1-1.

It seemed like an eternity although it was only minutes before the Bath police and the emergency response team arrived. Tucker and the owner were both going to live—unlike their two attackers.

Bath, Maine

Maya entered Tucker's Bath Memorial Hospital room with a White Knight, one of several who provided security at the Cherokee Estate. He guarded the room while Maya came to his bedside.

She hugged him and kissed his lips. Tears clouded her radiant eyes. She said, "Do I have to keep you by my side at all times to keep you out of trouble?"

Tucker said, "Yes, please keep me by your side. Where's Star? Is she guarded?"

"Yes, she's under guard, and Ram's with her."

"What do you know?"

"For one, that you are mortal—something you seem to forget from time to time. Another thing is that the 45 blew a hole through your thigh big enough for a Mack truck to drive through, but it didn't hit an artery. You won't be walking without a limp for a long time. But at least you'll walk."

Tucker said, "I mean do you know who did this? How did they know I was in Bath? What were they going to do with me if they succeeded in kidnapping me?"

"Neither attacker carried identification, and one can't be identified through facial recognition. A photo of the one who still had a face was introduced into the FBI facial recognition database. I also managed to get a photo to Tony Vinci. We'll know soon. We don't know the 'how', 'what', 'where,' and 'why' yet."

"How's Steve?"

"He's in a room down the hall. He was in the ICU for a while, but I understand he'll survive. The verdict is still out as to whether he'll ever regain full use of his arm."

"He saved my life."

Maya nodded, tears once again filling her eyes and leaking down her cheeks. She said, "We'll make sure he gets the best medical help available."

Maya's cell phone rang. She looked at the caller ID and said, "It's Tony."

"Put him on speaker."

Tony said, "Are you there with Tucker?"

"Yes, he can hear you. What do you have for us?"

"The hit came out of Boston. It was ordered from Washington. You know the buyer. It was Clayton West."

CHAPTER 54

"Do not fear the enemy, for your enemy can only take your life. It is far better that you fear the media, for they will steal your HONOR." – Groucho Marx, 1890-1977, comedian

The Hamptons, Long Island, New York – October 22nd

The Uber driver pulled up alongside the road in his six-year-old Nissan Sentra where he was instructed to pick up a customer, but he didn't see anyone. He honked his horn and flashed his lights on and off and waited a couple of minutes.

Out of nowhere, a man knocked on his driver's-side window, scaring the shit out of him. A man in his fifties, looking disheveled, moved his hands in the universal sign that told the driver to roll his window down.

Zimmerman said, "I'll tip you an extra hundred dollars if you break every land-speed record known to man to get me to the East Hampton Airport."

Upon arrival, Levi hustled into the airport and beelined to a bank of storage boxes used by frequent patrons. He opened one of the boxes and pulled out a fake driver's license, a fake passport, and credit cards that matched the name on the passport.

Levi had called his pilot even before he'd called Uber. The pilot had the Cessna Denali gassed up and ready to fly to the requested destination, Halifax Stanfield International Airport in Nova Scotia, Canada.

Wiscasset

Tucker was on the computer researching the basic psychology of physical therapists. He was damn sure that his PT was a sadist. The recovery was more painful than the initial gunshot wound.

While in his home office and on his computer, Tucker checked the electronic versions of the *Wall Street Journal*, *The Washington Times*, and *The New York Times*. He also checked the Liberty University website, FactCheck.org, HollywoodReporter.com, and HonestMediaMatters.edu. It had become part of his daily routine.

Surprisingly, it was the *NYT*'s headline and featured article that caught Tucker's eye: "Paradigm Change in Journalism School. Younger Professors at the Top Journalism Schools Teach Instead of Preach."

The article went on to rank Wichita State University and Liberty University in the top twenty-five journalism schools for the first time. Additionally, the article, written by Professor Orwell of UC-Berkeley, cited a Nielsen poll showing a marginal increase in reader confidence in journalistic honesty and integrity.

Tucker called out to Maya, "Sweetheart, we may be having an impact after all."

Mountain View

Lawrence Slaughter, CEO of California Media Group, listened to the interview between White Knight Personal Security, LLC, and Levi Zimmerman sent to him directly by the interviewers. He noticed all the law enforcement people the file was sent to and wondered why he was added to the list. Of course, so will the FBI wonder.

He could feel the hair in his ears grow. His hands shook, which caused him to spill brandy on his Hawaiian shirt. He was not surprised Zimmerman had sold him out. Levi must have figured that pointing the finger in Lawrence's direction would give Levi enough time to execute an escape plan.

Slaughter knew the FBI now had justification to start sniffing around and trying to pin something on him.

He thought, "And they'll find something. Just like that Israeli woman did. It's time to execute my own escape plan after the conference in Chicago."

Washington, DC

Senator Peter Enya reached a level of anger he'd not achieved since he was a teenager—he was blood-coming-out-his-eyes mad. It wasn't the fact that the chairperson of the Democratic National Committee had suggested that today's talking point be directed at Enya, but that his membership in the foundation had been disclosed. He knew by whom.

The chairperson of the Democratic National Committee: "Senator Enya is unstable. He is using his position as chairman of the Select Committee on Intelligence to undermine the First Amendment. I have it on good authority that he is a high-ranking member of a secret society whose dogma is to suppress the media from reporting pro-progressive news. Today's talking point is that the Republican Party leadership is unstable and opposes the First Amendment of the Constitution."

Editor for the *Chicago Tribune*: "Do you have a name of this alleged secret society?"

The chairperson of the Democratic National Committee: "My source advises me that the name of the group is the Foundation for Media Transformation."

President of Media Matters for America: "Who are other members of the anti-media foundation?"

The chairperson of the Democratic National Committee: "The other members we know for sure are Michelle Mallard, former Senator Powers, and his partner, Jorge Alvarez."

Editor for *The Boston Globe*: "Consider taking this new information and expand the talking point to 'Republicans may consider eliminating the First Amendment.'"

Senior Senator from Illinois: "Make it pithy, 'Republican Enya opposes free speech.'"

The chairperson of the Democratic National Committee: "Done. Any objections?"

Editor of *Los Angeles Times*: "Not an objection, just a comment. Since Jorge Alvarez was a person of interest in the death of Gabriel Lakatos, why don't we tie Senator Enya into it, say, "Senator Enya may be investigated in the death of philanthropist Lakatos.""

Editor for the *Chicago Tribune*: "Perfect."

The chairperson of the Democratic National Committee: "Even better. Any objections?"

None were forthcoming.

It took every molecule in Senator Enya to resist yelling, "I have an objection." It was a good thing he'd taped the call. It was going to be his primary defense when the FBI came looking up his skirt, checking under his bed, looking for an unsecure server, and reading his every e-mail, which he suspected they already did anyway.

Peter dreaded his next call, but he couldn't avoid it. He had to share this development with Tucker.

CHAPTER 55

If a secret piece of news is divulged by a spy before the time is ripe, he must be put to death together with the man to whom the secret was told. - Sun Tzu, 554 BC–496 BC, Chinese general, author of *"The Art of War"*

Washington, DC – October 23rd

Clayton West knew he was treading on thin ice, that he'd overshot the runway metaphorically. People inside The Media Transformation Foundation realized he was a traitor to his boss, Peter Enya. A few people also knew he'd given Tucker Cherokee access to the DNC daily talking point secure WebEx site.

He made the long walk at least once every week down the mall from the Senate Hart Building to the Vietnam War Memorial. It brought him comfort to stand before the dark wall, raise his right hand, and place his fingertips on his father's name. Nixon was president when Captain West was gunned down by a fifteen-year-old Viet Cong he was trying to save.

"What a useless war."

It was a political war, not a war necessary for America's survival. As he grew up, he saw politicians draw young American soldiers, marines, sailors, national guardsmen, and Air Force war fighters into new wars of questionable necessity.

He'd worked hard to get on the inside and observe how decision-making was done. The more time he spent in Washington, the more he detested the people who were elected to allegedly represent their constituents. These people thought they lived atop Mount Principle; he believed they suffered from cognitive dissonance.

"What a joke."

A man West didn't recognize stood next to him, placing his fingers on the name of another fallen hero. No one else was within ten yards of the two of them. He said to Clayton, "You're burned."

The man pulled his hand down from the wall, turned his back to Clayton and walked south in the direction of the Lincoln Memorial.

Clayton was frozen in place. He couldn't move. All his available synapses fired to think about what he would do when he brought his hand down from feeling the impression of his father's name. Should he return to the Senate Hart Building, grab his personal gear, and head out to the airport, or should he catch the metro to Union Station and take Amtrak to places unknown?

He chose neither option. Instead, he walked north on the mall to the Smithsonian metro exit, exited at Reagan National, and rented an Avis compact car. He drove south on Jefferson Davis Highway staying off I-95 until he reached Fredericksburg, Virginia, where he checked in to a Holiday Inn Express. Clayton caught the elevator up to his third-floor room.

Inside he turned on the TV, sat in a lounge chair next to the bed, pulled out his cell phone, and ordered a pizza to be delivered to his room from Godfather's.

He was pretty sure he was safe and no one had followed him.

Pretty sure.

Forty minutes later, someone knocked on his hotel room door and hollered "Pizza delivery." Clayton peaked through the peep hole and saw a teenager in uniform with a pizza warmer. He opened the door, accepted the box removed from the warmer, tipped the boy, and watched him leave the room. But a stranger's foot prevented the delivery boy from shutting the door completely. The man entered the room wearing an ancient Richard Nixon Halloween mask and held a pistol with a silencer extended from the barrel. The delivery boy ran to the stairwell in fear.

Clayton ran to the hotel room window and attempted to open it, but he was unable. The hotel locked the windows so no one could jump or fall out. Nixon emptied his magazine. Blood splattered the windows.

The next day an article was published in *The Washington Times*: "Washington, DC: Clayton Alexander West, chief of staff for Senator Peter Enya, was found dead in a hotel room in Fredericksburg, Virginia, only hours after he alleged that Senator Enya was a high-ranking member of an anti-free-speech secret society.

"Pending confirmation by the medical examiner, Fredericksburg police said he was shot sixteen times and that the murder had to be an act of passion.

"An unnamed FBI agent said Clayton West was also under investigation for the death of NORAD Commander Wes Blackstone and the attempted murder of Tucker Cherokee, CEO of Entropy, LLC, Boston, Massachusetts."

Halifax Stanfield International Airport, Nova Scotia, Canada

The chartered Cessna Denali touched down without incident. Zimmerman thanked the pilot and gave him directions to refuel and to schedule a flight plan to Boston Logan Airport. Levi deplaned with no intent to be on that flight. The passport control agent at Halifax Stanfield cordially accepted Levi's false identification without question.

Zimmerman breathed a sigh of relief. He was safely out of the United States. He calmed himself, thought about his next course of action, walked casually with confidence, and headed for the taxi stand. As he walked through the airport, he decided that his next move, even before he grabbed a bite to eat, was to go to the Bank of Nova Scotia where he had one of his offshore accounts and a safe-deposit box. He was a long-term planner and it paid off.

Until it didn't.

The concourse was crawling with law enforcement types. The cop with two Dobermans set off alarm bells for him. He had no luggage but decided to ride the escalators down to baggage claim. He noticed that the cop with the dogs grabbed an elevator. Zimmerman caught the escalator back up to the ticket counter level in hopes of ditching the K-9s. At the top of the escalator, Levi was greeted with a Royal Canadian Mounted Police badge stuck in his face.

He turned and ran back down the escalator only to see the cop with two Dobermans waiting at the bottom. He looked back up to the RCMP officer to see he was aiming a Beretta .40 APX in his direction.

Rod Nelson said, "Go for the dogs. That would be fun to watch."

New York City

Darrell Hammond announced, "From New York City, it's *Saturday Night,* with special guest, comedian Dennis Miller." The band played the traditional melody featuring the upbeat sound of a saxophone while Dennis walked onto the stage.

Miller bowed, spread his arms wide, smiled, and said, "I didn't think I'd ever be invited back on this show after I came out of the closet and admitted that I was a conservative. Did you know that the keyboards of comedy writers malfunction when they write jokes about the liberal press? I don't know how the Writer's Guild does that. This is my first opportunity to perform in front of an audience that wasn't given medication to resist laughing at jokes about the progressive media. This is exciting because I can't wait to tell jokes about liberals to a conservative audience. Let's start the first skit."

Wiscasset

At the end of the first skit, Maya turned off the TV after she watched the *Saturday Night Live* show and said to Tucker, "Why is it so hard to write comedy that makes fun of the liberal media?"

Tucker responded, "Because most of the writers have been programmed to be liberal. It's hard to make fun of yourself. But Liberty University has added a class in its school of journalism on comedy writing."

Maya asked, "Who is teaching the class?"

Tucker smiled conspiratorially and said, "I thought we needed a new challenge."

Maya said, "No way. I hope you're just kidding. I know my limitations. No way, Tucker."

"First class is in three months. We get to work on it together."

Maya said, "No way. Tell me you're just pulling my chain."

Tucker just smiled.

CHAPTER 56

"We tend to justify our actions, and in a sense, we color history to achieve that objective." Robert McNamara, 1916-2009, Secretary of Defense during Vietnam War

Salmon, Idaho – October 24th

"We have a common interest. We've assembled to right a wrong. Without pushback, the country—hell, the world—will devolve into a place where no one has an incentive to work, to invent, or improve life. The gap between the haves and the have-nots will widen. Health care will deteriorate and only a few will dictate to all.

"It's time to accelerate, peg it up a notch, get more aggressive. There's an upcoming Society of Professional Journalists convention in Chicago in two weeks. We all need to attend. Meet me here at the Sacajawea Interpretive Culture and Education Center this Saturday and I'll share the plan. We can eliminate hundreds of sick liberal puppies and lead investigators in the wrong direction.

"Thank you, and I'll see you then."

The fourteen followers of Craig Lakatos's Constitutional Militia hollered the fight slogan "Win or Die!" and exited the parking lot where they had assembled.

Craig turned to Dan Murphy and asked, "Can you make it happen in Chicago?"

The Australian said, "Damnit, Craig, haven't I proven myself to you yet? Didn't I plant a GPS tracking device on your Dad's rented Toyota Land Cruiser as promised right under the noses of his security team? Didn't I take him out for you, eliminate all witnesses, and make you a billionaire. Didn't I hire a student within six hours of your request who was willing to throw a Molotov Cocktail into *The Washington Post* headquarters? I even developed an escape plan for him. Didn't I take care of that New York Times' fag, Drake Pasqua, for you? And all these crimes are going to get pinned on that limp-wristed, weak-kneed, The Media Transformation Foundation."

"Ok, OK, Dan, get a grip. And I'm paying you a helluva lot of money to make things happen and get things done. Now share with me your plan for Chicago."

Dan took a deep breath, counted to five and said, "I've acquired three 40-millimeter laser-guided missiles and two M320 grenade launchers. It cost you a blooming' fortune but we got 'em. They're on their way to Chicago as we speak in a UPS truck that thinks they're delivering an exhibit booth to the conference center."

Craig said, "I assume it won't quite make it into the exhibit area?"

Dan said, "No, of course not. But it *will* make it to the Marriott Hotel across the street."

Craig responded, "I'm curious, how are you going to make it look like the White Knight guys are responsible for the attack on the journalists?"

Dan responded, "You let me worry about that. The Media Transformation Foundation is a perfect decoy— it's a good thing your Dad learned about them. One thing we need to make sure we do is to make reservations for hotel rooms in the name of Jorge Alvarez and Powers. Part of the plan is to have our militia visible but nowhere near Chicago. When we meet on Saturday, I'm going to send them to Portland, Oregon, where a protest the manufacturing of plastic straws is scheduled. I figure our guys can elicit a little violence by counter protesting. The Constitutional Militia will get national coverage at the same time Chicago police are sweeping up body parts of journalists in Chicago."

"Craig," Dan continued, "can we talk about Zimmerman?"

"What's to talk about? The dumb shit got caught. He knows nothing about the militia and nothing about my hatred of my father. He has no reason to suspect us and, therefore, is unlikely to lead law enforcement to our doorstep when they interrogate him. And I'm sure he doesn't know a thing about the secret account my dad left for me in a bank in Salmon, Idaho. Who would look here?"

Murphy said, "No matter. After the Chicago mission, I'm going to hide out for a while and enjoy all the money you paid me."

Hollywood

"Tank," said Powers, "you have to calm down. Pounding holes in drywall won't speed up Tony Vinci's effort to locate Rocky Watters.

"Rocky is probably somewhere on his way to Bali, Indonesia, or Buenos Aires. He knows he can't find a place in the United States where he can hide from law enforcement, much less you. We need to help Julienne, here, recover from the explosion instead of focusing on revenge. We'll eventually catch up with the son of a bitch."

Tank said, "OK, OK. Julienne, what can we do to help you?"

Julienne said, "Do you think we're out of the woods? Do you think this guy is done and out of the country and not hanging around planning on killing all of us?"

Tank said, "We can't be sure, so Tucker has authorized increased security for Real America

Productions. Our insurance coverage is good, so the studio will be rebuilt. We're going to relocate to a studio in Pasadena until reconstruction here is complete. How are the cast and staff handling the crisis?"

Julienne said, "The cast is tough. They are not willingly letting a domestic terrorist win. The staff is frightened but will follow the cast's lead."

"And you?"

"I am more determined than ever to complete this film. It's going to be a blockbuster."

Tank's satellite phone rang. It was Tony Vinci. Tank answered, "What do you have for me, big guy?"

Tony said, "To be called a big guy by you is interesting. The psychology behind it is worth exploring."

Tank responded, "Cut the shit, Tony. What do you have?"

"Seventh floor, Los Altos Villas, Vera Cruz, Mexico."

"Is he there under an alias?"

"Numb nuts didn't think of that."

Vera Cruz, Mexico

Officer Doug Butterfield had never been south of Calgary. The trip from Fort Chipewyan, Alberta, to Vera Cruz, Mexico, had exhausted him. He met up with Lucas Justice in Mexico City, where they strategized about how to tackle the arrest and extradition of Rocky Watters to Alberta for the murder of Kika Kisecawchuck. Butterfield had the authority to arrest Rocky in Mexico; Lucas had the muscle.

Butterfield said, "We blond guys look a little out of place down here. Watters will see us coming from a kilometer away. Your idea may work if we can secure the equipment. How good a shot are you?"

"It's not a skill I'm known for, but unless you have a better idea, we should give it a try. If I miss and he runs, we need a trap. Where would he run to? I bet he has a plan."

"Well, Lucas, you better not miss."

Rocky Watters sat at a table in the restaurant Ciobanus with his back to the wall eating mussels and sipping on his second glass of tequila. When his eyes weren't scanning the pages of a Lee Child paperback, he was eyeing the legs of the twenty-something senorita who waited on his table.

Rocky wished he spoke better Spanish but did his best to communicate with the woman. He raised his glass, winked at her, and placed a wad of cash on the table. Although she knew he was making a proposal to her, she pretended that he just wanted another glass of tequila. She brought him a clean glass from the bar, filled to the brim, leaned over his table to give him a good view of her cleavage, smiled, and winked back at him.

Encouraged by her response, he patted her rear end. She gave him another smile, tapped his watch with a rose-colored fingernail, and held up one finger. He interpreted her charade gesture to mean she was off in one hour.

Rocky went back to his paperback novel and sipped more tequila until he couldn't focus on the words. His vision blurred, he felt dizzy, the room moved on him, and his heart started to race. His forehead pounded the paperback on the table just before his body slumped to his right and off the chair to the floor.

Patrons in the restaurant ran to his side and yelled for help. The waitress told everyone to calm down and that she would call for an ambulance. Instead, she called Butterfield, who waited outside with Lucas. The two of them rushed in, picked Rocky up by his shoulders and feet, placed him on a gurney, and whisked him out and into a van.

Lucas said, "I've got to hand it to you, Doug, drugging his drink was a much better idea than my tranquilizer gun takedown approach. Let's cuff him before he wakes up."

CHAPTER 57

"A lot of the evil in the world is actually not intentional."—George Soros, 1930-present, liberal activist

Yellowknife, Northwest Territories, Canada – October 30th

Rocky Watters shuffled into the visitor's room wearing leg irons linked to his handcuffs. The large prison guard pushed him along until he reached the seat in front of the plexiglass window.

With both his hands linked together Watters picked up the phone to communicate with his first visitor since he became a guest of the Yellowknife Correctional Service of Canada.

Napoleon Drygeese picked up the phone on the other side of the plexiglass security and said, "Welcome to Hotel Yellowknife. You can go anytime you want but you can never leave."

"What the fuck do you want, Napoleon?"

"The guard that brought you in? His last name is Drygeese.

"The warden here is Kika Kisecawchuck's second cousin.

"The head cook at this prison is Chuck's sister.

"And you're going to spend the rest of your life here. You're going to wish Canada had the death penalty."

Budapest, Hungary

FBI Special Agent Michael Roberts and a US Treasury Secret Service agent entered the ING Bank on Dózsa György in Budapest, Hungary, with the Budapest police, Rendőrség, to check whether one of Gabriel Lakatos's numbered safe-deposit box keys fit the identical number at this bank where one of his offshore accounts resided.

The key fit. In the box were gold bars and an envelope addressed to Craig Lakatos. In the envelope was a letter: "Dear Craig, it saddened me beyond anything in my life to realize how much you hate me, my ideology, my passion to correct wrongs in the world, and my life priorities. You should know that I loved you unconditionally even after I learned that you formed a right wing radical group whose mission was to erase my progress in moving the world toward economic equality.

"Yes, I hypocritically used capitalism as a vehicle to garner funds for my mission.

"Yes, I ruined lives in my path to achieve the end.

"Yes, I could have been a better father, but you rejected me at an early age.

"I'm not asking you to follow in my footsteps, but please, don't erase all I've stood for. Don't destroy the Lakatos name.

"Watch your back. Trust no one.

Signed: Gabriel Lakatos"

Roberts said more to himself than the others in the room, "I wonder if Craig Lakatos hated his father enough to kill him? He formed a right wing radical group?"

Agent Roberts texted Rusty Winemiller with the new information and a question: "Where is Craig Lakatos now?"

Hauppauge, Long Island, New York

An irritated Detective Roger Sheppard confronted Suffolk County Medical Examiner Dr. Maverik Patton in his office in Hauppauge and said, "Looks like you dropped the ball on the Drake Pasqua murder case. I'm surprised that on such a high-profile case involving the editor of *The New York Times*, that you wouldn't give it more of your time. You're losing it, old man."

"Ah," said Dr. Maverick Patton, "my young investigator, your timing is impeccable. You must have smelled the news."

"What news?"

"Well, I haven't issued my report because I wanted to tie DNA results to somebody."

Roger said, "DNA results? Why didn't you inform me that you found DNA earlier?"

Patton said, "I didn't want to waste your time. I had no idea if the hair fiber I found wrapped in the newspapers on the mannequin was even human or in any way relevant. You would have stood over me for days, harassing me, until I had an answer."

"Terrible excuse, Doctor. What did you learn?"

"The hair fiber was human."

"And?. ."

"The person from which the hair fiber came is of Australian decent."

Sheppard said, "What does that tell us exactly? It could have been from the paper boy, the newsstand salesperson, or the person that read the paper before he threw it out."

Maverick Patton answered, "That's true, which is why I didn't give you a report that told us too little to be helpful."

Detective Sheppard said, "Doc, I can tell you're holding out on me. Your attempt to hide a smile is not working."

"The hair fiber belongs to Daniel Murphy."

Sheppard put both of his palms out with a questioning expression on his face.

"Murphy served time in an Australian stockade, was dishonorably discharged from the Australian Army, and is currently living somewhere in the United States."

Roger Sheppard said, "Good stuff. Do we know where he is?"

Doc was still smiling.

"I'm all ears, Mav, as long as you don't have any No. 2 pencils."

Patton said, "I'll get to that in a minute, but a contact of mine at the FBI said that Dan Murphy's name showed up in a Pittsburgh safe-deposit box that belonged to Gabriel Lakatos."

Sheppard's eyes widened, his forehead furrowed, and his head cocked. Asking a rhetorical question, he said, "What's the relationship between *The New York Times* Editor Drake Pasqua and Gabriel Lakatos?"

Maverick Patton said, "That, my good detective, became obvious when we read the information on the thumb drive that was deposited in Pasqua's anus." The medical examiner handed Sheppard a printed copy of the manuscript:

"You could be next. It is time to repent."

Sheppard said, "Why does this statement make anything obvious?"

Patton said, "You need to build a better rapport with the FBI. This exact wording was received by fifty or so people the day after the murder of Gabriel Lakatos. One of the recipients was Drake Pasqua. My guess is two liberal media activists down, forty-eight or so to go."

Sheppard said, "You were going to say something about the No. 2 pencils used to kill Drake by forcing them through his ear canal into his brain."

"Yes. Although no DNA or additional information was derived from inspecting the pencils, I can tell you that death was not immediate. The killer took his time, jammed it slowly, a millimeter at a time until the hemorrhaging drowned his brain. Pasqua died a very painful death. This Murphy guy is a sadist."

Sheppard shared his thought out loud, "I wonder if there is a connection to the bombing of the MSNBC headquarters? Were any of their executives on the list?"

"Good question."

Quantico

Special Agent Rusty Winemiller, Cybercrimes Division, sat in his motorized wheelchair directing the agent assigned to investigate *The Washington Post* cybercrime when his encrypted tablet energized. The name displayed matched the code name for Tucker Cherokee.

He said to his subordinate, "I've got to take this call. We'll reconvene in thirty minutes. Thank you."

Winemiller scolded Tucker, "This better be good. I'm in my office."

Tucker said, "Tony Vinci located the Australian, Daniel Murphy's, account. I've texted you the routing and account number at a Wells Fargo Bank in Tucson, Arizona. He received payments from an ING account in Budapest, Hungary."

Tucker let that sink in for a couple of seconds before he continued, "Jimmy Ma discovered that hotel reservations were made on a credit card linked to Murphy in Powers' and Alvarez's name. The hotel is right across from the conference center in Chicago where journalists meet starting tomorrow. They're setting White Knight up for something."

Winemiller said, "Let me call you right back. I need to contact the Chicago field office."

Fifteen minutes later, Rusty had Tucker back on the phone and said, "We've connected #MrCraig to Craig Lakatos. We've also connected #MrCraig to newsvigilante.org and the right wing radical group Constitutional Militia. What you've given us connects Daniel Murphy, the sniper who we think killed Gabriel Lakatos, to the ING Bank in Budapest where Craig Lakatos has an account and where we found an admission by Gabriel Lakatos in a safe-deposit box that Craig hated him. The stars have aligned—we now have enough to get a warrant for the arrest of Craig Lakatos. We already had enough to arrest Daniel Murphy."

Tucker said, "Ah, that explains how the killers knew where Lakatos was when he was secretly in Wood Buffalo National Park—he told his son."

"Now, if we can stop whatever they're planning in Chicago, we'll be ahead of the game."

CHAPTER 58

"The writer is the engineer of the human soul."—Joseph Stalin, 1878-1953, ruled the Soviet Union from the mid-1920s until his death

Pasadena, California – October 31st

Julienne O'Kray and the scene director reviewed the final script prepared for the next cut with Angie Harmon in her trailer when the assistant producer interrupted them. All three glared at the violator. Angie said, "Time is money."

O'Kray knew it had to be important or the assistant producer would not have slowed the process down. "What is it?"

"The chief operating officer of Metro Goldwyn Mayer is here and has asked if he could see you."

The director's eyes widened, and Angie Harmon said excitedly, "Chris is here, at my trailer?"

The actress went to the door, peaked out around the assistant producer, and said to Julienne, "It sure is him with one of your security people standing next to him like he's a spy or something. I'd talk to him if I were you."

Julienne said, "I'll be back in less than thirty minutes. Don't go anywhere, and read the script again in my absence." Julienne walked down the three stairs from the trailer, extended her hand to the MGM executive, and said, "Please, follow me to my office."

As they walked from the trailer to the office, the MGM COO said, "You overcame a lot of adversity to keep this film going. That's impressive."

"Thank you."

He continued, "I understand you plan to release *Unsustainable* in two months? Also very impressive."

"Thank you." She didn't know what he was up to but chose to listen rather than speak.

"I also understand that you've stayed within budget even with the high-priced cast and intense special effects. Sorry about your special effects director. I knew him and he was a great guy."

The security guard opened the door to the producer's office and followed Julienne in behind the MGM COO. She offered her guest a chair and nodded at the security guard—his signal to leave.

The guard cocked his head to signal "are you sure" but she nodded affirmatively. He stood right outside the door in case she needed him.

The MGM executive got right to the point, "I'm here to offer you a five-year contract at MGM at a salary twice what you are currently making, and a bonus higher than any other movie producer in Hollywood tied to the success of your productions."

Julienne said, "That's an exciting offer, sir. In principle, I accept pending my attorney's review of the contract and, of course, the completion of my current obligation to Real America Productions, which includes the release of *Unsustainable*."

"Ms. O'Kray—"

"Please, call me Julienne."

"Julienne, you would have to start next week and abandon *Unsustainable*. 'Leave it on the cutting floor' as they say."

They stared at each other for a full thirty seconds. He spoke first, "It's a spectacular offer and I'll review with you the movie script we want you to tackle first when you start next week."

"Sir, working for MGM is a dream come true. It would be my honor to accept your generous offer, but I must insist on completing the film I am currently producing. It would be unethical for me to leave at this time."

The COO said, "I'm sorry, Julienne, we need you right away to start a film I know you would love to produce. The director is well-known to you and the cast is first rate."

Another thirty seconds passed. Julienne stood, walked from behind her desk opened the door and said to the White Knight security officer, "Would you please escort this gentleman out?"

The MGM executive said, "I'm very sorry you made the decision you just made. Call me if you change your mind over the next forty-eight hours."

As he was leaving, she said, "You won't succeed at delaying the production of *Unsustainable* by hiring me, and you won't drive Real America Productions out of Hollywood with this sort of tactic. The people who run our production company are determined to succeed. Good day."

Five minutes later, Julienne O'Kray was on the phone with Tucker Cherokee.

Fifteen minutes later she was back in Angie Harmon's trailer reviewing the next scene.

Quantico

Special Agent Rusty Winemiller's assistant said, "Sir, you have a call from a Long Island, New York, homicide detective. He said the FBI New York field office told him to contact you."

Rusty signed and said, "Put him through."

"This is Winemiller."

"Uh, hi. My name is Roger Sheppard. I'm a homicide detective for the Suffolk County Police Department. I am the lead investigator on a case you may have heard about and one that maybe involves the FBI Cybercrimes Division. The case involves the murder of Drake Pasqua, the editor of *The New York Times*."

Agent Winemiller said, "Yes, I recall the case."

"Well, I am told that the guy who committed this murder, Daniel Murphy, may be the same guy that committed the murder of Gabriel Lakatos."

Winemiller said, "That's Special Agent in Charge Michael Roberts's case. It's not a cyber case."

Sheppard said, "Are you going to let me finish or not?"

Winemiller stayed silent.

"I have it on good authority that after Lakatos was murdered, fifty or so people received digital contact stating 'You could be next. It is time to repent.'

"I understand that Pasqua was one of the recipients. It is only logical that someone on the floor in Rockefeller Center, where MSNBC resides, is also on the list. Since it is a cybercrime to threaten someone digitally, you might want to start warning the others on that list. I assume you already know the names that were threatened?"

"Thank you, detective. I appreciate your input and will follow up. You've closed your case and may have helped us close a cyber case."

Winemiller signed off and wondered who might have access to Tucker and Maya's list of fifty-two names. He also wondered how many of the names were going to attend the Chicago journalism conference. Rusty immediately contacted Tucker.

"Tucker, this is Rusty. Who had access to your list of fifty-two names?"

"Let's see, Maya, Tony, and Jimmy. Why?"

"Because someone may have leaked the names to a right-wing radical group that is using it to take out leaders of the liberal media."

"Hmmm. I trust all three implicitly."

"Would you send me the contacted? We may need to warn the others who were contacted."

"Let me talk to the team first."

Wiscasset

Tucker asked, "Maya, do you think anyone besides Tony Vinci and Jimmy Ma ever saw our list of fifty-two who we threatened after Gabriel Lakatos's murder?"

Maya said, "I can't imagine anyone else. Why?"

"Because Winemiller thinks someone wants to assassinate each person on it."

Maya said, "Only Jimmy Ma and Tony Vinci had access. This is not an indeterminable problem."

"Let's get both of them on the line in a conference call."

Maya made the arrangement, and both were on the conference call six minutes later.

"Gentlemen," Tucker said, "we have a problem. The FBI thinks our list of fifty-two media liberals was shared with a right-wing radical group bent on eliminating each person we threatened. How could this be?"

Jimmy Ma said, "No way it came from my side. Impossible."

Tony Vinci said, "Same here."

Tucker asked, "What other explanation can there be?"

Tony asked, "How did you come up with the list?"

Tucker said, "I constructed it from known liberal media activists."

Tony said, "So, couldn't someone else come up with an almost identical set of names?"

Tucker and Maya said in unison, "Good answer."

Chicago

The annual conference of the Society of Professional Journalists opened its registration desk at 08:00 in the conference center. Name tags were handed out to preregistered attendees and the plenary session of the conference started at 09:30. The guest speaker was Lawrence Slaughter, CEO of the California Media Group and chairman emeritus of the Society of Professional Journalists.

The limousine carrying Chairman Slaughter arrived at the conference center at 09:10. Across the street on the roof of the Marriott were FBI sharpshooters. Two doors down was an FBI SWAT team ready to roll if Daniel Murphy was spotted.

There were other interested parties in the vicinity.

Murphy picked out the sharpshooters on the roof and decided to pass on this mission so as to fight another day. He left the hotel out the back through the truck bay. He left a 40-millimeter laser-guided missile and an M320 grenade launcher in his hotel room.

Craig Lakatos had made arrangements for their escape after the mission was completed. He'd reserved two rooms at a hotel two blocks away that matched Craig's fake passport. They would slide to the other hotel and have dinner there while the chaos ensued at the Marriott and conference center.

Lakatos went to join Murphy in his hotel room to discover that Murphy was gone. Craig looked at his watch and knew he was going to have to launch the missile by himself. He waited only five minutes. The limo carrying Lawrence Slaughter was a minute from arrival.

They had practiced using the grenade launcher back in Idaho. Although Craig Lakatos had not practiced operating the launcher, he'd watched Murphy do it.

He had thirty seconds until launch. "That fucking Murphy. After all, I paid him, you'd think he wouldn't bail on me."

An FBI sharpshooter on the roof of the convention center spotted Craig with the grenade launcher and asked, "Permission to act?"

"Stand down until we confirm unsub."

Craig fired and the limousine exploded in a fireball. Flames rose to seventy-five feet in height. The overpressure threw conference attendees against brick walls, and gunfire erupted.

Chicago Tribune: "The Chicago field office for the Federal Bureau of Investigation stated that a right-wing radical group called the Constitutional Militia attacked the Chicago Conference Center where the Society of Professional Journalists were conducting their annual meeting. Four people died as a result of the act of domestic terrorism, including the society's Chairman Emeritus Lawrence Slaughter.

One of the right-wing terrorists, Craig Lakatos, son of Gabriel Lakatos, was killed in a firefight with the FBI. Another alleged terrorist, an Australian named Daniel Murphy, was found dead behind the Marriott Hotel with two injuries consistent with wounds expected from large-caliber rifles. Thus far, the investigation concludes that munitions were fired from separate weapons and neither were fired from standard weapons carried by FBI sharpshooters or the SWAT team."

Colorado Springs

Tank drove Tucker from the airport to the Colorado Springs police headquarters to meet with Detective Slick White and MP Major Javier Castro.

Detective White said, "Thank you, gentleman, for coming all this way. Especially you, Tucker, with your leg wound and all. I know you didn't have to, but your coming, especially without attorneys, tells me a lot.

"The murder of your friend, Commander Blackstone, on Peterson Air Force Base, remains unsolved. Both of you remain persons of interest, although, frankly, neither Javier or I think the probability that either of you is the perpetrator is high.

"Having said that, there is a lot of drama that surrounds you two, and you're exposed to more violence than the average bear. A second murder, right down the road from DC, involved Clayton West, Senator Enya's chief of staff."

Major Castro said, "Do I have my facts straight that the man that shot you in the leg was attempting to murder you?"

Tucker said, "Yes, it seems that way. At a minimum, they were trying to kidnap me."

Castro continued, "Do I also have it correct that there is a connection between the late Clayton West and the hit man that attacked you?"

Tucker said, "Hit men, plural."

Detective White said, "Then you had a motive to have him killed."

Tucker said nothing.

White continued, "You are connected to both open murder investigations. You see my point. And Mr. Alvarez here was, at one time, accused of murder in Canada. A lot of smoke surrounds you two. I'm worried there is a fire somewhere."

Detective White looked over at Tank and asked, "Mr. Alvarez, where were you the evening Clayton West was murdered?"

Tank said, "Not in Fredericksburg. Not in Virginia. I was a guest speaker at the University of California, Berkeley."

Major Castro said, "You know we will have to verify that?"

Tank said, "No problem."

Detective White asked, "Mr. Cherokee, if, in fact, Mr. West did hire hit men to kill you, why? Why would he want you dead?"

Tucker put his hands flat on the table, stared into the eyes of Detective White without blinking for a full ten seconds. White waited and could see the wheels churning in his head. He was a patient man. Finally, Tucker said, "Both of you visited with the talk radio queen, Michelle Mallard. During your interview with her, you learned that both Ms. Mallard and Commander Blackstone belonged to The Media Transformation Foundation. My wife and I are the founders. Tank is also an important part of it. In short, the purpose of the group is to figure out how to move the media to the right and report news honestly.

"Mr. West had the opposite political view and wanted to shut us down. The best way to do that, in his mind, was to eliminate its founder. That's my best guess."

Major Castro asked, "Did Clayton West know that Commander Blackstone was a member of your foundation?"

Tucker answered, "I don't know. I do know he has a brother in the area. I think he works at the Pueblo Army Chemical Weapons Destruction Facility. You might want to ask him where he was the night Commander Blackstone was murdered. I'd check to see if he belonged to a softball team. I'd also check, if I were you if there was a connection between Clayton's brother and an Eboni Williamson at the Pentagon. She's an IT geek with a financial link to the same ideological team that the West family does."

Castro asked, "Who else might have the motive to have Clayton West killed?"

Tucker had an idea who it was but didn't want to share it with the detectives. Instead, he said, "There's a foxy lady in DC called Abigale that he mistreated. You might want to follow that thread."

Detective White asked, "Mr. Alvarez, you've been exonerated from the accusation that you were part of the team that assassinated Gabriel Lakatos. Congratulations. For my own edification: why did his son kill the golden goose, his own father?"

A question for which there was no sane answer.

CHAPTER 59

"If you don't read the newspaper, you're uninformed. If you read the newspaper, you're misinformed." – Mark Twain, 1835-1910, author and humorist

Wiscasset, Maine – November 1st

Star sat in her dad's office chair while he was away. Ram lay in his office bed. Maya pulled up a seat adjacent to her daughter. Both computer monitors were activated, one with FactCheck.org pulled up, the other with a webcast where Star was getting her indoctrination as an intern.

Tucker and Maya argued about how her internship was to be conducted, and they compromised to allow Star to work remotely from home during her first year as a summer intern rather than working out of Philadelphia. The approach had the added benefit that Star would not be able to use her mind-reading skills on the job. She was going to have to survive on her own like any other intern.

Her first summer's task was to observe the organization's process for determining what facts to check and how to check them. Star could choose which fact-check answers she wanted to read. Star picked the facts she was most interested in. She was pleased to learn that in all her search, no one mentioned the word "Amberdelic." It had remained a secret.

FactCheck.org Title: CNN Report About Gabriel Lakatos's Death Misleading

"CNN reported that billionaire philanthropist Gabriel Lakatos left $19.5 billion to his foundation, charities, and other nonprofit organizations. The fact is that of his $21 billion net worth in known accounts and real estate, only $7 billion made it to his foundation, charities, and other organizations. $14 billion of the account paid off back taxes and settled pending lawsuits.

Gabriel Lakatos left $500 million to his late estranged son, Craig Lakatos, who is alleged to have hired a hit team to assassinate his father. The son left no will. The executor of Gabriel Lakatos's last will said the law required the $500 million become property of the State of New York."

Title: Fox New Reports that Craig Lakatos, Son of Gabriel Lakatos Was Mentally Ill

"A psychiatrist pundit for Fox News Network stated that the late Craig Lakatos must have been legally insane to have had his billionaire father, Gabriel Lakatos, assassinated. Craig Lakatos's psychiatrist responded to a warrant requested by the FBI for the release of his records. The FBI stated that there was no evidence in the records that Craig Lakatos was a sociopath or psychopath, or that he suffered from delusions. The conclusion of the FBI investigation is that Craig Lakatos was of sound mind and body when he created the right-wing radical group Constitutional Militia, the website newsvigilante.org, and the plan to murder over fifty members of a left-wing radical group that allegedly controlled the mainstream media. FBI Special Agent in Charge Michael Roberts reported that Craig Lakatos led investigators to suspect that a competing group, The Media Transformation Foundation, was responsible for Constitutional Militia activities."

Title: *Hollywood Reporter* Wrong about *Unsustainable*

"The Hollywood Reporter incorrectly credited the revenue generated by the movie Unsustainable, by Real America Productions, at $75 million. The correct number is $175 million."

Title: *Enquire* Incorrect about Media Cabal:

"An interview with talk radio host Michelle Mallard of Colorado Springs by *Enquirer* misquoted Ms. Mallard in her claim that the media is controlled by a media cabal of left-wing moguls that included highly visible members, including Jeff Jorgensen, the world's wealthiest person and former owner of *The Washington Post*; the late billionaire Gabriel Lakatos; the late CEO of California Media Group, Lawrence Slaughter; the late editor of *The New York Times*, Drake Pasqua; the late chief of staff for Senator Peter Enya, Clayton West; incarcerated Executor of the Lakatos Foundation, Levi Zimmerman; and many other well-known ideologically left media editors and publishers.

"There is no proof that such a cabal existed or exists."

Title: NRA Wrong According to FBI

"In the latest issue of the National Rifle Association's *Shooting Illustrated*, the chief of police for Chicago Police Department stated that the weapons used to take down the Australian terrorist sniper, Daniel Murphy, remain a mystery. According to Royal Canadian Mounted Police Detective Rod Nelson, Mr. Murphy was the hired triggerman for the murder of Gabriel Lakatos.

"A report issued by the Federal Bureau of Investigation in response to a congressional inquiry stated that a .50 BMG round was fired from a Barret M107 sniper rifle estimated to have been fired from four blocks away. The striations from the round found lodged in a concrete block matched the striations of the round pulled from an oak tree on Jeff Jorgensen's property in Seattle.

"The second round that passed through Daniel Murphy's chest was reported to be from an IWI DAN .338 sniper rifle typically used by Israel's Mossad.

"The report further stated that neither rifles are standard weapons carried by the FBI's Chicago field office or the Chicago Police Department.

"Craig Lakatos died of multiple wounds suffered from the FBI SWAT team located on the roof of the conference center.

"The case will remain open."

Star wondered where Sonja McLeod was at the time of the shooting but decided to never ask her.

Pentagon

Major Javier Castro deplaned at Andrews Air Force Base across the Potomac River in Maryland, caught the military shuttle to the Pentagon, and met Brigadier General Ronald Zax in his office. Major Castro saluted the general and remained standing until Zax said, "At ease, Major. Please sit down."

Castro looked at the construction of the office chair and asked if he could remain standing.

Zax said, "I read the report of your finding surrounding the murder of my friend Commander Wes Blackstone. Good work."

Major Castro waited for General Zax to continue. "How confident are you that you got the right person? There remains a lot of circumstantial evidence and too little 'smoking gun' quality evidence."

"Sir," said Major Castro, "with all due respect, the blood residue scraped off Captain West's aluminum softball bat matched Commander Blackstone's DNA. True, it wasn't a 'smoking gun'; it was a 'smoking bat.'"

Zax responded, "Oh, I have no doubt Captain West committed the murder. I have no doubt Clayton West directed his brother to commit murder for their cause. What I don't know is who at the top directed Clayton West to take out Blackstone. I don't think your investigation is over. I've discussed this with your superiors and they agree to leave you on the case until we know who is on top of the pyramid.

"I further understand that the police in Fredericksburg, Virginia, has not yet identified the person who killed Clayton West nor the person that directed the assassination."

Major Castro said, "To the best of my knowledge, your understanding is correct. Sir, you didn't ask me to come here all the way from Peterson Air Force Base to congratulate me for closing the case on Blackstone."

Brigadier General Ronald Zax eyed Castro carefully. "I want to know why."

"Why what, sir?"

"Why Blackstone was a target by whoever orchestrated the murder. Surely you've learned something about motive."

"You knew Wes well, right? As a friend?"

Zax nodded his head.

"Then you know he was actively conservative. West was actively liberal. It was a clash of ideology. Everyone gets shit on them in a shit storm."

"Worth murder? I don't believe that. What are you holding back, Major?"

Castro added, "Are you aware that West also tried to murder another conservative, Tucker Cherokee? Is that not evidence that West was a little wacked? What is your suspicion, sir? Why do you think I'm holding back something?"

"My suspicion is that you investigated me, his friend."

Major Castro said, "My job is to rule no one out until evidence proves otherwise. Did you instruct West to kill

Blackstone? You felt betrayed, didn't you, when you discovered your name was on Blackstone's list of people inside the Pentagon with ties to the cabal run by Lakatos, Slaughter, and Zimmerman? You agree with the concept of a one-world military with no borders, don't you? You believe in international law with NATO enforcing the laws. Where do you fit in to a one-world-government military? Do you see yourself as chairman of the joint chiefs of staff who reports to a single world leader? Who was that leader going to be, Gabriel Lakatos or a European king? Yes, general, you were under investigation for suspicion of treason. We became even more suspicious of you after we interviewed the IT expert Eboni Williamson to learn she aided you by allowing all your private conversations with the NATO Frenchman to be conducted from her private residence."

Brigadier General Zax opened his desk drawer, reached down, pulled out a Glock 21 with a .45 caliber round in the chamber. Before he managed to lift his hand up to take aim, a powerful right hook from a 310-pound weightlifter caught the general's left ear, which was followed by a head butt to the nose. Zax dropped onto his desk in an awkward position and never again moved.

Major Javier Castro was immediately arrested by Pentagon Military Police and charged with the murder of Brigadier General Ronald Zax and spent two nights in the brig in Fort Belvoir. The Military Police Internal Affairs Officer reviewed the case in detail with Castro but the major was unable to prove self-defense.

On the third day after his confrontation with Zax, his appointed JAG lawyer said the military was dropping all charges and that he was free to return to duty.

Castro asked, "What happened?"

The JAG answered, "It came down from way high. I'm too low on the food chain to know the specifics. However, there is a civilian outside the gate in a taxi who has asked if he could give you a ride to Andrews."

The lawyer gave Javier Castro a ride to the Ft. Belvoir gate. The big man spotted the taxi and asked the driver if he was waiting for him. He climbed into the back seat to see a dwarf. The contrast in their size was comical to both of them.

Tony Vinci said, "I watched and recorded everything that went on between you and Zax. I'm the guy who invented the nanodevice that was placed in Zax's office by my boss, Tucker Cherokee. He managed to get the video to someone in authority to release you."

Major Castro reached out to shake the short man's hand to thank him. Big Javier Castro could not match the strength of Tony Vinci's handshake. No one shook Tony's hand twice.

New York City

The courtroom clerk said in a loud and authoritative voice, "Please stand for his honor, Judge Michael Levine."

All in the courtroom stood as the judge took his place on the bench. After adjusting his spectacles, he said, "I understand we have a major development in the case. Would the counsels for both the plaintiff and defendant approach the bench?"

The attorney for the defendant, with his long silver hair, wore the same deerskin sports jacket and turquoise bolo tie as he'd worn in the previous court appearance. The plaintiff's attorney wore a brand-new power suit.

Judge Levine asked, "Tell me you've settled out of court and that we can dismiss the jury."

The two attorneys smiled, looked at each other, and said, "Actually, that is exactly what we will tell you."

New York Times headline: "MSNBC Settles Claim.

"A source close to the case confirmed that the plaintiff agreed to drop the claims against MSNBC if the news organization agreed to be acquired by Real America Productions for an undisclosed amount."

Washington, DC

Peter Enya sat on a bench at the National Zoo and watched a 600-pound tiger prance around an exhibit area in which the Smithsonian intended to replicate its natural habitat. He wore a long wool coat and fedora to stay warm; the senator made no attempt to conceal his identity. It was too late for that. Some things couldn't be fixed.

Also watching the tigers and sitting next to Senator Enya was Tucker Cherokee—cane and all. Tucker said, "I'm twenty years younger than you are, but I'm feeling old."

Peter said, "OK, I'll bite. Why?"

"Maya teased me about my limp. I'm still in physical therapy with one sick sadist. Anyway, she playfully called me 'Chester.' Star asked who Chester was, and I answered that he was a character on *Gunsmoke*. She asked, 'What's that?'"

Peter said, "Is there a moral to this story?"

Tucker said, "It wasn't that long ago, the old West. Back then when good prevailed over evil, there was nobody to second-guess you. When the sheriff shot a bad guy, the town celebrated. Today, the good guy gets second-guessed by a zillion people on Twitter.

"The moral of my story is that a good guy can't kill a bad guy anymore without consequences. Eventually, a detective from Fredericksburg, Virginia, is going to question you. The world is a better place without Clayton West, who, by the way, tried to have me killed."

Tucker added, "How'd you know he was in a Holiday Inn Express in Fredericksburg? How'd you manage to find a hit man so quickly? You're more resourceful than I realized."

Enya smiled and said, "To protect you, Tucker, the less you know, the better." Peter Enya took on a menacing appearance, his eyes darkened as they narrowed, and his expression turned hateful as his fists clenched and unclenched repeatedly.

"So, Tucker, who else knows?"

The question metamorphized Tucker from a concerned friend to a warrior. His internal antennae picked up a signal from Enya that heightened his senses and awareness.

The Senator lifted his frame off the bench and said casually, "It's time for me to return to the Senate Hart Building."

Without warning, he smashed into Tucker's left ear with a vicious elbow attack as he pulled a key ring out of his pants pocket, held one in his right hand with metal key firmly between his pointer and middle fingers, and swung toward Tucker's throat.

Tucker minimized what surely could have been a devastating blow to the side of his head by falling away from the direction of the attack. Still, the blow caused Tucker some temporary dizziness. He rolled on the zoo's pavement and simultaneously swung his cane and connected with Peter's right hand before the weaponized key successfully dug into Tucker's throat.

The pain in Peter's right hand from the hit by Tucker's cane made him drop the key ring. The senator kicked Tucker violently in the back of his head followed with a kick to the kidneys. Enya then lifted his right leg to stomp on Tucker's head. Although dizzy and in excruciating pain, Tucker rolled into Peter's leg, placed his left hand behind the heel of the foot still on the ground and leveraged his right shoulder into his calf just below the knee.

Enya screamed at the pain when his knee was forced to bend in the wrong direction and dislocate. He fell onto his butt pivoting his back backwards to the ground. The momentum from the fall forced his torso and head to accelerate onto the asphalt—the back of his head hit with a load crack.

"Stop right there," shouted a young Hispanic man in an official-looking security uniform.

Tucker was fighting nausea and visual focus but managed to say, "Thank God you showed up. This man is Senator Peter Enya and murdered a man named Clayton West and was trying to kill me."

The security officer said into his two-way radio, "Request back-up and emergency medical support." He turned to the two men on the laying ground and said, "Stay where you are. Smithsonian Protective Services and Park Police detectives will sort this out."

The guard kneeled next to Peter, felt for a pulse, but found nothing. The security officer looked over at Tucker and said, "You just killed a senator."

Georgetown University Medical Center

In the emergency room, Maya sat across from a seriously wounded Tucker who suffered a concussion and kidney bruising. Tucker said, "We're going to have to quit meeting like this."

Maya was not happy—she just spent five hours with the Park Police clearing Tucker of any wrongdoing and convincing the authorities that Peter Enya had motive to commit the assault on Tucker. She said, "Damn it Tucker, running The Media Transformation Foundation and the Amberdelic Group has been as dangerous as we feared. We need to stay in our compound in Wiscasset and let Tank and Powers do the dangerous stuff."

Tucker said, "Sounds good to me."

Maya added, "And Tucker, you have a concealed carry permit. Try to remember to use it."

CHAPTER 60

"A cynical, mercenary, demagogic press will in time produce a people as base as itself."—Joseph Pulitzer, 1847-1911, Hungarian-American newspaper publisher and New York congressman

Keystone, Colorado – August 1st, eighteen months later

Tucker and Maya sat in cushioned lounge chairs breathing in the light, crisp, Rocky Mountain air, far away from the oppressively humid heat torturing the east coast. They took in the smell of the sagebrush and conifers; experienced the golden aspens and deep forest evergreens; and marveled at the beauty of the tiny white, yellow, and orange alpine wildflowers, columbines, and prickly pears. But they had only thirty minutes left before they had to go inside the resort conference room to chair the seventh meeting of The Media Transformation Foundation.

Maya said, "This is so much better than having these meeting in caves and underground bunkers. Here, I feel like we're seemingly at the edge of the world, just about to touch the sky. This is spectacular."

Suddenly, a shadow enveloped the two of them. Tucker said, "Tank, damnit, your blocking the sun and our view."

"Sorry, boss, but it's time. We need to secure the facility—so, you need to go inside. We don't have long before your meeting starts. You'll have all day tomorrow to enjoy this place."

Maya said, "Tucker you go on in. I'll be right behind you, but first I'm going to call Star to see how she is doing back home with the SAT tutor. She's determined to score well."

Tucker agreed and went into the meeting room to review, again, his initial presentation which identified specific progress the foundation has made.

Outside Keystone Lodge

"OK, men, its showtime. This is a ten-minute job; in and out." The captain of the mercenary team continued, "We'll make 100 grand each—for you mathematically challenged, we'll earn $600,000 per hour. Good wages, don't you think?" The eclectic group of former Special Forces veterans chuckled at the captain's joke but were too focused on the mission to truly enjoy the humor.

"Smith-1, recite to me your role."

Smith-1 answered, "Pin down their security team while the rest of you do your part of the mission. I'll be positioned in the forest, 75-yards away in direct line-of-site to the guarded entrance with my silenced rifle in hand. I'll stay there until the mission is over then retreat deeper into the woods and eventually to our rallying point. I'll fire the first shot, take out Powers and turn my attention to Tank. That leaves the third guy which we expect will be running in the direction of the two down guards. I'll take him out and wait to see if any others show up to interfere with our mission."

"Good," said the captain, "And be sure to take Powers out first. We don't need him spoiling our payday.

"Smith-2, recite to me your role."

Smith-2 said, "Sir, After Smith-1 fires the first shot and takes out the first guard, I'll lead Smith-4 and Smith-5 into the front door, through the lobby and through the meeting room entrance. I will focus on terminating Tucker and Maya Cherokee while Smith-4 and Smith-5 spray brass around the right side of the room. Then we exit out the front and make our way to the rendezvous point in the woods."

The Captain said, "Be sure your team doesn't fire into the back wall of the room."

"Smith-3, recite to me your role."

Smith-3 said, "Yes, sir. After Smith-1 fires the first shot and takes out the first guard, I'll lead Smith-6 through the kitchen and into the back entrance to the ballroom. If anyone is running for cover out the back door, we'll terminate them, then we will carefully enter the meeting room and take out any remaining attendees on our right side of the room. Then we exit back out through the kitchen and make our way to the rendezvous point in the woods."

"Good. As captain, I'll be watching for anything that may go wrong and provide contingency back-up. My priority, however, is to make sure the meeting security team is neutralized.

"Let's go."

Keystone Lodge

As he walked into the conference room, Tucker greeted new foundation members which included new congressmen, the Assistant Secretary of the Army, the president of *Police Magazine*, Professor Orwell from the University of California-Berkeley, and a board member from the Media Research Center.

Tucker thought, "I miss the members of The Amberdelic Group who need to maintain complete secrecy—people like the Hurt Brothers, Winemiller, and the Ambassador."

Ten minutes later Maya walked in with Julienne O'Kray, Michelle Mallard, and Maggie Mellon, all of whom gave Tucker a warm hug. Maya pulled up a chair next to Tucker at the head table and whispered, "The tutor said Star is going to excel on the SATs."

Tucker said, "Did you ever doubt that? Are the White Knight agents still on duty?"

Maya said, "Yes, of course."

Tucker stood, approached the microphone, tested it, and said, "OK, everybody, take your seats, we're ready to start the seventh meeting of The Media Transformation Foundation. This meeting is hereby called to order.

"First, I'd like to welcome all the new members. Our exclusive and vetted enrollment has reached 42 members. We're proud to have each of you. As all of you are aware, the foundation has been exposed and is now, unfortunately, well known to the public. We are no longer able to operate in secrecy which we once hoped to maintain. Your membership will be difficult to hide from our liberal media adversaries. So, be careful. There are crazies out there and hundreds of conspiracy theories about what the foundation does. Did you know that we are funded by the Russians?"

Everyone laughed.

"Having said all that, I'd like to remind you that what is disclose in this meeting must be held private and not discussed with anyone not in this room."

Tucker continued, "The first order of business, as always, is to discuss our financial situation, ensure we have adequate funding to continue our neutralization of the biased main stream media, and that we have invested your generous contributions wisely. Afterwards, we'll discuss progress on each of our war fronts.

"Maggie, are you ready to give us an accounting of our current status?"

Outside the resort conference center, Tank, Powers, Lucas, and Ram vigilantly surveyed the surrounding to protect the members from any unwanted guests. They carried weapons as discreetly as possible and maintained constant communication as they patrolled the premises.

Tank was very nervous about this meeting because they had no natural fortification like they had in the past and threats against the foundation had increased exponentially over the last few months.

Lucas said to Tank over coms, "It's eerily quiet. No civilians walking around. No resort guests milling about. Do you find that a little weird?"

Tank answered, "Well, it's a good thing, don't you think?"

Ram growled.

Tank asked, "Powers, how's it at your station?"

No answer.

"Powers, come in."

No answer.

"Lucas, check on Powers. His coms must be……..ahhh, fuck!" Tank took a shot to his left side, dropped to the ground and rolled to prevent a second shot from connecting. The walkway chipped as another round just missed Tank's head. He rolled behind a large rectangular concrete flower pot and said into his mic, "Lucas, Powers, we're under siege. Take cover. I'll warn Tucker."

Tank was bleeding badly, and his left side hurt like hell, but he managed to send a warning to Tucker by pushing *60 on his phone.

Three men dressed in black tactical gear, wearing helmets, ski masks, and body armor swung assault rifles back and forth as they made their way to the conference room entrance. Smith-1 held Tank in place behind the concrete flower pot with his silenced 7.62x39mm rifle.

Lucas found Power dead at his post with a bullet hole cleaning showing in the back of his head. Lucas then rushed to where Tank was positioned only to observe three combatants entering the building double-doors. Lucas unloaded his semi-automatic Glock 19x in the direction of the attackers. He took one out, Smith-2, and wounded another before Smith-1 hit Lucas in the back of his neck with a round. Lucas was dead before he hit the pavement.

Tank was able to get a couple of shots off in the direction of the attackers and hit one of the wounded invaders—Smith-4. Two down in the front, one to go.

The captain of the mercenary team positioned himself behind a façade column with a decent vantage point to take out Tank. His mission plan had not taken Ram into consideration—big mistake. Ram lunged at the captain's firing arm and damn near ripped the arm off before he let it go and attacked the captain's throat.

Ram heard and smelled Smith-1 escape into the woods and ran hard after the sniper.

Inside, Tucker's cell phone registered the warning with a siren-like sound.

Tucker stood up and yelled, "Everyone, out the back entrance into the conference kitchen area. This is not a fire drill. Go."

The new foundation members in the back row broke through the rear exit only to be met by two more mercenaries with assault rifles. The President of *Police Magazine* already had her concealed Ruger out and chambered, unloaded three 9mm rounds into Smith-3's head before she was met with six rounds from an AK-47. The Secretary of the Army also carried a concealed weapon but was unable to get off more than one shot that hit the chest protection of Smith-6.

Smith-6 with his assault weapon entered from the back while Smith-5 entered from the front. They began unloading indiscriminately around the room.

A Keystone Resort security guard who had called 9-1-1 appeared with his handgun in position to take-out the front door attacker and yelled, "Stop or I'll shoot."

As the killer turned to kill the guard, the guard ineffectively shot into the man's Kevlar.

Both Tucker and Maya carried concealed weapons and were well-trained by Powers and Tank. Tucker took advantage of the distraction caused by the security guard and shot the Smith-5 in the legs. The man sprayed bullets around the room until his magazine was empty before he collapsed to the floor.

Maya took her 9mm Barretta and put two rounds into the attacker's head. She proceeded to pick up the attacker's AK-47, pulled a new full clip from his vest, and looked toward the back of the room.

Sirens could be heard outside when Maya began to unload the assault weapon. Tank now dragged his bleeding body into the conference room with his weapon firing after determining that the sniper, Smith-1, left his post.

The sole remaining attacker, Smith-6, exited out the back door as rounds hit his body armor.

Suddenly, it was deafly quiet. Excepts for moans.

Maya looked around the room with gunsmoke still permeating her nostrils. She heard groans and cries for help. Without looking in Tucker's direction, she asked, "You OK sweetheart?"

He didn't answer.

She turned to see Tucker still on the floor. She ran to his side and asked with desperate fear in her voice, "Baby, you OK?"

Tucker was not OK. Nor was anyone else in the room. Maya was the only person both alive and uninjured.

Outside the conference hall, Ram whined as he lay next to his trainer with his head on top of Powers' unmoving chest.

Washington, DC

The Washington Times Headline: **Massacre in Keystone, Colorado** – "Police from both Breckenridge and Silverthorne, Colorado arrived at the site of the bloodiest crime scene in modern Colorado history. Nineteen high-profile attendees and three guards at the Keystone Resort Conference Center were killed by assault-rifle-carrying attackers. Twenty-one others were seriously injured—seven remain in intensive care. Six of the attackers were killed in the assault by either security guards, armed attendees, or a guard dog.

"Interviews with the lead investigator for the Colorado Bureau of Investigation revealed that the dead assault team was apparently mercenaries. The current theory is that the motive for the massacres was to eradicate The Media Transformation Foundation whose efforts to change journalistic culture had been effective at also impacting political voting trends. Neither the CBI nor the FBI would comment on the likely person or organization that contracted the mercenaries."

CHAPTER 61

"Revenge is an act of passion; vengeance of justice. Injuries are revenged; crimes are avenged."—Samuel Johnson, 1709-1784, English poet

Wiscasset, Maine- August 21st

Tucker spent ten days in the intensive care ward of the University of Colorado Hospital in Aurora, Colorado. Surgeons tried to save his larynx from the stray AR-15 round but were more concerned about saving his life—he needed six pints of blood.

Tank was released from intensive care after three days of constant attention for his small intestine stomach wounds.

But, at least, they both lived.

Maya's grief had turned into anger. Jolene, Tank's significant other, spent the last three weeks consoling Maya and Star after Tank and Tucker were released from a hospital and flown home.

Tank, Jolene, Sonja, Maya, Tucker, Star, and Ram sat around a coffee table awaiting a report from Jimmy Ma and Tony Vinci. Tucker's in-home nurse thought it best to allow Tucker to participate in the meeting although he could not speak. She said it might take a few more weeks of physical therapy before he could speak using an electronic device.

Chef Rhino served crabmeat filled mushrooms and Pinot Grigio wine to the guest at the Cherokee Estate to help achieve normalcy in a totally abnormal situation.

Sonja crashed—she had never cried. Powers was her only family and now she was totally alone. Sonja's grief had also turned to anger.

And Tank's grief turned to anger.

The beast of all that anger could only be fed with vengeance.

Maya took in a deep breath, swallowed hard, and asked with a little crack in her voice, "OK, guys, what have we learned? Tony, you go first."

Tony knew he had to be compassionate but concise and said, "The seven attackers were mercenaries. Three were Americans, two were Czechs, one was South African, and one was Ukrainian. All were Special Forces in their respective countries. The one that escaped was an American who was Special Forces in Afghanistan."

Tony looked Sonja McLeod directly in the eye and said, "I have located him hiding in a small town in east Tennessee."

All at the coffee table knew that one surviving mercenary was now a dead man walking.

Maya asked, "Have we learned who hired them?"

Tony said, "I defer to Jimmy on that subject." All eyes were focused on Jimmy including Ram's.

Jimmy had always been frightened of Ram so instead of looking at Maya he addressed his answer to Ram, "The mercenaries were advanced $700,000 from an account registered in Belize to "The Global Free Press Society."

Maya asked, "Jimmy, have you shared what you know with Winemiller about the, what was it, 'The Global Free Press Society.'"

Jimmy said, "No, not yet."

"Why?"

Jimmy was very uncomfortable, shifted in his seat, and glanced in Star's direction.

Star said, "You've got to be kidding? You know what that means, right?"

Ram inched a little closer to Jimmy Ma.

Everyone in the room waited patiently for Jimmy to share the information. Finally, he said, "The account owner is," Jimmy hesitated, "ah, the deceased Craig Lakatos."

"Apparently, the State of New York which was the recipient of Craig's estate never learned about this secret account. The only one that did know about the account was the incarcerated Levi Zimmerman."

Sonja asked the question to which everyone already knew the answer, "Could Levi pull this off from jail?"

Heads nodded in unison.

Sonja asked, "What can you tell me about the sniper?"

Tony Vinci answered, "He used a vintage 7.62x39mm Howa Mini Action Chassis Bolt Action Rifle with an OSS HX-QD 762 Ti Silencer. From everything I learned, he was positioned only 75 yards or so from the entrance to the meeting room double doors. Tank, you and the guys were easy targets. It looks like when he saw the mission go south, he bolted. But he couldn't outrun Ram."

Tony looked at Ram and said, "Good boy. He was bad-bad."

Tank asked, "What are the police and FBI doing?"

Tony said, "The police are trying to find the surviving mercenary. I haven't shared the information I have about him with the police—thought maybe we could use the information ourselves. Besides, I used some, maybe, questionable methods to learn his whereabouts.

"Winemiller says the FBI is totally focused on who financed the mercenaries."

Tucker wrote on a piece of paper, "Zimmerman and the leftist one-world government cabal."

EPILOGUE

CHAPTER 62

"Every day our leadership would listen to world news over the radio at 9 a.m. to follow the growth of the American antiwar movement." - Bui Tin, 1927-present, Colonel, North Vietnam

The Hamptons, Long Island, New York-A Decade Later

The sky was dark, clouds were swirling from west to east at an incredibly high velocity, and the wind was picking up. He looked at his watch for the third time in the last five minutes. It was after the scheduled two o'clock p.m. meeting. The hurricane was not forecast to make landfall for another nine hours.

"Sir." He jumped when his head of security startled him. "Your guests have arrived. We have patted them down; they are clean. Should I inform Stanley?"

"Yes, please. Have him serve coffee, tea, and some cheese. Oh, and have him bring a bottle of our best bourbon."

"Yes, sir."

Two men and a woman entered the study where an aged Levi Zimmerman sat. The first man extended his hand and said, "Levi, you look great for a man who spent the last ten years locked up with real monsters. How did you survive it?"

Zimmerman said, "I didn't survive it. But I was able to buy protection. The first thing I did was pick out the biggest bad-ass I could find and explained to him how I'd pay him on the outside if he kept the other psychopaths off me. He was able to get more conjugal visits from women all claiming to be his wife than anyone else in the pen."

The two men laughed, but the woman failed to find humor in the story, which brought unwanted attention to her. Zimmerman stared at her and asked, "Do I know you?"

The first man said, "I'm sorry, let me introduce Ms. Jennifer Rose to you. She is the no-nonsense chief operating officer of our organization. She came to us highly recommended and is amazingly knowledgeable about the history of our cause. She has proved herself to be a great tactician with uncanny foresight. Ms. Rose, meet Mr. Zimmerman. Mr. Zimmerman is the godfather of our movement to move the media to be more liberal and progressive in the way they report the news."

"Yes," said Zimmerman, "since my release, I have noticed a big difference in the tone of the news from news reported a decade ago. The way it's portrayed, the method of delivery and the sensitivity to accuracy is different. There seems to be a trend in the media where it is now cool or hip to be conservative. Editorial pages appear to be more pro-military, pro-law enforcement, and pro-America. Corporations are given the benefit of the doubt, American exceptionalism is touted as fact, and statistics that demonstrate the generosity of the American people are listed. Even *The New York Times* quoted the benefits of a smaller government and the stupidity of gun-free zones.

"What the hell happened during my incarceration?"

The second man spoke for the first time, "That's why we're here. We need to assemble a secret left-wing society to reverse the pro-conservative trend in the media. Since you are out of prison and confined to your estate with an ankle bracelet, we thought you should run the new group from here. It will not violate your parole to manage the group."

"Ms. Rose will administer the strategies we develop to move the media back to where they should be.

"The conservatives have declared war against us, and we must treat it like war. We need to take a scorched earth approach. Our first war front will be to deploy cyber soldiers against HonestMediaMatters.edu and somehow shut it down. The second war front must be to replace conservative editors with liberal editors and get the *The Washington Times*, *Chicago Tribune*, and *The Boston Globe* back to where they were more than a decade ago. The third war front . . ."

Ms. Jennifer Rose recorded the meeting and streamed it real time to Special Agent Rusty Winemiller at Quantico. Jennifer Rose was an undercover agent for the FBI that had an amazing resemblance to the grown-up Star Cherokee.

Waiting outside the Zimmerman estate, roughly 1500 yards out on an elevated platform constructed on a home recently acquired by an untraceable and non-existent buyer, Sonja McLeod lay patiently in her sniper position for Levi Zimmerman to show his face in her crosshairs.

THE END

Many thanks go to my beta testers:

Dawn Allen

Shere Day

Doug Hoover

Sonja Hurt

Ken Landon

Don MacIntosh

Brad Naylor

Paul Nice

Steve Unthank

Cover Designer: Sam Rotolo

Made in the USA
Middletown, DE
17 August 2019